Light from a Distant Star

ALSO BY MARY McGARRY MORRIS

The Last Secret

The Lost Mother

A Hole in the Universe

Fiona Range

Songs in Ordinary Time

A Dangerous Woman

Vanished

Light from a Distant Star

A NOVEL

Mary McGarry Morris

BROADWAY PAPERBACKS

NEW YORK

B
BROADWAY

Copyright © 2011 by Mary McGarry Morris

All rights reserved.
Published in the United States by Broadway Paperbacks, an imprint
of the Crown Publishing Group, a division of Random House, Inc., New York.
www.crownpublishing.com

BROADWAY PAPERBACKS and its logo, a letter B bisected on the diagonal,
are trademarks of Random House, Inc.

Originally published in hardcover in the United States by Crown Publishers,
an imprint of the Crown Publishing Group, a division of Random House, Inc.,
New York, in 2011.

Library of Congress Cataloging-in-Publication Data
Morris, Mary McGarry.
Light from a distant star : a novel / Mary McGarry Morris.—1st ed.
        p.   cm.
1. Child witnesses—Fiction. 2. Murder—Fiction. I. Title.
PS3563.O874454L54 2011
813'.54—dc22   2010039186

ISBN 978-0-307-45188-0
eISBN 978-0-307-45187-3

Printed in the United States of America

Text design by Lauren Dong
Title page photograph by Bernard Jaubert/Getty Images
Cover design by Monica Gurevich/Julie Metz Design
Cover photograph: © Lia G/Arcangel Images

10 9 8 7 6 5 4 3 2 1

First Paperback Edition

Dedicated to

Zachary M. Starkweather
Harrison D. Starkweather
Frank E. Starkweather
Michael D. Starkweather
Joseph M. Danisch
Margaret L. Danisch
John T. Danisch
William J. Pannos
Kristen P. Copell
Alexander W. Pannos
Timothy V. Morris
Katherine A. Morris
Mary Joan Lonergan
Jane M. Lonergan

with love.

Light from a Distant Star

Chapter 1

And you still think so? Even after all this time?
Absolutely.
How can you be so sure?

YOU KNOW HOW YOU JUST KNOW ABOUT A PERSON SOME-
times? He doesn't even have to look you in the eye or say a
word, and you know. Now, exactly what it is you know might
not be clear, but you still know. You just do.

That's the way it always was. Even as a kid. It wasn't any kind of
higher power or sixth sense, just her own God-given bullshit detector.
What surprised Nellie most was how few people had one. Or if they
did, how few bothered to use it—or trust it.

Like the first time she met Max Devaney in her grandfather's junkyard, though it wasn't until all the trouble that she even knew his last
name. She and her brother, Henry, were bringing Charlie his supper
that day. Charlie Campbell was their grandfather, but they always
called him Charlie, along with everyone else in town. In fact, his was a
household name in Springvale then. Once something broke down or
was of little use anymore, you'd say, "It's Charlie's now."

Charlie's house had always reminded Nellie of a choked weed,
struggling its way up through the junkyard's rusted mountains of scrap
metal. Close by was the tar paper–sided barn where his flinty transac-
tions took place, the few there were anymore. The junkyard was right
in the middle of town and so it was considered a blight, especially by
newer stores in the area. But with Charlie's own rumors of a big national chain looking at his three prime acres, no one dared push the
old man too hard. Walmart, he'd tell people, angling for a groundswell
of interest—from someone, *anyone,* Nellie's mother said. Yes, sir, it was
the only company he'd deal with, he liked to brag, basking in his own
self-empowerment. Of the fancied negotiations, one newspaper article
quoted him as saying, "A few more details, and they can do what-

ever the (. . .) they want, put up a (. . .) ferris wheel for all the (. . .) I care." The selectmen immediately appointed an advisory committee to study the impact of Walmarts that may have opened in other downtown business districts. Most of the junkyard was hidden by a sagging wooden fence, its rotted posts braced by random boards. An eyesore, but it did keep out intruders, real and imagined. Charlie thought everyone wanted to steal his stuff.

Nellie and her brother found Charlie in the barn that day, in the dim horse stall he called his office. Because of his personality and full thatch of wavy white hair, he had always seemed big to her—and scary. But her gangly six-inch spurt in the last few months had left her nearly as tall. Height, and stronger lenses in her glasses to keep her eye from turning, had given her new perspective on just about everything. Especially Charlie. What seemed a permanent sunburn was, she realized, a web of tiny broken veins in his nose and cheeks, and shining in the corner of his mouth was a thin trickle of spit. For the briefest fraction of a millisecond she felt bad for him.

"Here you go, Charlie." She held out the warm, foil-wrapped plate.

"Pot roast," Henry said, surprising her. They'd been working on that. Speaking right up and not waiting to be spoken to. As long as she was going to be saddled with him for the entire summer she didn't want to be constantly speaking for him or repeating the little he did mumble. In some ways it was like being a translator, though Henry was very intelligent, one of those little boys adults take to right away, all cowlicks and dimpled cheeks. It's just that then he was the shyest kid, always staring down at the ground when people were around, or when he had to make eye contact, blinking so rapidly they'd look away. She'd made up her mind. This was the summer to toughen Henry up. He had the brains, all he needed was confidence, and she'd recently found the perfect book in her father's study. Actually called *Get Tough!*, it had been written in World War II by Major W. E. Fairbairn to teach hand-to-hand combat to British Commandos and the U.S. Armed Forces. Every day she and her brother practiced new holds and "the various ways of securing a prisoner." So far, he had only thrown her once. He'd been getting tired of always being pinned, headlocked, and hip thrown, so to keep him interested, she'd let him take her down in a stranglehold that left marks on her neck for days and got them both in trouble. Now they practiced when no one else was home.

Distracted, Charlie kept peering out into the yard. He gestured for her to put the plate somewhere. She set it on top of one of the junked radiators lining the stall. A shadow darkened the bright doorway.

"Well, what d'ya know," Charlie said. "I figured that was it."

The entering man was broad backed and unshaven. There were deep pocks on his forehead and nose. His dark hair was wild and bushy. A black dog trotted alongside. The man didn't look at Nellie and her brother, but the dog did. His stare was yellow. His thick tail wagged, but hesitantly.

"Took longer'n I thought," the man said. "But it's done."

"Hour'n a half?"

The man shrugged. "Pay what you think, I don't care."

Bad move, she knew, seeing Charlie's grin. This sucker didn't know what he was up against. Last time here, out by the barn door, she'd found a half-buried quarter that Charlie made her hand over. He insisted it was his—he remembered dropping it in that exact spot. Probably why he had them call him Charlie; that way, he could treat them like everyone else.

Henry raised his shaky hand for the dog to sniff. They'd been working on that, too, biding your time, letting the animal know you weren't a threat. The dog gave an eager yip and Henry lurched back.

"Boone," the man's deep voice warned. "Down."

Down the dog dropped.

"Scared of his own shadow but pretty damn smart, I'll give him that," Charlie said. She thought he meant the dog until he introduced them as his daughter's kids, no names given.

The man nodded without meeting their gaze.

"How do you do, sir? My name's Nellie. Nellie Peck." She reached to shake hands.

He stiffened back. "Pleased to meet you," he said with a curt nod as if in pained acknowledgment of her far better manners.

"And this is Henry. My brother. And he's actually very brave." She shot a look at her grandfather, who just chuckled in that way he had, under his breath to show he was right and could say more but chose not to.

"That's good." Turning his attention to Charlie, the man said he'd piled the copper piping behind the barn, but the door wouldn't open. The padlock was rusted.

Charlie reached under the desk and gave him a spray can, WD-40, his answer to all life's problems, according to her mother. "Give it a soak and try later. And here." He handed over the dinner they'd brought. "Pot roast. Hot off the range."

His nose to the rim of the foil, the man actually sniffed the plate. She and Henry exchanged looks. Only animals sniffed their food, they'd been taught.

"Go ahead. Go on up before it gets cold," Charlie said.

SHE COULDN'T WAIT to tell her mother that Charlie had given her delicious dinner away to some guy in the barn. And that he'd scurried up into the loft with it.

"Oh yeah. Max," her mother said. "So he's still there, huh? Well, that's good."

"Sandy, who's Max?" her father called over the running water as he washed the last pan. Sharing chores had begun when her mother started working. She cooked and he kept the kitchen clean. He also did laundry and scrubbed the toilets, sinks, tubs, and floors in both bathrooms—small price to pay, she'd say with that edge in her voice. And her father was never a man to argue. With anyone.

"Some guy Charlie hired." She was still at the table with her coffee and the newspaper. "Creepy, if you ask me, but Charlie says he's a hard worker. He's up in the hay loft, that little room."

"That's good." Her father was rinsing the sink with the sprayer, which they weren't supposed to use. But leaky hoses mattered little. His were larger concerns: peace, kindness, truth, and in their brief time on this planet, the importance of leaving a mark, their imprint, making some difference to benefit those yet to come. "It's about time Charlie let up a little."

Her mother glanced over the paper. Didn't say anything. Just sighed. Henry was eating his pudding and didn't catch it, but Nellie did. In her mother's opinion her husband had let up long ago, if he'd ever really cared much in the first place. About business, that is, and making money.

Benjamin Peck was a fine man. Polite. Thoughtful. Well raised and probably the handsomest man in Springvale. For almost a hundred years Peck Hardware on Main Street had provided most of the community's workaday needs: nuts, bolts, gadgets, hinges, keys, and every manner of tool, paint supplies, ladders, even wallpaper, though most of the rolls Benjamin had stamped SECONDS, they were so old, and long after they were fashionable, glossy decals to decorate your walls, furniture, and cabinets. Peck's sold bird feeders and pails, lightbulbs and shovels, lawnmowers and rakes. Window shades were his specialty. MEASURE TWICE, CUT ONCE said the black-and-white tin sign over the shade-cutting machine, both sign and machine older than Benjamin, who took great pride in his shade-cutting skill, though not much else when it came to the cluttered store. For an impractical man caught in the most practical of lives, the past was sustenance enough.

Benjamin's true calling was the history he was writing of Middleton County, most especially, the town of Springvale. His small office at the back of the store was filled with old books, some stacked higher than Nellie was tall, which at that point in her thirteen years was way taller than she wanted, though she took care to always stand straight, shoulders back, head high like her father. For Nellie it was important to never show blood or weakness. For her father it was an inborn, natural stature, as erect of torso and limb as he was of character.

It was generally agreed that no matter how bad things got, Benjamin Peck was a decent man. A dreamer, certainly, and careless maybe when it came to the business, by that point in time on its last wobbly legs. In just a five-mile drive, three ways out of town in a triangle of Peck financial doom, there was a Sears; a Target; then two years ago, the orange-and-brown death knell, a Home Depot, where you could buy everything from a hot dog and orchid plant to a utility shed complete with shutters and window boxes, as well as crystal chandeliers and French doors, even a refrigerator if you wanted. Just cart it away.

Four generations of Pecks had served the hardware store, which was her father's problem. It had never really seemed like *his* business as much as the place he was still minding, all these years later, for his father, grandfather, and great-grandfather. From time to time people did come in and buy things, "pity purchases," her father's sister called them. Aunt Betsy had never wanted anything to do with the store. Even the shade business had fallen off. Maybe nobody could cut them like Benjamin, but when everyone else had gone to vinyl, all he stocked were more expensive paper shades in ivory and dark green, and of the latter only two had sold in the last five years.

But the solitude was fruitful. Without distractions he could continue his research and write for hours. An old cowbell would clang on the opening front door, and there was an etched silver school bell on the counter for customers to tap if he'd missed the first bell. Most people just went looking for him. Some helped themselves and left money on the counter. Some probably helped themselves and just left.

The history was almost finished. Only a few more chapters to go, he assured her mother. He'd finally made it to the war years, he declared one night at dinner, soon after she'd started working at the hair salon.

"Which war?" she asked.

"World War One."

"Are you serious?"

"It's fascinating," he said, waving his fork, striking key notes with a conductor's blinkered intensity. "I mean, even then, that something so very distant could have such an impact on this little part of the universe. Amazing, when you think of it, when you consider it in that light. How connected, how vital a part we are of one another, from then till now, down through the ages. And how brief it all is. I mean, here we all sit, thinking we're so important that every mistake, every disappointment is a disaster. Cataclysmic. When all we are, all we really are, is a mote, an infinitesimal speck, a pinprick in time."

Even Nellie could see the parallax effect: her mother thinking, perhaps for the first time realizing as she did indeed consider it in that very light, just how small, how isolatingly local and therefore remote, was the pinpoint myopia of her husband's life's work. But he was a brilliant man—everyone knew that—she surely must have reminded herself as she so often did her children, and far more educated than she was, which by Benjamin's own mother's admission had been the family's first mistake, sending him off to a fancy college, and then the second, when he graduated, insisting he come back home and take over the business when his father died, which had only made him a prime target for Sandy Campbell and her illegitimate baby.

Chapter 2

HEY LIVED ON OAK STREET. THE OLD PECK HOUSE WAS BIG
and kind of ramshackle compared to their neighbors', but the
inside was comfortable, even pretty thanks to her mother, who
did all the painting and papering herself, and a lot of the repairs. She
had sewn most of the curtains, duvet covers, and tablecloths. By Memorial Day weekend her flowers would be planted, the shrubs fertil-
ized, and the shade-patchy lawn limed. There were nine rooms not
counting the part of the attic that had been done over for Nellie's sister's sixteenth birthday.

Ruth always got special treatment. Because she's the oldest, they'd
say, but Nellie knew it was more than that. You see, Ruth was a "love
child," born when her mother was a senior in high school. Her birth
father's last name was Brigham, but she had always gone by Peck, until
that particular summer.

For reasons Nellie could not fathom, Ruth had become obsessed
with, in her words, "finding my real father," a lousy thing to say considering Benjamin had raised her almost from infancy. Danny Brigham
lived in Australia, and up to that point in time, had never laid eyes on
Ruth. His offspring. Little more than his seed, the way Nellie figured it.

His family had moved from Springvale halfway through his junior
year and Sandy's pregnancy. She had been older and a year ahead in
school, a fact that Nellie found *the* most disturbing of all. Unnatural.
Danny Brigham hadn't wanted to leave, Sandy had always been careful
to tell Ruth. It wasn't that he didn't care, only that being so young he
had no choice, his plight another of the bittersweet fairy tales that gov-
erned Ruth's life. In the only picture she had of him, he was seventeen
years old in a Hawaiian shirt, with a big honking nose, long wavy hair,

and a goofy smile. Nothing like distinguished Benjamin with his dark eyes and jet-black hair just starting to gray at the temples.

In the back of the house there was a three-room apartment that people always seemed to be moving into then out of when the young wife got pregnant or the grouchy old lady's tumble in the tub landed her in assisted living. So far, their best tenant had been Lazlo Larouche. Lazlo was an artist, though he supported himself by waiting on tables at the Mountain House, the most expensive restaurant for miles around. Lazlo's paintings were of prancing moonlit horses and mist-covered lakes and vague spectral images fleeing in billowy capes. He and Benjamin took to one another quickly and on Lazlo's rare evenings off would sit on the front porch sipping wine and talking. Each man was a good listener, particularly Lazlo, who avoided personal questions and was ever eager to steer the conversation back to Benjamin and his work, the history of Springvale. It was with Sandy, though, that Lazlo was more himself; they shared confidences and easy, sometimes helpless laughter together.

Eventually, Lazlo moved across town into a bigger, more modern apartment with James, his frequent visitor at Oak Street. Lazlo had come back to visit, but only a few times, and he was always in a hurry.

After Lazlo, came the downturn. The apartment stayed empty for a month. By then any vacancy meant financial hardship. With the store income a dribble at best, Sandy had counted on the rent to buy groceries and pay bills. Her job at Frederic's helped a lot and her client base was growing, though still small. She had worked right after Ruth was born, but quit when she married Benjamin, who shared her belief that a mother's place was at home. Most of her clients were still walk-ins, but people liked her, and her girlfriends were supportive, recommending her and coming in for touch-ups and trims they barely needed. The other stylists were Carolyn, Kris, and Lizzie, who used to do Sandy's hair. Frederic was a small, dramatic man with a blond goatee and a tan that was sprayed on weekly. He absolutely "adored" Sandy, and paid her minimum wage.

Warmhearted and generous, Sandy Peck was always ready with a helping hand, so what could she say when Lizzie asked if her niece could look at the empty apartment. She had just broken up with her boyfriend and needed a place to stay. Lizzie had had it with the girl's sleeping on her pullout couch. In spite of Sandy's misgivings, she had agreed to show the apartment to Dolly Bedelia.

"She's an entertainer at the Paradise," her voice rose past the open cellar door.

"The Paradise?" Nellie's father said.

"Out on Route Nine?"

She had called him down to remove the dead mice and reset the traps. The stiff little carcasses had been in them for days. Maybe weeks. It was his most hated chore.

"Entertainer, what's that mean?" He spoke nasally, probably holding his breath, Nellie thought.

"Singer? I don't know. But Lizzie's always saying how she's got this amazing voice."

A bag crinkled—her father opening the paper casket.

"Not that kind of place though, is it?" he asked.

"What I'm hoping is she won't like it, the old tub and no shower."

"Lazlo's works okay, the one he hooked up."

"Except for running out of hot water all the time."

"So, tell her that."

"Believe me, I will."

"Doesn't seem right, does it?"

"I know, but the last thing I need right now is some ditzy pole dancer moving in."

"I meant them. Look, they're not even full grown."

"They're still mice, Ben. Vermin. Coming up through the walls into the cupboards and—"

"What do you mean, ditzy pole dancer?"

"Oh, God, I don't know. How do I get myself into these messes?"

"Because you're very kind."

"No. I just talk too much, that's the problem."

"Speaking of which, guess who came in today?"

"Ben! I hate it when you do that. Just tell me."

"Andy Cooper."

"Oh, thank God! Did he say how much?"

"I turned him down."

With the furious stomping up the stairs, Nellie barely made it around the corner onto the recliner.

"For now!" Her father followed her mother into the kitchen, the bag of dead mice a dry rattle with every appeasing gesture. "Just for now, that's what I told him. I just need some time, Sandy. A little more time."

"To do what, Ben? To do what?"

"To finish."

And in the stark silence that pulled the walls together, she felt it once again, deeply, her mother's disappointment and her father's determination to overlook her desperation, no matter the cost.

An entertainer was moving into the apartment. She couldn't wait to tell Ruth. When she'd told Henry, all he'd said was "So?" It was Friday night and Ruth had gone out after dinner to meet her two best friends in the park. Supposedly they were going to Rollie's for ice cream, then to hang out at Brenda Hoffman's house afterward. The Hoffmans had an amazing playroom, with its own bar, pool table, Ping-Pong table, huge television, a conversation pit lined with leather couches, and sliding glass doors leading out to the Gunite swimming pool. Not that Nellie'd ever seen it, but at that point in life, Ruth was her Vasco da Gama, returning from her great adventures with detailed descriptions of exotic worlds, and if she was lucky and showed enough interest—but not too much—romantic relationships.

"I probably shouldn't be telling you this," she would begin, and Nellie'd already be getting that dull pelvic ache. Especially when it was about Patrick Dellastrando. Nellie wasn't sure why, because she truly found him repulsive—hairy arms and legs, a man's deep voice, and a perpetual five o'clock shadow. He was a grade ahead of Ruth, but he lived around the block, so their frequently crossed paths had long seemed a kind of cosmic destiny to both sisters.

Ruth was twenty minutes late. On weekends her curfew was eleven. School nights she couldn't go out except to the library. It was amazing how many projects she'd recently been assigned. Anyway, at 11:20 Nellie had come down from bed, claiming hunger, a plausible excuse because to listen to her mother tell it, all she did was eat. Constantly. Her mother was folding her work laundry on the kitchen table, mostly lavender towels and black smocks. Nellie was slowly eating toast with peanut butter, trying to drag it out, when Ruth came through the door. Even without glasses, the first thing Nellie noticed was her sister's rashy face, then her wrinkled shirt, and the funny way she was looking at them. Like through a fog. Her pupils seemed to fill her eye sockets.

"I'm sorry," she said, hugging herself with a quick shiver even though the June night's muggy heat still hung in the kitchen.

"That's twenty minutes off your next night out," her mother said.

"Mom!" Ruth protested. "That's the problem. Everyone's curfew's later than mine, so they're all having fun, and I don't know what time it is, and—"

"But you've got your watch," Nellie interrupted. Big mistake. Huge, she realized, following Ruth up the stairs.

"Where do you think you're going?" Ruth hissed at the door to the attic stairs. Her mouth tightened and her eyes swam with a drowsy, unfocusable disgust. She smelled funny. Sweetish, like dried herbs.

"I just want to tell you something."

"What?"

"Shh." Nellie pointed upward. To privacy.

Her room was brain-boiling hot. It would be awhile before the window air conditioner cooled it off. But that was the deal, it could only be run when Ruth was up here. Piles of clothes were everywhere, even on her unmade bed. She turned and pulled her shirt over her head. Her back was lean and tanned. She wasn't wearing a bra. Some girls didn't have to, they were so small, but not Ruth. She was like their mother—big breasts, small waist, and one of those rear ends so perfect that when she walked, it took on a life of its own. She put on her nightie, then stepped out of her pink shorts, leaving them where they dropped. She sat down hard on the bed. "So what's so important?"

Nellie's brain was fuzzy. Her face burned and her eyes stung. It wasn't just the heat, though. Ruth's bra was hanging halfway out of her shorts pocket. Needing to absolve her, Nellie asked if she'd gone swimming in the Hoffmans' pool.

"No," she sighed, collapsing back onto the bed. "We just kinda hung out."

"Where?"

"We ended up at Colleen's." Looking up at the ceiling, she grinned.

"Dellastrando?" Colleen was younger than Ruth, only two years older than Nellie.

"Yeah."

"In the house?" A forbidding place, muscled teenage boys jamming baskets, dribbling in the wide driveway, their music-thumping cars constantly coming and going. Passing by, Nellie would quicken her step, stare straight ahead. Things happened there. She just knew it.

"No, out on the deck. The screened-in part."

The gazebo. For Nellie, the most exotic structure in all of Springvale. "Was it just girls?"

"No!" Ruth crowed.

"So, who then?" There, again, that strange, deep ache.

"Some guys. You know. Patrick and his friends. They were showing off their . . ."—she lowered her voice—". . . tattoos."

Tattoos. So there it was, the beginning. Of what Nellie couldn't be sure. But her heart raced and she averted her eyes from the hard swell of nipples against the nightie's thin, blue cotton as Ruth described the red tattoo around Patrick's left bicep, a jagged design, like barbed wire. So what was the big secret, she wanted to know.

But now Nellie didn't want to tell her. The news gave her none of the pleasure she had expected. None at all. Only a dingy heaviness.

"Are you serious? Oh, my God, I can't believe it. Why would Mom do that? I mean, the Paradise! How cheesy is that? Even I know it's a strip club."

WITH ONLY A few weeks left before school let out for the summer, Nellie's mother still hadn't figured out what to do with her two youngest while she was at work. There'd been vague talk of overnight camps and different community programs and Ruth's babysitting them, but as the days dwindled, it had come down to Nellie minding Henry. Ruth had gotten a job scooping ice cream at Rollie's takeout window.

Nellie and her brother were walking home on one of their last school days when Jessica Cooper caught up with them. Jessica could be mean, especially to Henry, but she and Nellie'd been friends since kindergarten and if Nellie was nothing else, she was deeply loyal. And besides, Jessica didn't have an easy life. Not really. The fourth born out of seven, she was bookended by six of the best-looking and smartest kids in town. By this time, though, Jessica and Nellie had little left in common, other than huge appetites. But Nellie was death-march skinny, while Jessica was gaining so much weight so fast that she'd been put on a strict diet, which only made her more bitter about her mother and more furtive about food. Whenever they had money, they'd stop at the little grocery store on their way home, but that day Nellie refused. Last week Jessica had bought two Snickers bars and stolen two. Today in the cafeteria she had been caught taking an extra brownie. She'd been accused before, but this time the lunch lady insisted she turn out her pockets. Everyone snickered as fudgy chunks and crumbs fell onto the floor.

School had always been a trial for Jessica. She did well in math but could barely read. The language arts specialist took her out of the class-room every morning at nine-thirty. That daily walk to the door, then down the corridor was a trail of unending shame. On Saturdays from ten to twelve a private tutor came to the house to work with her. Fifty dollars an hour, but the Coopers were rich. Nellie thought so, anyway. Through the years she had overlooked Jessica's many failings except for one: her hatred for her mother. It was chilling.

"Sometimes I wish she'd just get cancer and die," Jessica would say.

You don't mean that, Nellie had long ago quit saying. Because she'd finally accepted that Jessica did. You could hear it in her voice—a malevolence that would curl her plump mouth into the most frightening smile. Maybe it was because Mrs. Cooper was so nice and so strik-ingly beautiful; maybe that's what Jessica couldn't bear—the contrast between mother and daughter. Mrs. Cooper was exquisite, her inky black hair a perfect widow's peak over her high-boned ivory complex-ion. Seven children and trim as a model, which, it was said, she'd once been—in New York City. She was the lead soprano at Sunday's eleven o'clock Mass, where Mr. Cooper and their well-dressed brood filled an entire pew.

Not that Nellie ever saw them there. Hers wasn't a churchgoing family. Benjamin and Sandy were friends of the Coopers, though not the socializing kind. Just people you'd either grown up with or known forever, and knew you could count on. The relationship had become especially important in the financial struggles of this last year. Her mother had finally persuaded her father to sell the store. The business was losing money daily and the only person even remotely interested in the property was Andrew Cooper. He owned the buildings on either side of Peck Hardware.

"Come on!" Nellie called back to Henry, who was deliberately lagging behind.

"He's such a little prick," Jessica said.

"Shut up!" Nellie snapped and came to a dead stop, waiting for her brother. She knew what he was up to. He wanted to lose Jessica so they could stop at the junkyard to look for boards. So far, though, there'd been no ditching her. Huffing breathlessly with a quick skip every few steps, she'd kept pace.

"See you tomorrow," Nellie said when they came to the tall wooden gate. The last time Jessica had been with them, she'd climbed up into the hayloft. Seeing her legs dangling through the opening, Charlie had yelled at her to "get the hell down from there!"

"I'm not doing anything wrong!" she'd yelled back, which enraged Charlie. He called Nellie's mother, who said they were never to bring anyone to the junkyard again.

Jessica said she wanted to come in, too. No, Nellie told her, she'd been fresh to her grandfather and she couldn't. Yes, she could, she said, it was a public junkyard. No, it was private, she told her. That's stupid, Jessica said, pushing open the gate.

"You can't go in," Nellie said, pulling it back. She pointed up at the sign. "See. Warning. No kids allowed." It actually said, WARNING. KEEP GATE CLOSED.

Her eyes narrowed and her lips moved as she peered up at the sign. Again, Nellie said good-bye, then followed Henry inside. For the last few weeks he'd been building a tree house in the enormous swamp maple tree in their backyard. With most of the floor done, he needed boards for the walls. The junkyard never got much lumber, but now Charlie was on the lookout and pleased to save it. Seeing Henry root through the teetering piles had sparked Charlie's interest in his only grandson. The skittish little crybaby might just be turning a corner. And who knows, he'd recently told his daughter, Sandy, the boy might even want the business someday. "Maybe," had been her kind but listless reply. With her husband and father running the two most dead-end enterprises in town, it was a painful thought.

While Henry rummaged through old metal signs and sheets of tin, Nellie went in search of Charlie. His empty chair was just inside the barn door alongside the rusted green TV tray that held a coffee can filled with sand and cigarette butts.

"Charlie's resting." The dark voice fell like a shadow. Max gestured toward the house. Charlie'd gone over to lie down. He was getting those pains again. Nellie didn't know what pains he meant. Every few years Charlie seemed to be having some new ailment or surgery. Did she want to go inside, he asked, meaning the house. She said no. Ordinarily she would have, but she didn't feel right leaving Henry alone behind the barn with this strange scowling man hovering around. He made her nervous. And a little scared, the way he'd seem to be looking at you yet wasn't, both at the same time. So she asked where his dog was, in a strong voice so he'd know she was not the least bit uneasy alone in here with him. He's around someplace, maybe out back, Max said, adding that Boone's favorite place was a worn-down spot in the dirt close by the barn wall where the sun shone from noon on. All those words seemed to unnerve him.

"Is it comfortable up there?" She gestured up at the loft, wanting to put him at ease. Actually, herself as well. Nervous chatter, her mother called it, but talking was her best skill, and a way to seem more confident.

"Pretty much."

"Must get hot though, huh?"

He shrugged. "It's okay."

"So you must be pretty adaptable then," she said easing past to get outside. She didn't want him to think she was looking down her nose, judging him just some loser, another of Charlie's transient laborers, skulking around the place for a few days or sometimes just a few hours—even if he probably was. She might not think all people were the same, but she did try to treat them the same.

"I guess."

"That's the most important thing of all. For us humans, anyway."

"Oh yeah?"

"It is, I read that. It's not just survival of the fittest; it's about, like, how you fit in, how you adapt to things when they change. Like *Homo erectus,*" she called as he walked away. She caught up. "That whole line's extinct, which is pretty amazing when you think how long they were here. A million and a half years, and now"—she clicked her fingers—"they're gone. My father says they never really developed the right tools."

"Tools, huh, well, your father oughta know then," he said, walking faster now toward the clanging that was coming from the back of the barn.

She trailed after him, one more person who found her annoying. Sometimes with so much to think about, so much churning in her head, it was hard to keep it all contained.

Henry was struggling to pull a board out from under a rusted snowblower. His face was red and his feet were braced under him.

"Hey!" Max hollered. "Don't do that! You're gonna—"

"It's okay!" she snapped. "Charlie said he could. Whatever wood he finds."

"That tips, he's gonna get hurt. Here," he said, lifting the snowblower off to the side so Henry could yank out the board. Its underside was black with mold and shiny slugs. "Careful the nails—they're all rust," Max warned, then said to wait a minute. He'd go get a hammer.

Seeing Max leave, the dog rose from his sun-baked hollow. He came over to sniff Nellie's outstretched hand. He looked at Henry.

"Tell him to go," Henry said through clenched teeth as Boone sat close, wagging his thick tail. Henry froze. She hated seeing his mind go blank like that, filled only with fear.

"He's just tryna be friendly, that's all," she said.

The barn's side door squealed open and Max returned with a long hammer. He banged out the rusted nails. The bent ones he had to knock straight, then wrench out. He wasn't saying anything and neither were they. Aside from hammering, the only sound was Boone's tail hitting the ground, reminding her of Miss Schuster's metronome the three months she took piano lessons, and how tense she'd feel with the relentless beat. Ruth was the musical one in the family, not her. It was stories she most cared about, even then. Mysteries of the human condition, something she'd heard her father say once. Lately she'd been thinking a lot about that, the way life could change so suddenly, like her best friend Paige moving to Maine last year and her mother having to work, which left her stuck with Henry every day now.

"So how old's your dog?" she asked, to make up for her rudely silent brother.

"Three or four. Don't know for sure, though," Max said.

"How long you had him?"

"A while."

"Couple years?"

He stopped hammering and glanced up. "Time." He shrugged. "Kinda runs together after a while."

"You don't keep track? Like the day, what month it is?"

"Eh," he grunted clawing out the last nail. He handed Henry the board, then began picking up the dropped nails.

What's that mean—*eh*? she wanted to ask but knew better. Instead, she put her hand on the dog's warm blunt head. "I'd say five or six, that's what I think."

Boone's growl shot up her fingertips to her elbow before she heard it. His wiry black fur stood on end, and he tensed, back arched, back legs bent, ready to spring, just as the ugliest dog she'd ever seen suddenly came charging at them from nowhere. With his liver-spotted white face and piggish little eyes and wide back, he looked to be a good part pit bull.

"Boone!" Max commanded as his dog strained for the attack.

But it was her brother the snarling, bandy-legged creature had targeted. Whether fear was the beast's quarry or the threat of Henry's instinctive step back with the board raised like a shield, it didn't matter. The intruding dog sprang, knocking him down flat on his back. "Now!" Max said, and with that, Boone leaped, his jaw closing on the dog's thick neck. Amazingly, Henry still clutched the board, covering his face as he screamed, and Nellie screamed, kicking now at both dogs whose vicious battle was being waged on top of her brother. Max kept swinging the hammer against the beast's back, but the blows had little effect. Henry shrieked and his torn shirtsleeve hung bright with blood. Bending, Max picked up the crazed dog as it kicked and struggled against him. Boone ran snapping at Max's heels as he slammed the dog hard as he could against the side of the barn, merely stunning him. The dog lunged, and Max swung the hammer into its head with a sickening, lethal thud. Its long dying squeals pierced the warmth of that June afternoon. There was a chunk missing from Henry's forearm.

"Help! Help! Help!" Nellie screamed, sickened by her little brother's torn flesh.

"It's okay, it's okay," Max yelled, running toward Charlie's house with Henry wailing in his arms. She chased after them past the open gate where Jessica stared in at the chaos.

It took twenty-two stitches to close the deep wound in Henry's arm. For weeks afterward he woke up with nightmares. All construction on the tree house stopped. His arm hurt too much. The thick scar would be with him forever.

Max's wrist and arm had also been bitten, but he wouldn't let the EMTs do anything. He was all right and would tend to it himself. The carcass was tested for rabies, but the results came back negative. With pictures of the bloody hammer next to the dog's crushed skull, the story was front-page news for two straight days. One more reason to close down the junkyard, some of Charlie's neighbors were quoted as saying. The place was an eyesore and getting worse. Trouble just waiting to happen. Charlie blamed the Shelbys, saying he'd chased that dog off before, but when her mother called, Mrs. Shelby denied it. Probably afraid of a lawsuit, Nellie's father said, which prompted Sandy to call Clem Billings, the lawyer who'd handled Ruth's adoption by Benjamin. She even went door to door in the old neighborhood of her childhood, but nobody knew for sure. Nellie knew one person did though. Jessica. She denied opening the gate. Denied seeing where the dog came from. Claimed she'd been waiting on the corner for them to come out. When she heard all the barking and screaming, she ran back and found the gate already wide open. Nellie didn't believe her. Somehow she knew Jessica was responsible for everything. Just as she knew Max was a hero straight from the brittle, yellowed pages of *Get Tough!* by Major Fairbairn. In that moment of danger, he had reacted with courage and self-reliance. That Max had beaten a living creature to death without so much as an outcry or shudder, continued to amaze and repulse her. It had given a chilling new meaning to the last sentence in the Major's preface: "Once closed with your enemy, give every ounce of effort you can muster, and victory will be yours."

Meanwhile, she had taken over the wood-scavenging detail. Under the swamp maple there grew a pile of two-by-fours and broken lengths of molding and baseboard harvested from construction Dumpsters she and Henry had located around town. He pointed and she did all the work. Getting his tree house built had taken on new importance. Dolly Bedelia had moved into the little apartment at the back of the house. And the tree house looked down on her windows.

Chapter 3

———

THINGS WERE GETTING INTERESTING. THERE WAS THE NEW boy from New York. Buckminster Saltonstall, who introduced himself as Bucky, so that's what she called him. He'd be spending the summer with his grandparents. Nellie and Bucky were the same age, but he acted a lot older. For one thing, he smoked. When she told him it was against the law, that he could get arrested for even trying to buy cigarettes, he said Springvale was the deadest place he'd ever been, and with his dad an Air Force pilot, he'd lived in a lot of places.

Most of what he said was bull crap, but whenever she saw him she got goose bumps. His eyes gleamed with intensity and a scary, thrilling wildness. He wasn't sure how many spy planes his father had shot down because the missions were so secret only the president was ever told about them. She gave that a *maybe.* He said his mother was a famous soap opera actress. That rated a somewhat shaky *maybe*—hard to prove because, believe it or not, the Pecks were the only family in the free world without a television. Two years ago when theirs went on the fritz, as Benjamin put it, he convinced Sandy that they'd be better kids without its insidious influence. All that did was leave Nellie pretty much out of touch, clueless, about practically everything normal kids talk about.

Which was probably another reason she'd stayed friends with Jessica. At her house she'd just hand over the remote and let Nellie watch whatever she wanted. Of course she hadn't seen Jessica since the attack on Henry, so she was way behind in *Survivor* episodes, but she did have some principles.

Anyway, Bucky had arrived just in time. He said he'd built tree houses all over the country. Some in Europe, even. At first Henry was jealous. After all, the tree house had been his idea. When he wasn't sulking below, he'd be hollering up criticisms.

"What's that board for?" He came charging off the steps.

"The window," Bucky yelled down.

"We don't have any windows!"

"An opening, then," Bucky called as he nailed the board in place.

"Well, that's stupid. It's just gonna let rain in," Henry said.

Bucky leaned out. "Aw, sorry, Hank, but last time I looked, we don't have a roof." He said it like a question, something they weren't allowed to do, ever. (Benjamin's rules of comportment, according to Ruth.)

"No, but I'm gonna." Henry stormed inside, slamming the door behind him.

"What's the hair across his ass?" Bucky asked. Another reason he seemed older, his foul mouth.

"Calling him Hank, for one," Nellie said. "And the tree house, he thought of it first, and now you're doing it."

"Jesus! You asked me!" He flung the saw over the side and climbed down the ladder. He hopped on his grandmother's ancient bike and pedaled furiously out of sight. Bucky was always taking off like that, either offended or angry.

Selfish maybe, but she didn't mind seeing him go. The tree house was almost finished. They'd run out of wood, so the back wall was only knee-high, but it was four o'clock. Perfect timing. The bathroom light went on in the apartment. Nellie sat down and rested her chin on the last board they'd just put in and watched through the glassless opening.

Dolly Bedelia leaned over the sink, splashing water on her face. She was just waking up. She usually left for work about six and didn't return until after midnight. Nellie's bedroom was in the rear of the house so when she'd hear her loud old car pulling into the driveway, she'd creep to the window and watch Dolly hurry up the steps onto her narrow porch.

With her platinum hair and long-legged swishy walk, she was the most glamorous woman Nellie'd ever met. "Anywhere you think, cutie," she kept sighing the day of her move. Nothing seemed to faze her. Nellie and Henry were helping carry her things into the tiny apartment. She'd arrived with nothing packed, her few possessions tossed into the backseat and trunk of her car—clothes, shoes, a frying pan, some dishes, and makeup. On the dashboard were her mouthwash and toothbrush, still wet. Her aunt and uncle came later with a bed frame and floppy mattress, a card table, two folding chairs, and a crooked floor lamp. Watching from the window, Sandy told Benjamin she'd made a terrible mistake. But then the next day she brought Dolly into the small barn behind their house and gave her a sagging wicker love seat to use until she got a couch. A few days later, when Dolly was at work, she had Max come over to help Benjamin carry an old mahogany bureau from the barn into Dolly's bedroom. Nellie wondered if Dolly even wanted the love seat and bureau, but she knew it made her mother feel better. Having the place furnished like a real apartment probably made Dolly seem like a real tenant.

Even in frayed jeans and a baggy sweatshirt, Dolly was beautiful. And barely out of her teens, according to Nellie's mother. After high school Dolly had given community college a try. Six weeks later she went to New York City, which to Nellie seemed another cosmic connection, this exotic creature entering her life from the same place, at the same time as Bucky Saltonstall. In the city Dolly and her roommates had shared a studio apartment. Nights, she'd worked in a pizza shop, devoting her days to auditions and acting lessons. The closest she'd gotten to her big break was as an extra in a mob scene, hundreds of panicky, screaming people running through Central Park. It was a science fiction horror movie that still hadn't been released. Prerelease, Dolly called it.

Dolly had come back home a few months ago, but after another fight with her stepmother she moved in with her old boyfriend. When that fell apart, she ended up on her aunt's couch. Though Nellie's mother pretended she was only trying to make the best of the situation, her tenant's girlish bewilderment was growing on her. One minute she'd be trying to prove how tough she was, then the next she'd be in hopeless, helpless tears.

A few days after she moved in, a young man came to visit. His shaved head gleamed as he rang the bell. There was a spiderweb tattooed on the side of his neck. From up here in the treehouse, Nellie had a perfect view. She and Henry were crouched low, spying on the next yard, hoping to see Tenley Humboldt burst from his house, pellet guns blazing. Louisa Humboldt had called last night with her annual complaint about the family of woodchucks living under the Pecks' old barn. Electric fences, smoke bombs, human hair, wads of chewed bubblegum, fox urine, traps—her poor brother had tried everything to keep them out of his vegetable garden, but they kept burrowing new tunnels under the fence. So if Ben and Sandy heard any loud noises, they shouldn't be alarmed. It would only be Tenley shooting at woodchucks. And just to be on the safe side, the children might want to play on the other side of the house, she had added. Nellie's father asked to speak to Tenley, and Louisa went to get him. She came back on, saying her brother was busy and couldn't come to the phone. Well, just tell him they'd be doing their best at their end to get rid of the woodchucks, Benjamin said. But Tenley shouldn't be out there shooting guns in his backyard. Not only was it dangerous, it was against the law. And as she did every year, Louisa had whispered not to worry. Tenley was feeling very frustrated, that was all. And besides, he couldn't stand loud noises.

Below the children the young man had grown tired of ringing the bell and was banging on the door. His back was still turned when Nellie scurried down and ran into the house. On the other side of their first floor bathroom was Dolly's tiny kitchen. Nellie knew from previous tenants that if she pressed her ear to the thin wall and the rest of the house was quiet enough, she could hear a lot.

"Stop it!" Dolly pleaded as the banging continued.

"I just want to talk! That's all," the young man shouted. "Please!"

"No. I can't have any guys in here, my landlady told me."

Nellie wasn't sure about that, but then again her parents had rules for everything, according to Ruth, so maybe. After the young man finally left, the radio came on with Dolly singing along in a high, clear voice. She never cooked except for instant coffee. When she woke up in the morning, she'd sit on the side porch in her purple bathrobe, smoking a cigarette while she sipped her coffee. Smoking wasn't allowed inside the apartment. A lifetime of Charlie's secondhand smoke stinking up the house and his daughter's clothes and hair and eventually killing his wife, who had died of emphysema, had made Nellie's mother hate cigarettes.

Nellie went back out and climbed into the tree house. Henry was behind the barn, checking the Havahart trap her father had set, though no woodchuck was ever dumb enough to enter it. Dolly's bathroom window had steamed up. All Nellie could make out now from her leafy perch was someone pulling open the shower curtain, then stepping out of the tub. A few moments later with the smell of cigarette smoke in the air, she climbed down and trotted around the back of the house, kicking the soccer ball.

Dolly's hair was wet and her silky robe was tied around the middle. Barefoot, she sat on the rickety green rocker with her legs crossed. She didn't say anything, just kept rocking and puffing away, but Nellie could feel her watching. She kicked the ball the length of the yard, then back again. She flipped it onto her knee, then bounced it high trying to head it, once, twice. Third time she did and her glasses fell off.

"That's cool," Dolly said.

"Yeah, I been working on that," she said fumbling to put her glasses on.

"You play on a team or something?"

"I used to. Not anymore though."

"How come?" After one long, deep drag, she flicked the butt over the railing. There was a circle of white filters in the grass. Obviously, Nellie's mother hadn't seen them yet.

"I like playing—I just don't like the whole game thing. The competition, coaches always yelling and saying I'm not trying hard enough." Actually, she wasn't very good, not coordinated enough, according to her more athletic sister.

"Yeah. I know what you mean. That's the part I didn't like either."

"You played soccer?" She'd been kicking the ball closer so that now she was right at the railing.

"Just gym class. Sports, it wasn't my thing. Dancing, that's all I cared about."

"So that's good. I mean, you're still doing your favorite thing then, dancing."

"Yeah. I guess. It's a hard life though. You know, performing, having to be, like, 'on' "—she made air quotes a lot—"all the time and . . ." Her voice trailed off. "We'll see."

"Do you sing, too? At the place? That place, where you work." Nellie couldn't get the word out. Maybe because they seemed to be talking about two different things and saying it would make her into someone else.

"No."

"How come? You've got such a nice voice. The other day you were singing and I thought it was the radio, I did."

"Oh, thank you! Thank you so much. That's so nice!" She sighed. "Sometimes I think people should just sing instead of talking."

"Yeah!" Nellie laughed. "That way there'd never be any fights, would there? Like politics. I mean, everything'd just sound funny, like—"

Saying she'd better go in and get ready, she stood up and opened her door.

"Thank you," Nellie called up just in case someone had warned Dolly against getting stuck in a conversation with her. "Thank you for talking to me. For taking the time. That was very nice of you."

Turning, Dolly glanced back with that watery weariness her eyes always seemed so full of.

For a few days after that, she avoided Nellie, hurrying in and out of her apartment, head down. So Dolly did think she was a weird pain in the ass, which was all right because she was. But it was a weirdness some adults, at least, could relate to. Maturity, they called it, which even she knew it wasn't. Her peers either liked her or they didn't, which, she understood on some level, was more a test of their mettle than hers.

BUCKY HAD BEEN coming by a lot. For the past few days, every time he skidded into the driveway it was on a different bike. Some were his grandparents', he said, and some, people just gave him because they were sick of them. Sounded reasonable enough to Nellie and Henry. Everyone they knew had more money and more stuff than they did. So when Bucky got the idea for the bike business, they eagerly cleared out the front of the barn. No one had parked a car in there for years and their mother was glad they were keeping busy. After a childhood in the junkyard, she hated clutter. Benjamin was the saver, the Peck family pack rat.

Their first day in business they sold two bikes, ten dollars each. Eric Strasser and Kenny Brown were their first customers. Bucky had wanted twenty-five apiece, but ten was all they could come up with. He had met them at the park after riding around looking for customers. Bucky kept ten and she and Henry split the other ten. With the next few days so rainy, business was way off. They had three bikes left. One was a bright yellow-and-black Mongoose that Bucky said was worth at least a hundred dollars. Because no kid Nellie knew walked around with that kind of pocket money, she made three signs describing the bikes, the prices, and their address. She hung one in the park, one on the Stop & Shop bulletin board, and one on the big community affairs board in front of the town hall. The next day Bucky showed up with another bike. It was a red Tonino Lamborghini Toro mountain bike. A price tag dangled from the handle bar: $385.

"You stole that, didn't you?" she said as he wheeled it up the ramp into the barn.

"Jesus, no! What the hell? You think I'm a thief or something? My grandfather, he just never took it off, that's all." He ripped the tag off, then pedaled down the driveway on his own bike to look for customers. She'd never met his grandparents but knew they were retired. She wondered what someone that old would be doing with such a cool bike.

Hours later Bucky returned with a teenager. Jimmy Clemmons, a boy in Ruth's class. He was interested in the gleaming Mongoose. Henry had just finished waxing it. A hundred twenty-five, Bucky told him.

"You gotta be kidding," Jimmy said.

"No, that's it. I told you, one twenty-five and no haggling."

Jimmy walked around the bike. He squeezed the gears and brakes. He squatted down and checked the chain, then stood up and swung his leg over the seat. Gripping the handlebars, he stared at Bucky.

"I know what you're doing," he said.

"What?" Bucky stared back at him, and in the heat of the musty barn, she and Henry glanced at each other, then looked away, past them, out over the dandelions growing through the cracked asphalt driveway. Suddenly they knew, too. They were trapped, but in what they weren't exactly sure. But it was criminal, and so were they.

"I'll give you seventy-five," Jimmy said. "And no questions asked." He smirked.

"We have to go in now." Before money could change hands, she grabbed Henry's good arm.

"A hundred," Bucky said as they hurried out of the barn.

Inside the house they stood close and watched from the window. They spoke in whispers though no one was home, only them, and next door, Dolly, who was probably still sleeping.

"We could get arrested," Henry whispered, his gentle lisp returning with fear or nerves. Both, this time.

"We didn't take them—he did," she whispered back.

A sickening streak of yellow sent Jimmy Clemmons pedaling down the driveway into the street. Bucky was at the door. She opened it but wouldn't let him in.

"Eighty bucks!" He was still counting crumpled bills. "Here, ten each."

Keep it, she told him. And he had to get his stolen bikes out of their barn.

"C'mon, Nellie, quit being such a bitch. I didn't steal those bikes. They're my grandfather's, I told you. Here." He held out the money, but she shut the door.

The minute he left, they ran to the park. She ripped the sign off the tree. Next they went to the supermarket, took down that sign, then hurried to town hall. But the sign she'd so securely tacked and taped to the community affairs notice board was gone. Only a scrap of yellow paper under the thumb tack remained.

Bucky not only didn't take the bikes out of the barn but the next day added one more, without telling them.

THE HUMBOLDT HOUSE on their left was the oldest one on the street, and the nicest. They hardly ever saw Miss Humboldt and her brother.

They were shy people, "skittish," her mother said. With their driveway on the far side of the house, they could drive straight into their garage, then enter their house, undetected—by the Peck children. For that's how they perceived them: as two very suspicious people. The beauty of the tree house was its perch over Dolly's apartment, and the unobstructed view it allowed over the Humboldt's fence and tall hedges. Nellie and Henry could see down into their deep backyard, half of which was wooded and at its far end abutted Chestnut Street. Theirs was the biggest lot in the neighborhood, almost two acres, according to Benjamin.

Tenley Humboldt kept two gardens, the larger plot, flowers, and the other, vegetables, where he'd be first thing in the morning, weeding and watering before the high heat of day. Then, in late afternoon, he would meander through the rows, pausing to pinch off fading blossoms and unwanted stems, dropping them into a blue bucket caught in the crook of his arm like a purse. It wasn't until the haze of early evening that Louisa would appear from the French doors onto the brick patio in her wide-brimmed straw hat. She stretched out on one of the fancy iron chaise longues. Her brother followed with their drinks and crackers on a shiny black tray. He set the tray on the table between them and sat down.

High above, peering through a slit in the tree house boards, Henry whispered, "Look, her seat, it's almost touching the ground, she's so fat."

"I wonder what kind of cheese that is." Stomach growling, Nellie adjusted the binoculars.

"There's hardly any left, she's eating it all." Henry had the old pair of binoculars, bigger and stronger.

"He always gets more," Nellie said, and sure enough, Tenley rose from his chaise longue and went into the house.

He was a slight man, surely half his sister's width, but it was the long ponytail halfway down his back that particularly fascinated Nellie. Tenley was the same age as her father, but never seemed to work. He didn't have to, her mother told them at dinner. Clearing his throat and straightening his shoulders, her father picked up the narrative. The Humboldt family was one of the oldest and richest in Springvale.

Railroad money, Benjamin said, eager to spur his children's interest in local lore. Right after the Civil War, Thomas Humboldt laid the first tracks on the line from Springvale to New York City. A few years later he committed suicide and his son, Thomas junior, sold the line to the Boston and Maine.

Ruth was kicking Nellie's foot. Henry was busy transferring broccoli into the paper napkin in his lap. Only their mother seemed to be listening.

"Look," Ruth whispered, flashing her palm below the table. The handwriting Nellie saw on the pink Post-it note was her sister's.

> *Daniel S. Brigham*
> *2942 Higgspost Lane*
> *Brisbane, Australia*

Ruth made that "can you believe it?" face, then excused herself; she had to go to the bathroom, her cue for Nellie to follow, but it seemed so disloyal. Benjamin had reached the Great Depression in his tale of the Humboldts. "The town's only hospital was about to close. Lack of funds. But it was Gerald D. Humboldt, great-grandson of Thomas, who not only secured the bond but gave a good deal of his own money to keep it going. He was an eccentric man, largely unremembered today, but if you drive out Crown Road to where the original spring runs . . ."

Sandy had gotten up and was quietly clearing the table. Henry's hand slipped into his shorts pocket, broccoli transfer complete. Nellie could hear the impatience in Ruth's overhead pacing. But how could she leave to hear news of her sister's other father? Benjamin's usually calm, deep voice pitched higher with confidence and excitement. It was this transcendence that she loved. No one else was like him. No one else could make her feel so centered and, still, so alive. His eyes gleamed and his hands flew as facts and dates swarmed him like startled bees. So much to tell. So much he knew and was desperate to share. With them.

"The little brick pump house—now that was built by Gerald. He deeded it to the town so that future generations could avail themselves of the purest, sweetest water in the state." He thumped the table with both hands. "We should do that! Yes! What do you say, Sandy, should we start filling our own jugs again? You're always saying we've got to save money, right? So why buy water at the supermarket?" He grinned. "So from now on, save the jugs!"

With Lazlo gone, they were his only forum, so Nellie nodded eagerly.

"We use tap water, Ben," her mother said with quiet annoyance.

"Well, all the more reason then!" he proclaimed, then began a clattery search through cupboards for containers. So far, he'd found two plastic pitchers with lids and from the trash a gallon milk jug he was rinsing in the sink. "There. That should do it," he said.

"Do what?" There was no mistaking the sting in her mother's voice and yet her father didn't notice.

"Come on, kids," he said, handing Nellie the pitchers and Henry the jug. "Let's take a ride." He knew better than to ask Ruth, who considered herself long removed from such juvenile jaunts.

Neither of them wanted to go. The night's plan was to move the bikes out of the barn, under cover of darkness. But they sat on the steps, waiting, shocked when their mother's voice rose sharply from the kitchen. They seldom argued, mostly because with any disagreement their father would simply go silent, for days afterward slipping in and out of rooms like a mistreated animal.

She couldn't bear to live like this anymore, she was saying. Last month their only income had been the little she'd brought home. Now she was faced with paying the store's bills as well, out of household money. In two more years Ruth would be going to college and where on earth was that money supposed to come from? "You've got to do something, Ben. We can't go on like this. It's embarrassing."

"I know. You're right. You're right. It's my fault. I've gotten too bogged down on the research. I've just got to be more decisive instead of going off on tangents every—"

"No! Forget the damn book! I'm talking about the store, Ben. You've got to sell it."

"I'm so close, Sandy. You have no idea how close I am. If you can just . . . just bear with me. Please. I've . . . I've . . . I've . . . even got query letters out."

His nervous stammer infuriated Nellie. How could her mother do this to him?

"That's great, Ben. But how's that going to take care of this? A shutoff notice. Six months, that's how far behind we are."

"I'll call Wally Miller. He practically runs the gas company."

In her mother's silence, she felt her father squirming with regret. Henry drove a stick deeper into the dry rot on the step's riser. He groaned.

"There's only one call I want you to make. Andy Cooper." Her soft voice quivered, whether on the edge of tears, shame, or rage, Nellie couldn't tell. "And I want you to tell him that you've made up your mind—"

"But—"

"And if you don't, if you can't do that for me and for your children, if you're that self-centered, then you're forcing my hand. And you know exactly what I mean. You do, don't you?"

THEY RODE IN silence. Nellie's chest hurt. It felt as if she'd been holding her breath this whole way. The last half mile to the spring led down a bumpy one-lane road so overgrown by poison sumac and blackberry bushes that when they parked, they could only get out one side of the car. The knob to the pump house door was missing, so Henry climbed through the window to let them in. It wasn't the expedition her father had envisioned. With blackflies around his head and enthusiasm strained, he read the plaque above the dripping spigot.

"This pump house is given to the citizens of Springvale in the communal spirit of good people looking out for one another. Gerald D. Humboldt." He lowered his eyes and sighed.

They filled their containers with the cool spring water. They were all quiet but her father was also remote. The dank dirt floor smelled like skunk and muddied their shoes, and when they came out to the car, the front tire was flat, which took awhile to change. When they got home, it was too late to move the bikes out of the barn. Nellie ran upstairs to her sister's room. Ruth was so annoyed. There she was, with the most amazing news, and she'd had to wait all this time.

She had gone online at her friend Allie's house and found her real father's name. His telephone number was unlisted, but she finally had an address. In fact, she'd just written a letter. "Sounds ritzy, huh?" she said, reading the address as she wrote it on the envelope.

"What if he comes here?" Nellie could just picture the horror of it, especially at this delicate time, her mother and Ruth swept off their feet by some wealthy, tanned guy with curly hair and a goofy smile in a Hawaiian shirt, and Benjamin's devastation. And worse, what would happen to Henry and her?

"I know," Ruth said, grinning. "I was thinking the same thing."

Chapter 4

PPARENTLY, THE CALL HAD BEEN MADE. THE NEXT DAY HER father came home early from the store. Her mother rushed in moments later. Her last appointment, Lisa Small, a color and cut, had been late, so she'd had to leave her under the dryer. She was taking off her smock when Mr. Cooper knocked on the door. He was wearing a dark suit and white shirt but came in unloosening his tie. It had been in the eighties for the last two days. The Coopers' whole house had air-conditioning, but the Pecks' didn't, just up in Ruth's room.

They were sitting at the kitchen table. There was a fizzy pop as her father opened a can of ginger ale for Mr. Cooper. Store brand, of course. Lately everything was generic. Not that it mattered to any of them, only Ruth, who said it was just the chintziest way to live.

"Thank you, my friend," Mr. Cooper said in that smooth way he had. Overbearing, her mother thought, but then her father would remind her of Andy's difficult childhood, an abusive father and mentally ill mother, so there was a lot he'd had to overcome in order to be successful.

Nellie had positioned herself in the living room near the kitchen door. So far, it hadn't been a very good day. Bucky had stopped by at noon with Raymond Doyle, a boy in her class she couldn't stand. They were going fishing at the pond, but Bucky didn't have a pole. He asked if he could borrow one of the two he'd seen in the barn. She wanted to tell him that if he didn't get the bikes out of the barn, then they'd have to dump them somewhere. But she couldn't very well say it in front of Raymond, so she asked Bucky to come in the house for a minute. As she held open the door, Henry started up the steps and for some stupid reason she told him to wait, that they'd be right out.

"Whoa, Nellie!" Raymond whooped and she glared back at him.

"Sure," Bucky kept saying inside. "Okay, all right. No problem." He'd come back later and move the bikes himself. But that'd be it, he said, the end of the bike club. From then on, all the profit would be his. He had until tonight, she warned, opening the door. He came down the steps, fumbling with his belt buckle, which sent Raymond hanging over his handlebars, hooting with laughter. Henry had dragged the two poles out of the barn, one for Bucky, the other for himself. No, she told him. He couldn't go. Not without permission, and as it slowly occurred to her that they were laughing about her and that it was lewd, she felt the strength of her authority fade.

"You're gonna be in big trouble for this!" her shaky voice threatened as they rode off, the older boys laughing with Henry pedaling double time in their draft. Anything, even under threat of doom, would be better than another boring day with his sister.

So here it was five o'clock and Henry still wasn't home. Both in their distraction and trust, neither parent had asked yet where he was. Nellie felt sick to her stomach. She was praying he'd make it home from the pond before they both got in trouble.

From the kitchen Mr. Cooper's voice carried like a whoosh of air, soft and hard to grasp. Sandy laughed nervously, uneasily, at everything he said, while Benjamin's assurances grew more expansive.

"No need to rush . . . however long it takes, Andy . . . don't want you feeling pressured here . . ."

"But—" Sandy started to say. Just then the doorbell rang, once, twice, three times, followed by an insistent *tap tap tap* on the glass.

Certain it was Henry, Nellie ran to the door. It was Dolly Bedelia in her purple bathrobe and bare feet. Wet hair dripped onto her shoulders. She'd been taking a shower when the water turned ice cold, she complained as she followed Nellie into the kitchen.

"I was just, like, putting the shampoo in!"

"Oh, Dolly!" Sandy grabbed the emergency flashlight she always kept plugged in to its charger. "I'm so sorry. It's that old tank." She opened the cellar door. With the flashlight shining up into Sandy's face, Nellie saw how lined it was, how old her pretty mother suddenly looked.

"Same problem Lazlo had," her father said, shaking his head, content to let her mother handle the problem.

Mr. Cooper just sat there with a dazed smile, looking up at Dolly. Bubbles glistened in her hair. The front of her robe was soaked, revealing every swell and hollow of her body.

"Benjamin!" her mother called up the stairs. "Get some matches."

"Matches, matches," her father muttered, fumbling through drawers, unable to find any.

"Maybe in the pantry closet." Nellie went to look. "There aren't any," she called back.

"I got some. Here." Dolly pulled a book of matches from her pocket and gave them to her father, who hurried down the stairs, holding them out in front like a flag. "I just started shampooing. That's, like, what I do first. Then after, I wash. I mean, you know," she said, waving a hand down the front of herself. As if for the first time, she seemed aware of the thin purple cloth so darkly plastered against her naked wetness. Slipping into the chair, she crossed her arms on the table.

"Isn't that always the way, huh?" Mr. Cooper said. He seemed amused.

Oh, Nellie could just imagine his version of this and Jessica's snarky questions about the strip club dancer being in her kitchen with nothing on under her sleazy bathrobe.

"I knew I shouldn't've waited so long to get ready. Now, I'm gonna be late for work again. Oh, Jesus, that's not the right time, is it?" She pointed to the wall clock.

"Ten minutes fast," Nellie lied so she wouldn't swear again and offend Mr. Cooper, who not only attended church every Sunday but had recently had his picture in the newspaper getting some award from the bishop. From downstairs came tapping on pipes and her parents' voices calling to each other like underground miners searching for a way out. After the canary died.

"Where do you work?" Mr. Cooper asked.

"The Paradise." Dolly cocked her head with a perky smile.

"Oh. Well. Maybe you should call and tell them you're running a little late then," Mr. Cooper said.

"Yeah, lotta good that'll do. My boss, he's a real . . ." She glanced at Nellie, raising thin eyebrows that were blond instead of yesterday's thick brown.

"Dolly's a singer. She's got a really nice voice," Nellie said quickly. She knew from listening at the bathroom wall that she swore a lot. Mostly on the phone, though. So far she'd only had a few visitors. That guy she'd turned away had come back again late one night, stayed a while, then after another argument had stormed out, slamming the door behind him, which her mother considered one of the rudest things one person could do to another—in this house, anyway. Two women who seemed to be Dolly's age had stopped in last week. They had the same mussed look, like dolls that had been handled too roughly. They didn't stay very long. Even their walk was similar, teetering down the steps on high wedge-heeled sandals, carrying out armloads of clothes on hangers.

Dolly winked at her. "Nellie's one of my biggest fans."

"Of whose numbers I'm sure are legion," Mr. Cooper said.

"Yeah," she said uncertainly, as if it might be an insult.

Nellie's mother and father emerged from the cellar with cobwebs in their hair. Her mother's cheek was smudged. She apologized again to Dolly. The pilot light had gone out and they'd had a hard time getting it lit. It was probably going to take a while for the water to heat up, so if Dolly wanted, she could use their shower.

"Oh, gee, that'd be great," Dolly said, jumping up to follow Sandy.

"Excuse me!" Mr. Cooper said, quickly pushing back his chair to stand. He held out his hand. "Here we've been talking and I never introduced myself. Andy Cooper."

"Dolly Bedelia. A pleasure to meet you," she said in that breathy, sing-song voice with a tilt of her head, and when she leaned to shake his hand, Nellie couldn't believe her eyes. The front of her robe slipped open, exposing a dark rim of left nipple. In Mr. Cooper's sly smile Nellie glimpsed their future, and it was bleak. She didn't breathe again until Dolly was upstairs. The clunk in the pipes as the shower went on wrenched in her chest. Her father and Mr. Cooper resumed their discussion. Her mother had obviously told him to stay on message. First, the building would need to be inspected, Mr. Cooper said. Oh, of course, her father agreed. And that price he'd mentioned, Mr. Cooper said, well, that was just a ball park estimate. Naturally, her father agreed. Mr. Cooper said he'd feel more comfortable having a commercial appraisal done. That makes sense, her father said. Especially now with real estate values down so much, Mr. Cooper said, adding how he'd probably end up taking a beating, but he did want to help out however he could. Her father didn't say anything. She wondered if he was already sorting through history, his grandfather and great uncle building Peck Hardware ninety-five years ago, tools as firmly in hand as their confidence in future generations.

"That Miss Bedelia, she seems like a pleasant young lady," Mr. Cooper said, interrupting their resumed business discussion as Nellie listened around the corner. But she'd lost interest in their talk of inspectors, purchase and sale agreements, lawyers, closing dates.

It was six o'clock. Dolly was gone, Henry was still not home. Something awful had surely happened. She never should have stood there watching him go. Afraid of Bucky's foul mouth and Raymond's dirty mind, she'd thrown her brother to the wolves. Maybe even literally. Coyotes had recently been spotted on the outskirts of town. Her little brother had been entrusted to her care and she had become exactly the kind of person she couldn't stand. A phony. A coward. She was setting the table for dinner when Henry's bicycle brakes squealed down the driveway. Relieved, but still the coward, she ran out to warn him not to say anything. Their mother thought he'd been in the tree house all this time.

His face was sunburned and dirty and his eyes were bloodshot and red, though he denied crying. Bucky and Raymond hadn't been fishing too long when they'd gotten sick of it. They told Henry about this amazing place they'd discovered. A sacred Indian initiation site. Sworn to secrecy, he'd been led deep into the woods, to a clearing littered with smashed bottles and burned beer cans. In the middle were charred pieces of wood and ashes from old campfires. First they'd made him take off his shirt, then they'd cut a length of fishing line, and according to ancient rite, tied him to a tree with his hands behind his back. With Henry begging him not to, Bucky yanked down his shorts and underpants. They threw his clothes high over his head into the tree branches.

"This is what you get for tryna get out of the club," Bucky hissed in his ear. "Next time's your sister's turn."

They'd run off with Henry screaming and begging them not to leave him alone. He said he stood like that, for a long time, his bare back and rear end rubbing almost raw against the rough tree bark.

"Look," he said, raising the stitched arm. The scar was fiery red and bleeding at two of the stitch points. He wasn't sure how long he'd been there, three or four hours anyway, he thought. His rescuers had been an older couple holding hands as their dog trotted ahead. The dog, a greyhound, had found him first. It came running at him, then stood inches away, barking. Listening, Nellie could feel her brother's terror, helpless, tied to a tree, certain the frantic dog was attacking him. The man used his pocketknife to slice the line on Henry's wrists while the woman shook the tree to get his clothes down, all but his underpants. They stayed caught on a branch.

"They wanted to call the police, but I said, 'No, please don't. They were just fooling around.' 'What kinda fooling around?' the guy said. 'They do something to you?' he kept asking." Henry looked sick.

"What'd he mean?" Nellie asked, and for a moment they couldn't look at each other.

Henry shrugged, and suddenly she pressed him against the wall, demanding he tell her, because if he didn't, she was going to have to tell Mom, which, of course, she had no intention of doing.

"He said he was going to—"

"What?"

"Pee on me," he whispered.

Enraged, she charged out the back door.

"But he didn't! He didn't!" Henry called after her.

The Brickmans lived only a few blocks away, in the small cottage behind the Universalist church and the parsonage. The church's wide circular driveway was where they'd first met Bucky. His grandmother smiled when she saw Nellie at the door. Oh, come in. Come in, she said. Bucky was just finishing dinner.

"Thanks," Nellie said. "I'll just wait out here till he's done."

But no, she wouldn't hear of it. As Nellie was led into the turquoise-

and-pink kitchen she felt her vengeful mission losing steam. Please, Mrs. Brickman said, insisting Nellie sit down. Like his wife, Reverend Brickman had pure white hair and looked to be as old as Charlie. His cup trembled as he raised it to his powdery lips. He was unshaven and there were food stains on his T-shirt. Delighted to meet a friend of Bucky's, they offered her applesauce cake, lime Jell-O, a soda. So far, Bucky hadn't said a word.

"Peck. Peck," Mrs. Brickman mused. "Are you the hardware store family?"

"Yes," she said, adding that her father was Benjamin.

Reverend Brickman said he'd known her grandfather Peck. They'd been in Rotary together.

"Really," Nellie said, staring at Bucky. Caught in his grandmother's fond gaze, he faked a smile.

"Yes," Mrs. Brickman said. "The reverend always made a point of keeping parish business in town."

"Think globally, act locally," the retired parson said with a lift of his cup.

Right. But Nellie was too well raised to say what she was thinking. Bucky's chair scraped away from the table, and she made a move to get up. He had to go to the bathroom, he said. He'd be right back.

After he left, Mrs. Brickman asked if she was enjoying the summer so far. Oh, yes, Nellie told her, straining to hear a toilet flush or a door open. Bucky's made so many nice friends, his grandmother was saying. A blessing, considering all the poor boy's gone through.

With more to come, Nellie thought, looking past her, hands clenching the chair seat. She'd already made up her mind to hit him if she had to. They were the same size and that was one thing she wasn't afraid of—a fight. Not that she'd ever been in one, but she'd memorized most of the holds illustrated in *Get Tough!* The book had belonged to her great-uncle Seth, who was killed in World War II. She had practiced the "handcuff hold" so many times on Henry that she knew it by heart, but he was sick of always being on the losing end, so he wouldn't be her enemy victim anymore. The Bent Arm Hold was trickier. According to the major, the movements had to be done in "one rapid and continuous motion." The blows were in the beginning of the book. She particularly liked the Chin Jab; so far, though, she'd never tried it on anyone. If she had to, Bucky would be her first victim.

Wondering what was taking so long, Mrs. Brickman went off looking for her grandson. "Bucky. Bucky? Bucky!" Nellie heard her voice pitch higher as she tapped on a door. "Answer me! Answer me right now, young man!"

"We don't," Nellie, meanwhile, answered the reverend, who had asked what congregation the Pecks belonged to. He seemed puzzled. Mrs. Brickman had scurried back into the kitchen. She removed a metal skewer from a drawer. Water was running in the bathroom, but Bucky wasn't answering and the door was locked.

"He must be sick," the reverend said, shuffling after his wife, Nellie next down the hallway.

"I thought he looked awful peaked," Mrs. Brickman said. Her hands shook as she kept trying to poke the skewer into the tiny hole in the knob. "I'm coming, dear," she called as the lock finally popped open.

The embroidered hand towel fluttered on the rack. Water was running into the sink and the window over the toilet was wide open.

"My Lord!" she exclaimed, staring for a moment, trying to make sense of it all. She looked back at them. "Why did he do that?"

"He's a troubled child, Florence. Who knows why he does anything?" the reverend scoffed with surprising bitterness.

Mrs. Brickman snatched her straw purse from the closet shelf. She would drive around until she found him.

"Let him go," Reverend Brickman said with a weary sigh.

"No!" she declared on her way outside. "We gave our word."

Her slammed door sent a shudder through the old clergyman. Seemingly unaware of Nellie's presence, he shuffled along the dim hallway, back toward the kitchen, feeling along the wall. If this was a test of his spiritual mettle, he wasn't looking up to the task. He sat down with a groan.

"I guess I better go, sir," Nellie said, standing over him.

"Randolph. That's his name. Your grandfather," he said, spoon clinking as he scraped the last green Jell-O bits from the footed bowl. "He liked the horses."

"I never met him."

"Here, have some." He pushed a bowl of it across the table.

With little choice, she sat down. If Mrs. Brickman didn't find Bucky, *she* would. Eventually. The Jell-O was very good, she told him. "My mother used to make it but not anymore. She works, so now for dessert we mostly have cookies."

"What?" he demanded irritably. "What?" He peered past her.

She glanced over her shoulder, but no one else was there. "Cookies!" she repeated, louder. "Store-bought," she added because he looked so confused.

"We don't have any," he called back. "Just applesauce cake." He pointed toward the domed cake stand on the counter. "Cut me a piece, too. Good size." With two fingers he indicated how thick.

So she did, and they ate in strained silence. She could barely swallow with Reverend Brickman scowling at her as he chewed. Crumbs flecked his chin whiskers. That was very good, she said when she was done.

"Say what you want, but your grandma's a pretty fine cook, gotta give her that," he said.

"You knew my grandmother?"

"Don't get fresh with me, boy. I've just about had it with your mouth."

"Sorry, sir, I thought you meant my father's mother."

His head snapped up. "Doing it again, aren't you? Trying to mess me up, aren't you?"

"No, sir. I'm sorry, I better go. My mother, she doesn't know I'm here."

"Doesn't know where you are! Let's get something straight here, she doesn't care. That's how you ended up here. We're the ones calling the shots now. We're the ones you better be concerned about, not *her*!"

Nellie waited a respectful moment. The old man of God was either crazy or senile, and it wasn't her place to try to set him straight. This time she wouldn't say anything, just leave. He concentrated on eating his cake again. She slipped from the chair and eased toward the door.

"Sit down!" he bellowed, pointing his buttercream frosting–smeared fork at her. She froze. "And don't move until I say so!" he warned, un-buckling his belt. He snapped it on the edge of the table, and that's when she took off. Running. Straight home. Good thing for Bucky it was getting dark.

A FEW DAYS later Max showed up at the house. He'd come for Char-lie's mending, frayed shirts that needed collars turned and buttons re-placed, stained work pants with balky zippers and torn seams. Most everything belonged in the rag bag, Nellie's mother had said the other night, but if she didn't mend them, he'd just keep wearing them in their sorry state. In the past she'd been able to buy him new clothes whenever he needed them, but now she could only at Christmas. Nel-lie was telling Max all this when Dolly knocked on the door.

"Hey!" she called through the screen with her perky-jerky little wave that Ruth was now imitating. Dolly asked to borrow some bread for toast. Sure, Nellie said, as she let herself in. Max's eyes moved so hungrily up and down her body that it was embarrassing, for Nellie, at least. Dolly wore skimpy black shorts and matching sequined halter top and, as usual, was barefoot. Raving about what great toast their oatmeal bread made, she opened the wooden bread box on the counter and took two slices from the bag. She'd done the same thing the other day, which had really annoyed Nellie's mother.

"I'm getting ready and all of a sudden I have an attack of the munchies," she said, twirling the plastic bread bag before fastening the twist tie. When neither adult acknowledged the other, Nellie figured they were waiting for her to make the proper introduction.

"Dolly, I'd like you to meet Max. And Max, this is Miss Dolly Be-delia. Ms., I mean," she added, hoping Dolly wasn't offended. She re-alized she didn't know Max's last name and he didn't offer it.

"Hi," was all Dolly said, which even Nellie knew was inadequate.

He gave a stiff nod back.

"I gotta go eat fast," she said on her wiggly way to the door. "Or I'll be late for work. Nice meeting ya!" She waved back with a breezy flap of the bread that sprayed crumbs onto the floor.

"An' you," Max grunted as the door banged shut.

Nellie continued what she'd been saying before, that her mother said to tell Charlie his pajamas weren't in the bag.

"Where's she work?" he interrupted.

"Frederic's. But she doesn't have them there. They're not worth mending, she said. She's just gonna get him some new ones."

"I mean . . ." He nodded at the door.

"Oh. Up on Route nine. The Paradise. Yeah, Dolly. She's a dancer. And a singer, too. A really good one." Nellie was enjoying her moment of authority. "She used to be in New York. You know, like, Broadway or something."

"Hey, mister!"

With the burst of Dolly's voice through the screen, they both glanced back.

"Your friggin' dog—he's on my porch and I can't get in."

"He was in the truck," Max said.

"Yeah, till he jumped out the window."

Muttering, Max hurried outside and pulled Boone by the collar into the truck. A moment later he returned for the mending. First time Boone'd ever done that, he said, seeming oddly flustered as he lingered in the doorway. He most always left the window open and Boone just knew to stay put. Every time. Maybe it was the bread, Nellie suggested, not wanting him to be too disappointed. Or angry. She still remembered his attack on that other dog. Probably smelled it and just wanted some. Here, she said, starting to open the bread bag, but Max shook his head; that's no kind of lesson, he said, rewarding him for doing the wrong thing. Maybe he just saw a squirrel or something, she said, and he just forgot for a second, that's all. With animals, it's all about instinct. One going after the other. She was on a roll, and best of all was having an adult listen to what she had to say. Like that time in the junkyard, she continued without pause for breath, the pit bull, remember? And the way Boone charged right at him. That was different, Max said. He'd acted on command. He said he'd had a lot of dogs and Boone was the smartest one yet.

"Like, some things he just knows, like some kind of . . ."—he tapped his chest—". . . thing inside. He just knows."

"Yeah!" she said, warming to this, one of her favorite topics. "And some people're like that, too." *Like me,* she'd been about to say.

"Like Charlie," he was saying. "He's that way. I'll be tryna think of something, next thing I know he's saying it. He's good at that."

"Charlie!" She couldn't help it. "He never talks, not to me, anyway."

"He's just kinda worn out, that's all. Early morning, now, that's his good time." He laughed. "Four-thirty, five, come then, he'll fry up a sunny side and tell you whatever you need to know."

"About what?" she scoffed, making his eyes flash.

"All the stuff you don't get in books," he said sharply.

"Like junkyards?" She squirmed with her own smart-assiness, but talking to Max was different from talking to most people. She'd pushed past some barrier. And he liked her for it.

"Yeah. And, like, how everyone's always after him about it, but like Charlie says, here we are on a dying planet, and they just keep on making things to break down, for the economy, so if it wasn't for him, where would it go, all the broken stuff? Everything'd be an even bigger mess when you think about it."

She tried considering Charlie in such heroic light, unappreciated and performing a service to humanity with his haphazard mountains of useless goods right in the heart of town. But she couldn't get past the cranky old man part, the grandfather who'd admitted he didn't like kids.

"Well, anyway," she said, wanting to turn the conversation back to herself and Max, "that thing with Henry, I mean, you were really brave, and me, I just froze. I couldn't do anything."

"Just wasn't your time, that's all," he said as Boone began to bark.

"Hey!" Dolly was at the screen door again. "Hey, can you give me a hand?" Her car wouldn't start. She'd called her girlfriend for a ride, but she wasn't answering her phone.

"How 'bout I take a look?"

"Yeah. Jesus, that'd be great. Stupid car. I been late so many times now, it's not funny." She followed Max outside, then went into her apartment. Nellie stood on the side of the driveway while he tried to start her car. But Dolly was right. It was dead. Boone watched from inside the truck, frozen in chastisement, though alert to Max's every move. When Max climbed back in, Boone sat so close the two dark profiles appeared to be one as Max inched the truck nearer Dolly's car. He got out and popped the car's hood then attached jumper cables from his battery to hers. That done, he sat in her little car, one long leg stretched through the open door. He turned the ignition. Nothing. He kept getting out, adjusting clamps, going back, sliding half onto the seat—still wouldn't start. He turned off the truck, then asked Nellie for a cloth and some rubbing alcohol, so she ran inside.

She hurried back with a bottle and rag. Dolly came out then and Boone's head rose through the window in a whiny howl.

"Quiet!" Max snarled and the gleaming black dog froze. Nellie stuck her hand in and stroked Boone's warm silky ear. Poor animal. He hadn't done anything wrong. All he'd wanted was a little attention. Some kind of connection. And Nellie knew that feeling well, the dull ache of the ignored. There was Dolly chattering away at Max, who would have picked up her car and carried her to work in it if she wanted, while Boone and Nellie looked on.

Dolly waited with her arms folded while Max leaned over her engine cleaning the leads on her battery with the alcohol soaked rag. She was telling him how the club was just temporary, for now. Her agent in New York really wanted her to come back. She was still thinking it over. The thing is, she'd needed a break.

"You're going along fine, and all of a sudden it's like, whoa—I don't want to do this anymore. You know what I mean? People're going, 'Don't quit! C'mon! I got this great gig for you.' So you leave what you're doing and after all the rehearsals with hardly any pay, you end up in this show and it only goes for six days. Crazy!" she sighed. "Just crazy, the whole thing. But that's what happens."

With the uplift in her voice, Max turned. He covered his mouth, smiling so hard his eyes were all crinkled up.

"Sounds pretty exciting, though," he said behind his hand.

"Being paid woulda been even more."

"Yeah, I guess." He chuckled.

"Hey!" Dolly grabbed his wrist.

"What the—" Max growled, recoiling as if he'd just been stung. He seemed startled, as much by her touch, as by his anger.

She twisted his hand to see his watch. "Jesus!" she squealed, her hand still on his. "I didn't know it was this late!"

A coldness had overtaken him, and for some reason, Nellie thought of Patrick Dellastrando's ignoring her on the street yesterday when she made a point of saying a loud and pointed hello to him and his girl-friend.

"Get behind the wheel," Max told Dolly. He walked quickly back to his truck and started it. He gestured over the wheel for her to turn the key. When she did, her engine sputtered to life. She backed out of the driveway onto the street.

"No!" Max yelled out his window, waving for her to stop. "Let it run a minute!"

But she was on her way, then gone.

Chapter 5

———

JESSICA WAS AWAY AT CAMP, "SPECIAL" SUMMER CAMP, SHE'D told Nellie bitterly. The seven Cooper kids had always gone away together for the same two weeks: Camp Lewis, somewhere up in New Hampshire. But this year Jessica was being sent to a camp for special-needs kids—one more reason to hate her mother. Nellie felt bad for Jessica being singled out like that, but she knew her brothers and sisters were probably relieved. Nellie certainly was. As much as she missed keeping up with her shows, she didn't miss Jessica. Right before she left she'd been acting so nasty that Nellie'd hide in the house when she came banging on the door. Her moods were hard to take, especially when Nellie was feeling pretty low herself.

The "hot" bikes, as she now thought of them, were still in the barn, hidden way in back, omens of disaster. Somehow they had to get rid of them, but Henry wouldn't even discuss it with her, much less do anything about it. Ever since the incident in the woods all he did was work on his tree house. Life was changing all around Nellie, and no one was doing anything about it. Her family was coming undone. Or at least that's what it felt like. All Ruth cared about, besides finding her "real father," was getting Patrick Dellastrando to notice her. She traipsed around the house in bright red lipstick and black mascara so thick her lashes would actually get stuck together. Dolly Bedelia had shown her how to highlight her mouth with deep purple liner, which gave her a kind of clownish desperation and made Nellie sad to look at her. She went out at night in tight halter tops and skimpy skirts with half her butt hanging out. She got away with it by leaving the house wearing a loose shirt and pants over everything. Her sister was teetering on the edge of a dark abyss only Nellie seemed aware of.

Meanwhile, her father was clueless, racing against time, working day and night to finish the history, as if that would solve all their problems. Nellie was beginning to think her mother didn't want to know what was going on. In fact, she'd even started saying it, that there was only so much she could handle. Because it was summer, business at the beauty shop had slowed down, but the bills hadn't. Dolly came over all the time now to use their shower. Her hot water was just too rusty, which probably meant a new hot-water tank, her mother worried. The latest bad news came when the store's ancient key-cutting machine "started going on the fritz." Key cutting had never been a big moneymaker, but it did bring in customers, who'd roam the aisles while her father fiddled with the temperamental settings, and sometimes they'd even buy things they hadn't even known they needed. The repair estimate was almost as much as buying another machine, which her mother said made no sense when they'd be selling the place soon. It was clear that their future was in Mr. Cooper's hands, though he still hadn't called. Every day when her mother raced home from work to check the answering machine, Nellie wished she'd been nicer to Jessica. Maybe this was her father's payback.

Even Dolly Bedelia had lost some of her mystique now that she was coming over so much. She loved hanging around the kitchen talking to Nellie's mother, or if she wasn't home, to Ruth, who was beginning to laugh just like her and throw up her hands in the same fluttery exasperation when she couldn't quite get the right words out. Yesterday Ruth had even ordered Nellie out of the room so she and Dolly could speak privately. Nellie tiptoed down the creaky cellar stairs, then teetered on a milk crate directly below them, with her ear at the musty old beams. It was hard to hear much. Dolly was doing most of the talking. About protection. Nellie knew exactly what that meant, and it made her stomach queasy.

THE JUNKYARD HAD been in the news again. One of the mountains of rubber tires had caught fire—arson, Charlie insisted, people trying to drive him out of business, mainly the Shelby twins, he told his daughter, which made little sense beyond the fact that their family's property abutted the far end of Charlie's. The Shelby twins were Nellie's age and generally regarded as odd. In school they spoke only to each other, so they were pretty much ignored, but she'd been studying them for years and knew they were harmless. Roy and Rodney had dark hair and identical cowlicks. They towered over everyone else and were the clumsiest boys she'd ever seen. Gym classes were agonies of tripping and falling. They always seemed to be getting hit by balls. They weren't the best students, though their flashes of genius and wit intrigued Nellie. Their science-fair projects might combine the usual elements but in the most unique ways. When their volcano erupted, the spew of colored lava launched a rocket hissing through a tunnel out onto a pad that began to play the "William Tell Overture." Their mother was at least six feet tall; her white hair was pinned back in a messy bun and she wore yellow tinted aviator glasses. She picked the twins up every day after school and the minute they climbed into her ancient tan Cadillac, Nellie just knew they morphed into different people. She would see them drive off laughing and talking, two of the handsomest and cleverest boys a mother could have, Mrs. Shelby surely thought. It made Nellie feel better knowing that in the safety of their home, Roy and Rodney were gregarious and funny, probably computer geniuses who would someday be programming the universe. For her, it was all part of needing to know people's secrets, filling in the backstory, as her father called it. Because in the end people were always more than they seemed to be. But then she was often the only one who recognized the "more." By investing even the most difficult people with some measure of hope and dignity, her own guilty inertia was somehow diminished. And that way she could continue to distance herself from Roy and Rodney. Jessica Cooper was all the burden she could handle.

Acrid smoke from the smoldering tires enveloped the downtown streets for days until a twelve-hour torrential downpour doused the last of the fires. Investigators discovered countless safety violations, which were bad enough, given Charlie's many citations through the years, but the worst blow of all was what they dug up about Max. Before drifting into Springvale, he'd been in jail. Her mother told Charlie he had to let Max go. People in town were upset enough about the junkyard, but an ex-con in their midst was just too much.

"That was three years ago," Charlie scoffed.

"And what was that for?" her mother sighed. She was getting worn out. Her father's gall bladder was acting up again. He'd had two attacks in one week, but refused to go to the hospital.

"A fight or something," Charlie said. "But it wasn't his fault."

"Get rid of him," her mother said.

"He saved your son's life." With his sly look he might have been haggling over the price of a tin pail or a new car. Charlie was master of the upper hand.

"He's a criminal!"

"I judge a man for who he is. Not what he was," he declared in his loftiest tone. The truth was that he'd found someone with a strong back willing to work for a roof over his head and the privacy of the fenced in junkyard for him and his dog. Kind of like jail, in a way, or so it seemed to Nellie.

"You enjoy this, don't you? You're just asking for trouble and you know you are," her mother warned in a low voice. Max was by the front gate, helping a man push two large cast iron radiators up a ramp into a plumber's van.

"You sound like your mother." He grinned, savoring, if not his daughter's misery, then the memory of some familiar rebuke.

"Please, Dad. People're just looking for something, a way to get rid of you, you know they are."

Charlie chuckled and looked around. "Well, Charlie's got a surprise for them. Little something up his sleeve." He motioned her closer. "I'm in negotiations."

"What do you mean? For what?"

He held out his arms. "This. All of it. Andy Cooper. Don't say nothing, but he wants to turn this into one of those intown malls. Two stories. Fancy shops, places to eat."

Instead of going home as planned, Nellie and her mother walked quickly to the hardware store. Surprisingly enough, there was a customer. They waited at the end of the scarred counter. The young man kept glancing at her mother and smiling while her father dropped the four toggle bolts he'd bought into a small paper bag.

"Three dollars and fifteen cents," he said, not even bothering to ring up the purchase. The young man paid him and her father slipped the money into his pocket.

"Hey," the young man said to her mother as he started to leave. "Sandy, right? You cut my hair. Couple weeks ago. I'm Anthony, Lizzie's friend."

"Oh sure," her mother said, distractedly. "I remember. Still looks pretty good."

"Getting a little scruffy." He touched the back of his neck. "How 'bout tomorrow? Got anything at four? That's when I get off work."

"I'm not sure. Maybe you should call."

"Okay!" He flipped the bag of clinking bolts in the air and caught it. "What's your number?"

"Call the shop—that's what I meant." Her mother's face was red.

"Okay, I'll do that then," he said.

Her father's long stare at the departing young man confirmed Nellie's uneasiness. It bothered her that someone other than her father found her mother so attractive, though it had certainly gotten her father's attention. "Anthony. What's his last name?" he asked.

"I don't remember," she said with a little smile. "Why?"

"Nineteen thirty-nine!" He tapped the side of his head. "It just came to me. Before you came in we were talking about the old Brewster Bridge—he used to live near it—and I couldn't remember the year it was rebuilt. Oh well," he laughed. "I guess he'll just have to buy the book."

"Ben, you've got to call Andy. He's trying to buy the junkyard. I just found out. That's why we haven't heard anything." She relayed Charlie's news, though her version contained big-name stores like Gap and Talbots, as well as an expensive French restaurant.

"Well, that's exactly what this town needs. New blood. A rising tide to lift all our ships. It'll be a boost for everyone, including this place," he said.

"Wait outside, Nellie," her mother said through tight lips.

She did but watched through the front window, long ago lettered PECK HARDWARE in shaded gold leaf with black edging. With one hand on her hip and the other pointing, her mother appeared to be shouting. Whatever her ultimatum, it was just a while later that Mr. Cooper came to the house. He was still interested, though not at the price he'd originally quoted. Too much time had passed. All the banks, appraisers—it was the same story everywhere. The market was shaky and real estate had taken a nosedive in the last year.

"Everything's down. Way down," Mr. Cooper said.

"That's the truth," her father agreed. "I see it every day. People trying to—"

"How down?" her mother interrupted. "What do you mean?"

"Twenty, maybe even twenty-five percent."

"So how much is that?" she asked.

"A hundred twenty, anyway," Mr. Cooper said. "And dropping by the day."

Her mother was stunned. A hundred twenty thousand dollars, which meant what, the store was only worth five hundred thirty thousand? If that, Mr. Cooper sighed, thumbs working his fancy cell phone. And don't forget, as part of the original offer he'd naturally calculated the worth of the business itself. Which was a lot less now with all the big box stores. Not to mention depreciation, the equipment, inventory.

Into the silence, like the beat of a distant heart, pulsed the faint *thump thump thump* of music from the third floor. Ruth had bought an iPod with her tip money. Nellie was the only one who knew because she'd seen it. And Henry, whom she'd sworn to secrecy. And Dolly, because Ruth told her everything. All the late-night confidences, the coveted daily reports from her teenage wasteland, she now shared with Dolly.

"No, Andy." Her father leaned forward on the table. His dark eyes gleamed, and she was struck by how handsome he was. And how stern he sounded. "That wasn't part of it. All we talked about was the property, the building itself."

"That may be your recollection, Ben, but that's not how it went." Mr. Cooper almost seemed offended.

"That's exactly how it went." Her mother's voice trembled. "I remember that day. Every detail. Ben came home and he said you'd been in the store buying a new drill and, by the way, you said, if he ever wanted to sell the building you'd pay him six hundred and fifty thousand for it. There was nothing about—"

"Three years, Sandy. Those were the good times. A lot's changed since then. I'm sorry." Mr. Cooper checked his cell phone. Mrs. Cooper had just texted him again. She was waiting to be picked up. They had early dinner reservations at the Crestshire Club, then afterward a movie. Nice to have a night out without worrying about babysitters, he sighed. Her parents looked up, their expressions numb, lifeless. Nellie was trying to remember the last time they'd gone to a movie together or out to dinner. "It's still not a bad offer," he said. "Talk it over, the two of you, and let me know. We can do this." He opened the door. "Just don't wait three more years, my friends," he said with a quick glance back. "Or months even."

"He's not a nice man," Nellie blurted when he was gone. "He takes medicine for his temper, but Jessica said he still flips out. Once he even threw a shoe at her."

"Go in the other room," her mother ordered. "Please."

Well, it was true, but she knew better than to protest. Jessica had sworn her to secrecy, but why should she protect someone who was trying to rip off her mother and father? Mr. Cooper was not the pleasant man people thought. He had a dark side only his family and she knew about. At home he was always screaming at Mrs. Cooper and the kids—and most especially, at Jessica. As a result, she said, her mother took everything out on her. Up until now Nellie'd thought that it was just more of Jessica's desperate lying for attention. She stood behind the sheer curtain watching Mr. Cooper stand by his car, talking on his cell phone. A moment later Dolly came down her steps, carrying the soiled pink back pack that contained her work clothes. Her car had been dead in the driveway for a week now. She couldn't afford the repair, so she'd been walking the mile or so downtown where she caught the six o'clock bus to the Paradise. If Mr. Cooper had been hurrying to meet his wife, he wasn't in any rush now. He and Dolly were on the sidewalk talking and laughing. Nellie hadn't realized Mr. Cooper could be so amusing. Or, at least, Dolly thought so anyway. She kept running her hand through her hair. Nellie wondered if they were talking about the shower water turning cold that day while she still had shampoo in her hair. Probably comparing notes about what losers Benjamin and Sandy Peck were—no money for a new hot-water heater or movies or dinner out or camp for their kids or even a new television to replace the one that had died ages ago. Nellie leaned over the windowsill as Dolly slipped into Mr. Cooper's slick little sports car, and off they drove. She had that funny feeling again inside.

THE HOUSE HAD been deeply quiet. For two days the only voices had been Nellie's, her brother's, and her sister's. And for Ruth, make that just barely. She seemed, as Nellie's father would say when her mother accused him of not listening, preoccupied. Now Nellie knew for sure who Ruth's preoccupation was: Patrick Dellastrando. They were dating—but secretly. No one could know, Ruth confided. No one on earth. She hadn't even told Allie, her best friend.

"Why's it have to be secret?" Nellie asked, though she was pretty sure she knew.

"Because he still has to break up with Diane." Diane James, his steady girlfriend forever.

"Yeah? So why doesn't he?" As if he'd want to. Diane James was beautiful. Even Henry had a crush on her.

"It's not a good time." Ruth sighed as if Nellie wouldn't understand. "She's got personal problems. Stuff at home. Her parents."

"Same as you. I mean, Sandy and Ben aren't even talking," she said. As long as Ruth insisted on calling Nellie's father Ben, she had begun referring to their mother by her first name as well. Not that it made any sense. But they were fast approaching strangeness anyway.

"That reminds me. My letter, guess what? I mailed it," she announced with shivery delight. She figured it would be three weeks before she heard back. "A week for the letter to get there, a week for my father to get over the shock, and a week for him to get back."

"What do you mean, shock?"

"He doesn't even know I exist! I mean, think of it."

Yes, he does—why do you think he and his whole family took off, leaving their mother in such a lurch, Nellie wanted to say, but her father was shouting to them from the front door.

"Ruthie! Nellie?"

Alarmed, they ran into the kitchen. His shirt was plastered to his sweaty back and his thick hair was wild in the humid air that had hung over the valley for days.

"What'd Mr. Cooper want?" he panted as if he'd been running. He'd just seen Mr. Cooper's car come around the corner. Obviously, from here. Not from here, they told him. Well, maybe Mr. Cooper had rung the doorbell and they'd been upstairs and hadn't heard it, he said. No, because they'd been down here the whole time.

"Maybe that's it then. The bell," he said. "Maybe it's not working again." He opened the door and pushed the button. His shoulders sagged with the sharp buzz.

Now, why her father didn't just keep calling Mr. Cooper or go to his office, Nellie didn't know. Puzzling, like so much else in the world of adults. After all, it had been Mr. Cooper who had first approached her parents and gotten them all excited and hopeful, so why was he backing off now? She couldn't help thinking of all the times she'd taken a different way home from school to avoid Jessica, or the phone calls she'd answered disguising her voice, "This is Ruth. I'm sorry, but Nellie's not here."

"I know that's you, Nellie, and don't think I don't!" Jessica would scream back.

She must have told her parents of Nellie's cruelty and this was their revenge. The chickens had come home to roost. And yet this was the third day in a row that Mr. Cooper had been in the neighborhood. She'd seen his car yesterday and the day before, parked in front of Dr. Reese's dental office down the hill. So maybe that was it, she told her father. Maybe Mr. Cooper was having a root canal or something done.

"Maybe," her father murmured on his way into the kitchen to start dinner. Even the clang of pans and water running into the sink sounded thin and dispirited. And that was scary. If her father was getting worried, then things were a lot worse than she'd thought.

She had finally convinced Henry. They couldn't wait any longer. They had to get rid of the five bikes. Their opportunity came on a hot moonless night. Their mother had finally given in. They could sleep in the tree house as long as their father covered the unfinished roof and window openings with mosquito netting. Slick with bug spray, they lay in their damp sleeping bags eating and hearing the leaves tremble as bats swooped in and out of the trees. They weren't supposed to have any food because their mother said it would attract the band of rac-coons that had been pillaging the trash barrels at night. But what was a night in the tree house without supplies, so Henry had smuggled out a box of Cheez-Its and some brownies. They each had a water bottle and a flashlight. And for protection, a baseball bat. They'd been waiting for the Humboldts' floodlights to go out; one shone directly on the barn door. But it was getting late, so they climbed down the ladder and ran into the barn.

With each one riding a bike, it took two trips. They hid them in the bushes between the church and the cottage. Nellie and Henry rode double on the last bike, brother behind sister, holding on to the seat, bitching about the wobbly ride, until she got mad and ordered him off. She pedaled slowly as he jogged indignantly alongside. He kept trying to get her to talk to him, but she wouldn't. She hated it when he got all whiny and wimpy like that, so she ignored him, which only made things worse. Now he was telling her in a high, breathless voice about that day in the woods and how scared and ashamed he'd been, alone and naked, how every time he moved, the fishing line cut into his ankles and wrists, how the sweat poured down his forehead into his eyes, blinding him with the salty glare. His voice broke.

"Are you crying again?" she asked disgustedly. He denied it, but he kept sniffing and wiping his nose with the back of his hand. She sped ahead, going as fast as she could.

"Wait! Wait for me!" he bawled through the darkness.

She stopped, straddling the bike as he ran toward her, sobbing, head down, fists clenched. He kicked the bike, knocking it out from under her. As it fell, the pedal scraped her ankle. With a painful yelp, she punched him in the chest and he kept trying to hit her back, but she managed to hold him at arm's length. He was kicking the bike again.

"Cut it out, Henry! Just cut it out! You're acting like an idiot, like some kind of two-year-old!" He lunged for her glasses, an old countermeasure he hadn't pulled in years, but she shoved him away. Back he came in all his fury, fists raised, and she shouldn't have, but as she delivered Major Fairbairn's Edge-of-the-Hand Blow, chopping hard into his bony shoulder, she really, really wanted to hurt him and didn't regret it one bit. Crying harder, he held on to his curled shoulder and started walking away. "Go ahead, Henry, keep wimping out. Just keep wimping out!" she called after him, but he kept going. She stood there for as long as she could, watching his skinny, pathetic figure drag down the street, farther into the shadows until she had no choice. She ran after him and said she was sorry. She shouldn't have said what she said and she shouldn't have hit him. But there were a lot better ways of getting back at someone than crying and trying to hurt the person who was only trying to help him. She would have said more, but she was afraid she might cry, too. And besides, it was getting late.

By the time they got to the church, the steeple clock said five of ten. The lights were off inside the cottage. She steered the last bike into the bushes.

"Wait," Henry whispered. He pulled out the longest blade on his Swiss Army knife and slashed the front tire of the bike they'd just delivered. Nellie grabbed his arm before he could slash the back tire.

"Let goa me!" He struggled to free himself.

"They're not his bikes," she whispered, holding on with both hands. Somewhere nearby a dog started barking. "It's vandalism. You can go to jail for that."

"I don't care!" His voice cracked.

"Henry! Stop it!" She held on tighter as he tried head butting her away.

"He peed on me! In my face even!"

She let go. She watched him move from bike to bike sobbing and stabbing away at the tires, the bikes sinking flat on their rims. She couldn't see her brother's face through the darkness, but his anguish cut deeply into her, and for the first time in her life she understood what pure hatred felt like. Bucky Saltonstall had destroyed something vital and pure in her little brother. One way or another he would pay for that. And the cost would be a lot more than ten tires.

CHARLIE WAS ON another new medicine, which she had to pick up and deliver to him. Henry had been gone for the last three days. He'd been invited to go to the lake for a week with Kip Kruger, a boy in his class. When Mrs. Kruger called to make the arrangements, her mother had to close the door on Henry's shouts that he wasn't going to the lake with creepy Kip Kruger and no one could make him, and if they did, they'd be sorry.

Nellie shivered hearing how frantic and hateful he sounded.

"He'll be fine," her mother said later when she tried to tell her, actually warn her that Henry was serious. He really meant it.

"He never wants to go off on his own, but then when he does, he always has a good time," she declared in her forced, upbeat voice.

"No, he doesn't," Nellie said under her breath.

Her mother's head snapped up. "What is it with you, Nellie? Why do you have to be so negative? I know things are hard for your brother, but he still has to do them. He can't always be hiding in some dream world like—"

Like your father, Nellie knew she'd almost said.

Her mother took a deep breath. "Because I know what that feels like. When I was little, all I wanted was to not be scared."

"What were you scared of?"

"Everything. Everyone." She sniffed and cleared her throat.

"Did you tell your mother?" Telling Charlie would have been useless.

"Well," she said, wiping her nose with the back of her hand. "She was pretty sick, so—" She shook her head and tried to smile.

"Oh, Mom!" Nellie said, hugging her mother, who seemed to tremble in her embrace.

"Listen to me!" she said, easing free. "I'm turning into one of *those* kind of mothers, dumping everything on their kids. My Lord!" She peered closely, then took off Nellie's glasses. "How can you see through these? They're so dirty," she said, fogging them with her breath, then wiping each lens on her shirtfront. Nellie stood perfectly still while the glasses were slipped back over her ears. "Look at you, almost taller than me now," her mother murmured, adjusting them, then smoothing down her hair. "And nothing ever bothers you, does it?" She patted her cheek. "You're so lucky."

Nellie's smile ached. It wasn't that her mother didn't know her; it was her mother not wanting to know that made her feel bad.

———

APPARENTLY, DOLLY'S PHONE had been shut off. She had come over last Monday on her night off to ask if she could have a cat in the apartment. Someone had offered her a kitten, but she wanted to check first to see if it was all right. Nellie'd been making chocolate pudding, stirring it on the stove and holding her breath, praying her mother would say yes. Because of Ruth's allergies, they'd never had pets, but a kitten next door could be a kind of step-pet. No, her mother told Dolly. She couldn't risk cat dander in the house, not with Ruth so sensitive. That led into the long history of Ruth's close calls; bee stings, rabbit fur, even certain laundry detergents could trigger the histamines that had more than once landed Ruth in the emergency room.

"Yeah, right, I know how that goes," Dolly sighed. Interesting, Nellie thought, how she could turn any subject around to herself. Such a useful skill, a kind of conversational veering through an obstacle course of dull topics. And being a kid, who wasn't allowed to interrupt adults no matter how boring they were, Nellie was fascinated, even by Dolly's detailed description of her pneumonia last winter: the green mucous and hacking cough, the creepy intern who kept coming in to listen to her lungs without a stethoscope, pressing his ear to her chest. At the stove Nellie mimicked her exaggerated shudder that had made her mother giggle. "Yeah, two and a half days I was in the hospital until they found out I didn't have any insurance, so they kicked me out. Sick as a dog—they didn't care," Dolly said, even her pout seductive.

Lips also pursed, Nellie turned off the burner. A face like Dolly's made secrets impossible. Her childlikeness was surprising to Nellie, who had never known an adult like her. Later, when she thought back, she would realize how much Dolly reminded her of Jessica. They were incapable of masking their emotions. Everything showed, every feeling and nuance, like a throb of blue veins just under the skin, a pulsating glyph of vulnerability.

Nellie poured the pudding into four sherbet bowls instead of the usual five. A package went further with Henry gone. She did miss him, though, but in the way you'd miss your shadow. Not something you needed or wanted, but not having one seemed strange. She hoped he wasn't freaking out the Krugers with his weird moods and balky silences. Especially if they tried taking him into the woods.

"Lately I been getting this, like, spotting, I guess you call it." Dolly's sunny voice drifted on the fringe of Nellie's bitter reverie. She'd been imagining what she'd say to Bucky when she saw him. It was becoming an obsession, all the possible scenarios worked out, the brutal force of her anger reducing him to pleas for forgiveness, her cruel words so brilliantly insightful that in the end he'd turn his life around, and for that his grandparents would honor her with their gratitude. She wasn't sure exactly what form that honor would take or even what the phrase meant, but she'd heard it on NPR yesterday. And as the middle child, honor and gratitude didn't come easily.

". . . then, last month I wake up in the middle of the night, and the sheet's, like, covered, soaked in blood, the mattress, everything. It's like, nothing for two months, then next thing I know, some kinda geyser's going off."

She had Nellie's rapt attention. So sweet and pretty and not even caring that she could hear every word of her most intimate details. Ruth was big into menstrual details, because it was another way of feeling superior to Nellie, so she wasn't shocked. But there was an innocence about Dolly's confidences that drew you into her life. Or maybe her into yours. She needed something, someone, anyone.

"You should see a doctor," her mother was telling her, and Dolly agreed. Yeah, she should. Like, she knew that, and she was going to. She really, really was. Because the worst part of all were the clots, she said as Nellie scraped the last lumps from the bottom of the pan. Ruth could have her bowl. In fact, she was pretty sure she'd never eat pudding again. Dolly jumped up and said she'd better get going. A friend was taking her out to dinner tonight. She wasn't sure where, though. It was supposed to be a surprise.

"Who's your friend?" Nellie's mother asked, and Dolly answered with a wink.

"Oh, that smells so good." Dolly paused to look over Nellie's shoulder. "And it's from scratch."

"No." She showed her the box.

"Same thing. Kinda, sorta. Cooking it, I mean," she said, with a quick look as if Nellie'd hurt her feelings.

"Here, have some." She held out one of the warm bowls.

"Oh jeez." Dolly seemed disappointed. "If I do, it'll fill me up and I'm gonna have dinner."

"Take it with you," her mother said from the table. "You can have it later."

"Yeah! That's a great idea." Dolly left, bearing the bowl in two hands, like a rare potion.

"Poor kid," her mother sighed on the closing door.

"Why? What's wrong with her?" Nellie asked.

"She's . . ." Her mother paused to reconsider, which Nellie resented. Now if she were Ruth she would have come straight out with it. Her mother and Ruth were soul sisters, Sandy liked to say, two peas from the same pod, which always left Nellie wondering what pod she'd come from. "She's had a hard life, that's all."

"Is that why she sounds so . . . well . . . kinda dumb sometimes?" she asked, and was stung by her mother's reaction.

"Why're you so judgmental all the time, Nellie? You make people feel very uncomfortable. You sound like your aunt Betsy when you say those things."

Whoa! How many times had she heard that? She used to think it was a compliment. She thought Aunt Betsy was a very important person the way people always seemed to have an opinion about her. Now that she was older, though, she realized what a knife in the back the comparison was.

"It's not a very nice trait," her mother said, getting up when she heard Ruth race down the stairs. If her mother didn't give her a ride, she'd be late for work again.

Nellie was hurt. She was a very kind girl and careful of everyone's feelings, but if being a quick study of people meant she was judgmental, then there wasn't a thing she could do about it. And she could see what was happening here. Yesterday Ruth and her mother had been sitting on the side steps with Dolly. The minute Nellie came around the corner, their chatter and laughter stopped. Her mother had been painting Ruth's and Dolly's toenails and they all sat there with cotton balls between their toes, looking back at Nellie as if they'd swallowed the wrong way. She had become the outsider. In her own home, which was only turning her into more of a Dolly stalker than she already was, listening for footsteps, latenight car doors, laughter and tears, with her ear at the bathroom wall trying to make out the murmurous voices.

LATELY CHARLIE WAS spending less time in the junkyard. He'd taken up fishing. Max was teaching him how. In the middle of the afternoon they'd padlock the gate, and with the old, dented metal canoe lashed to the top of the truck, they'd drive down to the Hawnee River, which ran through the center of town. Max preferred lake fishing, he was telling Nellie, as he tossed a second bungee cord over the canoe. She followed him to the other side of the truck. With Henry gone, she was bored out of her mind being stuck in the house all day. She'd even started looking forward to Jessica's return. She'd asked her mother if there was anything she could do at the beauty shop—sweep the floor, fold towels—she didn't care. Her mother didn't think so, but she'd ask Lizzie.

"Another one! Two's not enough," Charlie called from the shade of the barn and Max waved in agreement.

"You should go to Lake Branmore," Nellie said on Max's and Boone's heels, back around the truck. "That's where my brother is. Maybe they took him fishing. The family he's with, the Krugers. I should tell Charlie."

"He doesn't like the feeling, not being close to land," Max said, attaching the third cord.

"How come?" It was hard to hide her pleasure when Max talked to her. Whenever she delivered meals or medicine to Charlie, she went out of her way to be friendly to him. After all, he'd saved her brother's life, which she made a point of mentioning every time she came, and her grandfather trusted him, which she suspected had more to do with cheap labor than anything else. But most important, Max was one more of those people she found strangely fascinating. Kind of like Bucky, who'd come to the house yesterday, banging on the door, but she hadn't answered. Max had that same kind of edginess. The difference was that Max often seemed so skittish. She wasn't sure if it was shyness or fear. Maybe both, but she could tell she was making inroads. Today when she'd come through the gate, he'd said hi first instead of pretending he hadn't seen her.

"Charlie can't swim. Least, I don't think so," Max said from the back of the truck. Just when you thought he hadn't heard, he'd answer your question.

"You're kidding," she said, watching the gruff old man who'd always considered his grandson such a whiny pansy.

"Okay!" Charlie called as he limped toward them.

"You got a sore foot?" she asked.

"My damn hip," he said, patting his thigh. "Junk, like everything else here."

"Spare parts," Max said, getting behind the wheel. "That's all it takes. They can pretty much fix anything nowadays."

"Yeah. Well. One of these days." With a heaving groan Charlie hauled himself up into the truck.

"Hey!" she called before he could close the door. "Can I come? I love fishing, but nobody ever takes me."

"Hell, no!" Charlie barked.

"I'll be really quiet. I won't even talk," she said, and Charlie gestured for Max to go.

Max looked over at her with an apologetic shrug. She knew right then and there that deep down inside he was a nice person. And sooner or later she'd be right where she wanted to be, sitting in the middle of that canoe on her way down the Hawnee, pole in hand.

It was the hottest day so far. Almost 90 degrees. Henry was coming home tonight, two days early. It was mostly his stomach, Mrs. Kruger had said. Nothing she could pinpoint. Strange, because his appetite seemed okay, and yet he'd been complaining of cramps. And bad headaches again. He'd told Mrs. Kruger that lately he'd been having a lot of headaches at home. Not true, but her mother didn't rat him out as the wimp he really was. Though, Nellie had to admit, the Bucky incident in the woods had made her a lot more sympathetic.

Nellie was at the beauty shop when Mrs. Kruger called. It was her second day on the job, not that she was getting paid a cent, though. Her mother had told Frederic it was just to keep her busy. Ruth and her friends were going swimming practically every day, either at different pools or driving to the lake. Her mother didn't like her being alone in the house all day.

After sweeping up all the hair from the floor, folding three loads of towels, cutting squares of tinfoil, polishing mirrors, and straightening magazines for the tenth time, Frederic called Nellie into the rear salon where he coiffed only his best customers, those ladies and a few men who wanted their work done not just privately but in utmost secrecy. He sent Nellie to the luncheonette with ten dollars for his lunch, ice tea and a Greek salad with extra feta. When she returned, he told her to keep the change. Her mother took her into the back room and said she had to give it back. Two dollars and twenty-five cents.

"It's not pay, it's a tip," Nellie protested.

"He's doing me a favor," her mother hissed, staring at her. "I should be paying him."

Insulted that she considered this babysitting, Nellie stalked out front and sat in the small waiting area and read the latest *People* magazine. If no one appreciated all her hard work, then what was the point?

Her mother's two o'clock had just arrived. Lisa Glickstein. Her daughter was Ruth's age and her son had just graduated from high school. Billy Glickstein, a real jock—she'd seen him around.

Nellie was seeing a side of her mother she wasn't sure she liked: friendly and as upbeat as ever but way too agreeable with everyone in a breathy voice she only used here.

"I don't blame you," she said for the third time as she painted gloppy brown paste onto a strand of Mrs. Glickstein's hair, then rolled it into a tinfoil square. "I would've called them, too."

"I just felt so bad," Mrs. Glickstein said. "I mean, the Brickmans, they're both so sweet. They were so upset."

"But I'll bet it was an expensive bike," her mother said.

"Oh, God, yes. Almost a thousand dollars. Billy's aunt, for his graduation. Just something to get around campus with, I told her, but that's the way she is."

"At least he's got it back," her mother said.

"But he's going to pay for the new tires with his own money," Mrs. Glickstein said. "It's his own fault for leaving it on the front walk like that."

"Kids, they think—" her mother started to say.

"You got some here." Mrs. Glickstein pointed to the dark stain on her forehead.

"Sorry." Her mother dipped a cotton pad into a jar, frowning as she dabbed at the spot.

"Last time it didn't come out for two days."

"I'm sorry." She leaned closer, rubbing. "So what're the police going to do?"

Nellie's eyes burned as a jackhammer drilled between her temples.

"Nothing they can do, I guess. Not as long as the grandson keeps denying everything. I'll tell you, though, he's a bad seed, that one."

MR. KRUGER BROUGHT Henry home at six. Never had she been so glad to see her brother. Maybe it was the news of Bucky's grilling by the police or maybe Henry had just saved his vomiting for the privacy and comfort of his own toilet, but when Nellie went to bed he was in the bathroom again, gagging.

SHE'D SPENT THE next afternoon searching for Bucky. She'd even left a note in his grandparents' mailbox. His face, now inches from hers, gleamed with sweaty flecks of grime. They were on a bench in the park.

"What the fuck did ya cut the damn tires for?"

"I didn't cut any tires," she snapped back.

"Yeah, right. So now I got the stupid cops on my ass all the time."

"You shouldn't've stolen the bikes in the first place."

"Oh okay, Miss Law and Order, like you didn't know, right?"

"Right! I thought you were getting them from people to fix up."

"Oh, Jesus! C'mon! And the moon, you probably think that's just some guy up there." He was jiggling a rock in his hand.

"You know what your problem is? You don't have any respect for anybody." On message, she was moving in for the kill, which seemed to amuse him.

"I respect you." He grinned.

"Like what you did to my brother, that was so disgusting."

"What? What'd I do to your brother?"

"You know what you did."

"Tell me."

"No!"

"They're sending me back to New York."

She looked at him. This wasn't going according to plan. "When?"

"Soon as they find some place that'll take me."

"What about your parents?"

"That didn't work out." He sidearmed the rock off the side of the bandstand. "My mom's a cokehead."

"I thought she was a soap star."

"That, too. She just likes her drugs better'n me, that's all."

"Did you ever ask her to stop?"

"Like a million times."

"Wow. That sucks."

"I tried it once." He picked up another rock and threw it at the trash barrel. It pinged off the metal like a gunshot. "In her bathroom, that's where she does it, the lines, on the counter. I rubbed some on my gums, but all it did was sting. I thought of doing it here." He pressed his finger to a nostril and sniffed. "But . . . I didn't."

"What if you got addicted? I mean, think of it, your whole life'd be ruined. You'd probably end up in jail or—"

"Or what? Dead?"

"You could."

"Would you feel bad?"

"No. Not if you were stupid enough to do drugs."

"I'd feel bad if it was you." He threw another rock. "I wish I could stay. I really don't wanna go back there."

"Ask your grandparents. Tell them you won't get in any more trouble."

"I did, but they said only if I tell who slashed the bike tires and put them behind the church. Then they'll let me stay." He leaned close, his leg jammed into hers. Her heart thumped as he moved closer. His mouth had to be almost touching her ear as he whispered, "But I don't wanna get you in trouble. I really like you a lot, Nellie. And not just in a friend way."

She jumped up. "I gotta go."

"I really mean that," he yelled after her.

Just in case he was following her, she took all the back alleys until she came to the hardware store. She didn't like the way she felt, guilty and angry and sad that Bucky had such a miserable life, and yet her own life had taken a dangerous turn. One word from Bucky, and she and Henry would be dragged down to the police station. Interrogated, arrested; *oh my God,* she prayed as she ran the last block, *please, please help me.*

"Well, look who's here!" her father declared, warning with false heartiness as she raced inside. "The great Nellie Peck!"

Stepping into the store from the sun's glare had blinded her. She couldn't see his face and couldn't tell who else was there. Her arresting officer?

"Come here," the stout woman said. "And give your auntie B a big hug." She smelled fruity. Her huge breasts smushed against Nellie's flat chest. As her eyes adjusted to the dimness, she saw her father's concern. She'd obviously interrupted an important conversation. Well put together, her father had said once of Aunt Betsy, and today was no exception, in her bright pink pantsuit and chunky white necklace, matching earrings, even pink-and-white open-toed heels, as she peppered Nellie with the usual adult questions. Was she glad school was over? Yes. What was she doing with all her free time? Not a whole lot. Mostly reading, she added quickly, to please her aunt. Right after college Aunt Betsy had been a schoolteacher for a few years until she married Uncle Phil and didn't have to work ever again, though she'd kept her hand in town affairs through the years. Aunt Betsy was one of those people who expect their importance to be acknowledged, and Nellie wasn't doing a very good job of it, especially under the circumstances, her brain so riddled with the shame and guilt of being a thief. Her aunt was some kind of local official. Library trustee, that was it. Yes, because now she was telling Nellie that if there was ever a book the library didn't have, she should tell her and she'd have them order it for her. Or any overdue fines—just bring the book to Auntie B and she'd take care of it.

"Thank you, that's very nice of you. I'll remember that, but the library's really good. They have just about everything." She tried to think of something else that might please her and make her father at least smile. "Movies. And all kinds of books on tape. Well, CDs, really. Not that I've listened to any. Not yet, anyway. But I'd like to."

They both stared at her.

"Nellie," her father said, "can you wait out back for a minute? We'll be—"

"No. No need for that, Ben. I understand. And I want to help, I do. It's just, well . . ." She glanced in her niece's direction. "Phil."

"Of course," her father agreed, shaking his head, almost wincing. "Of course. And I'm sorry. The last thing I want is to cause you any problems."

Her great poufed head drew back. "Generosity is not a problem, Ben. Have I ever once questioned your inheriting the house? And the business, have I ever put an ounce of pressure on you? But you still owe us from the last loan."

"I know, and it tears me apart, but this one wouldn't be for long. I'm almost finished with the book. Just a couple more decades, and those're the easiest, the more modern ones. So many people to talk to. Last week I ran into Salvie. Remember Salvie? He gold-leafed the weathervane on town hall, and you know what he told me?"

Her father began telling the same story that last week at dinner had held them spellbound. It was about the significance of the streaming-haired woman on the hundred-fifty-year-old weathervane made by the itinerant artist who had fallen in love with the daughter of one of the wealthiest families around, only to be run out of town by the young woman's brothers, who had locked her in her room. That night she opened her window and dropped a bundle of clothes onto the brick courtyard below. And then she leaned out the window and grabbed hold of a tree branch, but it broke and when she fell—

"She broke her back and was an invalid for the rest of her days, though she outlived everyone in her family. I know from my Civics Committee report for the bicentennial. Really, Ben, I don't know why you think this history of yours is going to be any kind of salvation. A few copies, that's all you're going to sell. I mean, who outside of Springvale gives a good fig about this town's history?"

Something Nellie'd wondered herself, but her father seemed genuinely surprised.

"An awful lot of people." He spoke with that conviction that always sent something soaring inside her, eagles and rockets' red glare, her *Get Tough!* book, even though the major was British. "Because our story's universal. It's every town's story. Good plain people, struggle and hard work, exactly what's made this country great."

"Do you know how hard it is to get a book published? Just last month in the *Library Journal,* it said how only one out of ten thousand manuscripts ever even get read."

"Well then, count me among the lucky few." He grinned. "Luminosity Press, they've got a few chapters, and they're very interested. And as soon as they get my . . . my . . . check, I'll know more." In spite of his stammer, her father's voice held strong. It was his head that seemed to have the slightest tremor, as if with his words air or conviction were leaking out of it.

"That's what you need money for?" Aunt Betsy asked, but her brother didn't seem to comprehend her question. "Ben. Oh, Ben." She gave a long sigh. "Don't tell me you're *paying* to have it published. Not when you've got a family to support. What you need right now is a job. A steady income with benefits. Look around you," she said, the sweep of her arm like a spotlight's glare over the tired dusty merchandise. "This beat-up, old place—it's run its course. Like Phil says, the small businessman, he's either a martyr or a fool. Corporate America, that's the reality."

Like a gently falling veil, a look of serenity was settling over her father. Transcendence, *his* reality, so she could talk all she wanted. Why argue or hurt her feelings when he knew things she didn't. He had a plan, a secret, a rare trove, and if his sister had little faith or understanding, well, that was all right, because as long as a man stays focused and true to his life's work, no harm can come to him. And as always, his confidence was sanctuary enough for Nellie. Even Bucky seemed very far away.

Chapter 6

It was Sunday morning, and her mother was addressing invitations to the jewelry party she was having for Ellen, her girlfriend. It really bothered Nellie whenever her mother said that—"my *girlfriend*." By the time a mother got to be a mother she only needed friends. *Girlfriends* sounded silly and flighty and undignified. If her mother had girlfriends, then *she* was a girlfriend, which of course she wasn't, being a grown woman as well as Nellie's mother, whose life was supposed to be about her kids, not girlfriends and their secrets. But of course she could never say that because then she'd be accused of sounding like Aunt Betsy again. Anyway, Ellen, Mrs. Heisler, had just bought a Royal Palais Gems franchise, and Nellie's mother had agreed to host her friend's first party.

"Here, go put this in Dolly's mailbox. If you can get it in," her mother said, licking an envelope. "One less stamp," she muttered. Nellie'd heard her fretting at breakfast about all the money this was costing. Had she known she'd be paying for all the food and invitations herself, she never would have agreed to host the party. But then when it came her turn, her father reminded her mother, someone else would be doing the same for her. Her mother was also interested in buying a franchise. With all her contacts at the beauty shop, it was a no-brainer, she'd said last night as she and Benjamin pored over company brochures and the bonus points catalog. In addition to a percentage of each sale, reps earned incentive points toward gifts, which ranged from a set of multicolor juggling balls to a blender, right on up to a new Ford Matrix. When her mother got her own franchise, the car would be her goal. Their ten-year-old Odyssey had more than a hundred twenty thousand miles on it. "On second thought," she called after Nellie, "slip it under her door."

Dolly's mailbox was jammed full of mail, mostly bills. Her mother had warned Dolly that if she didn't start bringing it in, the mailman would stop delivering to her. He'd already complained about it. "Sounds like a plan," had been Dolly's breezy response.

Just as Nellie was slipping the invitation under her door, it swung open.

"Leave me alone! Just leave me the fuck alone!" Dolly screamed. Her face was sunburned and her bloodshot eyes were puffy. A cold sore festered on her lower lip.

Stunned, Nellie held up the envelope and tried to explain, lapsing into the same nervous stammer her father had. Dolly listened a moment, tilting her head this way and that as if struggling to comprehend, and then burst into tears. She felt so sick, she wept. She had just the worst, most friggin' awful, sunburn, and the guy she'd been on the boat with wouldn't even call back to see how she was doing. She was chilled and sick to her stomach, and she hadn't slept in two nights, and she was sorry, so, so sorry. She shouldn't have yelled like that. In a million years, she never would've, except she thought Nellie was someone else, that's all, that's what happened, she sobbed into her hair, holding her so tight, her shoulders ached.

"That's okay," Nellie said, but she either didn't hear or was too distraught. She'd never seen anyone bawl like this before; Ruth, maybe, but never an adult. And certainly not one in a black thong bikini bottom and cutoff sleeveless T-shirt. Begging Nellie's forgiveness, she pulled her into the apartment. She was such a good kid, she gasped, and she didn't want her and her nice family thinking any less of her.

"That's okay," Nellie repeated, looking around, shocked. Nothing like Lazlo's perfectly neat living room. The shades were down. The dim little place was a mess, clothes and takeout food bags everywhere along with bloated, half-filled soda cups, straws still in them. If her mother saw this, it would be the end of Dolly. She could smell stale beer and warm, fruity garbage. The kitchen trash basket was overflowing. Teetering piles of dirty dishes filled the sink. The bedroom door was open.

Her bare mattress was crooked on the frame. There was a red-and-black sheet on the floor.

"It's just things're so screwed up right now," she tried to explain. "Oh, God, what am I saying?" she sighed, falling onto the tattered wicker love seat. "Things are always screwed up. I'm such a loser. That's all I am, just a stupid-ass loser," she bawled into her cupped hands.

"No, you're not," Nellie said, perched primly on the edge of the wooden folding chair. She thought of the old Naugahyde recliner out in the barn. Dolly could certainly use it. "You've got such a nice voice and I'll bet you're a really good dancer."

"Oh, God," Dolly moaned, crying even harder. She looked up, shaking her head. "I don't know how I got myself in this mess. Every time, it's the same thing. It's like you know exactly how it's gonna go, but you just think, oh, okay, what the hell, maybe this time'll be different. You know what I mean?"

"Yeah." She nodded.

She looked at Nellie for a moment, then, for at least the tenth time, asked how old she was. The answer brought more tears. Oh, God, if only she could be thirteen again, she wept. If only.

"It's really not that great of an age," Nellie said, wanting to make her feel better. "There's all kinds of things I can't do, and then people're always saying, 'You're thirteen years old, Nellie, act your age.'"

She threw back her head and laughed as if that were the funniest thing she'd ever heard, as if no one had ever said that to her before, which made Nellie feel weird, even more uneasy than her crying had. She said she'd better get going. There was a concert in the park this afternoon, and they were all going to walk there, she explained. All except Ruth, that is, though she didn't tell Dolly that. If they went in the car, Ruth said she'd go, but their whole family walking together was just way too lame.

"Wait!" Dolly said. She raced into her bedroom, returning with a large pink-and-blue bag. She took a floppy orange sunhat from it and a receipt fluttered to the floor. Nellie picked it up. The hat had red polka dots and an orange-and-white flower tucked into the red ribboned band.

"It's yours! For making me laugh. You're just too cute," Dolly said, plunking it down on her head. Perfect for a concert in the park. She'd bought it at a fancy boutique in Hyannisport, she said, fussing with Nellie's hair, trying to arrange it under the hat.

"It's nice." Nellie didn't want to hurt her feelings. "But it's way too expensive," she said, glancing at the receipt. Ninety-nine dollars. "My mother—she'd never let me keep it." The scribbled signature caught her eye. The first name was illegible, but the last looked like Cooper.

"How's this then," Dolly said, taking the slip. "You can borrow it. Anytime you want—it'll be fun."

"But I might wreck it or lose it or something," Nellie said. "And it's special, like a souvenir, right?" She wanted to see the receipt again, but Dolly had dropped it into the bag. Maybe Cooper was the name of the store.

"Here's the best one, though, best souvenir of all." Dolly lifted the back of her shirt. On the fiery skin just above her tailbone was the tattoo of a small blue star.

"Oh." Not knowing what else to do or say, she shrugged.

"Matches: east, west," Dolly laughed, pointing, breast to breast. "Now, I just gotta get north."

"Yeah. Well, anyway, I better go. They're probably looking for me," Nellie said, fearing what might be shown next. And then as she opened the door, Dolly asked the strangest question. So what was Claudia Cooper like? One of those worlds-colliding questions, it took Nellie a moment. *Claudia? Like, Jessica's mom, Claudia? Mr. Cooper's wife, Claudia?* Oh. "Very nice," she said. "She's always smiling." Though how that could be with Jessica for a daughter she had no idea but, of course, didn't say that. "And they have seven kids," she added, for that was always mentioned whenever the Coopers' name came up. Whether because it made them special, somehow more blessed than everyone else, or whether it was explanation enough, she'd never been sure, maybe both.

"Is she pretty?" Dolly asked so apprehensively that, for some reason, Nellie could not tell the truth—that, in fact, she was beautiful.

"She's okay. You know," she said with a shrug. It seemed to be the right answer.

———

So THERE IT was. Inklings. But of what she wasn't sure. She couldn't wait for Jessica to get home from camp, though her reasons were purely nosy.

THE LIVING ROOM and dining room were fragrant with vases of her mother's peonies and roses. Preparations had begun the minute she ran in from work: extra chairs carried into the living room, linen on the dining room table, Grandmother Peck's cut glass punch bowl and ladle washed and dried, the dainty cups arranged on its mirrored base. And candles everywhere, even in the bathroom. Thanks to Ruth, Nellie had already gotten in trouble for dipping her fingers into the melted wax, so she could peel it off, but they were soon kept busy, answering the door for the ladies in their pretty summer dresses, passing hors d'oeuvres, and keeping the white wine chilled in the ice buckets. Benjamin and Henry had gone to a movie. Boys' night out, her father said. Her mother looked so pretty. Lizzie had come early to do her makeup. She did Ruth's, too. Nellie got lip gloss, which tasted like strawberry soap.

Fifteen ladies came, though twenty-eight invitations had been sent. At first her mother was disappointed, but the party turned out to be a success. The ladies bought more than twelve hundred dollars' worth of jewelry. Dolly spent the most, three hundred dollars on a necklace of chunky turquoise and glinting yellow stones with matching earrings and bracelet. Nellie thought it was pretty ugly, but Ruth called it bohemian, something an entertainer would wear. Nellie noticed how quiet Dolly was all through the party. She had on a red-and-white striped sundress that tied behind her neck, and her sunburn had darkened to a tan that made her look very glamorous with her streaky blond hair. In this setting a rare specimen, Nellie thought, like one of the Agassiz Museum's exotic birds in its airless glass case. Compared to her, everyone else at the party just seemed so pale and drab. Dolly kept looking around at the other women, watching, as if she were studying them. Nellie heard her tell Miss Humboldt, from next door, how in New

York she'd been all set to audition for *The Producers,* but on the day of the tryouts she had "two of the biggest shiners you ever saw."

Miss Humboldt seemed to be searching for the appropriate response. "That must have been a letdown," she finally said.

"Yeah, I guess, but that's how life is, right? Up one minute, down the next—you never know."

"No, you don't. You certainly don't," Miss Humboldt said, fingering the black-and-gold beads of the long necklace she'd bought. Nellie's mother had been amazed when Miss Humboldt called to say she was coming. She and her brother never socialized, as Sandy put it. Nellie's leafy surveillance of the Humboldts had fallen off lately. Dolly's life had taken precedence. Compared to her, the Humboldts were dull. They went to the supermarket and drugstore, but that was about it. Even Mr. Humboldt's evening gardening had lost its mystique.

Hard to believe that after all her years of spying on Miss Humboldt, here she was, ensconced in their living room, her doughy body filling the big easy chair. Surprisingly, she seemed just as normal as everyone else. She and Dolly made a unique pair as the night wore on, each seeming more grateful for the other's company. Even as the party was breaking up, they kept talking. Ellen Heisler had packed up her jewelry display boxes and gone home, but Dolly and Miss Humboldt were still here. In the kitchen, Ruth was noisily loading the dishwasher, her signal for them to leave. The entire evening had been a forced march for Ruth, who kept disappearing with the phone into the bathroom. Nellie finished off the last of the pastries as she helped her mother clear the table. Limp mint leaves and orange slices floated in the frothy sherbet dregs of the punch bowl. There were eight empty wine bottles in the recycling basket. A lot of jewelry had been sold, and the ladies had all had a fine time, growing loud and silly by the end of the night. Nellie's mother was pleased, but she looked really tired. She'd already put in eight hours at the shop, on her feet all day, and now these last two partiers wouldn't leave.

Dolly continued to do most of the talking, growing only more animated, hands flying, her girlish voice pitched higher. She was telling Miss Humboldt about some guy her best friend was dating. Even though he was a lot older, like twice her age, he was so much fun. Last week they went to Hyannisport for the day and rented this amazing boat and just floated around the harbor until sunset. Then they went to dinner at a little Portuguese restaurant, and she had white anchovies for the first time ever.

"White anchovies!" Miss Humboldt gasped. "Imagine."

It hadn't escaped Nellie's notice that she had polished off an entire plate of finger sandwiches herself, declaring, with every reach, "I really shouldn't."

Her mother had turned out two of the three lamps. Well, Miss Humboldt announced with a great heave up from the chair, she'd best be on her way. Her brother was such a light sleeper and she didn't want to get in too late and disturb him. Some nights he didn't sleep at all, she said. The slightest sound, sometimes even leaves rustling in the wind, would keep him up.

Warm milk? Dolly suggested. Sleeping pills? Nothing works, Miss Humboldt said. Always been that way. Even as a baby, awake all night, never napping.

"Jeez," Dolly said on their way into the kitchen to say good-bye to their hostess. "If I couldn't sleep, I'd kill myself."

A visible shudder tore through Miss Humboldt. "I'm very careful," she said.

LATER THAT NIGHT Nellie's parents were talking in the hallway on their way to bed. Her mother sounded upset, something about Dolly and the jewelry party, and she didn't know how to handle it. "It's the right thing to do," her father kept saying, principle always the simplest measure of a solution. A few days later, when her mother went next door for the "talk," Nellie was not only ready, ear at the wall, but for Dolly's sake, praying she'd cleaned the place up.

Her mother began by saying that while it might not seem to be any of her business, in a way it was, both because of her friendship with Dolly's aunt and because Dolly was her tenant, so she'd come to the conclusion that she had no choice.

"What?" Dolly shot back, without even knowing what Sandy was talking about. "What'd I do? I didn't do anything wrong!"

Nellie couldn't believe her tone, worse than Ruth's, almost vicious, but her mother didn't sound angry. If anything, she was straining to be kind.

"I didn't say you did. I'm just concerned, Dolly, that's all. I mean, well, all your bills and your car out there, and your phone's still shut off—"

"Yeah! Because I got my cell. That's all I need!"

"I know, but what I'm trying to get at here, the point is, you're hardly working, even your aunt's—"

"Oh, okay! I get it, so that's what's going on. Well, you just tell Lizzie to butt the hell out!"

"Well, is it true? Are you? Are you still working or not? Are you still at the club? Did you get laid off? What?"

"I'm taking a little break, that's all. I been getting these, like, spasms in my back so bad I can't even—"

"Have you been to the doctor?"

"What do you care? I mean, fuck! I don't get this!"

For Nellie, the silence was profound. "Dolly," her mother finally said in a firm voice, "the other night at the jewelry party you spent three hundred dollars, and that was very sweet and so generous of you, but I can't keep that money. Not in good conscience, not when I know how difficult things are for you right now. So, here. I'll take the jewelry back, and this way you can pay some of your bills."

"I like you a lot, Sandy, but right now I think you're really stepping over the boundary line here."

"I just want to help, that's all."

"No! I don't need any help. Everything's fine. I been saving, I got money. I just gotta get my act together, that's all. I mean, I just moved. Look at this place. With my back, I can't even bend over. I still don't know where anything is here, my checkbook, the bills even."

"Let me give you a hand then. I'll go get Nellie. Between the two of us—"

Grinning, Nellie shot out of the bathroom, then sat in the front hall, waiting to be summoned. Instead, minutes passed, and when her mother did return, she looked upset. Nothing, was all she kept saying as Nellie followed her around, asking what was wrong. She couldn't admit that she'd been listening. During Lazlo's tenancy she'd gotten caught in the act, along with Henry. Not only was eavesdropping a vile invasion of someone's privacy, according to their father, but it was a loathsome character flaw, almost as bad as giving her younger brother such a poor example.

Her mother's bad mood spilled over into the next day; she snapped at Henry and sent him to his room when he said he wasn't going to the playground activities she'd already signed him up for and paid for. Things crashed and banged overhead—Henry trashing his room again, a desperate ploy that never worked and always got him in even more trouble. And then he'd just have to pick it all up, anyway. Nellie was almost enjoying the commotion. Earlier, when Ruth had been told to walk to work, she accused her mother of caring only about herself as she stormed out of the house in her brown Frostee Freeze uniform, slamming the door so hard the screen fell out. Yes, Nellie knew, compared to those two, she was a wonderful, loving child.

With the next crash, Benjamin bounded up the stairs. He so seldom ever raised his voice that now it seemed a thunderous shock, God roaring from the heavens at Henry to pick up everything in his room and when that was done, he was to come downstairs and apologize to his mother. And if he ever dared speak to her like that again, he could just pack his bags and go—the weakest of threats, in Nellie's opinion. First of all, Henry had no bags to pack. He'd used his backpack and Ruth's duffle bag to go to the lake, and second, there wasn't a place on earth he'd ever have the guts to go to.

"Your mother's got enough on her mind right now without having to put up with your nonsense!" he barked.

Nonsense. Henry had been guilty of far more than nonsense. But then, so was her father.

The night before, with the frantic banging of pipes in the cellar, had come the first of two cracks in her mother's world. In a moment of misplaced confidence, Ruth began telling her mother about the letter she'd written to her "real father."

"Real father!" her mother snapped. "Your real father is that poor man downstairs trying to fix the hot water heater! Your real father is the wonderful man who's raised you for the last fifteen years and has never considered you anything but his real daughter!"

Only an hour later, her "real" father, that poor and wonderful man with the worst possible timing, would eagerly tell his wife, in an effort to boost her spirits, that Luminosity Press had been so impressed by his query letter, outline, and sample chapter that they wanted to publish his book.

"You're kidding!" she'd gasped.

"No, it's the truth."

"I can't believe it!"

"Neither could I."

"So what happens next?"

"Well, now they want the rest of the manuscript."

"So send it!"

"Well, I'm going to. I just need to finish. That last chapter. And some edits, here and there. And then, um . . ."—he coughed—"the sixty-five hundred."

"Sixty-five hundred what?"

"Dollars."

"Why? For what?"

"That's what it costs."

"You mean you have to pay *them*? What kind of publisher's that?"

"Vanity press, it's called. That's how it works. So I was thinking, maybe I'll ask Charlie—"

"Don't you dare!"

"Just a thought, that's all."

Chapter 7

—

Jessica was finally home from camp. She seemed much happier. She'd gone out with two different boys and they were both going to write to her. Nellie asked exactly what "gone out" means at camp. It's just the way it works, Jessica said. What? The way what works? Nellie persisted. Dating, she said. Dating! Nellie couldn't help squealing. What kind of dates can you go on in a camp?

"Oh, my God," Jessica groaned. "See! That's because you've never been. But lots of stuff happens." She fixed her peevish, squinty-eyed look of superiority on Nellie. "Believe me."

"Okay. Like what?"

In the end, Nellie came to understand that at the camp social a boy named Carver had danced with her. Slow-danced. Close, she said, gesturing with a bump and grind. Like, really, really close. And then there'd been Seth in her therapy group, who'd always sit next to her. One day, during the group hike in the woods, she and Seth wandered off the trail. With everyone out of sight, they crawled under a huge fallen tree. Seth tongue-kissed her and then he asked her to do it to him. Tongue-kiss *him*? Nellie asked. No! Jessica scoffed. *Do it!* To him. Oh! Nellie said. As if she knew exactly what she meant. Jessica's experiences had made her more confident and critical of Nellie. She treated her like a jerk. As if she didn't know anything.

But at least Dolly Bedelia liked her, one day declaring that Nellie was very mature for her age and a really good listener, which most people weren't. Oh, they'd act like they were interested in everything, when they were really just waiting for an opening so they could start talking about themselves. Like Tessa from the club, for instance. She'd been the worst of all, because of the way she took every single thing Dolly'd told her in "privacy"—in *Private,* but Nellie chewed her lip rather than correct her—and used it against her. Apparently, Tessa had spilled Dolly's secrets to Tray, the guy Dolly used to date, and now he was jealous out of his mind. Instead of attracting the guy to Tessa, though, it had turned him even more crazy jealous over Dolly.

Dolly's breathy confidences always had a soothing effect. Her voice was like background music. Unintrusive melodies that made no demands on Nellie's own reveries while she moved around the apartment, pretending it was hers as she picked things up. She'd just started washing the sink full of dishes when Dolly came up behind and began fiddling around with her hair.

"I got an idea," she said, then hurried into her dark bedroom. She returned with a purple spray bottle and a set of electric rollers. She unplugged the clock above the table so she could plug in the rollers. What Nellie needed was a new look, she said, chattering excitedly as she set her hair on the hot rollers. Then she slipped off Nellie's glasses so she could pluck her eyebrows and curl her eyelashes. The price of beauty, she said when Nellie's nose began to run and her eyes teared up. The tweezing really hurt. Nellie declared she'd never do that again, and Dolly laughed.

"Yes, you will," she said. "Someday. That, and a lot more."

Nellie panicked, seeing the mass of crimped tubes and bottles, brushes and tools Dolly was dumping out of her soiled makeup bag. She couldn't, she told Dolly, she'd get in trouble. Ruth hadn't been allowed to wear makeup until ninth grade, though she'd secretly put it on in sixth grade on her way to school, but Nellie didn't tell Dolly that. Oh, just for now, in here, Dolly assured her, lifting off Nellie's glasses. And much better to learn from a professional. She'd had training. At the club she always made up the other dancers. They'd wait for her, she was that good. "It's all about lighting," she murmured. "And shadows. Some people just reflect different; it's this thing they have, this special kind of glowy thing. It, like, comes from the gut, works its way out."

Nellie held her breath, wanting to be told she had it, the glowy thing. "Plus, this way," Dolly continued, "you can see how you look—in privacy. Then after, I'll show you how to get it off. Baby oil and witch hazel, that's the trick. Mine, anyway."

Sounded reasonable enough to Nellie as she sat, heavy eyed, with Dolly's whispery breath feather-tickling her skin while she stroked her face and neck with soft, damp cotton balls and swirled fruity cream concoctions onto her cheeks and lips, talking all the while. She was being lulled into a dream, a haze of sleep and drifting wakefulness. Near blindness only heightened the spell. She had really good bones, Dolly told her, which Nellie took as pity praise, like when people admired Jessica's tiny, little feet.

"And your mouth," Dolly said, patting her lips with a gauze pad before outlining them, "it's just perfect. I'll betcha guys are always tryna steal a kiss, huh?"

"No!" she said, and Dolly laughed.

"Oh, all right, one guy then. What's his name?"

"Bucky," she blurted, despising herself, despising him, wanting the word back, but it was too late. She'd just made real every vile ache she'd so far been able to subdue.

"Bucky. That's cool. Bet he's cute, huh?"

"No!"

"But you like him."

Just then a knock came at the door. Dolly froze. Her eyes darted past Nellie, who quickly put on her glasses. The knocking became banging.

"Dolly!" a man called. "It's me! Open the door! C'mon, I know you're in there. I just wanna talk, that's all. I promise. Just open the door. I won't even come inside. I just wanna ask you something. About him, that guy you been—"

She was already at the door, throwing it open. It was the same man with the shiny shaved head and the spiderweb on his neck. Diamond studs glittered in both ears. He wore faded jeans and a snug black T-shirt that strained over the muscles in his chest and huge arms.

"Hey, Dolly-doll." His soft voice crept through a scowl. Nellie could tell from Dolly's tightly crossed arms that she was afraid.

"Not a good time, Tray. My landlady's kid, she's here. I'm taking care of her. Like babysitting." She tried to close the door.

"That's okay." He eased past her into the apartment. "We can still—"

"Nellie," she interrupted. "Whyn't you go home and come back later." Holding Nellie's shoulder, she steered her past the man. Nellie ran next door, straight into the bathroom and pressed her ear to the wall. Upstairs, Ruth was playing music in her room. The dull boom in the walls was more vibration than sound, enough to muddy every other word. First it was the man who got mad. Then it was Dolly. She didn't care, she said. It was her life and she could do whatever the hell she wanted. She damn well better care, he shouted. Unless she wanted to be a dumb-ass pole dancer the rest of her life.

"You'll see," she kept saying. "You'll see."

"So why's it such a big fucking secret then?"

"Cuz it's none of your fucking business, that's why!"

"No, cuz he's probably married and you're the only one that'll do him, that's why."

"Get out! Just get the hell out!"

"Same as before, right? And you keep falling for it."

"Just so you'll know, I'm in a very serious relationship."

"Jesus, then you're even stupider'n I thought."

There was a thudding scuffle and then a door slammed. Nellie ran into the living room. Through the curtain she watched the man storm down the walk. Suddenly he stopped, picked up one of the large rocks bordering her mother's hostas, and threw it, crashing right through Dolly's window. He jumped into his red pickup truck and roared off.

Talk about synchronicity. Ruth ran down from her room. Henry charged around the side of the house from the barn, where he'd been sawing down the legs on a wooden table he wanted to put in the tree house. Nellie arrived to find Dolly trembling on her narrow porch. "Bastard! No good bastard!" she sobbed. Daggers of glass glimmered in the window.

"Jesus!" Nellie and Ruth whispered. They'd heard stories about drunken Mr. Teehan shooting out the street lights on Commercial Street, and the time he kicked a hole in the front door when his wife wouldn't let him in, but things like that never happened here. Not on Oak Street. Not to them.

"What the hell happened?" Ruth yelled over Dolly's wails, thrilling Nellie with this chorus of curses, the entire scene more X-rated drama than anything she'd ever in her whole life been part of. The three Peck kids seemed more competent than the adult.

"We better call the police!" Henry shouted. He looked as scared as he was pleased by the excitement.

"No!" Dolly pleaded. "No, don't! I'll take care of it. I'll pay for it. I'll get it fixed!"

"But what if he comes back?" Nellie asked from the bottom step, shocked by the bruises already showing on Dolly's arms.

"Who?" Ruth kept asking. "What if who comes back?"

"Tray," Nellie said, and that's when Ruth looked at her sister, closely.

"What'd you do? Your face! All that makeup! And your hair! Oh, my God! You're gonna be in such big trouble!"

EVEN AFTER COUNTLESS scrubbings that left her mouth and cheeks raw, there were still traces left, vile stains making her mother wince whenever she looked at her. From that point on, Nellie was forbidden from ever entering Dolly's apartment again. But with her eavesdropping still a secret, no one could tell her not to listen at the bathroom wall. Dolly's television seemed to be on night and day. A few times Nellie heard her pleading with someone on the phone. Later, when Nellie would try her best to remember every detail, she couldn't recall exact words, just sounds—sad, sad sounds of being scared and alone and not knowing what to do about it.

Her father cut the new pane at the store. Saying it was the least she could do, Dolly made Benjamin a cup of instant coffee, then stood on the drizzly porch watching him putty the glass into the window frame, then touch up the trim paint. As he was leaving, she tried to tuck a twenty-dollar bill into his shirt pocket, but he refused, assuring her it was no big deal, not to worry about it. After all, he was in the business. When he came back in and told her mother this, with what even

Nellie recognized as a boyish grin, she was furious. Twenty dollars. The materials, plus his time, easily came to more than that.

"She's just a kid," he said. "And plus, she felt so darn bad, I don't know, I just wanted to make her feel better."

"Feel better!" her mother said. Kind as her mother was, family had to come first. And with their own finances so thinly stretched, Dolly had become one more risk. A burden.

Chapter 8

L IFE SEEMED QUIET FOR A WHILE, QUIET IN THAT TENSE WAY
adults have of going silent the minute she'd come into the
room. But Nellie knew what it was, the same old problem,
money and her father's unconcern about their lack of it. Her mother
had looked into Luminosity Press. No one had ever heard of their six
published books. None had ever been sold in a bookstore. She begged
Benjamin to forget about finishing the history, or at least put it on
hold for a while so he could concentrate on selling the store. "You're
probably right," he'd agree, then continue for hours in the office, typ-
ing away, so lost in the work that customers often came in and left
without his ever knowing.

One day her mother rushed home from the salon with exciting
news. She had this great lead on a job, she told him on his way out
to light the grill. It was a wonderful opportunity, selling cars. Not just
cars, but Cadillacs. The brother of one of her clients managed the
dealership on Route 82, and she said she'd be more than glad to call
him about Benjamin. Her brother was always on the lookout for good
salesmen. Benjamin seemed confused. Selling cars, he repeated. All he
knew about cars was how to drive one, he added.

"Plus, the really good salesmen are always getting bonuses," her
mother continued, in her hopeful breeze around the kitchen, grabbing dinner ingredients from cupboards and the refrigerator. She
chopped the stems off the green beans before dropping them into boiling water. She poured olive oil and lemon juice into a dab of mustard
and whisked up a quick French dressing. "Cash, gift certificates, even
trips," she said, seasoning the pork chops for the grill.

It had been a long time since Nellie'd heard such lift in her mother's voice.

"Nancy said last year her brother went to Hawaii. Free! His wife, too, all expenses paid. For the most sales or something like that. You'd be so good at it, Ben. I know you would." Pausing, she held out the platter of chops, an offering that with the urgency of her words might change everything. "People trust you, Ben. And that's key."

"To what? Being a good liar?"

"Being a good salesman," she said with a narrow stare.

"Sandy, I never once in my whole life sold anyone anything they didn't already want or need."

"Everyone needs a car."

"But not a Cadillac."

"Well, then, for the ones that do," she said in such a cold, mocking tone that even Nellie knew he should just be quiet.

But he couldn't. Couldn't contain himself. "How would I do my research? When would I write?"

"I don't know." Her voice quavered. "And you want to know something? I really don't care. I don't." She set the platter down just hard enough that it rattled a moment on the counter. Her gauntlet, from a woman who'd spent a lifetime avoiding such moments. And now there was no turning back.

For the rest of the night her father was very subdued. But come morning he seemed his old, chipper self again. Whistling on his way into the bathroom. Whistling as he came down the stairs to breakfast. Whistling "Oh, What a Beautiful Morning" in spite of the monsoon outside. Sheets of blurry rain ran down the windows. Brooding thunder rumbled in the heavy dawn sky. He poured a cup of coffee. Instead of sitting at the table where her mother was reading the paper, he stood by the sink, sipping coffee while he looked out at the mock orange branches lashing the window with spiteful fury.

"Once in the '38 floods," he said, "the streams and river rose so fast through the night, my mother said, that when they came down in the morning water was already coming in under the front door."

"Where? Here?" Henry asked, peering down as if for seepage through the floorboards.

"This very house. So they started moving everything up to the second floor, she and my father, as much and as fast as they could. But then a call came and my father had to leave. The store was flooding and he had to get there while he still could. So there my mother stood, looking around, not sure what to do next, and she realized the one thing she really wanted to save more than anything was her mother's spinet piano that she and my father had already tried to move but couldn't get past the first step. So, there she was, ankle-deep in water, but she got on the other side and managed to pull it up the one step. Then she came down around, and with her shoulder braced hard to it, she pushed, not just with all her might, she said, but with all her anger and determination, and the strength she needed just came. It poured out of her, little woman that she was, just enough to get the piano up one more step. Then one more. Then on up onto the landing. When the flooding was over, the water'd stopped one inch shy of the landing."

"What happened to it? The piano?" Nellie asked.

"They ended up having to sell it. The Depression. Times were tough then."

"Still are," came her mother's low voice from behind the paper.

"That reminds me. I've got a call in to Andy Cooper, asking him to come by the store sometime today," her father said.

Her mother's hands fell and with them the newspaper pages. "Thank you, Ben. It'll be for the best. You'll see." She tried to smile, but her mouth was way too trembly.

THREE DAYS OF rain had turned Nellie and her brother into caged animals. They'd played crazy eights, Monopoly, checkers, and chess and practiced practically every hold in Nellie's *Get Tough!* book, the nonlethal ones, that is, until they were as sick of each other as they were of being stuck inside. Ruth, their supposed babysitter, was either asleep or on the phone up in her room. The most they knew of her authority was the heavy metal music thudding through the house. Without parents home she amped it up full volume. Even Dolly had complained. In a nice way, though. She came over in her silky bathrobe to say that she wasn't feeling too good and needed to sleep, so could they please not play the music so loud. Hungry for information, Nellie asked if she was sick. All she said was that her stomach was upset.

"Hey!" Nellie called before she could turn away. "The other day, I didn't get to say thanks." *Because of what happened. That guy?* the real message in her widened eyes.

"When? For what?" Dolly seemed confused. She kept blinking.

"For all the . . . the makeup. And my hair. Everyone really liked it."

For a moment Dolly only nodded as if assuring herself of something or maybe working up the courage to finally speak the truth. "I wasn't cross-eyed, but I used to wear glasses, too, you know." She cupped her hand under Nellie's chin and drew it close. "And no matter what anyone said, four-eyes and all that crap, I never let it bother me."

Gee, thanks, I really needed to hear that, Nellie thought, watching her lift her robe as she tiptoed across the wet lawn. And yet she knew Dolly meant well. She was just the first of many adults who would be, one way or another, just enough off the mark to make Nellie feel bad for them.

She couldn't wait to deliver Dolly's complaint. Ruth didn't believe her, but when Nellie threatened to call their mother, she finally lowered the volume. Lucky for her because her mother called right then. She had a very important errand for them to run. Charlie needed his medicine. He was sick again, some kind of "plumbing" problem. Obviously just something to keep them busy, Nellie figured, but it was better than being stuck in the house. So when his prescriptions were ready at three-thirty, they picked them up and made their slow way through the soft drizzle. Nellie could feel the warmth of blistery wet sun swelling through the gray sky. There was a funky smell in the steamy air. They kept sniffing as they splashed through puddles.

"Worms!" Henry declared of the fishiness, and he was right. The sidewalks were alive with them. Long, fat, wet crawlers, many already squashed under passing feet. Outside the coffee shop Henry pawed through the trash bin until he found a tall cup with ice still in it. Now as they walked, they picked up the liveliest worms and dropped them into the cup. They were for Charlie. Maybe he'd be so grateful they'd take them fishing, Charlie and Max. Probably today. Everyone knew the best fishing was right after a rainstorm. Soon the cup was full to the top, a mass of writhing bait they hoped would entice Charlie. Or more likely, Max.

The minute they turned the corner they were surprised to see the junkyard gate wide open. Max's truck was gone.

"Must've left in a hurry," Henry said, sniffing the cup, for signs of death.

"Damn!" she said. They'd probably just missed them. Soon as the rain stopped they'd probably headed to the river. Just in case, they looked in the barn, but when Boone didn't come charging out barking, they pretty much knew for sure.

They climbed up into the hayloft, not that they expected to find anyone there, but because Charlie had forbidden it since the time Henry fell through the opening and miraculously wasn't killed. Just banged up. It was hot in the loft, but a lot neater than before. Still, there was the two-hundred-year-old whetstone Charlie used to get mad at them for spinning because it was worth a fortune, he said. There were the same rusting milk cans, but now, in the far corner, a sagging cot and crate. Henry pointed and she nodded: Max's bunk. They continued their silent investigation through boxes of old pitted bottles, some with plugs of dirt in their necks, stacks of brittle newspapers and magazines bundled in twine, a wooden box of rusted handsaws, another of lug wrenches, and a large musty trunk. Henry lifted the domed lid. Shirts, socks, underwear, a metal box were all they saw because the creaking hinge had triggered a flutter of small brown wings through the rafters, which sent them running down the stairs. Just then, there was a high *beep beep beep beep* outside. A large black-and-white truck was backing down the wide weedy driveway. It continued onto the narrow dirt road past the barn then stopped close by the first scrap metal pile. The driver jumped out. He was a big-bellied guy with a yellow baseball hat on backward, a look she and Henry both scorned. The driver let down the tailgate, then hoisted himself up onto the back of the truck and, fast as he could, began tossing insulated pipes onto the rusted heap. Nellie could tell by his furtive glances that something, as her father would say, wasn't quite kosher.

"Memorize his plate number," she whispered behind the bag of medicine.

"He's not stealing anything," Henry whispered over the worm cup clutched to his chest.

They watched for a moment.

"Hey, mister!" She stepped out from the doorway.

His head whipped around, but seeing two kids, he just smiled. Relieved. "Hey! How's it going?" he said.

"What're you doing?" she called back.

"What's it look like? Working!" he grunted, reaching down for more pipes.

"My grandfather's not here," she said, and he glanced back.

"That's okay. He said just dump it here."

"Hey! Hey, Becker!" From the distance came Charlie's thin voice. Barefoot and holding up the waist of his baggy pants, he limped out of the house. His white hair was stiff and unruly. It had been less than two weeks since she'd last seen him on his way fishing, but he looked years older. And frail. With a shaky stream of curses, he told the man "to put it all back in his truck and get the hell out of here!" Becker jumped down and clanged up his tailgate. He said he was just leaving, that he'd only been checking for any galvanized he could buy. By the time he'd reached the side of his truck Charlie was jabbing him in the chest and yelling, best he could in his weak state, for him to get all his shit out of there. No way was he getting stuck with asbestos pipe.

"Don't know whatcher talking about, old man. Sorry," Becker said. He swiped away the old man's hand and opened the door, but Charlie grabbed the back of his shirt. Becker gave him a quick shove that sent the old man reeling.

"Leave him alone!" Nellie shouted as she helped steady her grandfather, who charged right back at the man. She couldn't believe it, half the man's size, but Charlie kept trying to pull him down. She picked up a thick stick, holding it over her shoulder like a bat, determined to use it if she had to, while Henry pleaded with her to stop.

A red truck rumbled through the gates. It was Max, with Boone in back and grocery bags on the front seat.

"Some guy's fighting Charlie!" she yelled over the commotion of the two engines. Max was already out of his truck and running with Boone barking at his heels. Becker had scrambled into his truck, and was trying to turn it around. Max threw open his door and told him to get out.

"No!" Becker yelled back. "I'm just leaving! I got no problem with you."

"That asbestos's his. Idiot's tryna dump it on me!" Charlie shouted. His voice seemed stronger now with Max here.

Again Max ordered Becker down from the truck, but he refused, and who could blame him with the muscular dog snarling and baring his stained fangs? Max grabbed Becker's arm and yanked him out. Becker was taller, and younger, but Max wasn't fazed. He wanted all that asbestos pipe put back in the truck, and he wanted it done now. Becker stood his ground—the pipe wasn't his and that was that. Enraged, Charlie flew at him, but Max held him back. It was the same as that there, what was already in the truck, Charlie yelled over Max's restraining arm. Yeah, Becker said, because he was just starting to load up and then he realized what it was.

"That's a lie!" Henry erupted, gesturing with his cup of worms. "Nellie and me, we saw him put it there."

She was shocked by her brother's intrusion into the fray. His eyes gleamed like Charlie's. Cagey and eager. For the men it wasn't as much about the asbestos now as wanting the fight. Which they were getting. The man was trying to climb into the truck, but Max kept pulling him back. This time he got one leg behind Becker and yanked him down so hard he fell to the ground. She and Henry looked at each other. The Hip Throw, the exact same, number 18 in the major's holds. In all the times they'd tried it, never had it gone so smoothly as what they'd just witnessed. Becker was flat on his back, Boone straddling him. The dog's muzzle quivered inches from his face.

"Get him off me!" he pleaded.

"Back!" With just that one word and Max's raised hand, Boone sank onto his haunches and crept away. There was something loathsome in the dog's cowering retreat, yet impressive.

Becker scrambled to his feet and raised his fists. "Okay, come on! Come on! You want it so bad, so come on. Come on, asshole!" he growled, and Max lunged, fists flying so fast all the man could do was try to cover his head. Blood spewed from his crooked nose. He sank to his knees, but Max continued pummeling him. Nellie'd never before seen two grown men fight, their groaning, grunting struggle sickening to watch. Finally, Charlie stepped forward. He'd been yelling at Max to let the bastard go, but there was no stopping his frenzy. Just as Charlie touched his shoulder, Max's arm swung back, knocking him onto his rump. He sat for a moment, looking almost amused to find himself in a scuffle again. Shocked that he'd knocked the old man down, Max's fight was over. He lifted Charlie to his feet, then stood there with the strangest expression, as if flash frozen in death. Only Boone seemed to understand. Gazing up, he whimpered.

Holding his bleeding nose, Becker lurched toward his truck. Charlie did what he later said should've been done right off the bat: he grabbed Becker's keys from the ignition. So now Becker had two choices. He could either load all his goddamn pipe back onto the truck and get his keys back, or Charlie was calling the cops. Mindful of their mother's anger, Charlie sent the kids home, so they didn't actually see the rest: Max loading the asbestos-bound pipe back onto the truck. He had to. Becker had a broken nose and dislocated jaw.

Chapter 9

———

I T WAS ONE OF THOSE SLOW SUMMER DAYS, CLOUDLESS AND HOT, with just the gentlest breeze swaying the pink-and-white hollyhocks against the barn. Even the birds sounded lazy. Max was coming for the old recliner in their barn, the one Nellie'd had her eye on for Dolly, but no matter. Charlie needed it, and besides, it wasn't looking as if she'd be with them much longer anyway. The broken window had been bad enough, but now her mother was even more suspicious. According to Lizzie, at the salon, her niece was living a very secretive life. No one knew what was going on. None of her relatives had heard from her. Every call to her cell phone went straight to voice mail. And yet whenever Nellie ran into Dolly, she was her old self, sweet and always interested in what she was doing.

She'd been talking to Nellie through her kitchen window. It was trash day and Henry had pulled a moldy blue tarpaulin from someone's barrel. He wanted to use it as a temporary roof on the tree house. With his arm feeling better, work had resumed. Nellie'd been helping him, but every time she suggested anything, he scoffed, so finally she just quit, she was telling Dolly as she watched for Max's truck. She was supposed to unlock the barn. Now that her mother knew he was an ex-con, Nellie figured she was afraid he'd take more than the chair. They hadn't told her about the fight with Becker. Henry was dying to but knew if he did, they'd never be allowed back to the junkyard.

"You guys ever sleep up there?" Dolly asked.

"That's the plan," Nellie called over Henry's banging hammer. "If he ever gets the tarp on right."

"Yeah, but then you can't see the stars. And that's the best part, laying there with your eyes wide open. I did that once," she said with a smile of shivery delight.

"Sleep outside?"

"Yeah."

"Were you camping?"

"Kinda. Sorta. It was on a boat. Out on the deck. I never saw anything like that before. We just laid there. It was, like, the stars, you could almost reach up and touch them. They're way closer over the ocean."

"They're not closer. Just brighter. Cuz there's no light pollution."

Nellie knew by her quick glance that Dolly thought she'd made it up. Especially the part about light pollution. She'd noticed that before, how when Dolly was unsure of something, she'd look hurt, almost afraid.

"Well, anyway," Dolly said to end the conversation. Somehow, Nellie'd made her feel bad. Before she could close the window, Nellie invited her to come on out and see the tree house. Within moments Dolly was following her up the rickety wooden ladder, built just narrow enough to pull up after them. For protection if need be. Word had gotten back that Bucky was after them.

"No!" Henry protested, seeing Nellie climb in. "You don't want to help, then—"

"Hey, cutie!" Dolly giggled, hoisting herself up next and in. Henry glared at his sister as Dolly walked from side to side. He had nailed tall posts into the four corners so that even with the tarp on you could stand up. "Cool! This is so cool. My first tree house! I never been in one before. You did this, made it yourself?" she asked Henry, who blushed and nodded. And she wasn't just saying things to make him feel good. She was really impressed. And delighted. You could always tell with Dolly. Everything showed. She asked if they ever ate up here. Just crackers and stuff, Nellie said. Her mother was afraid food would attract skunks and raccoons. Dolly said she'd love sleeping up here some night. Her mother hadn't let them yet, Nellie lied. She knew her mother would say no and then Dolly's feelings would be hurt. She said it would make her mother too nervous, between rabid animals and prowlers. A house on Tremont Street had been broken into last winter.

But that was in broad daylight, Henry said. But they never caught the guy, Nellie said, which meant he was still out there, looking for his next victims.

"Why would he break into a tree house?" Henry asked, logically enough but with a dismissive scowl.

"Yeah, especially this one," Nellie snorted. "No roof, no door." She didn't like being shown up in front of the only adult she could impress.

"Then leave!" Henry snapped. "Why're you even up here, then?"

"Nice, Henry. That's really nice." She rolled her eyes for Dolly's benefit. "God, he's so anal."

"Nossir! He's just a really hard worker. I see you out here every day, Henry, tryna make this the best tree house ever, and guess what? It is! Hey, maybe your mom'll let you sleep up here if I'm here. I mean, with you guys." Then she lay down and stretched out. She told them to come lie down and see if they'd all fit. Nellie lay down next to her. But not Henry. Looking down at them like that, he reminded Nellie of her father. "Come on," Dolly coaxed, patting the rough board next to her. "We gotta see if this'll work."

"That's okay," Henry mumbled. He seemed embarrassed for them. Her brother wasn't one to cave in easily, Nellie knew, even if the pesterer was an adult. Even then, he had scruples.

Laughing, Dolly raised up on her elbows, a position that made Nellie realize for the first time just how big her supposedly fake breasts were—Ruth claimed to know by their perfect roundness. "I don't bite, you know, and I like little boys. Specially ones as cute as you," she teased in a breathy whisper.

In his full body slouch, Henry was about as miserable as Nellie'd ever seen him. His face was red, his shoulders so hunched they almost curled, one into the other, and he couldn't look at her.

"How 'bout tonight?" Dolly said she'd ask their mother, and if it was all right, they'd meet up here when the sun went down. She'd bring the snacks, bug spray, and some blankets. But they'd need a flashlight, which she didn't have. That was easy enough, Nellie said. Because of the store they had a ton of flashlights.

"Three," Henry muttered and began nailing a corner of the tarp onto the post.

That's when Nellie heard Max's truck backing into the driveway. She climbed down the ladder and hurried toward the barn with the key. Max jumped down from the cab. Nellie hadn't seen him since the fight. Something was different about him, but at first she wasn't sure what. The first whiff of sweetness came as she was unlocking the padlock. Cologne. He was clean shaven with his hair combed. Instead of his faded T-shirt he had on a regular shirt, tight and shiny black, with small silvery buttons. She really wanted to tell him he looked nice but was afraid he might take that to mean he usually didn't. She asked where Boone was.

"Back with Charlie." He followed her into the barn.

The recliner was just inside the door, where her mother had asked her father to put it. The more her mother was learning of Max, the less she trusted him, no matter how good he was to Charlie. Nellie'd seen the effort it had taken her father to drag the big old chair, so when Max just picked it up and hoisted it into the back of his truck, she was impressed. She followed him as he clamped the truck gate shut, then slipped the cotter pins into place. She asked if he'd gone fishing again with Charlie. Been a while, he said. Charlie hadn't been up to too much lately but maybe tomorrow.

"Said he'll give it a good try, anyway. See what happens," he added, looking toward the house.

"Can I come? I'll be real quiet. I wouldn't say two words, really. I mean, I know how important it is when you're fishing, being quiet, that is."

Max seemed amused. "Well, you tell *him* that, then. He's *your* grandpa after all." He smiled and tried to cover his mouth, his two broken bottom teeth jagged and discolored.

"When're you leaving?" She was elated by the possibility of finally going fishing.

"After lunch, maybe. One or two." Squinting, he peered past her.

Dolly was climbing down the ladder from the tree house.

"Hey, Nellie! We're gonna go get ice cream!" she called, waving both hands in that little girl, wait'll-you-hear-this way she had as she came closer. "I just told Henry. We're gonna walk down to Rollie's and—"oh, hi," she said as if only just recognizing Max. She folded her arms.

"Hi," Max said, grinning and quickly covering his mouth. "The other night. At the club. You were—"

"Yeah, I had to go," she said. Her face was white.

"You were the best one. That was good dancing."

"Yeah, well. Anyway," Dolly sighed, and for a moment no one spoke. It was obvious she didn't like him talking about her job. Or at least, not in front of a kid.

Saying she had to call her mother about going fishing, Nellie excused herself and ran into the house. She winced when Frederic answered. He sounded annoyed. Her mother was in the middle of a process, he said, and couldn't come to the phone. When Nellie came back out, Dolly immediately stopped talking. Max looked upset. There was an uneasy silence. Henry watched from the tree house.

"Hey, guess what!" Nellie blurted, never at a loss for words herself. "Tomorrow I'm going fishing. Max said I could."

Dolly stared at him. "Maybe Max oughta find some other fishin' buddy," she said in a low voice. "Somebody a little older."

"Well, my grandfather—" Nellie said quickly because if Dolly went there wouldn't be room for her.

"What's that s'posed to mean?" Max broke in.

"—he's going too," Nellie continued.

"Whatever you think," she answered with a smirk.

He just stood there looking at her, head nodding, almost panting, it seemed, as if something inside was going way faster than he wanted. He turned suddenly and jumped into his truck, shifted into reverse, then sped backward out of the driveway.

"Creep," Dolly said, as he peeled down the street.

"No. Max is nice," Nellie said.

"Yeah, right, staring at my boobs the whole time," she said.

No, he wasn't, she wanted to say. He kept looking down at the ground because he was quiet. That was all. A man of few words, but a nice man, before it had turned into something else. There was no denying he'd left angry, though Nellie wasn't sure why. And thinking back, later, when every word and detail would seem so freighted with meaning, she would understand that the fancy shirt and sweet cologne had been worn to impress Dolly.

THEY DID WALK down to Rollie's. Henry didn't want to, but he couldn't stay home alone, so in the end he had to come with them. Nellie and Henry were still in shorts, but Dolly had changed into a lacy blouse and ruffly skirt, the same bright yellow as her purse, and very high heels. Seeing her so dressed up made Nellie feel bad for her. They were only going for ice cream, but Dolly was excited. The whole way there she never stopped talking. Everything seemed to fascinate her. Kitty Lowry's three-legged dog, Rusty, chained to his sagging porch, barking and lunging at them was "just the most bravest thing," and the straggly pink-and-lavender petunias in the shaded stone planters in the park were "just, like, so precious," she sighed, leaning to smell them. She broke one off. "Shit!" she cried, recoiling from the sticky stem. She spit on her fingers and rubbed them furiously on her skirt. Her heels kept sinking into the grass, so now she was carrying them. Henry looked at Nellie, each poker-faced glance conveying the weirdness of it all.

"Hey, let's go sit on it," Dolly said, heading barefoot toward the Civil War cannon in the far corner of the park. She hoisted herself up sidesaddle on the long, black barrel. Nellie and Henry watched from the path. Only little kids ever sat there. "C'mon!" she insisted, holding out her hand.

"That's okay," Nellie said.

"C'mon, Henry!" she called. "C'mon up here!"

"No, thanks." Bitter enough about this roundabout route for ice cream, he groaned as Dolly tapped a cigarette from her pack. Her eyes glazed over as she lit it. After each long drag, she blew smoke straight at them. They stepped off to the side. Coughing, Henry covered his nose and mouth, but she didn't seem to notice. It was almost as if she'd forgotten they were there. Finally she gave a deep sigh and flicked the butt into the grass. Henry rushed over to stamp it out, which seemed to break her spell.

"Come on, you guys, let's have some fun!" She slid off the cannon barrel, then pranced along, swinging her arms and calling back loudly. "Sometimes you just have to do things! Take the friggin' bull by the horns!" At the sidewalk she had to balance, wobbling on one foot to put the other heel back on. Continuing her march, she grew short of breath, even a little wheezy. "Get outta your comfort zone. People're always going, 'Oh, I don't know. I don't think so.' But, jeez, what kinda life's that? I mean, you at least gotta die trying, right? That's what I say anyway." A passing car honked its horn and she waved both hands high over her head.

"She nuts or what?" Henry whispered.

"Happy, that's all," Nellie whispered back, but something was off-kilter, like static in the air, invisible but prickly.

As they walked down Linden Street, Dolly grew subdued. Her skinny heels clicked between them. They were all feeling the heat. No one was talking. Every time Henry tried lagging behind, she'd stop and wait for him to catch up. At the end of the street she turned right then left, then right again onto Harlequin Circle. Nellie and Henry froze at the mouth of the cul-de-sac.

"Whose house is that?" Dolly asked with a slight nod at the large gray cape at the end.

"My friend. Jessica," Nellie said with the uneasy sense that Dolly had deliberately led them here. Well, then, why didn't Nellie go ask her friend to have ice cream with them, she said. No, she told Dolly. She didn't want to. Why not? Because, Nellie said. She just didn't.

"Let's go see if she's home." She gestured for them to follow. "C'mon, it'll be fun," she teased, almost whining. "The more the merrier!" Nellie could feel Henry's disbelieving stare with Dolly's pouty insistence. "We came all this way, and now we're here, so why not? Why?"

"Because I don't want to, that's why," Nellie declared in a tone she'd never before dared use to an adult. But right then Dolly was acting more like a child than a grown woman, petulant, and determined to have her way. No matter what.

Stepping off the curb, Dolly tucked the back of her blouse into her waistband, then squared her shoulders and marched across the street right up onto Jessica's front porch. They froze, watching her ring the bell. Nellie couldn't understand why she was doing this. Maybe her mother had put her up to it, hoping if she was nicer to Jessica, then maybe Mr. Cooper would finally make an offer on the store. But that wasn't her mother's style. She was way too direct. And Dolly didn't even know Jessica, although Nellie did remember her asking about Claudia Cooper. Maybe that's it, she thought, relieved when no one answered and Dolly started back down the steps. Dolly was on the serpentine brick walk when Mrs. Cooper opened the door. She was drying her hands on a dish towel. Her dark hair was pulled back and she wore a tight white tennis outfit. Three-year-old Annie, the youngest Cooper, peered out from her side.

"Can I help you?" Mrs. Cooper called down to Dolly, who hurried back onto the porch. Whatever she said caused Mrs. Cooper to look past her with an exuberant wave. "Hi, Nellie!" she called over the railing.

Groaning, Nellie managed a limp wave.

"I just told your sitter, Jessica's not here. She just left for her appointment, but she should be back in an hour or so."

"Oh," Nellie called back weakly.

"I'll tell her you came by! She'll be *so* happy!"

Again, Nellie waved.

"I'll have her call you!"

Faking a smile, Nellie backed off, waving.

"That was weird," Henry said under his breath as Dolly crossed the street. They continued on to Rollie's. Instead of going inside, they stood at the takeout window where Ruth was. Store policy didn't allow workers to wait on family members, so Ruth not only pretended she didn't know them as she jam-packed their triple chocolate cones, but she asked Henry what his name was. Ronnie-Don Rufus, he said, and she burst out laughing so hard she could barely scoop. Ronnie-Don Rufus was one of the characters in the made-up stories their father used to tell them when they were little. No matter the calamity, hapless Ronnie-Don was usually nearby, both cause and victim, the family catchphrase for those what-can-go-wrong-will-go-wrong moments. Ruth and Henry's laughter made Nellie realize how long it had been since they'd enjoyed one another. But what had changed? And why? Was it money? With hard times upon them, were they turning on one another? Pulling apart? Coming undone? Wasn't that when families were supposed to stick together? Right then and there she resolved to do everything in her power to keep them strong. Ever since Ruth's search for her birth father, Nellie'd had the feeling that *she* was the lynchpin, true firstborn of the real family.

Much to Ruth's disappointment, Dolly didn't want anything. Not a sundae, a frappe, freeze, or even a cone. Just a cup of water. She didn't have much to say on the trek back, which took even longer because she seemed so tired. Her earlier zest had fizzled. She'd pulled her blouse out of her waistband and was carrying her heels. Sighing, she trudged barefoot up the hill, behind them.

"You gonna call her?" she asked when they got home. She meant Jessica. Henry had already thanked Dolly and fled into the house before she could suggest any more excursions.

"I don't know," Nellie said, licking her sticky fingers.

"She seems really nice," Dolly said.

"She wasn't even there."

"I mean her, the mother," Dolly said, looking not at Nellie but past her.

IT WAS MONDAY night and Ruth still wasn't home. Her mother and father had been up for hours, waiting. They thought Nellie didn't know, but she'd been waiting too, listening. At three in the morning the front door finally squealed open. Nellie crept to the top of the stairs, straining to hear every word. Accusations, the tearful denials, and in the end her mother telling Ruth she was on "a quick trip to big trouble, drinking and running around with a fast, older crowd!"

"I wasn't drinking!" Ruth shot back in thick-tongued protest.

"Of course you were! You reek of alcohol! And God knows what else!"

With that, Ruth must have tried to rush past them for the cool sanctuary of her room. The sounds of a brief scuffle only darkened the shadows below. Nellie leaned closer. The hair on the back of her neck pricked up and she was queasy with the thrilling horror. Never had such shocking events taken place within her own family. She ducked back. Ruth was halfway up the stairs.

"Get back here! Get down here right now!" her mother demanded. She must have grabbed Ruth then. A thud came on the stairs.

"Oh! My God! Are you all right?" her mother gasped.

"What do you care, you bitch!" Ruth screamed.

"Don't you dare speak to your mother like that!" Her father sounded about as angry as she'd ever heard him. "After all she does for you, you should be ashamed of yourself, young lady."

"Leave me alone. I don't have to listen to this. You're nothing to me! Nothing!"

And with that she half ran, half stumbled up the stairs, sobbing and moaning, past Nellie hunched in the dark alcove by the bathroom.

Nellie lay in bed awake for a long time after that. She hated her sister and suffered a deep sorrow for her parents' pain. Their lives, she realized, were false, counterfeit. They were just like everyone else. It was all a lie. Her father was weak and so was her mother. High above, from her air-conditioned perch, Ruth had always ruled their family, and now would destroy them. At four A.M., too agitated to sleep, Nellie turned on the light and wrote her a long letter. In it she said how sorry she felt for Ruth, that it must have been hard all these years, being a stepchild and half sister and never a 100 percent real member of the family, but that didn't mean she was different from the rest of them, meaning, of course, herself and Henry. No, because they loved her as much as they loved each other, but if she kept on acting this way, then she was going to have to stop caring about her. And, soon, so would Henry. It was up to her, her choice.

Nellie sealed the envelope, tiptoed to the third floor, and slipped the letter under her door. She returned to bed, relieved and empowered. She felt good about everything, especially about herself. Upon reading her letter, Ruth would realize she had to start acting better. The future of their family depended on it, which she'd also stated in her letter.

RUTH WAS ASLEEP when Nellie left the next morning. Because she'd be home all that day with "a touch of the flu," as her mother called it, Nellie'd be free of Henry. As he'd so gratefully be of her. The day would be hers to do whatever she wanted.

She rode her bike to the junkyard. The canoe was lashed to the top of Charlie's truck. Max was digging a trench along the front of the barn. A few more feet, then they were going fishing, he said. She asked if she could go and he said it was up to Charlie, who watched from his chair just inside the shade of the barn. She went over and asked, but Charlie was in a foul mood. He just kind of waved her off, saying how "pissed" he was. For one thing, the more Max dug, the more rot he was finding in the sills. Oughta just shovel it all back in. Goddamn place could fall down, for all he cared. Last night someone kept throwing firecrackers over the back fence. Twice he'd called the police, but soon as they'd leave, it'd start up again. His third call, they told him "to deal with it." They had more important things to do. Charlie said he knew who it was, so he damn well would deal with it his way, and nobody'd better say a damn word after.

Still muttering, he got up and limped toward the truck. She followed eagerly. Max tossed his shovel in the trench and started tying Boone to his stake by the gate. No, Charlie called back, bring him. But the canoe wouldn't take all three and the dog, too, Max said, but Charlie insisted. Max put Boone in the back of the truck. Nellie climbed in between the men. Duct tape patched the split leather seats, but the inside of the cab was immaculate. Excited to finally be going fishing, Nellie knew better than say much, which fit right in with Max being his usual quiet self. Not Charlie though. He was talking a blue streak. It started the minute the old pickup rumbled onto the street.

The damn Shelby twins, that's who was making his life miserable, setting fires in the woods, which is how the tires got burning, and stealing from him because their parents couldn't control their two strange kids; not only that but the father, whatever the hell his name was—Mort, that was it—Mort Shelby'd been on his case since day one, and he was damn sick of it—turn left—another left—down there—that road there, dammit . . .

They were rattling down the narrow washboard road, right toward the Shelbys'. Their house sat at the very end, starkly tall, the weathered clapboards a paintless gray. She'd seen it once or twice, years before, from the backseat of a crowded minivan or station wagon, filled with squealing kids being driven home after someone's birthday party. But now no one was inviting the Shelby twins to anything anymore.

Go knock on the door, her grandfather ordered Max, and tell their kids to get the hell out here so he could set them straight about some things.

"No." Max looked past her, right at Charlie.

"What the hell you mean, no? You wanna job? You wanna keep working or you wanna be picking your skinny ass up off the goddamn street again? Is that what the hell you want? Well? Is it?" Charlie's tinny voice churned the heat inside the cab. She squirmed between them.

"Can't, Charlie," he muttered, looking down at the wheel.

Licking his lips and breathing hard, Charlie studied him for a moment. "Goddammit!" he finally barked, opening his door. With a groan, he removed himself from the truck in sections, one foot, a leg, hip, an arm. "You! Come on down!" He gestured. To Nellie. Just go knock on the door, he said, and ask the twins to come out for a minute, which, when she thought of it later, was probably his plan in the first place, the only reason he'd let her come. She said the same as Max: no. "Why?" He was enraged. "Why the hell not?"

"I know them. They're in my class."

"Even better then."

She refused to get out of the truck. Now, Charlie insisted, or he'd damn well pull her out. Beside her, there came from Max a low, deep sound, a drone, almost. Arms folded tight and feet braced to the floorboards, she stared back at Charlie. He tried a few more threats: telling her mother, her father, never allowing her back in the junkyard again, her or her piss-ant brother.

Finally, he stormed, as best a limping man can storm, up to the house. He was still banging on the door when it opened. Boone's barking started in the back of the truck the minute Mrs. Shelby stepped out. A tall woman, she was older than Nellie remembered, and skinnier. She endured Charlie's tirade, from time to time straining her head back in disbelief. She said something, then went inside. Moments later, with Boone's even more frantic barking, she reemerged with her sons. They towered over their mother, squinting, as if from sunlight they hadn't seen in months. Even with the engine running and Boone's barking, Nellie could hear Charlie's shouting. The Shelbys just stood there taking it.

Nellie slid low on the seat. "They didn't do anything. I know they didn't," she said over the dog's commotion.

"Boone's pretty riled," Max sighed, proof enough for him.

"They're just different, that's all. They're really smart."

Max leaned over the wheel.

"They're always getting picked on," she added.

Whatever Mrs. Shelby was saying now incensed Charlie even more. His hands flew in the air. Nellie could tell from the way she looked at her boys that she knew they were different, too. She spoke to Rodney, then to Roy. Suddenly they both turned, in such a rush that one seemed stuck to the other as they hurried inside.

"They your friends?" Max asked.

"No. I mean, I know them, but—"

"They have any friends?"

"Uh-uh. Just each other."

He nodded. "I had a brother."

"What's his name?"

"Merrill."

"Merrill. He live around here?"

Mrs. Shelby stood her post, watching Charlie's labored retreat down her steep steps. No matter what, they were good, good boys, she was surely thinking.

"No. Merrill's long gone."

"What happened to him?"

"He died."

"How?" she blurted. Not a polite question. And sometimes you got way more information than you could handle. Like Jessica's description of her cat's crushed head after it was run over. That time, Nellie threw up on her kitchen floor.

"Got shot. Tracking deer."

"I'm very sorry to hear that." She felt dizzy.

As soon as Mrs. Shelby closed her door, Boone stopped barking.

"They come out at night." Max's dark voice in the sudden quiet sent a chill through her. "Over the fence. I seen 'em. Mostly just looking for spare parts."

It took her a minute . . . he meant the twins.

Charlie climbed back in with new vigor. He'd told her all right, the beanpole. And she'd backed right down. Next time he saw her boys anywhere near there, he was to call and she'd come get them herself.

Charlie didn't want to go fishing. He said she and Max could still go, but then Max changed his mind, too. He said they'd go next time Charlie felt more up to it. They offered to drop her off, but instead, she hung around the junkyard, watching Max throw a threadbare tennis ball for Boone to spring after, then fetch back in his sticky muzzle. Charlie was fanning himself with a broken fly swatter, half the stick missing. He was telling about the old days, how busy it was here, especially weekends. He'd had two, sometimes three men working for him. And a dog in the yard, useless as it was.

"People took better care then. Something broke down it got fixed, and the only place in town for parts was right here," he said swatting the chair arm. "Still, you had to keep an eye out. I mean, human nature, take what you can and the hell who owns it. Best one though was Armand Lussier. Butcher at the A&P. Stole the place blind and married to the homeliest woman around. One of them, you know—he demonstrated—jutty-out jaws. Anyway, she took in laundry for all the fat cats in town, probably even your grandma Peck—pretty sure Charlotta wasn't doing up her own undies and sheets," he said, his inclusive wink meant to keep her from telling on him. "The peckity Pecks," he explained to Max, who'd just thrown the ball again, "they always lived high—new car, new clothes. Anyway, one day Armand comes in and he's telling me how the old mangle's gone Democrat and the missus, she wants a new one. 'No way,' Armand said he said; he'll just fix the one she's got. 'I know you got one inside,' he tells me. Says he'll pay for parts. 'Well, I got one, sure,' I tell him. 'Old as hell—thing is, though, it works.' Told him I'd sell it to him. Fifteen dollars and his in trade. He acts like he can't believe it. Next day, back he comes, only this time with a bag of bones and gristle for the dog. Same thing, he says, by the way, dumping the bag out for the dog, coupla parts, that's all he needs. Fifteen dollars and your old one, I say, so off he goes. Next day, guess who's back? Armand! Same bag of bones, same offer, so I refuse. Well, next couple days the old dog, he's dragging around, shitting his brains out. But I don't think much of it. Then he's dead. That very night, the gate chain's cut. Next morning, guess what's missing? The fucking mangle!"

"He fucking poisoned your dog?" Max asked, hand resting on Boone's tensed head. "I mean, Jesus, what'd you do?"

"Fucking poisoned his!" Charlie yelped with a pump of his fist that Nellie just knew was dirty. He leaned close to Max and whispered behind his hand. ". . . didn't get near as good as I gave," was all she heard. Both men erupted in the kind of wheezy snickering that kept them from looking her way. She felt bad. Charlie's swearing was one thing. Even though she was used to it, she still didn't like it, and knew not to tell her mother, because that's just the way he was. But Max's swearing in front her, now that was a disappointment. She'd really thought he was better than that, a finer person. And why that was, she couldn't begin to explain, other than that skill she had, that keen sense of a person's worth.

"Best part, though, was the fucking mangle!" Charlie gasped. "Overheated one day and burned his house half down."

"Sweet Jesus!" Max's arm reared back.

If a dog can be ecstatic, Boone surely was. Waiting, his tail beat the dirt, then with the ball's release, he took off, grinning, she thought. A few minutes later, Charlie said he was going in "for a snooze." After he left, Max slapped his thigh and said, "Well." He looked slowly around the yard. Well, what? she wondered, slowly realizing *well* meant it was time. Time for her to go. Whimpering low on his haunches Boone kept picking up the ball and flipping it into the air, desperate for Max to throw it again. Max just sat there. She shared Boone's hunger for the dark-eyed man's attention. A word. A look, anything.

She picked up the ball. Wanting to engage both dog and master, she threw it hard as she could down past the barn. Boone whimpered and wiggled, but never stood or chased it. Max's wait continued in the uneasy stillness. As much as he wanted her to leave, she was determined to stay.

"How come he won't go get it?"

"He knows not to."

"How?"

"I got work to do," Max said.

"That's okay. I can help. I'm a pretty good worker."

"You better be going now." He gestured at the house. "Charlie's inside."

"I'll just wait. I don't care. Nothing else to do," she said.

He got up. Boone stayed put, but she followed Max into the barn. He turned.

"Go on back out!" he said. Ordinarily, his pock-whiskered scowl would have sent her running, but not then.

"I'll be quiet."

"You shouldn't be in here."

"Charlie lets me."

His mouth puckered with sourness. "Well, Charlie ain't here."

"So?"

"Don't be talking to me like that, okay?" he growled and went outside.

"I'm sorry," she said close on his heels. She really was. "I was just wondering about your brother, that's all. What you said, about tracking deer. How'd he get shot?"

He started digging again. The shovel's scrape and ping through the gravelly dirt gave her the shivers. She knew she should go, knew he didn't like it, but leaving would be an admission. She just wasn't sure of what. Mostly she felt let down, sad, without knowing why. Something needed saying, but it wasn't up to her. She was the kid, after all.

"We were going over a stone wall. Him first, then me. He was a year younger'n me. Twelve, but always faster. Smarter, too. We'd been out all day. By then it was getting late."

In spite of the way it played out in his voice, distant and labored with the rhythm of methodical digging, she saw them, the two brothers, burst from the dusky woods, panting, the dry crunch of brush underfoot as they raced each other.

"Almost suppertime. Not that it mattered," he grunted and dug, his back to her the whole time. "I mean, Merrill, he'da lived in the woods if he could, eating squirrels and snakes. Frogs, he didn't care. But not me, all I wanted was to get back. I started running. He went first. Nothing to it, I mean the wall couldn't've been but two and a half feet, but I mustn'ta been looking. My foot caught, snagged kinda, in between the rocks, and down I go. Which is when it happened. The gun going off. Just that one shot. I don't know." He paused, foot on the shovel. "Hard to figure."

The gun blast. She'd heard it, too. Still was, in her bones. "That's awful," she finally said.

"Yeah. They never got over it, specially my mother."

"But it wasn't your fault."

"To them it was," he said, jamming his foot down on the shovel, hard.

She must have left soon after that. She wasn't sure what more was said or even if she said good-bye. The most she'd remember were the sweat circles darkening his back as he kept on digging and digging, not for, but against something.

WHEN SHE GOT home, they were waiting, her mother by the sink, arms crossed, staring out the window, and her father next to her, peeling carrots.

"Sit down," she said, then called up the back stairs for Ruth to come down, which seemed to take forever. Nellie kept asking what was wrong? Had something happened? What had she done? Where was Henry?

"Just wait," her father said. He peeled another carrot into the mound of thin orange strips.

"Why? For what?"

Her mother followed Ruth into the kitchen. They couldn't look at her. A crime of enormous proportions had been visited upon their house. The damn bikes, it had to be. The fact of Henry's absence made her knees go weak. Had he been arrested? Was she next? This might be their last private time together. Her poor parents. Last night with Ruth, and now this. Her father cleared his throat and put down the peeler. Surprisingly enough, *he* would be enumerating the charges.

Insensitivity, they wanted to think, and, they hoped, not out-and-out cruelty. He put on his glasses. His orange-stained fingers removed a once-crumpled sheet of lined paper from his breast pocket. He unfolded it. "Stepchild," he read. "Half sister, never a 100 percent real member of the family?" He shook his head. "Ruth is your *sister*. Your *sister*! Nothing else. Plain and simple." Looking over his glasses, he stared at her.

"I know!" she cried, overwhelmed with relief. She grinned at Ruth.

But they continued staring, as if at some vicious intruder who'd stumbled into their lair.

"How could you? How could you say those things to your own sister? Your *only* sister." Her mother sobbed, then tried to stop, and with her shuddering gasp Nellie's father drew her mother into his arms.

"But I didn't mean it that way," she tried to explain.

"Not a 100 percent real part of the family." Ruth wiped her nose. Now, she was crying. "What way did you mean?"

"Legal. You know. I mean . . . not being . . . from birth," she stammered, mind racing and weak with the futility of it all. What could she say? That she had tried to help her family, who now, in their wounded solidarity, believed the worst and had turned against her? It hadn't been intended as cruelty.

But to them it was . . . to them it was.

Chapter 10

——

I T WAS A HOT SATURDAY NIGHT. THEY'D GOTTEN PERMISSION TO sleep in the tree house again. Not with Dolly though, her mother said, cringing at the suggestion. Nellie had asked, just in case. She was already worried that Dolly'd feel bad if she saw them up there. No food, her mother said, just water, they both had to be covered with bug spray, and they were to pull the ladder up after them. She'd even had Nellie's father cut a section of plywood that fit over the opening. They had fresh batteries in their flashlights. Then suddenly, at the last minute, they had Jessica Cooper. Earlier that afternoon she had called to invite Nellie to the movies with her and her older sister Patrice. It was with great relief that Nellie'd told her she *had* to sleep in the tree house. Her mother was making her because Henry needed someone up there with him. Why can't Ruth do it? Jessica asked, adding how unfair it was that Nellie always got stuck minding Henry. Ruth had to work, Nellie said—only partially true. Her shift would end at eight, but ever since her poorly received letter, Ruth was barely speaking to her, so she sure as heck wouldn't be doing Nellie any favors. And she was making the most of her new role: the misunderstood outsider. No one dared look at her the wrong way.

"We can't even have snacks," Nellie complained to underscore her regret. This was Jessica's fourth invitation she'd turned down in as many days. "Just be nice. Please," her mother had whispered yesterday when Jessica called again. They were still waiting for Mr. Cooper to get back to them with an offer. Every time the phone rang they'd look at each other. Her mother couldn't understand why they hadn't heard anything.

"Just call him," she'd said earlier at breakfast. "Find out what's going on. Maybe he's getting cold feet."

"These things take time," Nellie's father assured her. He opened the newspaper. "Market analysis, appraisals. You know Andy—he's a stickler when it comes to details."

"And *I'm* a stickler when it comes to losing the house because we're so far behind in the taxes."

"That's not going to happen," her father scoffed.

"How can you say that?"

The children all looked up.

Her mother's voice had pitched to a new level of shrillness. "How can you sit there calmly reading the paper when the only money coming into this house is what I make?"

He put the paper down. "It's going to be all right, Sandy." He stared up at her. "Trust me."

"I am. I have been. I want to." She stared back.

He put his hand around her wrist, and she winced. If it weren't for the tenderness in his voice, Nellie might have thought he was hurting her. "This is a small town. We've lived here all our lives. We know people. They know who we are. And that's what this is about. A level of trust, and maybe it's not something you can add up in dollars and cents, but it's still there. It's *moral* tender, that's what it is." He smiled but she looked away, quickly, too quickly.

NELLIE AND HENRY had been hauling their sleeping bags up into the tree house when Jessica called back. She told Mrs. Peck that she'd asked her mother if she could come sleep in the tree house, too. Her mother said it was fine with her, as long as Mrs. Peck approved.

"You what?" Nellie gasped.

"I thought you asked her. That's the way it sounded."

"Well, I didn't! And I'm not going to! No way am I spending the night with Jessica Cooper!"

"You have to." Her mother was white lipped. "Besides, she'll be here any minute. Her sister's driving her."

No sooner said than the bell rang. Red cheeked and giddy with delight, Jessica stood in the doorway, hugging her pillow and carrying two grocery bags.

"No food in the tree house. Sorry," Nellie said, ready to close the door.

"That's okay," her mother said from behind. "Come on in, hon."

Patrice Cooper couldn't get Jessica's sleeping bag and flashlight out of the car fast enough.

Henry stared in horror as Jessica climbed into the tree house behind her. But she had arrived well supplied: a box of Oreos, a large bag of Fritos, Gummi Bears, a bag of Snickers bars, bubble gum, and a six-pack of Coke. She'd had Patrice stop at the supermarket on their way, which of course her sister had been only too willing to do. Better than having to drag Jessica to the movies with her and her friends. Bouncy and sweet with a broad toothy smile, Patrice had been class president, salutatorian, varsity basketball captain, queen of the senior ball, and in another month she would be going to Notre Dame on a tennis scholarship. She stood in the yard talking to Nellie's mother, who was congratulating her on her many achievements. Behind them, a curtain fluttered in Dolly's window as she peeked out at the fabled Patrice. At the time, Dolly had seemed so much older, though Nellie would later realize that they were probably only two or three years apart.

Earlier, before Nellie knew Jessica would be coming, she'd brought out Ruth's old CD player. She wasn't going to play it at first, because she didn't want to have to listen to Jessica's snickering disbelief that Nellie didn't even have an iPod when she was on her second one. But as darkness enveloped their leafy aerie, they had already eaten half the Oreos and all of the Fritos while Jessica entertained them with wild tales about her two weeks at Camp Crazy, as she called it. Nellie and Henry were as repulsed as they were fascinated by her detailed accounts of near drownings and getting lost in the woods; having to ride the wildest horse and being bucked off; the mountain cave where counselors smoked pot and had sex; a fistfight between two schizoid girl campers, which she broke up and, in the process, got a black eye; and then the night the boathouse caught fire and burned to the ground before the fire trucks could even get there. And romance—she was still getting love letters. Her mother had read one last week. When she realized that Jessica's boyfriend was sixteen, she forbade her from writing back.

"But my friend Krissie says he can write to me there. That way the bitch won't know."

Nellie bristled. Krissie Potek was her friend, too. Jessica's snarl had backed Henry against the wall. He crouched in a corner, his headlamp shining on *Harry Potter and the Prisoner of Azkaban.* The weekend before, her mother had bought the set at a yard sale. Henry's goal was to finish the series before school started, which might well happen at the rate he was going, reading night and day, Nellie mistakenly told Jessica.

"So he's got OCD, then," she said.

Ignoring her, Nellie turned the music on low so it wouldn't bother Dolly or the Humboldts.

"Now what do we do?" Jessica sighed, popping open another Coke. "Jesus!"

"Look!" Nellie showed her the stack of magazines. *People* and *Us, Glamour* and *Vogue,* all from the salon. Her mother always brought them home before they got thrown out.

"They're all, like, old!" Jessica said, checking dates and flipping them aside.

"They're still interesting," Nellie said. She should have known better. Enthusiasm, it was like showing blood.

"Yeah, if you've been in a coma for six months."

Getting through the rest of the night would be rough. Nellie opened *People* and read, intently, for Jessica's benefit. It was the story of a boy who had disappeared from his family's campsite near Lake Tahoe. His mother had zipped him into his sleeping bag, kissed him and his older brother goodnight, then went into her own tent, where her husband was reading. (Henry's headlamp was giving her the creeps. Every time he moved, jagged light streaked off the walls.) In the morning, when the family woke up, the boy was gone. Sleeping bag and all. Just disappeared. No one had heard a thing. Not even his brother beside him on the mat. She closed the magazine. Barely a breeze, and yet the wind chimes on the Humboldt's patio kept tinkling. The green bulb in their garden lamppost cast a creepy glow through the trees and bushes.

Lights still burned in Dolly's apartment, but it had been a while since there'd been movement inside. Footsteps were coming down the driveway, Nellie aimed her flashlight into the yard. Her parents both waved. They'd gone for a walk, her father said, and wanted to check on them before they went inside.

"Oh! And a warning!" her mother called up and Nellie's hair stood on end. She reminded them of the rabid skunk that had been spotted in the neighborhood recently. If they heard anything, they weren't to come down. No matter what. What if it comes up here, Jessica asked. Nellie's father assured her that skunks can't climb trees. Prowlers can, Jessica said. Trying to keep her voice down, her mother came closer and asked Jessica if she was scared. Maybe sleeping out here wasn't such a good idea after all. No, Jessica said quickly. She wasn't scared— she'd be fine.

After Nellie's parents went inside, Jessica pulled out her pink cell phone and dialed a number.

"It's Jess," she said in a muffled voice. "Call me." She flipped the phone shut then picked up a magazine. "Think fast!" she said and threw it right at Henry's face.

"What's your problem?" he asked, rubbing his cheekbone as he tried not to cry.

"You."

"Then leave," Nellie said.

"I can't. Nobody's home and Patrice is at the movies," she sighed.

"My father'll drive you. I'll go get him." Nellie jumped up to push back the plywood cover.

"No! I was just kidding. Jeez." She rolled her eyes.

"That's not kidding. That's insulting. I mean, this is Henry's first night in his tree house and he lets you be here, and you're throwing stuff at him?"

"I'm sorry! All right?" She ripped the paper off her fifth Snickers bar and tossed it out the window opening.

Nellie and Henry looked at each other.

Her phone rang. "Yeah," she answered. "Yeah, we are . . . I don't care . . . Okay . . . Sure, if you want . . ."

"Who was that?" Nellie asked when she hung up.

"Nobody."

Jessica refused to tell her, and besides, it wasn't any of Nellie's business.

"It's my business when you're on my property," Nellie said.

"It's not your property."

"Well, whose is it then?" Nellie asked uneasily. Jessica just might know more than she did.

"Your parents, of course," she crowed.

"Same thing," Nellie said, relieved.

Henry had retreated into his sleeping bag. He lay with his back to them, headlamp on, still reading. Nellie was unrolling her sleeping bag, straightening it, getting the zippers to work smoothly.

"Jesus!" Jessica said from the window opening where she knelt. "Your friggin' house has bats. They keep coming in and out of the chimney."

Nellie crawled over next to her. Things were swooping down into the chimney, then darting out again. Quick black things. Lots of things. "Those're just chimney swifts. Every house has them." Grateful Henry didn't contradict her, she returned to her sleeping bag.

"Mine doesn't," she said, still watching. "Jesus, what do you live in, some kinda haunted house?"

"Shut up! Just shut up, Jessica!" Nellie was sick of it. Sick of her.

Jessica turned back, grinning. Nothing pleased her more than pushing people to the edge—especially Nellie. She used to think it was the only real happiness Jessica could feel. But now Nellie wondered if it was the only feeling she could understand—someone else's pain. Because she had so much of her own, being so negative, mean, unhappy, disturbed, Nellie didn't know which, and right then, didn't care. "Least my house doesn't have bats," Jessica said, leaning out the window opening. "Hey!" she called down in a whisper.

"Hey!" a voice answered, and before Nellie could stop her, she had pushed back the plywood cover and dropped the ladder down.

Bucky Saltonstall's head popped through the opening. "Hey!" he laughed.

"You can't come up here!" Nellie couldn't believe his nerve. And Jessica's.

"I'm already up."

"No! My parents don't want anyone in here. Just us," Nellie said.

"Then, shh!" Squatting on his heels, he gestured them closer. Somebody was chasing him, he whispered, this weird guy named Gussie who thought he owed him some money. For what? Jessica asked, grinning with excitement. Bucky looked around as if he'd heard a sound. A bike, he whispered. Right after the guy bought it from him, someone stole it from his garage.

That was his problem, Nellie said. Not theirs, and if he didn't leave, then she was going to go get her father. Henry's headlamp faded. Nellie knew he was holding his breath, wanting to disappear into the green-tinted shadows. With this bad mix of people there was bound to be trouble. And they couldn't risk their parents or, God forbid, Jessica with her big mouth, finding out about their own dark foray into stolen bikes. She could threaten to tell the disgusting thing Bucky had done to her brother, but that would be too humiliating for Henry, especially in front of Jessica.

"Shh!" Jessica whispered, ducking low. "What's that?"

"Wind chimes," Nellie said quietly, immediately regretting it. Scared enough, she might leave and take Bucky with her.

"No, listen!" she whispered.

"Bats?" Nellie whispered. "In the tree it sounds like."

"Somebody's out there," Bucky said. He crawled to the opening that overlooked her house. Nellie couldn't see anyone either, but the sound was more than wind chimes. Bucky moved to the opposite opening and peered out. With a sudden rustle through the leaves, he ducked back.

"Definitely bats," Nellie hissed, enjoying his cowering. In the corner, Jessica huddled, knees to her chin. Henry hadn't moved.

"Down there," Bucky whispered, pointing to the floor.

Maybe the weird guy named Gussie was right under them, waiting to make his move. Waiting to strike. Nellie scrambled onto the plywood cover, with herself as ballast. Henry gave an approving nod. Just then, a strange, muted gasp pierced the leafy darkness, and a bright light flared in Jessica's hand, her cell phone. She was calling 911, she whispered.

"No!" Bucky snatched her phone.

Below them a strange woman had appeared on the Humboldt's brick path. Her blond hair streamed down her back. Tall and very thin, she wore spike heels, an ankle-length dress with a high ruffled collar, and a satiny billowing cape that glowed in the lamplight. At the edge of the patio, she wobbled, then steadied herself. Just then, the back door of the house opened and out lumbered Louisa Humboldt. Arms outstretched, her nightgown moved over the path like a great floating tent.

"Tenley!" she hissed, and he stepped back. "Come inside, please. Please, Tenley, before someone comes out. Please, you don't want that, now do you?"

"I don't care!" he gasped. "I don't! I really, really don't!"

"You don't mean that, dear. You know you don't."

"Stop telling me what I mean or what I know or what I think!"

"I'm not. Of course I'm not," she said, slipping an arm through his.

"Then leave me alone. Please!" And pulling free, he flung himself down into a chaise longue. He sat with his hands clasped behind his head and ankles crossed. His sister leaned close, still entreating him to come inside, but he would have no part of it.

They were all at the window opening. Nellie didn't say anything. Mostly because she didn't know what to say. She'd heard of such things, but this was right next door.

"What's going on?" Bucky asked, watching Louisa Humboldt lower herself down onto the sagging chaise longue next to her brother's. She sat facing him. Head turned, he twirled his necklace impatiently as she spoke. It was the same one Miss Humboldt had bought at the jewelry party.

"No!" he erupted, swinging his feet over the side. "Because I don't! I just don't care anymore!"

"Who the hell're they?" Bucky whispered, shoulder pressing against Nellie's.

"Miss Humboldt and her brother," she whispered, and in his quiet nearness, felt a stirring in her heart. So many troubled people. Like Bucky. Poor Bucky, such a tough life, no wonder he was so messed up. All he needed was a friend, someone to be kind to him, someone to help him stay out of trouble.

"Cool," he said, and she liked him even more.

"My father says they're, like, really strange," Jessica said, wide-eyed.

"He doesn't even know them," Nellie shot back.

"Are you kidding, he knows *every*thing about *every*body," she said. "Like how much money they have, and their houses, all that stuff."

"So he must know about Mr. Humboldt being in plays then. He's, like, some kind of actor. Like in Japan, how they look like ladies, but they're really men," Nellie lied to keep Jessica from telling how little money her family had and how desperate they were for her father's help. "And that's his costume. Probably going over his lines. He does that sometimes." Fueling her bluff was her sudden loyalty to the Humboldts. As her life-long neighbors they were hers, no matter how strange, and she would not have them scorned.

"Hey, freak!" Bucky suddenly cried. He threw a Snickers bar through the opening. Mr. Humboldt ducked as it whizzed by his long moonlit hair. "Here, fag, suck on this!" Bucky shouted, firing off another candy bar, then another. Mr. Humboldt's hands flew to his face. Miss Humboldt peered up at the tree. "Stop that! You just stop that right now!" she screeched, flinching as the next one hit her arm.

"That's my candy, asshole!" Jessica was trying to wrestle the bag from Bucky, but he kept firing candy bars. Mr. Humboldt was a sorry sight struggling to get up in his long, tapered skirt. His ankle must have turned because he sank down on one knee. Nellie had to stop Bucky. The Sentry Hold! She and Henry had practiced it before, though never on a kneeling opponent. From behind, she locked her left forearm against Bucky's throat and delivered a sharp jab in the small of his back, hard as she could. He fell against the boards, gagging. For an awful moment she thought she'd really hurt him.

"Very likely the blows on his throat and in the small of his back will cause him to drop his rifle or will knock his helmet off his head. Retaining your hold around his neck with your left arm, drag him away backwards," the major wrote.

There would be no dragging Bucky away. "Bitch!" he cried, turning on her with fists raised. "I'm gonna smash your fucking ugly face in."

"Try it," she growled, instantly realizing just how confining an arena was their little house in the night sky. "Go ahead, just try it!" she warned, mind racing through fragile pages to The Bent-Arm Hold.

"Your opponent has taken up a boxing stance. . . . Seize his right wrist with your left hand, bending his arm at the elbow, towards him. Continue the pressure on his wrist. . . . Immediately step in with your right foot, placing your right leg and hip close in to your opponent's thigh. . . ."

She was readying her left hand when Bucky lunged across the creaky floor, knocking her into the rough wall. A long board popped out and the whole tree house shook, propelling Henry into the action. On her knees, she groped along the floor for her glasses.

"Let her go!" Henry shouted, lashing Bucky's back with his head-lamp.

"Stop it!" Jessica screeched, trying to scoop up the spilled candy. "Jesus! Stop it, will you stop it!"

"What in God's name is going on out here?" her mother shouted from below.

"Nellie!" her father's voice boomed. "You and Henry, get down here! Right now! And you, too, Jessica," he demanded a little more kindly as she peered out at him.

Last one down the ladder was Bucky. No one spoke as he ran from the yard.

THE NEXT DAY they were sitting with their father in the Humboldt's brilliant living room, heads hung both from shame and the glare as they waited for Tenley Humboldt. Sunlight poured through the picture window sheers onto the gilt-streaked mirrored squares covering the walls. The tables were glass topped and all the furniture was white, even the carpeting, while everything else was golden: lamps, vases, picture frames, and an assortment of birdcages in which lifelike yellow canaries stared out vacantly from lacquered perches.

Their parents had explained that Tenley Humboldt was a very nice man who in the privacy of his home dressed in women's clothes.

"Nothing wrong with that," her father had said, her mother nodding as Nellie and Henry dared not make eye contact.

Last night, as Miss Humboldt had earlier told them, she and her brother had disagreed once again about selling the house. The big old place was just too much work for her. She wanted something smaller, preferably one of the new town houses being built out on Riley Road. She blamed herself, she said, for not easing into things the way she'd always done with Tenley. Instead, she'd just told him flat out that a real estate agent was coming in the morning to give them an appraisal, which just pushed poor Tenley over the edge. And then, to be taunted and pelted with missiles (*MISS-eyels,* she pronounced it), well, that had been devastating.

"I don't know—I don't think he's coming down," she sighed, looking toward the wide staircase. "I told him he didn't have to, but . . ." Her voice trailed off.

"If he doesn't, that's fine," Nellie's father said. "Don't worry about it, Louisa."

"Well, I do, Ben, I do. You have no idea how much I do."

"We can always come back."

"It's . . ." Her hand flew to her quivering mouth.

"Same as a thank-you—it's never too late for an apology."

"It's all just such a shame." She struggled to contain her tears.

"I know. Their friend . . ." Her father cleared his throat. His embarrassment was painful to see. And now on top of it, he and her mother were barely speaking. She thought he'd been too hard on Jessica Cooper, who'd gone home last night, sobbing. Actually, he'd barely said a word to Jessica, but that was her way, having such a meltdown that no one would dare reprimand her. "But still," he continued, "they were the ones in charge. Their responsibility—"

"I mean, the whole thing, and now . . ." She gestured at them. ". . . this," she said weakly. "They're just children. They shouldn't have to—" She wiped her puffy red eyes.

"Oh yes, they should, Louisa," he said sternly. "They have to. Better learn now, than go around thinking anyone different from them's not quite right. We're all odd ducks, every single one of us, and they know that. Right?" He peered down at his children.

"Yes, sir," Nellie and Henry answered softly, in guilt and giddiness, afraid to look at each other. Their father saying they were all odd ducks had always been their signal to quack.

A door squealed open above them. Tenley Humboldt stood at the top of the stairs for what seemed the longest time, wearing men's clothing, Nellie was relieved to see. He descended each step slowly, head trembling slightly as he tried to look their way but couldn't. Her father nodded and they jumped up.

"Hello, Ben," he said. His small, raspy voice reminded Nellie of something fragile—wings, she realized, the brush of moth wings close to the ear. Even his handshake seemed more flutter than grasp. Never having been this close, now she was alert to every detail. The man looked faded, his skin the same drabness as his shirt and pants that hung on his skinny frame in folds, his fine hair pulled tightly back in a thin ponytail. He was wearing a narrow turquoise bracelet, but no necklace. They'd come to apologize, her father said, patting her arm, and so she began. Mr. Humboldt couldn't make eye contact, which only prolonged Nellie's stammered apology. He seemed so delicate, in such distress that she was desperate for him to know that *they* hadn't thrown the candy bars at him, they'd never do something like that, and that the person who had wasn't even supposed to be up there with them and never would be again, he could be sure of that. He and Miss Humboldt both.

"And as far as I'm concerned, people should do exactly as they please. Which means wearing what they want to wear, and . . . and . . . doing what they want, because we're all the same underneath . . . the clothes we have on, whichever ones they are, I mean." She looked around wide eyed, relieved to see everyone staring down at the floor.

"Henry," her father said softly.

"And I'm sorry, too." Henry's voice was so shaky she was afraid he might cry. "Sometimes I get picked on and I don't know why." He swallowed hard. "It always makes me feel bad. But then . . . then, I think, well, maybe it's them. Maybe they don't have a nice life or something. I don't know." With his timid shrug, her father rubbed Henry's head, and she knew that never again would she tolerate unkindness or injustice, especially to someone as good as her brother.

"That was very nice," Miss Humboldt said, touching her cheek.

"Some things just need saying from time to time," their father said. Nellie knew he was feeling the same about Henry that she was.

"They certainly do," Miss Humboldt agreed.

A moment of uneasy silence followed as they each fixed on a place to look, anywhere but at poor Mr. Humboldt's misery. Head trembling, he reached into his pants pocket, twice. "Here." He held out two handfuls of Snickers bars. When no one took them right away, he dropped them onto the glass coffee table then slipped into the next room and closed the door.

"He's afraid of animals eating them. Chocolate's not good for them. In fact," Miss Humboldt added, trying for a perkier tone, "some even die from it."

"Dogs." Henry nodded.

"Yeah, but that's if they eat a lot," Nellie said, grateful to be making their way back from such dense, prickly woods into a conversational clearing.

"Probably depends on the size dog," her father said.

"Yes," Miss Humboldt said absently. She was looking toward the door. And Nellie felt her yearning—Tenley, her brother, in there needing her to keep him safe, and for as long as she could, she would.

DAYS LATER, IN the early morning, Nellie opened her window and saw something on the lawn. She ran outside and picked it up, a cellophane-wrapped bouquet of pink carnations wet from the dewy grass. Never too late for an apology, her father had said. Bucky, she thought, dropping it into the wastebasket, his cowardly way of telling her he was sorry. When her mother came down for breakfast and found the flowers in the trash, she took them out and arranged them in a vase of water.

"I just found them," Nellie answered honestly when her mother asked who'd brought them.

For a week their fragrance filled the kitchen, sometimes making her smile for no reason at all.

Chapter 11

SO THIS IS WHAT HAPPENED, THE WAY SHE REMEMBERS IT, ANY-way. Funny how some details seem so compressed. Like the letter, for instance. Maybe it did come a while before, but once she started keeping secrets and trying to make strangeness seem perfectly normal, then pretty soon, events started running together, exactly what was said and by whom, and the reason for this or that, eventually all twining together like a house built of twigs, fragile and unsecured, because each enfeebled fact depended on another, and that one on the one before, until in the end nothing seemed true anymore.

With almost another week of rain, they'd been pretty much stuck inside, she and Henry, that is. Ruth was back and forth to work, though most days she got out early. The ice-cream business slowed way down in bad weather. Maybe if Ruth had come home instead of lying and going to Patrick Dellastrando's house that day, then she might have gotten the letter herself. And it wasn't as if Nellie'd been looking for it. Bringing in the mail was about it for excitement. That and listening to the drama that was Dolly's life with her television droning in the background. It was hard to untangle the soap operas and reality shows from her own misery, sobbing in bed, sobbing into her phone, pleading, demanding to be taken seriously. She was sick of waiting around, doing nothing while he did exactly as he pleased. It was way more than money and if he dared say that again, ever, then she was just going to call the bitch, that's what she'd do, call the bitch and tell her exactly what was going on here. After all, she had a life to live, too, and he better get used to the idea because she wasn't going to be treated like this anymore. And there wasn't a thing he could say or do that was going to make her change her mind. Had he ever once said *that* to the bitch? *Timing!* What the hell's that supposed to mean? Silence. And this time, a thud. Something hitting the wall.

"I'm a good person," she began to wail. "Doesn't he know that?"

Nellie couldn't tell whether she was talking on the phone again or to someone in the apartment. She pressed closer. Her ear so often at the damp bathroom wall had made a grease mark on the wallpaper.

"Why's he doing this? It's not fair! It's so fucking not fair! Why? Why?" she moaned, then fell into hysterical sobbing, and no one answered or spoke a soothing word back.

Ruth's letter must have come during that same rainy week. The ink on the damp envelope was smeared. She remembers standing on the porch, staring at the blurry postmark. *Australia.* She ran to put the letter in her bottom drawer, under her shorts. Ruth was in trouble again for missing her curfew two nights in a row. She'd been grounded, and with her resentment so deep it seemed simpler to hide the letter than have her on the next plane to Brisbane. The following day Nellie took it out and held it up to a lightbulb, but she couldn't see through the envelope. Next she tried slipping a knife under the seal. All that did was rip a ragged tear in the flap. That left her little choice. She ripped it open the rest of the way. She would read it and then decide what to do next.

Dear Ruth,

    What a surprise, hearing from you. And thank you for the picture. I see more of a resemblance to your mother than me. Actually, I don't ever get to the states anymore. My work and family keep me firmly anchored here. I'm glad that you're such a good student. Lord knows, I wasn't, so there again you take after your mother more than me. No, I don't surf or ride a motorcycle anymore. I work for a supermarket here. I'm a manager. Not very exciting but secure. I know you'd like to come for a visit, but this wouldn't be a good time. The trip's a long one and quite expensive. I haven't told my wife or children about you, so that would be a problem. Oftentimes the past is best left buried. I know that sounds cold, but I only mean it in a practical way. I'm sure you can work out your problems with your family if you try. I know one thing, I'd never want to go through being a teenager again. If you do write again, please use the address below. Be sure and write PERSONAL on it because it's where I work.

I'm sorry I don't have a picture to send. Just as well, I'm not much to look at.

Sincerely,
Daniel Brigham

And not much of a pen pal, Nellie decided, relieved. She peeled back the brittle flap of linoleum on her dusty closet floor and slipped the letter underneath the loose board, then piled her shoes and junk back on top. Daniel Brigham's lack of interest would only hurt Ruth's already frazzled feelings, so really, what was the point? He had tried to be polite, but he might as well have been writing to a perfect stranger, which, in a way, he was. He didn't know her, didn't care to, so that was that. Why make things any more tense around here? And they certainly were tense. Mr. Cooper still hadn't called, and Dolly had been right on the verge of being evicted when she'd somehow come up with two months' rent, both pleasing and frustrating her mother, who only wanted to be rid of her.

And at the store the motor on the ancient key-cutting machine had finally burned out. Her father had tried fixing it but couldn't, and this morning he had stunned her mother when he said he guessed he'd just have to get a new one. Why in God's name would he do that? she'd asked, rushing out the door for her nine A.M. Lazlo Larouche, a trim and highlights—and a big tipper. Her father merely stared at the closing door. He knew better than admit that he'd already inquired about a new machine. He'd pretty much given up on Mr. Cooper's saving the day but couldn't bear to burst her mother's bubble the way his had been. The publishing company he'd sent six hundred dollars to wasn't returning his calls. Nellie'd heard him on the phone telling Uncle Phil, who was going to send them a threatening letter.

———

THE RAIN FINALLY stopped, only to be followed by hours of howling wind trying to dry out their soggy world. All through the night Henry tramped back and forth past her door to the hallway window. He kept checking to see how his tree house was holding up. Early in the storm the tarp had blown off, over into Humboldt's yard, but that was all. One gust had ripped down a huge limb from the oak tree near the barn. Amazingly, there wasn't any damage, but the driveway was blocked, pinning their car in. Their parents had to get to work. Benjamin had been out since dawn with his chain saw, but it was slow going. Two blades had already broken and he needed help moving the little he'd cut. Her mother called Charlie and asked if Max could lend a hand. He arrived within minutes. By then other neighbors had ventured out. They stood around, coffee mugs in hand, some of the women in bathrobes, catching up on neighborhood news. A few men pitched in, dragging wet leafy branches out of the way. Old Mr. Fuller shuffled over from across the street with his own chain saw and started cutting the smaller branches, which made everyone nervous because he could barely see. He still drove, so staying out of his way had become a kind of game. The minute kids saw his old white Pontiac coming down the middle of the street, they'd ride their bikes up over the curb or dive into bushes. "Be respectful," her mother would say, whenever she caught them doing it, but Nellie was sure he never noticed.

Anyway, in the midst of sawdust flying and the buzz of dueling chain saws, Dolly appeared on her little porch, shading her eyes as she squinted toward the hubbub. She was wearing gray sweat pants and a skimpy T-shirt, with nothing on under, it was plain to see. Miss Humboldt had also trudged over. The bright blue tarp had landed on Tenley's antique roses, not that she was complaining, because it was, after all, an act of God, she said, a concept that delighted Henry—God lifting the tarp and dropping it into the next yard. But in any event, she wondered if one of them could come by later for it. Tenley had it all folded on their front steps. If it wasn't so heavy, she would have carried it over herself, she said.

With the enormous limb finally cut up, Max, to everyone's amazement, effortlessly heaved the sections into the back of his truck. It would take two and a half truckloads for him to move it from the driveway into the junkyard, where he would chop it all up into firewood, then stack it to dry for burning next winter in Charlie's stove in the barn. Nellie wasn't sure if he noticed Dolly that day, watching the excitement. Probably not, the way he was working, a man possessed— no, more machine than man, all smoothly turning gears and moving parts. What she would remember, though, was their interaction days later when Max returned with some of the split wood.

It was late afternoon and Henry was up in the tree house, reading. She'd spent a good part of the day in a search of Ruth's room. She was looking for her journal, which she hadn't read in months. Sweat trickled down her sides, but she was afraid to turn on the air conditioning because then she wouldn't hear anyone coming up the stairs. Deep in a bin of wool sweaters, she found a book about sex positions, but she'd seen that before in other raids. Her next discovery was Ruth's school backpack, stuffed behind her bureau. In it was a bag of makeup. She didn't understand until she saw the price tags. One lipstick alone cost twenty-nine dollars. There was a tiny jar of blush that cost thirty-five dollars and an eyeliner pencil for fifteen dollars. Nellie didn't know whether she'd hidden it because she'd stolen it or because it was so expensive. Both, she guessed, remembering Ruth's seventh-grade shoplifting bust. To get past Walgreens' security alarm, she had taken a curling iron from its box and slipped it up her sleeve. The only problem was that a clerk saw the whole thing and waited until Ruth got outside before stopping her. It was awful. Her mother and father had to go to the police station, where they found Ruth curled in a ball, sobbing hysterically. Her father called Uncle Phil, who was a Grand Knight with the police chief, who, at Benjamin's request, gave her a stern talking to before sending her home. For a long time after that Ruth left the house only to go to school. She'd learned a most humiliating lesson. But her mother had been even more deeply affected. She cried a lot, wouldn't eat, and couldn't sleep. Benjamin finally got her to see some doctor in Boston. She went every Tuesday morning at ten until her coverage ran out. Benjamin wanted her to keep going—the money was well worth it—but she insisted she was better. In fact, she said, it was the best thing she'd ever done. She'd learned a lot about who she was and how she had to live her life. And for a long time she did seem a lot happier. That is, until lately, and all their money problems.

Anyway, Nellie's most shocking find came next, three thong underpants in the pocket of Ruth's bathrobe, two red and one black. She felt dirty just for having touched them. Her sister was some kind of deviant. She couldn't stop thinking of that strip of cloth lodged—stuck—between her bum cheeks. Disgusting. Why? What was the point? The way it felt? Or for someone to see it on her?

She finally found Ruth's journal in the most obvious place, right under her mattress. It wasn't at all what she expected. Instead of juicy details about Patrick and his wild friends, she mostly wrote about how sad it made her that "aside from *those* times, he hardly even talks to me." She said her old friends had dropped her, "and all these new ones do is make fun of me because I'm so into Patrick, and I know it's because they're so jealous of him caring about someone younger than them." She wrote about how ugly she felt and how the first thing she was going to have done as soon as she was out on her own with a real job was get a nose job and implants. Her boobs were smaller than anyone he knew, Patrick had told her, which she knew for a fact wasn't true, but then when she got mad, he'd just laughed and assured her that she more than made up for it in other ways. She couldn't understand why her real father hadn't written back. If only she had his e-mail address, then they could be in touch every day, writing back and forth and it could be like a normal conversation almost "instead of all this phony shit me and Benjamin have to have all the time. Like he really cares about me, when we both know it's to make my mother happy, that's the only reason. He's so annoying. All he does is talk about the most boring things. Sometimes I think we'd all be better off if my mother divorced him. It'd be like a movie, just me and her flying to Australia. Imagine meeting my real father after all this time. The problem is she can't afford a lawyer. Maybe she can, when they sell the building to Mr. Cooper. She thinks I don't know what's going on, but I've heard them enough times now to know . . ."

Just then, a car door slammed shut down in the driveway. Nellie's limp, sweaty hands shoved the journal back under the mattress. Divorce. Her world was falling apart. She couldn't think straight. On top of all her other fears, now there was her parents' marriage to hold together. She raced down to the kitchen. She still hadn't done any of the chores on her mother's list. Nellie could hear her up in her room changing out of her smock. She had just jammed the last of the breakfast and lunch dishes into the dishwasher as her mother came into the kitchen. Through the window she saw Max's truck backing slowly into the driveway. He pulled close to the barn, then jumped out and took the back steps in a bound. The bell was still ringing as her mother opened the door. She seemed as startled to see him there as Nellie was pleased. A familiar face to pull her back to reality.

"Gotcher wood," he announced, grinning and covering his teeth. He gestured back over his shoulder. "Good half cord, anyway." He must have rushed over soon as he'd split the last log. Wood chips and bits of bark flecked his hair and sweaty shirt back.

"But we don't need it," her mother said.

"Just doing what Charlie said, that's all."

"Well, it's . . . it's not a very good time," she stammered through the screen. Now *she* gestured back. "I'm trying to start dinner."

"Sure." He nodded, his eyes hardened to stone. "I only rung it so you'd know. That's all. I mean, you're cooking," he said, backing down the steps. "I'll just get to it."

She stared after him. Her unsmiling mother, not only kind to everyone but kind to a fault, could not hide her dislike of Max, a dislike bordering on revulsion. Nellie figured it was her difficult childhood growing up in the town junkyard with a father like Charlie, who didn't give a damn what anyone thought of him or his dealings. So to her, Max's unsavory past was probably a reminder, another embarrassment, maybe even a threat to the orderly and respectable life she finally had.

"A small pile, that's all then," she called after him. "By the barn. Just dump it, that's all."

As soon as her mother went back upstairs, Nellie slipped outside and found him muttering as he tossed logs from the truck, so heedlessly she knew to stand back. "Hi!" she said, but he didn't even look up. She could tell he was riled and trying to work past it. "We don't burn too much! Just every once in a while! In the family room fireplace!" she called, hoping to make up for her mother's coolness.

"Usually just those fake ones, the kind you buy!" she hollered over the clunk of falling wood. "We can't use the other two fireplaces. The chimneys, they're not safe. Fact, we even had a fire one time a couple years ago. A chimney fire. That was wicked scary. Thanksgiving morning. Yeah, the firemen said we were lucky it wasn't the middle of the night." Her voice quavered with the strain of needing to pierce his dark intensity.

"So then we had to go eat at my aunt Betsy and uncle Phil's. They were supposed to come here, but the whole house was, well, you know, full of smoke. Course they didn't have a turkey, so we brought ours. My mother finished cooking it there, but, I don't know, it just didn't taste right. 'Our first smoked turkey,' my father said. His idea of a joke, but my mother, well, she didn't think it was too funny."

"No surprise there," he grunted with a look she didn't like, a sneer almost, a sneer he seemed to expect her to share.

"Well, you can't blame her." She was annoyed he'd think she would criticize her mother, especially to him, someone she barely knew. "I mean, all that work, and then the house, it could've burned down, you know. It almost did. That's what the fire chief said, and now she's, like, got this thing about fires. A phobia, almost."

"Chimneys probably need a good cleanout, that's all." He jumped down and picked up a log. She could tell he knew he'd said the wrong thing. "Gotta be careful what you burn," he said, sniffing the cut end. "This here oak's never gonna leave pitch—harder the wood, hotter the fire." He began stacking the wood next to the barn, but not close enough to touch, he pointed out. She picked up a log and laid it on his first row.

"Okay for you to be out here?" he paused to ask.

"Well, yeah," she said, laying down another log. "It's my yard, after all."

"I mean with her." He gestured toward the house. "Your mother."

"She likes me doing stuff like this." Log after log, she was picking up speed. "Idle hands're the devil's workshop, right?"

"Whyn't you go ask, just to be on the safe side." He was turning some of the logs she'd placed.

"Why? Am I bothering you?" she blurted, wishing she hadn't, but her feelings were hurt.

He continued working. His silence made her feel worse.

"Or am I just doing it wrong?" she asked to give him a way out, he looked so troubled with his head down and shoulders hunched.

"The point's a tight stack," he said. "Space enough for drying, but no gaps. Too many and the whole thing'll fall down. Wind, frost heaves," he grunted, hands a blur of motion. "Animals even. Burrow in, building nests, next thing you know it's all collapsed."

"You know what you told me, that story about your brother? I keep thinking about that—"

"Well, don't."

"No, I don't mean *that* way. I mean, some things're just important to know. That's what my father says, anyway. He—"

"Oh, my God!" her mother screamed, and Max jumped back. She ran toward them carrying a laundry basket. "The basement!" she was shrieking. "It's all flooded!"

The bottom had rusted out of the hot-water tank for Dolly's apartment. Her mother had started down cellar to do a wash when she discovered the water, inches high in some places, and still rising. Nellie and Max followed her back to the house, but she stopped them at the cellar door. Afraid he'd be electrocuted, she wouldn't let Max go down. The fuse box was almost within reach of the stairs, so with a broom handle he was able to throw the switch. Her mother called Benjamin at the store. Benjamin called the fire department, who apparently thought they had another blazing chimney because two trucks, the hook and ladder, and an ambulance arrived, all sirens wailing, lights spinning.

Startled by the commotion, Dolly burst into the Pecks' kitchen. She'd been watching television when the power died. Convinced the house was burning down, she was hysterical. Everything she owned in the whole world was in her apartment and she needed help getting it all out. Nellie and Henry had to go with her, she insisted. It wasn't a fire, Nellie tried telling her, but she wouldn't listen.

"I need help! I need help! Don't just stand there, goddammit, I need help!" she cried, pounding her fist into her palm like a crazy lady. Afraid she'd be beating on them next, Nellie and Henry stared at her from the other side of the table, relieved by the trudge of footsteps up the cellar stairs. Max came in, carrying two tall boxes of wrapping-paper rolls. He'd started retrieving what he could from one end of the cellar. His pant cuffs and boots dripped mucky puddles onto the white tiles. He set the box down and asked what she needed help with.

"All my stuff!" Dolly cried. "I gotta get it out!"

"No, you don't. Just water, that's all. Never gonna get that high. Listen. They're down there now, shutting off the main." Barely moving his hand, he pointed toward the underworld of voices and clanging pipes. Dolly's wild eyes darted around. She was panting. Her hands shook in her struggle to cross her pale, bony arms. Max stood there, like them, trapped, caught in Dolly's vision of flames and ruin.

She sniffed the air. "I smell something," she said in a strained voice.

"Exhaust, that's all," Max said. "The trucks, they gotta keep running."

"I thought it was a fire," she said weakly.

"Just water, that's all." He reached out, whether to pat her shoulder or just to make a point, but she punched his hand away.

"Keep your dirty, fucking hands off me!" she exploded, fist raised.

"Don't you—" he warned, glaring down at her.

"Yeah, right," she said, then was gone, slamming the door behind her.

Nellie and Henry still weren't sure what had happened, but now Max seemed short of breath. He kept nodding.

"What's her problem?" Nellie said, not expecting an answer, but needing to say something.

"Crazy bitch," he said.

Whoa. They stared at each other as Max stomped back down the cellar stairs.

Later, when they talked about the incident, they agreed that Dolly hated Max, but they didn't know why. Henry scoffed when Nellie said maybe Max had a crush or something on her. Kind of like the way she felt about Bucky, though she'd never admit that to her brother. But the nasty exchange was disturbing. Not Dolly's end of it, as much as Max's. He might work in their grandfather's junkyard and sleep in the barn with his dog, but he'd saved Henry's life, which made him a real hero. So what if he'd been in jail and been blamed for his brother's death and had a quick temper and always smelled of sweat and wet dog and could barely hold a person's gaze when spoken to, he still had goodness in him. And courage. Those were the things you just know. Especially when you're a kid, when the world is still pretty much black-and-white, because that's the way she'd been raised, the way she'd been taught, the way she had to believe, with all the murk yet to come. So of course she held him to a higher standard. Max was a man of principle, however unpolished. Or primitive. Or distant.

After the firemen pumped the water out, everything had to be hauled outside to dry, the mess spread over the yard for all the neighbors to see, throw rugs, Christmas decorations, long strips of pink fiberglass insulation covering every shrub and post, humiliating her mother. The foundation windows and the cellar door had to be left open. Benjamin rented two huge industrial fans that ran day and night to prevent mold, her mother's other big fear. In the meantime, Dolly had no hot water and now with her rent up to date she could afford to be indignant. Actually, she was mad as hell, swearing when Nellie's mother said she was doing her best to get another water heater. Dolly demanded rent money back for every day she was forced to go without hot water. She even complained about the fans, saying they sounded like jet engines. It was true. Like a giant hive, the walls buzzed with a powerful hum, which had cut Nellie off from the drama of Dolly's world.

Except for one very puzzling visitor. It was four A.M. and too hot to sleep. A skunk had sprayed somewhere down the street. With the cellar windows open the sharp night smell had easily seeped inside. Hearing a door close, Nellie peeked under the shade just as a man hurried down from Dolly's porch. When he reached the sidewalk, she recognized him in the pinkish glow of the street lamp. Speed-walking, Mr. Andrew Cooper disappeared around the corner.

Later, that next day, Uncle Phil stopped by the house in his new car. He was on his way home from the office. Still no word from the publishing company, he said, but he wanted Benjamin to read the draft of his letter threatening a lawsuit. Not that Uncle Phil was a lawyer, but as the office manager in a law firm, he probably knew more law than any of them, Aunt Betsy liked to say.

Benjamin handed the letter back. "Let's give it another couple weeks," he said with Sandy biting her lip. "No sense alienating them."

They followed Uncle Phil out to the driveway, their technologically deprived family watching him shout at his silvery leather dashboard. "Home! Home!" he kept demanding. "Home! Home, goddammit," until his address finally appeared on the GPS grid. "Not used to my voice yet," he explained. Both red faced, Nellie and Henry were remembering Charlie's tale of his grandfather's late night stumblings out of the tavern into his horse-drawn wagon. "Home! Home!" he'd bellow, snapping the leads while the stubborn horse just stood there. Finally, "Home, goddammit, unless you wanna end up a goddamn pot'a glue!" Then off they'd go, with the old man soon snoring all the way.

Her mother's cheeks were flushed, probably remembering the same story, or so Nellie thought until the gleaming black BMW disappeared around the corner. "No sense alienating them?" she gasped. "They've got our money! Six hundred dollars, Ben!"

"They're a small house. Probably just a few employees. The editing alone'll take some time." With that, her father gave a brisk salute to Mr. Powell driving by. "Say what you will, but that's independence," he declared in a jaunty attempt to change the subject.

"Editing?" Her mother walked alongside. Nellie knew that hard stride, the combative tilt of her head. Her father's daughter, she would not be put off. "You haven't heard anything from them, nothing at all?"

"They probably haven't gotten to it yet. I mean, I'm sure I'm not their only author."

"But you're not—"

"They probably date stamp the—."

"—an author, Ben. Not until you're published, anyway."

Nellie knew by his somber nod and their uneasy glances away from each other that a wound had just been gouged. They both felt bad, her father for having heard the truth and her mother for having spoken it.

They had just started dinner when Dolly arrived with her shampoo and conditioner bottles, razor, and frayed towels. Every night it was the same thing. She didn't even bother knocking, just ran up through the cellar into the kitchen, then with a frosty hello raced upstairs to take her very long shower. She preferred using Ben and Sandy's bathroom because she didn't like the water pressure in Nellie and Henry's, and it was too dark to see well enough to shave her legs.

They ate in silence. Between the fans' drone in the walls and the running water overhead, Nellie could feel the room shrinking around them. Thin shoulders hunched, her mother picked at her food. A pile of chicken bones barely concealed Henry's spinach, a skirmish neither parent was up to. Upstairs the bathroom door slammed. Her father winced and ate faster. Dolly always left the room a mess, shade crookedly down, water on the vanity counter and floor and strands of her long hair in the tub. That night, though, instead of hurrying back to her apartment, Dolly lingered by the table, in her bathrobe and wet hair wrapped in a towel.

"Is something wrong?" Her mother pushed her plate away.

"No. I just wanted to tell you, I mean. . . ." Dolly shrugged. "Just so you'll know. What I said. It's okay, there's no rush. I mean about the hot water. Actually, I kinda like coming over. Makes me feel like part of the family, like, you know, *don't pay any attention, it's just me, Dolly coming through,*" she laughed, hands waving in her childish way.

"Well, that's awfully nice to hear," her father said. "And you're always welcome." His quick smile faded. "And soon, of course," he added, under his wife's pained stare, "you won't have to. You'll be back in business over there. Hot water anytime you want it."

"Yeah, I know. But like I said, no fuss, no muss, no rush, that's all. Okay? See ya guys," she called, opening the door, then banged it shut, sending a visible shiver through Nellie's mother.

In the silence Henry slid his napkin over the bones and wadded it up. His mother jumped up from the table, and they all froze.

"I just thought of something," she said, going straight to the phone. She called her father and asked if there might be an old hot-water tank at the junkyard that still worked. Just to tide them over until they could afford a new one. As a matter of fact, Charlie said, there were two. He'd pick out the best one and send Max over in the morning and he could hook it up, too, if she wanted. She could pay him whatever she thought the tank was worth, which made her mad, but she knew better than say so.

———

Nellie was annoyed. Here it was the hottest day of summer so far and she and Henry were stuck inside, waiting for Max. As soon as he arrived with the hot-water tank, she was supposed to call her father home from work. Her mother didn't want Max "having free roam of the house." Actually, Ruth had been left in charge, but at 11: 35 a.m. someone from Rollie's had called. They were really busy and needed her right away, she yelled in her giddy rush through the door. The plan had been for Nellie and Henry to take a bus to the mall, get a slice of pizza, then just walk around and hang out in the air-conditioned stores until her mother picked them up after her last appointment. They'd done that on other brutally hot days. Nellie called Charlie and asked if Max had left yet. He had, Charlie said, early in the morning, but to go fishing. As soon as he got back he'd send him right over with the tank.

At 2:00 p.m. Max still hadn't come, but Henry didn't even notice. He was working on the LEGO 1,500-piece *Star Wars* Galactic destroyer he'd started at noon. Her mother had gotten it at one of her client's yard sales. The lady had let her come early to have first pick. Henry finished the destroyer at 2:45—as best he could with three pieces missing. Still, no Max, so Henry went up to his room, looking for his old ant farm. That was at 3:00. Because Nellie'd been watching the clock since midmorning, she was acutely aware of the time. Afterward, it seemed odd to people that she would know the exact minute this had happened or that, but the truth is, she did. *How can you be sure?* they'd ask, one after another. Because she kept checking, that's how she knew when the first noise was—3:10.

What do you mean, noise?

Just that, noise.

Voices? Yelling? Screaming, what?

No, like banging, but not even that.

Not even what?

Not that it was loud, just kind of, maybe—like, you know, scuffling. Like a commotion or something.

Which? Scuffling or commotion?

More like thuds. Like, maybe something fell.

Like what? What fell?
She didn't know.

NOT THEN, ANYWAY. Not with those big fans droning down in the cellar.

So, when you heard the first sounds at or about 3:10—
At 3:10. It was.
Okay, so maybe Max Devaney was already there.
But he wasn't!
But maybe he was, and you just didn't know it.
But I know he wasn't. He didn't come till after. Like, five of four, something like that.
So, you're not sure.
Not of that, the exact time that he came, I mean.
But isn't it possible that's what you were hearing, the noise? Mr. Devaney, down cellar, working?
No. Because he still wasn't there. We kept waiting.
But you're so sure when other things happened, so why not that?
Because.

Because this was the part she couldn't tell anyone, except her mother. And then, not all of it, not right away. She still thinks it came from knowing too much, more than she understood or could accept. She needed her world to be safe, and if bad things happened, she had to work them out first in her head, then only later, inside, deep, deeper than she could ever have imagined.

When she heard the noise, she raced into the bathroom and pressed her ear to the wall. She wasn't sure what she was hearing but knew what she was feeling. Dread, like needles jabbing the back of her neck. Maybe Dolly's television was on. Day and night, it usually was. Maybe that's why the voices didn't seem real, if there even were voices. The best way to describe it now that she's older is that whatever it was, whatever she was hearing was human. And horrible. Horrible, as death must be when you're fighting it, clawing, kicking, gagging for breath. And then, as suddenly, it stopped, whatever it was, whatever it had been, it was over, leaving not quiet, not stillness, just nothing. And the drone through the walls.

Maybe Max had come, she thought, and she'd missed him. So maybe that's what had been going on. Maybe he'd been down cellar working the whole time. But his truck wasn't in the driveway. Maybe he'd parked on the street. Opening the front door and seeing nothing, she went outside. The heat stung like a fiery blast as she walked around the sun-beaten house. When she came to the side yard it took a moment before her eyes adjusted from the glare on her glasses to the stingy shade of the house's shadow across the lawn. And there, close by the dusty lilac bushes, sweaty, disheveled, red faced, pressing his left hand to his neck, and his right hand in his pocket as he gauged her myopic approach, was a man. She jumped.

"Mr. Cooper!" she gasped.

"Yes!" he declared with almost theatrical calm. He stepped away from the branches. His fixed, glassy stare made her think he couldn't remember her name, which happened with adults, especially one with so many kids of his own to remember. "Your dad . . . I don't see his car."

"He's at the store," she said, noticing his scratched chin—*from the bushes must be,* a conclusion rendered not in actual thought, so much as a flash, an impression, a child's need to impose logic on confusion.

"Oh. Well. Just some papers. I'll come back."

"I can give them to him if you want," she offered uneasily, recalling Ruth's journal entry linking their parents' possible divorce with the sale of the store. At that moment she wasn't even thinking of Mr. Cooper's furtive trot down the street only nights before.

"No, that's okay. I'll try him at the store." And then he was gone.

It was another half hour or more before Max finally pulled into the driveway. She called the store to say Max had come, but the line was busy. Boone was so excited he leaped out of the truck. He wiggled against her, but she ignored him. Wanting to be petted, he kept butting his snout up under her hand to lift it. She folded her arms. He, too, would pay the price of her annoyance.

"He's real happy to see you," Max said, patting the dog's head.

"You're late," she said.

"I am?" Max had arrived clean shaven with slicked down hair, which got her mad to think that after fishing, instead of coming straight over, he'd taken the time to spruce up in hopes of seeing Dolly.

"Yeah, we've been waiting, Henry and me. And now we can't go to the mall."

"Want me to ride you there? I can do that. If your mother says."

"It's too late."

"Mall's open till nine. I'll drop you off."

"We were supposed to go at noon. After you got here."

"Well, I didn't know that, now, did I?" Max chuckled as he followed her to the outside cellar door. He seemed to enjoy her irritation and Boone's goofy need for her attention. "Charlie didn't tell me till I got back," he said with a glance up at Dolly's window.

"Last night he said you'd be here first thing. He told my mother."

Max shrugged. "Musta forgot. Only thing he said last night was maybe I oughta stay in the house from now on. 'Not him though,' he goes. 'Not that fleabag.' And poor old Boonie, he knew. That's why he's so hyped today. Fraida bein' set loose again."

She ran her hand along Boone's hard bristly tail but not so Max could see. All his chatter was for Dolly's benefit, especially since she wasn't saying a word. *Maybe, she's looking out the window,* he was probably thinking. *Maybe if she sees me being nice to the kid, she'll treat me better.* Which only irritated her more, being used like that.

As far as she was concerned, the day had been ruined and it was all his fault. He'd been off having a great old time fishing, without taking her, which she managed to be bitter about even though she knew her mother never would have allowed it.

The hot-water tank from Charlie might look pretty beat up, Max was saying as she unlocked the cellar door, but it was in decent enough shape. Could last a couple months or a couple years, he said, then drew back, startled by the roar of the fans as they entered the cellar.

"Can't even hear yourself think," he shouted, turning them off.

Only three bulbs lit the long, dim cellar. It had dried out but with a harsh damp odor. Their stairs were at the front end, with Dolly's at the back, near her rusty hot-water heater. In the sudden quiet Max's voice seemed to boom—for *her to hear,* Nellie figured. Why else was he was telling her all that the job entailed? "Yeah, that's what we'll do," he said, shining his flashlight on the cobwebby pipes above the failed tank. "Just take a look here—see how much work we got, getting this old sucker out." *So he does,* she thought; *he wants her to know he's down here, at this very moment right under her feet.* "I'm gonna have to shut the main off. You maybe should go tell her." He tapped a pitted copper joint. "The young lady up there," he said loudly.

Whether it was that quick clang or some other sound that set Boone off, suddenly he charged up the stairs. He sniffed under the door to Dolly's kitchen, snuffling his nose along the narrow gap with whiny yelps that upset Max.

"Come!" Max called, but Boone ignored him. It wasn't just odd, but creepy, Boone's flattening himself on the stairs, as if in desperate need to squeeze under the door. "Come!" Max kept demanding, then he'd swear under his breath. "Goddamn it! Jesus Christ! Come!" More than mad, he seemed nervous, as was Nellie, fully expecting Dolly to come raging out at them. "Come!" Max smacked his hands together, agitating Boone even more. He began to bark and wouldn't stop. "Get! Get!" Max shouted, bounding up to him. "Get down here!" He grabbed the dog's collar and dragged him, yipping down the stairs. And every bony strike of Boone's legs hitting the steps was a jab in the pit of her stomach.

"Don't hurt him!" she pleaded.

"Hurt him, I'll damn well hurt him if I have to," Max growled pulling the struggling dog along with him.

"But he stopped. He's okay now," she said on Max's heels through the cellar.

"Not when he don't come he ain't!" he said with a vicious yank through the door, out to his truck. He shoved the whimpering dog up into the cab and closed the windows. His face twisted with the same rage she'd seen when the truck driver wouldn't pick up the asbestos pipe he'd dumped.

"It's too hot! He'll suffocate in there."

"Then he'll learn, won't he?" Max muttered, stomping off to the back of his truck. Boone was panting. Strings of drool dangled from his tongue as they regarded each other, she through smudged eyeglasses and he through the nose-smeared window. How utterly sad his watery eyes were. And humiliated. Suddenly, she disliked Max. She understood how he'd been able to crack that pit bull's skull open. He just hadn't cared. He didn't have normal feelings like other people. He could be one person one moment, then entirely different another. Just like that. And while he may have saved her brother's life, anyone who'd treat his own dog like that was not a good person. And with his hot temper, it was her guess that Boone had seen his share of hurt. And maybe his family'd been right, maybe he had shot his own brother on purpose. Wrenches and a small saw in hand, Max headed toward the cellar.

"That's not right, that's just cruelty to animals," she called after him and he spun around.

"He's gotta obey. The minute he hears my voice."

"Well, that's not how to teach him. Putting him in a hot truck."

It was a long glaring moment. There was a struggle going on inside his head, too. He didn't like her much either, right then, only difference was, she knew, he couldn't afford to show it. "He's my dog. And how I raise him's my business."

"Not if you don't treat him right." Her heart was pounding, but she stared straight back into his squinting meanness. "There's a law about that."

"Lemme tell you something." He gave a close gesture with the lug wrench. "Obeying, that's the most important thing. Only thing'll keep him safe."

He disappeared inside. And for a long time after, she would remember that, those exact words. Because maybe obeying can get in the way of things, of a life, she would later think. And because maybe when Boone barked, if they'd opened that door at the top of the stairs and looked inside together, then everything might have turned out different.

She marched into the house and looked up the number of the Springvale SPCA. The phone shook against her sweaty ear, she was so mad and so indignant.

"Helloo," she said in a low, deep voice to the woman answering. "I'd like to report a dog that's in a boiling hot truck."

"Could I have your name, please?"

"No. This is anonymous. But—"

"I need a name, that's all."

"Louisa Humboldt."

"Okay, all right then, so where's the dog? I need the address. Can you—"

She hung up. Not only would she get in trouble for using Miss Humboldt's name, but Max would know it was her, not that it should have mattered, she knew in her *Get Tough!* principled heart. She might have brought down Bucky Saltonstall with one of the major's holds, but standing up to an adult was a different kind of toughness, one that went against everything she'd ever been taught, and now she couldn't very well call back saying she was someone else. She could hear Max working downstairs. Unnerved by the spiteful racket of banging, clanging, rattling pipes, the cellar door opening and slamming shut, she went outside and asked Henry to come in the house with her. She needed his help. It would take only a minute. She wanted him to call the SPCA, but she didn't tell him that.

"Can't," he grunted from his squat on the sidewalk. He was pinching ants as lightly as possible from a teeming sand hill in the cracked cement, then flicking them into a jar. Never had she been so resentful of his single-minded intensity that everyone else called brilliant, but she knew the truth. Her brother was a selfish creep and she was through sticking up for him. She needed help and he wasn't the least bit interested. She went back inside. She took a bowl from the cupboard and held it under the faucet, but only a drip came. So instead, she filled the bowl with milk and carried it out to Boone. The truck doors were locked. She pressed her forehead against the window, wanting the poor creature to know someone cared, which only got him howling. She set the bowl on the ground and went into the cellar. Max stood on a wooden box aiming a small blow torch at a water pipe.

"The Springvale SPCA just called," she said breathlessly. "Something about a dog barking. Somebody complained. A neighbor, they said."

"Jesus!" He turned off the flame and she noticed the cloth wrapped around his hand, green and white striped, from her mother's ragbag, which hung by the clothes dryer, and the thin blood streak on the front of his shirt. He hurried out to the truck, then returned with Boone. But the dog shot right back up the stairs and started whining and yelping under the door.

Before he could drag him back down the stairs again, she asked if Boone could come with her. He let her take him up their stairs into the kitchen. She was having fun rolling the tennis ball to Boone and wasn't noticing the time, so she wouldn't know how long Max was alone in the cellar that time either. But it couldn't have been more than a few minutes, insignificant enough, it would seem, to keep to herself. Even Henry wouldn't recall her trip out to the sidewalk, so focused was he on his ants. And besides, what happened next seemed logical enough, except for Max's agitation, charging up their cellar stairs, banging on the door, and yelling that he needed to get in Dolly's apartment and she wasn't answering the door.

But the way she told it, she'd been down cellar the whole time with Max and Boone. Partly, it was guilt for taking the dog into the house when she shouldn't have because of Ruth's allergies, but then came fear. She'd already told everything that needed telling to the first policemen on the scene. They knew her parents and kept assuring her and Henry, who were both crying, that they were safe. Nothing else bad was going to happen. They even made taking Max to the police station sound routine. A few questions and he'd be back for Boone. Before the State Police crime scene unit arrived, she was questioned by Detective Des La Forges, a large man of no little self-importance. He also knew her father, but he was all business, terse and suspicious. He kept pressing the same questions on her, rephrasing them this way and that, as if he thought she was lying.

So what about Max's cut? The one on his hand. If you were down there the whole time, you must've seen him do it then.

No. I told you, I was at the other end, playing with Boone. (But upstairs, the part she left out.)

Did you ask how he got it?

No. He just said. From a jagged pipe.

Did he yell or swear or anything?

No.

What about the blood on his shirt?

Same thing. He even pointed to it, the jagged pipe.

I mean, what'd he say?

He didn't. I just figured it was from his hand.

He didn't tell you he'd already been in the apartment?

No.

But you said he seemed upset.

No, I didn't. I said, bothered. Like he had to get in there so he could finish.

Bothered, upset—that's not the same thing?

No. It was the pipes. He was having a hard time.

He said it was the pipes?

I could tell. He was, like, flustered, that's all. Because of the pipes.

And that's why he wanted you to go inside the apartment with him? To help with the pipes?

No! He just wanted me to unlock the door, that's all.

But it wasn't locked, was it?

No.

BUT OF COURSE she hadn't known that. She told Max she wasn't sure where the apartment key was, but that she'd go look. The last time Dolly had locked herself out her mother had been really annoyed. She told Dolly there was only one spare key left, so she'd just have to go get her own made. There had to be one here somewhere, Nellie said and kept pawing through drawers and cupboards. Maybe there was one at the store—her father always used to cut extras, she said. But when she called the store, the line was still busy. She waited a minute, then tried again. Still busy. Max didn't seem to be in a hurry or anything, just quiet. He stood there, by the kitchen door, staring down at Boone, who sat at his feet, the perfect dog, not wanting to be punished again. She finally found the key in a bank envelope in the pantry junk drawer. When she went to give it to him, he said she should come, too, so they headed back down cellar. Boone tried slipping out with them, but Max stopped him.

"Stay, boy! Stay, now!" he ordered with a thump on his broad back.

Max followed her up the stairs to the apartment. She felt a little giddy, wondering what fireworks would happen when Dolly saw him again. She figured that was why he wanted her there. He even stood behind her while she knocked on her door. No answer. She called Dolly's name, knocked again. Still nothing, so she put the key in the dead bolt.

"It's not locked," she said.

"Go on in," he said.

"I don't know if I should."

His hand brushed past and turned the knob. The minute the door swung open she saw Dolly. On the floor. Curled on her side, legs drawn as if to protect herself from whatever hulking rage had intruded before them. The bottoms of her feet were soiled, the glittery toenails, fuschia. Her card table and two folding chairs had been knocked over. There was a broken plate and bowl on the counter. A red mug on the floor, the toaster in a spill of burned crumbs. The white trash can had been tipped over. A greasy black plastic takeout container had spewed its noodly Chinese entrails near her blond ponytail. A trickle of blood ran from her nose and the corner of her mouth.

"She's dead," Max said from the step below.

Nellie turned and ran, through the cellar, stumbling on all fours, back up the stairs to her own orderly kitchen, where she lurched back and forth, gagging. She had to do something, couldn't think what. Call, call her father. He came home. The Springvale police arrived next, then her mother. She brought Nellie up to her bedroom and held her so she'd stop shaking. Then the detective needed to talk to her. He sat in the rocking chair and let her huddle on the bed with her mother while he asked questions. Questions only she could answer. Questions about time. Time, when all of time had stopped.

Max stayed in the back of a cruiser for a while before they drove him to the station. They left Boone tied up outside, so Henry wouldn't be nervous. Her mother wanted the dog brought to a shelter, but Nellie begged her not to. Instead, her father took Boone to the junkyard, then he went to Rollie's, but Ruth wasn't at work, hadn't been all day. Afraid Max had done something to Ruth, too, her mother was inconsolable. Nellie told them to try Patrick's house. Her father drove Ruth home dripping wet and shivering in a beach towel. In Nellie's mind, this was all her sister's fault. If only she'd been here, everything might have been different. A part of Nellie felt dead. Ruth was grounded, forever, she hoped, as her sister sobbed up in her room. She'd gotten exactly what she deserved.

DOLLY DIDN'T HAVE a real funeral. Just a memorial service at her aunt Lizzie's house. Only a few people came. Tray, some dancers from the club, and the manager. And Nellie's mother and father. "You were, like, her only family," one dancer told Nellie's mother. "She'd tell us things, stories, like about Nellie, how she was like a little sister or something. And stuff they'd do. Like that time, the night she slept in the tree house with them." Not true, but poor Dolly, Nellie hurt inside for her. And for Max, too. With the truth being turned every which way, it was easier to keep certain things to herself.

THERE'D BEEN TROUBLE between them from before. Max swore he'd been fishing, but couldn't prove it, so he'd probably come earlier than Nellie knew. Dolly'd probably let him in because of the plumbing work, and for some reason he'd snapped. He'd hit her, and in the struggle they'd both been cut. And then he'd put his strong hands around her neck and strangled her before going back to Charlie's for a shower and fresh aftershave. Needing to cover his tracks, he'd returned with the used hot-water tank, then come next door so Nellie would think he'd just arrived. So there it was, the pieces fitting just right. Motive. Opportunity. A man with a violent past, who'd been in jail a few times. A cousin came forward to say she remembered hearing how as a boy he'd shot his own brother to death.

Everyone said how lucky Nellie was. It could have been her, too. If she hadn't run.

She didn't know what to think, so she tried not to.

Chapter 12

STRANGE HOW QUICKLY THE MOST HORRIFIC, THE MOST UN-imaginable events manage to find their place in a life. The family's new norm was evasion and pretense. If on the surface everything appeared to be all right, then perhaps in the end it would be. Nellie's mother continued going to work. She even had a few new clients. When pressed for the juicy details, she begged off, saying she couldn't discuss it because of the upcoming trial and also out of respect for Lizzie, who had the chair next to hers. Lizzie, however, was eager to defend her niece. She wanted it known that Dolly was in no way the slutty little stripper the newspapers had made her out to be. If Dolly had a problem, it was always being too naive, and trusting.

One day, after going to the movies with Krissie Potek and her cousin from Wyoming, Nellie had taken the bus uptown to the salon. She didn't like being alone in the house anymore. None of them did. Their family home, their haven, was now a crime scene, the back half wrapped in yellow police tape. Cars still slowed down out front. Police investigators had returned three days ago to see the apartment again. They had taken measurements of each room, which, her mother complained to Detective Des La Forges, had already been done. But apparently not to the enormous man's satisfaction because, as he told her through the door screen, he "was all about details, especially when a life's at stake."

A life. Whose? Max Devaney's? No longer did Nellie press her ear to the clammy bathroom plaster, not even to listen to the detectives' terse voices. Far safer not to know, numbed as she was by her paralysis of dread and hope. She feared what might happen, all the while certain it could not. She couldn't think about who had actually killed Dolly, but knew it hadn't been Max.

Ruth had taken Henry to the town pond at noon, her reprieve from being grounded. He was her reluctant companion, because all she did, he complained, was ignore him and hang out with her friends. But then again, she did supply him with as much candy and soda as he wanted. And she let him go into the swampy woods at the far end of the pond to catch frogs.

Jessica had been calling constantly, begging Nellie to do something with her, anything. What Jessica really wanted, though, were the gruesome details. "All right, just tell me one thing then," she whispered into the phone. "Was her tongue, like"—she made a gagging sound— "sticking out? Cuz that's what happens when you get strangled."

Nellie repeated the party line: because of the trial, they couldn't talk about anything; they weren't allowed to. That might squelch most probing, but not persistent Jessica's, who blind as she was to most social cues, just didn't get it. Tragedy conferred a twisted celebrity, Nellie was discovering. It was like living in a bubble, both transparent shield and showcase. People were fascinated but also uneasy around them. And yet, as she would realize that day in the salon, everyone wanted inclusion, however peripheral their role.

She'd been speed-reading her way through the salon's magazines. Her mother was in the back room folding the last dryer load of towels before going home. Lizzie's client was a homely older woman in lavender pants. When Nellie first came in, she'd been struck by her teeth, how big and square they were, like horse teeth. Not wanting to make her feel bad, she'd looked away quickly. Lizzie was cutting the woman's hair. Lulled by the soft music and the close blur of female voices, Nellie hadn't been paying attention until she heard Max Devaney's name.

"Even the first time she met him he tried coming on to her," Lizzie was saying. "But it was, like, weird. Like something was wrong with him. Like, really wrong. The things he said, his whole . . . you know, it all just creeped her out."

"No!" she blurted over the magazine. "That's not what happened."

Lizzie paused midcut, her full mouth caught in a sour pucker. She and the woman stared back through the mirror. "Excuse me, Nellie, but I think I know a little better than you."

"But I was there. I know what happened. Everything."

Now Lizzie turned to face her. "Maybe you think you do," she said with peevish deliberation. "But some things're probably a little over your head, if you know what I mean." Lizzie and her client exchanged glances.

"He fixed her car, that's what happened. Her battery, it was dead." Nellie held her breath in the silence. *Dead*—bad word. She was beginning to understand: more than sorrow and personal loss, this was Lizzie's exclusive story to tell. But facts were facts, however damning or trivial. "He was very nice to her. He was!"

"Really." Lizzie's stare was withering. "In any event," she sighed, resuming her story and the cut, each *clip clip clip* punctuating her tale with impending menace. "So the very next night he shows up at the Paradise, and plunks himself down at a front table, big as life so Dolly can't miss him. 'Come sit with me,' he says when she's done her act. 'Sorry,' she says, but she can't. So what's he do but wave three twenties in her face. Says he'll gladly pay for her time. Well, Dolly gets all insulted, of course. Who the hell's he think he is, coming in to her place of business, treating her like she's some kind of hooker or something. And then *he* gets all bent out of shape. 'No, no,' he keeps saying. 'That's not what I meant.' So then, of course, one thing leads to another. And he starts saying, like, the most nasty things. And that's when she tells him, just get the hell out, which he does, jumps up and storms out. Then, later, when she's leaving, she spots his truck, and him in it, waiting next to her car, so she sends the manager out to get rid of him."

Nellie flipped the magazine onto the table. Lies! But she kept her mouth shut as the story went on.

"But then what happens, the very next night Dolly's leaving work and he jumps out from the shadows and says how he sorry he is, and how all he wants is to apologize for bothering her. 'Okay,' she says, 'well, if that's true, then how come you're bothering me now?' Which, she can tell, really ticks him off, but as much as she hated to, she said she had to do it, cuz if she didn't, she knew she'd never get rid of him.

So then a few days go by and a knock comes on her front door, and when she opens it, it's him. He's tryna give her some flowers, one of those supermarket bouquets, you know, wrapped in cellophane. She not only refuses to take them, but she tells him she doesn't want him coming to her house anymore. And if he does it again, then she's gonna have to call the police, that's all there is to it. He didn't say anything, she said, just kind of drops the flowers on the mat and takes off down the stairs. "Hey!" she yells. "I told you I don't want them." And she throws them on the ground. Not the smartest thing to do with a psycho, but anyway, he turns around and glares at her, hard, like he really wants to hit her, you know, but he's tryna control himself, and then he gets in his truck and just takes off.

"From that point on, the poor kid, she was like petrified, but what could she do? I mean, he hadn't actually done anything," Lizzie said.

"She should've called the police anyway. Put the bastard on notice," the woman declared with shaky vehemence.

"Someone should've," Lizzie agreed, then with a quick glance toward the backroom door, lowered her voice. "I mean, he's on the list, and no one says anything? What's that all about?"

Nellie closed her eyes and took a deep breath. The flowers on the lawn. So that's where they'd come from. If that was true, what else had she been wrong about? Even her confusion about Mr. Cooper seemed to be exactly that: confusion. After seeing her in the yard that day, he had called her father saying he was ready to make an offer. That's why the line had been busy when she'd called the store to tell him Max was there. He'd been on the phone for a long time with Andy, he'd told her mother. Talking, haggling back and forth on the price, her father was proud to report. He'd driven a pretty hard bargain.

"Have a good night, Sandy," Lizzie said when her mother emerged from the back room with her purse. "And you, too, Nellie," she added, and Nellie knew by the long look she and her wet-haired client shared that there was more to tell.

She and her mother were walking home. Good therapy, her father liked to call it, though the truth was the car was being repaired again for the third time in a month. She slipped her arm through her mother's and felt her tense up. Nellie's mind raced, trying to think of something to make her feel better, but every subject seemed tied by invisible thread to the murder. When they got to their corner, her mother stopped and said she'd heard what she'd said to Lizzie.

"From now on, if you need to talk about what happened, would you please tell me and not everyone else?"

"Okay," Nellie agreed slowly and a little hurt. Whenever she tried to, she'd wave her off, saying that she just wasn't up to it yet.

"Something's wrong, isn't it?" her mother said. "I can tell. Whenever his name comes up, you look so . . . so upset."

Nellie thought a moment. Well, because the more she defended Max, the more upset everyone got with her. "I don't know, it's just all so kind of, you know . . . freaky."

"Freaky?" her mother gasped. "What do you mean? Something happened, didn't it?" She put her hands on Nellie's shoulders. "He did something to you, didn't he? And you're afraid to tell me."

"No!"

"Listen, hon. You can tell me anything, you know you can. Please, just get it out."

Nellie stared back. There was a lot to get out. But it wasn't about Max.

"Tell me!" she insisted. "Whatever happened, whatever he did, you've got to talk about it. You have to."

"He didn't do anything. Honest!" Her voice broke. It scared her to see her mother so frantic, so intense. "He was just nice, that's all. He always was."

"What do you mean?" she asked, her voice faint with dread and accusation. "How? How was he nice?"

A familiar car was coming up the street. It slowed at the corner.

"Hi, Sandy. Hi, Nellie," Barb Horton, their neighbor, called through the open window. The Hortons had been among the few to come by after the murder, wanting to help, whatever they could do. "Beautiful day, isn't it?"

"Sure is," her mother called back. "Oh, God, God, God," she groaned through a frozen smile, waving to the passing car.

"And not just nice, he was brave," Nellie continued. "Like how he saved Henry that time with the dog. He got bit, too, you know. His hand and his arm, and he never said anything. He was just, like, that's what had to be done, you know what I mean?"

Her mother didn't answer. *Because she's made up her mind, just like everyone else,* Nellie thought as they walked the rest of the way in silence.

THEY WERE STILL at the dinner table. Along with Henry's annoying interjections of facts, Benjamin had been telling them about Venus, Mars, and Saturn, the triangle of planets in tonight's sky. Ruth kept checking her watch and her mother was staring down at her plate. She'd barely eaten. Nellie's struggle to look interested was waning when her father suddenly got up and said they should drive to the pond. Much better viewing there without any streetlights. Ruth's mouth gaped open, but before she could protest, her mother said that only Nellie would be going, which confused Nellie and sent Henry into a bitter tirade. After all, he was the one who wanted to be an astrophysicist, not *her,* he yelled, running upstairs and slamming his door.

Her father'd hardly said two words on their way here. Probably feeling guilty about leaving Henry behind, she thought. Maybe they should go back and get him, she suggested as he pulled into the empty lot.

"He'll be fine."

"Yeah, after he gets done trashing his room," she laughed, but he didn't say anything.

As they came along the fringe of the woods, the leafy darkness seemed to swell with chirping crickets, which made her even more aware of his silence. The crunch of their footsteps over the gravelly sand echoed across the still black water. Hoisting themselves up onto the large flat rock that marked the far end of the town beach, they sat facing the last, faint rim of western twilight. Pointing, her father named each glow in the triangle, the brightest being Venus, the closest to Earth and also the closest to the sun. The evening star, he added.

"Must be a million other stars," Nellie said, squinting up at their brilliance in the inky blue sky.

"Actually, only five thousand can be seen with the naked eye," her father said. "Twelve thousand with binoculars."

Fireflies flickered around them. She'd forgotten how soothing his voice could be, his nearness. Her eyes kept closing. There's the observable universe, he was saying, and the unobservable universe.

"And right now, the two of us, we're at the center of our observable universe," he said.

"What's that mean?" she yawned, letting his explanation of cosmic horizons and worldlines and events drift into the night. What mattered was how much he knew and cared about things that no one else did. Someday people would appreciate just how brilliant he was. Ruth, for instance.

". . . particles and galaxies that last over long periods of time, but an event, now an event is just that, brief, a flash!" He snapped his fingers. "Like those fireflies. And that's what so much of this is, Nellie. Something that surely happened, but now it's over. It's gone. Do you know what I'm saying?" He picked up a stone and scaled it plinking three times across the water.

"I guess so." She scaled a stone. Hers plinked once.

"Mom's afraid you're holding things in, that maybe you're not telling us everything. She said when she tried to talk about it, you got upset."

"*She's* the one that got all upset."

"She's worried about you. And so am I." He put his arm around her.

"I'm okay. It's just hard sometimes, that's all."

"It must be, being there, seeing what you saw, then everything afterward. But I just want you to know, Nell, that there's nothing, nothing on the face of this earth that you'd ever have to hide from me."

"I know!" she said with a rush, dreading the thing she couldn't even think about: Mr. Cooper. That's what she needed to tell.

"Nellie, did . . . did Max Devaney ever touch you in a way he shouldn't have?"

"No! That's disgusting! That's so disgusting! Why're you asking me that?" She struggled to pull free, but he wouldn't let go.

"Listen to me! Listen to me!" he pleaded. "I had to ask you. I had to." And then he told why. Max Devaney was a convicted sex offender. It was with stars glimmering above the pond water as it gently lapped the gritty shore that she first heard the words statutory rape and consensual sex. When Max was nineteen, he'd been sent to prison for having relations with his fifteen-year-old girlfriend, which, disgustingly, made her think of her eighteen-year-old mother having sex with seventeen-year-old Danny Brigham.

"That's sick. That's so sick," she said with a shudder. Her father thought she meant Max, but it was everything, everyone around her, this whole life that felt soiled. She kept rubbing her nose. Rot, the stink coming from inside her head, her brain, even though she knew it was the pond.

He was still talking. "I remember the day you were born, I vowed that I'd never, ever let anything bad happen to you. I meant that. But that was an impossible vow to keep, because bad things happen. They do, and they did, and they always will. So all I can do is tell my little girl how much I love her. Try and keep her safe that way."

His shirt button was rubbing her cheek raw, but she didn't care.

Chapter 13

———

EVEN THE PROSPECT OF SELLING THE STORE COULDN'T LIFT her mother's spirits. No one knew how depressed she was. Death's taint was everywhere. She blamed herself for renting to Dolly. She blamed her father for taking in Max. The one person she really wanted to blame for her life of disappointment was Benjamin, but she couldn't. For one thing, she loved him, and for another, Mr. Cooper had, after all, agreed to buy the hardware store. Their financial situation was bound to improve. But until then, without rent from the apartment, every day was a struggle. Detective Des La Forges had finally said she could run a For Rent ad in the paper. Of course, once prospective tenants learned there might be a jury visit to the premises, they wouldn't be interested. Not that there'd been a single serious inquiry, anyway.

Sandy Peck felt marked, as shamed by the murder in her own home as she'd felt growing up in the middle of the junkyard. Even her fledgling jewelry business had been ruined. Days before the murder, she'd been planning her first party but then had to cancel it. She grew very quiet. At home she went about her usual routine but without her old spark. Nellie and Henry tried to stay out of her way. Ruth, however, had turned into the most loving, considerate daughter a mother could have.

Though he looked terrible, Lazlo Larouche brought the first glimmer of brightness into Nellie's mother's life. There were pouchy circles under his eyes and he hadn't shaved. Their old tenant sat at the table while her mother chopped green peppers and onions for her meat loaf. Nellie listened from the hallway.

His life was in turmoil. He couldn't think straight lately, couldn't concentrate, and hadn't picked up a paintbrush all summer. He suspected that James was seeing someone. James had been denying it, but for the last two nights he hadn't come home. And to make matters worse, the Mountain House had just been sold and the new manager didn't like him, so who knew where that would end up. Lazlo told her mother he hated bothering her at a time like this, but he'd been feeling so alone. He'd just needed someone to talk to. And now that he had, he felt like such a vulture, swooping in after the—"carnage," he said—something like that, because her mother gasped and then he was apologizing all over again while she kept assuring him that it was all right. It was her—she'd just been having a hard time dealing with it all.

"Of course, you are. I mean, who wouldn't?" Lazlo agreed in his sweet voice.

"It just makes me sick inside. I keep seeing it, picturing it. How it must have happened. Him killing her, and then he comes back and he gets Nellie? My God! I mean, she was right down there with him." Her voice cracked. "And what'll that do to her?"

"She'll be fine. Kids're resilient."

"But she's really bothered. I can tell."

"Then maybe she should talk to someone, a therapist or something."

"That's what Ben said. But we don't even have insurance right now."

"It's just going to take time, that's all," Lazlo said. "For everyone."

"And it's all my fault. Everything's so ugly now. Everything! Everything I touch." And she began to cry. Finally, for the first time, that Nellie knew of, anyway.

"Oh, Sandy. Oh, poor Sandy. Things'll get better. They always do."

Nellie peeked around the corner to see her nodding and rubbing her eyes with a dish towel and blaming the raw onions while Lazlo hugged her and patted her back, and she felt the same resentment as when her mother went off with her girlfriends.

"Well, just remember," her mother said, sniffling, "the apartment's yours if you ever need it."

As Lazlo was leaving, he asked to see the tree house. Nellie and Henry followed him outside, reluctantly. They hadn't ventured into the side yard since the murder and certainly not into the tree house.

This had become Dolly's side of the house now, the darker side. They stood below looking up, realizing, they would later admit to each other, how uneasy they felt. Its helter-skelter construction could come crashing down on them at any second.

"Oh, my Lord!" Lazlo said. "This is so amazing. It's like I've seen this before, in a dream or something."

Henry's eyes shifted to hers. They'd forgotten Lazlo's easy fervor, how annoying it was.

"I can just picture it," he continued, swirling his hand above his head, "caught in a storm, blowing, twirling, spinning round and round and round before it finally comes to rest, there, there, right there. A perfect landing." He stood for a moment, hand over his mouth, gazing up. He took a few steps back, squinting with one eye. "Beautiful," he sighed.

HER MOTHER COULDN'T get over it, not a word from the Humboldts. She asked Nellie's father if he thought they should call them or go see them or something. How horrified they must be, living next door to—

"To a house where someone died?" he said it for her.

She nodded.

"Well, guess what, Sandy, these are old houses. Every house on this street's had someone die in it, at one time or another."

"But they weren't murdered."

"But we don't know that, do we? I mean, who knows, in the old days, dyspepsia, a little arsenic slipped into the tea for good measure. Reset the gas light in the bedroom. Oops, poor papa. Didn't quite make it through the night. Believe me, these things happened."

Ooh. A huge blunder. Nellie squirmed.

Silence around the table.

"Something's wrong with you, Ben. Seriously wrong."

"I'm sorry," he said with a clownish grimace.

"It's almost like you live on a different planet from the rest of us." Her stare was awful, as if suddenly seeing him for the first time.

"Well, maybe that's not such a bad thing," he said slowly.

"For you maybe."

Eyes lowered to their plates, they ate fastidiously. Except for Ruth, whose gaze flickered with hope.

NELLIE'D JUST PICKED up Charlie's prescriptions at the drugstore. The day was sunny but chilly with a wind that rattled the heavy junkyard gate, which made it hard to lift the hasp. After finally prying it open, she was disappointed not to be met by Boone. Charlie wasn't around, either. He had called her mother the other night, complaining that the police kept stopping by and asking him the same questions, over and over, even though his answers were the same every single time. He'd warned them to leave him alone or he'd sue the entire department for harassment and loss of income for driving his customers away.

After Nellie looked in the barn, she went over to the house and knocked on the door. From inside came the low, deep rumble of Boone's bark. She kept knocking. Nothing. Turning the knob with a sweaty hand, she fully expected to find another body inside. Charlie's. Boone whimpered happily as she slowly opened the door.

"Hey, hey, Boonie," she whispered, staggering a little as he jumped against her. With his paws resting on her shoulders, she put her arms around his powerful head. "Hey, how're ya doin?" They stared into each other's eyes, and she could have sworn he looked like he was crying.

"Where you been?" Charlie asked, coming out of the kitchen. "Hey! Get! Get down!" he scolded, snapping a towel at Boone, though she assured him it was all right, Boone wasn't doing anything wrong. "Goddamn dog," he muttered as Boone retreated to a far corner, whimpering from the dusty shadows. "If it wasn't for the goddamn Shelbys, he'd be long gone, believe me."

She gave Charlie his bag of pill bottles and followed him into the small, cluttered kitchen. The cracked green flooring was sticky underfoot. Hard to believe her mother ever could have lived here. The metal topped table was covered with newspapers, as were the chairs. She cleared a seat and sat down. She figured she'd get right to the point. At the counter Charlie was emptying half-filled bottles into the new ones. The rusty dish drainer next to the sink was stacked with what had to have been a week's worth of clean dishes. Charlie probably just kept washing them until he either ran out of room or ran out of dishes. She asked if he'd heard from Max. Nope, was all he said.

She got up from the table and pulled the stiff dishtowel from the cabinet knob. She began drying his dishes and putting them into the cupboard.

"Leave 'em. Don't bother," Charlie said.

"That's okay." She continued drying. A couple of the plates were her mother's. She set those aside, though she knew she couldn't carry them back on her bike.

"Just don't get old," Charlie said, tossing the emptied bottles into the trash. "Cuz this is what it comes to."

"Yeah, but you're not that old." She kept checking the flatware for food bits as she dried. Most went back into the sink for rewashing.

"What're you after, my money?" Charlie peered at her, trying to scowl away a smile.

"Sure, if you got any!" She laughed.

"How much you want?"

"I don't care, whatever you wanna give me."

"Here," he said, digging deep down into his pocket. He held out a dollar bill.

"No, no," she immediately protested. "I was just kidding, that's all."

"No, you weren't."

This, she knew by his squint was some kind of test, one she was bound to fail.

"No, really."

He studied her a moment before slipping the bill back into his pocket.

"You think he did it? Killed her?"

"I don't know." No one had asked her that. It was her most honest answer.

"But you were there. Right there with him the whole time, right?"

"Pretty much."

"Pretty much what?"

"The whole time."

"They keep asking when he left here. How the hell'm I s'posed to know?"

"He was late. He said you didn't tell him till after fishing." She hadn't thought to tell the detective that.

"Well, that's his story."

"I know, but did you?"

He snorted. "Like it makes any difference?" Now his eyes narrowed to slits. "Maybe he did go before, ever think of that? Probably only takes a couple minutes to kill someone like that. Leave. Come back later."

"I don't know," she said, shrugging. Though she'd never actually done the Japanese Strangle Hold, she knew there weren't many steps involved. She wanted to leave. She'd come here expecting support as Max's ally, but Charlie's suspicions were too unsettling. Like hearing Max called a sex offender. In order for Max to be innocent, she needed him beyond everyone's reach.

"Just doesn't make sense, that's all. Him and his dog, that's all he cared about. Never even talked about a woman."

She asked Charlie if he'd been to the jail to visit Max. He hadn't, he said, but he'd thought about it. Well, if he did go visit, would he take her with him, she asked.

"You can't go!" He looked surprised. "You're the star witness."

After she left Charlie's, she rode her bike in the complete opposite direction from home. The Hillman County Jail was on the outskirts of town and she'd seen it plenty of times on their way to the lake. But never with someone she knew inside. The jail itself was a dark three-story building of reddish stone blocks and barred granite windows. A tall chain-link fence topped with razor wire surrounded everything. She slowed down, standing high on the pedals as she coasted past. She had this feeling that Max was staring through the bars at her, so she lifted one hand from the handlebar, but couldn't do it. She couldn't wave. And it was more than not giving him false hope. She was disappointed. Max had let her down. He was different from any adult she'd ever known. Like her father, Max was brave and decent and honest. But the one thing she couldn't reconcile was him making her open that door if he knew what was inside. He was the adult and she was the kid, and he'd dragged her into it. He shouldn't have made her see that.

The next day she and Henry were walking downtown. He wore a baseball cap to hide his hair, or lack of it. His mother had cut it the night before, but with the trimmer on the wrong setting, way too short before she noticed, so she'd had to do his whole head like that. Everyone else in the family said he looked great, except for Nellie, who'd called him a skinhead, which made them all mad. He knew what he looked like, and besides, as she tried to explain, she'd want him to tell her if she looked strange.

"What's the point of lying? It just makes him feel worse. And then when it's true he won't believe it."

"Yeah," Henry had leaped to her defense. "Like when your eye crosses, and they all pretend it's not, I always tell you."

Ruth had burst out laughing.

"Why? Is it now?" She had strained to see in the distant mirror.

"It's not crossed," her mother had insisted, glaring at Ruth. "It turns a little, that's all. Just when you're tired. Or you get too excited."

Anyway, they'd already taken three detours through backyards and alleys to avoid kids Henry knew. Instead of being home alone all day, they'd been sent to the store to help their father. He gave them a few chores, sweeping and emptying wastebaskets, then retreated to his office, which had never been neater. All his research books had been packed into boxes. There were twenty or so brown accordion folders bulging with papers. While he wedged the folders into large plastic bins, Nellie wandered through the store, not really doing anything yet still managing to look busy, a skill she'd mastered in these last few weeks. Henry had found a box of old brass plumb bobs and had been carefully attaching them to the spools of linked chains on the back wall, apparently trying to see how many weights it would take to get the spools turning. Six on the larger links and four on the smaller links, because they both began spinning at once. As the spools of chain clattered to the floor, her father rushed out of the office.

"What's going on? What happened?" Relieved to find no injuries and nothing broken, he cleared off the folding table next to the counter and gave them a worn deck of cards, each one stamped with the old store logo from her grandfather's time, a cartoonish woodpecker sitting on the "P" in a sign that read PECK HARDWARE. They could play rummy if they wanted, he suggested. They didn't want to. Well, what did they want to do, he asked, looking perplexed. Henry said he was hungry. Her father gave them what money he had—eight dollars—to buy lunch, even though it was only ten in the morning. They walked around the corner to the coffee shop and each ordered a thick slice of chocolate cake and a large chocolate milk.

When they returned, her father was talking to someone. Mr. Andrew Cooper. He wore a pink-and-white striped tie and a pale green summer suit that had a kind of swampy sheen under the fluorescent lights. This was the first time she'd seen him since that day in the backyard. Her father called them over to the counter to say hello. He reminded Henry to remove his cap.

"Well, hello," Mr. Cooper said in his mind-racing, wide-eyed way of trying to remember her name. She didn't help him out. "Hello, sir," was all she said. "And how're you doing, big fella?" he said, knuckles rubbing Henry's fuzzy crown. "Or should I say cue ball?" he added, laughing. Henry's face reddened. Her father shot her a warning look. But in a million years she wouldn't have had a comeback. She could barely think straight.

"Anyway, just give these here a look-see," Mr. Cooper said, as he removed papers from his leather folder and fanned them out on the counter. "Any questions, I'm a phone call away—you or Sandy—I'm easy to get. We're not as far off as you think. And remember what I said, Ben, any gap is bridgeable. Long as we keep talking. Dialogue, that's what it's all about." They shook hands and she couldn't help noticing how tired and worn and rumpled her father looked compared to Mr. Cooper. He followed him to the door.

Mr. Cooper turned on his way out. "You be sure and give Jessica a call now," he said, looking back at Nellie. His long, cold stare cut right through her. He was telling her something. Ordering her.

"Course she will," her father said with his hand on her shoulder. "Won't you, Nell?"

She tried to smile.

"As a matter of fact," Mr. Cooper said, "Jessica's home right now. I was just talking to Mrs. Cooper on my way here, and she said if I run into you, I should tell you you're welcome anytime."

"Oh." She nodded.

"In fact, I've gotta make a quick stop home. I could drop you there right now."

"That's awfully nice of you, Andy." Her father looked at her. "More fun than hanging out here, right?" One of those questions he did not want an answer to.

"Give Claudia a break," Mr. Cooper agreed. "Tough duty tryna keep that one entertained."

Nellie sensed her father's uneasiness. *He'd* never be disloyal about one of his children.

"So Henry and I'll start clearing out the storeroom," he said, delivering her to the door where Mr. Cooper waited, folder tight under his arm. The back of her neck prickled, her fate now somehow contained in the papers her father had received from Mr. Cooper, who was already on his cell phone with his wife.

When she opened Mr. Cooper's back door, he insisted she ride up front with him. At first he drove in silence. She stared out the side window. How about some music, he asked, turning on the radio. Jessica's favorite station, he said. His slender fingers ticked the beat on the shiny steering wheel. She wondered if he could see how bug-eyed she was.

"So!" he announced over the music. "This'll be your last year of middle school."

She nodded.

"Hope you and Jessica stay good friends." Fingers *tick, tick, ticking.*

Nodding, she hoped he didn't notice her hard swallow.

"Like your dad and me. Known him since we were kids together."

"I know." Not really, not details anyway, but she couldn't just keep nodding.

"Too bad, everything that's going on right now. Lotta strain on everyone. On the family." With a touch of a button on the steering wheel, he lowered the volume.

She nodded.

"Can't be a very good feeling, I mean, something like that in your own house." He kept glancing at her. "Especially for you, being the first one in." He wanted her to say something, but she couldn't think what. "Must've been pretty awful, huh?"

"Yeah."

He sighed and hit the directional long before the corner. Its *click click click click click* beat in her sternum. When he did turn, he lifted his foot from the gas. The car crept along, with his voice. "Like being in shock, I guess, huh? The details, they must all run together, huh? Same thing happened to me once. Probably just about your age, too. I was in a car in the front seat and this man was driving; he was crazy mad out of his mind, and he just kept going faster and faster. Next thing I know the car's flying through the air, and that's all I remember. They said I was talking after, making perfect sense, or so everyone thought, but it was all messed up. All the details. I was telling things that happened weeks before like they'd just happened, that day, right before I got in the car."

They'd come to a complete stop, in the middle of the cul de sac. "You know what I mean?" She could hear the scratch of his tie rising and falling on his starched shirt front at each little pant.

"I guess so."

"Some things, they're just not worth it, all that trouble and pain." With a flick of a smile, he patted her arm. "You know what I'm saying?"

"Yes, sir." She didn't dare move.

"You're a good kid." His hand felt hot. She wasn't breathing. "So go ahead in." He nodded toward the pretty house with its terraced front lawn and serpentine flower beds edged with white alyssum. "Jessica's waiting for you. And remember!" He hit the unlock button and she jumped at the sound. "Things're bound to get messed up. But that's okay. That's just the way it goes."

She opened the door. "Actually, I remember everything," she said with one foot on the ground.

"You mean, you think you do."

"No, I do. I'm going to be the star witness."

"Who told you that?"

"Detective Des La Forges," she answered without hesitation.

———

SHE PUT IN two hours with Jessica. Two rather pleasant hours, in the beginning. She knew the drill, with Nellie's arrival, Jessica would hand her a can of Cherry Coke and the remote. All Jessica wanted to talk about was the murder, but having again declared herself the star witness, she felt buffered, protected. It was the official legal moat no one could cross, though Jessica would keep trying.

"Well, tell me about him then, that guy, the one that killed her," she said, when the next commercial came on. They were downstairs, catching up on *Survivor* episodes.

"I told you, I can't."

"I remember him. He was that guy, right, the one that saved Henry?"

"Yeah." Safe enough. Unwilling to forfeit control of the TV, Nellie would have to answer *some* questions. She aimed the remote, ready to click back to the show. She'd been scrolling through the ads.

"They're probably gonna electrocute him, right?"

"I don't know." A chill ripped through her.

"That's what they usually do. Or an injection. I saw that once. Or gas. They, like, seep it into this, like, box thingie with him in it."

She hit the button and the show resumed.

"Or poison. Like in his food or something."

She'd stopped listening.

Off on one of her riffs, Jessica leaned close. "Wanna know a secret?" she whispered. She got up and closed the door, then hurried back to the sofa. "Well? Do you or don't you?"

"What?" She tilted her head, trying not to miss any of the show.

"I did that. I mixed all these powders from my mother's pills. So now I have my own supply."

"Of what?"

"Poison. Wanna see it?"

"That's weird. Stop being so weird, will you?"

She laughed. "You don't know, maybe I put some in your soda."

"Jesus, Jessica, here." She stood up and flipped the remote onto the sofa.

"I'm only kidding. Don't go, c'mon!"

Nellie sat back down, but couldn't help feeling Jessica had meant it.

They watched the show in silence, while beside her Jessica twisted her hand backward to better gnaw on a hangnail.

"What if he didn't do it though," she mused, and Nellie hit the pause button. "You ever think about that? Like, how, maybe people just thought he did because he said things or did things, or maybe they just didn't like him, so they just blame things on him? Like sometimes the way people treat me. I mean, like, my own family even. It's, like, always my fault. Everything. I'm just one of those people, you know what I mean?"

"No," Nellie said. But she did know. It was the same in school, too. Jessica was like a magnet for negative feelings. And so, in a way, had been Max. "You just think about that stuff too much," she said.

"Yeah." Jessica settled back with her chubby arms behind her head and her feet up on the coffee table. "Like about how to kill people. Put them out of my misery."

"That's it!" Nellie jumped up and hurried upstairs.

"Is everything all right?" Mrs. Cooper called after her.

"I have to go pick Henry up," she called back from the door.

For days after, she kept thinking of Mr. Cooper trying to convince her that she'd probably been in some addled state of shock the day Dolly was murdered. And she was beginning to understand why. In a way, he'd been right. Sometimes, the most important facts aren't the ones you've forgotten but the ones you just don't know what to do with.

Chapter 14

I N HIS LETTER TO CHARLIE, MAX DEVANEY said he'd only laid
a hurting hand on one woman, a long time ago, and he'd always
been ashamed of that. He swore he hadn't killed Dolly. Maybe no
one else believed that, but he wanted Charlie to know the truth so he
wouldn't think he'd taken advantage of his kindness and generosity. He
was grateful that Charlie had given him work and a place to stay. And
if anything should happen to him, would he please see to it that Boone
was taken care of. He understood that Charlie didn't care too much
for dogs. Lots of people don't, he wrote. Especially an old fleabag like
him—Charlie chuckled reading her that line. So if it looked like he
wasn't going to get out, then he wanted Charlie to do him a really big
favor. He couldn't stand the thought of Boone having to go back to the
pound.

"Every time I think of him squeezed into one of them tight metal
cages again, it just about kills me inside." So would Charlie see to it
that Boone got put to sleep. As peacefully and painlessly as possible.
And to cover the cost Charlie should open the metal box in the trunk
by Max's bed. Should be enough there to pay for it.

"Which I already did," Charlie said, folding the sheet of loose leaf
back into the envelope.

"What?" She looked around feeling sick inside. She hadn't seen
Boone since she'd been here. She found it chilling that Max could so
easily request the death of his closest companion.

"Took it. More mine, I figured, than any cop's. That's what they do,
just slip it in the back pocket, and who the hell's gonna call 'em on it?"

"So where's Boone then?"

"Down back—that's where I keep him now. No way the Shelbys're getting by him there."

Boone was tied up to a junked truck, Charlie explained. The rope was long enough for roaming and still being able to jump up onto the truck bed come nightfall.

"That's not right," she said, and Charlie assured her the animal had plenty of water and food.

"A lot better'n the alternative, don't you think?" He waved the envelope.

THINKING, THAT'S ALL she was doing. Especially now after Max's letter. If he had killed Dolly, then he could be sentenced to death, which also meant Boone's death. Everyone she knew thought he'd done it. Even Max's own lawyer, or so it seemed. Eggleston Jay Wright. His name made her expect a neat and slender man, like her father. Wasn't a public defender a man of principle and tempered appetites, eager to save the less fortunate from any injustice? Well, not this one—at least, this was her first disappointing impression. His office was a mess, and so was he. The unmanned reception desk in the outer office was covered with legal boxes. Every time the phone rang, Attorney Wright answered it himself, seizing it midsentence, hungrily, desperately. His thin, reddish hair was parted just above one ear in a sad attempt to cover his shiny, freckled pate. His short-sleeved white shirt was wrinkled and there was a soil line rimming his sweaty collar above his loosened tie.

Her father had brought her here. Attorney Wright had offered to come to the house, but her mother couldn't bear the thought of it, everyone knowing, all the neighbors. As it was, Patty and Kirk Lane-Bush, the young couple from across the street, had gone public with their displeasure. They had sent a letter to the zoning board complaining about the apartment in the Pecks' house. They said when they bought their house last year, they'd been told it was zoned an A-1 neighborhood, for "residence only." And now this, "a murdered stripper in an illegal apartment," the letter went on to say, which devastated Nellie's mother, even though Benjamin insisted the apartment had long ago been "grandfathered in."

Nellie was beginning to see just how complicated life could be. Nothing stood alone. Every action had a reaction, and every reaction had multiple reactions, on and on, in a chain of insidious combustion they couldn't quite pin down, much less prevent, and now was everywhere. Their own nuclear fallout, for here they sat, right in the center of the blast radius, still trying to seem normal, she and her father, across the desk from the pasty-faced lawyer. He had a copy of her statement to the detective. He kept looking at different pages and rephrasing the questions, or he'd repeat her answers, then ask if that's what she'd told the police.

"So the whole time he was in the cellar, you were there, too?"

"Uh-huh."

"Then how come he says you left a couple times?" Squinting, he wet his finger and flipped the page. "'To mind Boone,' he says." He looked up.

"I don't know, maybe he didn't see me, that's all." So that's why the police kept returning to that same question. Her answer was harmless, not so much a lie as the only way to prove Max's innocence without turning this into a bigger mess than it already was.

"See you where?"

"Down there, in the cellar." She'd twisted the drawstring on her shirt tightly around her thumb.

"So Mr. Devaney'd already been in the apartment, then, before you got there, right?" He kept reading.

"I never said that."

"Well, he knew she was in there." He sounded exasperated. "Dead."

"He didn't say that." She unwound the drawstring and examined the ridges it had left on her finger.

"Well, what did he say?"

"Just that I should open the door."

"And he wasn't surprised that it was unlocked, right?"

"Why would he be? I was the one that told him." She rewound the drawstring again.

Her father's feet scraped. She knew by his look he didn't like her tone.

"All right," the attorney sighed. "But then he tells *you* to open the door. He tells *you* to go inside. That's what it says here, anyway."

"Because it was *my* house. He was like that. You know, polite."

He glanced at her father with raised eyebrows. "Polite," he repeated with a caustic snort. "So how'd he know she was dead then?"

"Because she was?" *Such a dumb question.* "I mean, there she was. On the floor. You could tell. We just knew." Her fingertip was turning purple. It felt numb.

"Okay," he said, nodding. "All right." His chair kept creaking. The office was getting hotter. The air-conditioning was temperamental, he had already told them twice. He was reading again, clucking his tongue as he ran his finger from line to line, his nails bitten to the quick. Like Jessica's, which always sickened her. But an adult doing it seemed like a real character flaw.

"Well, I guess that about does it," he said after a moment. He closed the file and tapped it on the desk. "I think we've covered everything." He pushed back his chair and got up.

Her father stood then. She undid the drawstring, checking for marks again. The two men shook hands and talked about another lawyer, some long-ago, mutual friend who'd gotten caught embezzling from his client. Apparently, they knew each other from another time, which whenever adults did that, seemed to shunt her aside, as if their earlier attention had been merely to humor her. Her father asked Attorney Wright how his wife was doing.

"Good as can be expected," Wright said. "After enough zaps, there's not much left."

She could see that made her father uncomfortable. "Sorry to hear that," he said. "Anyway, tell her I was asking for her."

For all the good it'll do, Wright's listless harrumph seemed to say.

"And thank you, Ellen—"

"Nellie," she corrected, and his eyes flashed. He didn't like it. He didn't like her.

"Well now, in the courtroom, I will be calling you by your given name. If that's all right with you." He winked. And that's when she understood. This wasn't even for real. The questions were routine, the answers didn't really matter.

"Are you going to ask me those same questions?" She pointed to the folder.

Fleshy lips pursed, he nodded with a slightly amused shrug. "I should imagine so." He smiled at her father.

"Well, what's the point then? I mean, they already know all that." Still seated, she looked between the two men.

"Nellie," her father gently warned.

"No. No, Ben. That's what I'm here for. And besides, what does she know? I mean, think of it. Young girl like her caught up in something like this. Of course she's going to be nervous." He eased back down into his creaking chair and stared into her unblinking eyes. "Now, listen to me. There's nothing for you to worry about. Nothing at all. No surprises, no questions you can't answer. It's not gonna be like some crazy TV thing with people yelling and browbeating you. It's all pretty cut-and-dried. So don't give it a second thought. You'll be fine." He looked up at her father. "I'll take good care, Ben, don't you worry."

"I know you will, Egg."

"So you think he's guilty too?" she asked the attorney. Seemed like a fair enough question, though she'd never seen a grown man's face burn so red so fast.

Unmoving, he seemed to stretch across the desk. "Of course not," he said through clenched teeth.

The car door had barely closed, and even though her father spoke sternly, she didn't think he was angry, at least not at her. "Nothing about this is going to be easy. Nothing." He was straining to see over his shoulder as he backed out of the narrow parking space. "And as much as I wish it had never happened, the fact is that it did, and now everyone's got to do the right thing and see it through to the end. I'm going to do everything I can to make sure that your mother's all right and that you're all right, and that this isn't any uglier for any of us than it has to be." They both jerked forward a little as he braked in the middle of the lot. He turned to her. "But, if you think for one minute this somehow entitles you to say whatever you please anytime you want, then you're in for a very rude awakening, young lady."

She was stunned. She didn't know what she'd done wrong. She really didn't. "I was just trying to answer the questions."

"You could've done it in a lot nicer way. And the next time an adult speaks to you, I expect you to be respectful, do you hear me?" He started driving again.

"I'm sorry," she said, though only sorry to have him upset with her. Because she knew that for him that was hardest, not her disrespect but that he'd had to sink to that sorry level, of scolding her. And so she felt bad for him.

"I hope so." Well, he never should have said *that*.

"He didn't do it. He's not guilty."

"You don't know that. No one does. Not for sure, anyway."

"Yes, I do. Because someone else was there. Before Max even came. And I saw him, too. In the side yard, by Dolly's back door. It was Mr. Cooper. He said he had some papers for you. But he wasn't acting right. It was like I scared him or something." Her brain was a jumble of moving parts, flashing, squealing into place. Just saying it was an enormous relief.

"Nellie." He could only look at her. "That's a terrible thing you just said. I mean, Mr. Cooper, he's—"

"He used to go there. I know he did. He'd, like, sneak in, late when nobody was around. He was her boyfriend. That's what she called him."

"Who? Dolly? She said that? She called Mr. Cooper her boyfriend?"

"Something like that." No. But now Nellie knew that's exactly who she'd meant.

"Nellie, do you have any idea what you're saying? Do you understand what could happen? The damage to an innocent man's reputation? His family? Once something like this is spoken, its mere utterance becomes a kind of reality. It takes on a life of its own. And no matter how hard you might try to change it later on, it keeps growing, giving off energy. Negative, vicious energy."

Well, it's true, she wanted to interrupt, but didn't. Trees, houses, cars blurred past, everything speeding up and strange—even the way he was driving, racing up to the stop light then sitting there until a horn sounded behind them.

"And as a matter of fact," he continued, almost breathlessly. "He *was* looking for me that day. Because that's when he made the offer. And a very generous offer, at that. We must've been on the phone for an hour anyway. I remember I came home and told your mother. Even with that nightmare going on, it was the one bright moment for her. Relief after a long, hard struggle. She hasn't had an easy time of it lately," he added, and Nellie couldn't help feeling he was trying to convince himself more than her.

"I know, but still . . . it was weird. It was like he was trying to hide behind the bushes. And his face!" She suddenly remembered. "He had these, like, scratches."

"Nellie, please. You mustn't do this. I'm begging you. One word and it'll turn into a witch hunt. Think of the fallout from this, the lives you could destroy. An entire family."

Unnerved by the way he kept blinking, she had to look away. Whose family was he begging her not to destroy? The Coopers'? Theirs? Or both?

So THERE IT was. She thought she knew but wasn't sure. And the one person she needed to believe her could not.

Chapter 15

———

MONEY WAS TIGHTER THAN EVER. WITH WORD AROUND town that Peck Hardware was as good as closed, a good day might mean ten or fifteen dollars in sales. Some days there were none. Business was also slow at the beauty shop. Many of her mother's clients were away on vacation. Or maybe, she worried, they'd gone elsewhere. And now without rent from the apartment, things were going from bad to worse. Yesterday her mother had had to borrow money from Ruth for the electric and telephone bills. Her father had spent the previous weekend painting the apartment, and at her mother's insistence, he'd even put down new vinyl tiles in the kitchen. Not that there was anything wrong with the old floor other than its violation by death. The apartment was ready, her father said, so now they could put an ad in the paper. They were eating dinner as the conversation went back and forth across the table. As soon as Ruth finished eating, she ran up to her room. Her friends were picking her up soon for a pool party. Every time Henry wiped his mouth, he spit more broccoli into the napkin, but Nellie was the only one who'd noticed. She envied her little brother's invisibility in the family. With all the turmoil, he could do pretty much what he wanted.

"But what about all that yellow tape?" Her mother pointed toward the window. She'd called Detective Des La Forges about it last week, and he said he'd come by as soon as he could.

"Just take it down." Her father sounded impatient. Andy Cooper wasn't returning his calls. And when he'd dropped by his office on Monday, the secretary had said he wasn't in, even though his car was in the parking lot.

"The police have to do that," she said.

"Who said?"

"Detective Des La Forges."

"That's ridiculous. The police haven't been here in two weeks."

"But they will, you know they will," her mother said.

"The investigation's over," he said with rare, thin-lipped finality.

"Maybe not," Nellie piped up. "Maybe they're just waiting for more clues. Maybe there's some new evidence."

With both hands gripping the table, her father stared at her. "They've got the man they want."

"Well, they're wrong then." She stared back.

"Don't say that," her mother gasped with a shudder. "Oh, my God, just the thought of it."

Her father stood up then and marched outside. He started ripping off the barricade of yellow tape strung from the trees and bushes to the porch railing.

"Don't, Ben. Please, please, don't, her mother pleaded on his heels around the back of the house. "We don't have permission yet. Why?" she said as he continued rolling up the tape. "Why're you doing this?"

"Because this is our home. It's not a crime scene," he declared, tossing the balled up tape into the trash barrel.

NELLIE HAD BEEN sent up to the third floor because the downstairs lights kept flickering.

She waited a moment on the landing, then knocked on Ruth's door again.

"Just a minute!" Ruth shouted over the music. She held on to the opening door so Nellie couldn't come in. "What?" she demanded, holding her fuzzy green bathrobe closed. Half her hair was set with heated pink rollers. The rest of the house was hot, and it was freezing in there.

"Turn something off!" Nellie shouted. "Mom's afraid the fuse'll blow again!"

"Yeah, and, like, it's my fault, right?"

She shrugged, always best with her sister, that and a blank stare. After a long, pained sigh, Ruth stomped back in, with Nellie close behind. Racing around the room, she turned down the iPod speakers and yanked out the plug for the electric curlers. She climbed onto a purple milk crate, and pulled out the extension cord to the string of Chinese lantern patio lights tacked along the highest peak of her gabled ceiling, a touch that hadn't been here during Nellie's last ransacking, which hadn't happened in a while. Not since . . .—she still had a hard time saying it—the murder. Next, Ruth turned off two lamps, but not the air conditioner.

"Okay?" she snapped, snatching an electric roller from the set on her dresser. "I hafta finish before they cool off."

"Just don't shoot the messenger," Nellie said under her breath, and Ruth scowled at her through the mirror.

"Do you mind?" she growled. "I'm tryna get ready."

"Okay." Nellie nodded, perfectly willing to endure her annoyance. At least it was attention, more than she'd gotten lately from her. Or from anyone else for that matter. They'd all closed themselves off, not just from prying outsiders but from one another.

"Like I need an audience, right?" Ruth grumbled.

Not wanting to look too ensconced, she half sat, half leaned against the bed. "She said to turn off the air conditioner. It's not even hot out," she added to soften the command. Just being here was contentment enough. Watching her sister's nimble fingers twist and turn her blond hair onto the rollers was almost as hypnotic as when she used to set Nellie's hair like that and polish her nails—when Ruth used to like her, before she realized what a loser she'd become.

"Can you? I'm late. I'm so wicked late."

Nellie turned off the air conditioner, then crept back to the edge of the bed, motionless in the sudden silence, expecting imminent eviction. With her long hair away from her face, Nellie saw how pretty Ruth really was. Looking into the mirror was like watching someone from a long time ago. Their mother, Nellie realized, her eyes the same bright blue. A party, she said, when Nellie asked what she was late for. A pool party, Ruth continued, surprising her. It had been a long time since she'd shared anything with her, air space or information. Catherine Larson was having it. Of the four girls invited, Ruth was the only junior. Catherine's sister was Linda, who also worked at Rollie's.

"Their pool's all curvy, like some kind of lagoon, black stone with this, like, waterfall at one end. All lit up and ripply," she said, spearing the last roller with a long silver pick.

"How come you're setting your hair then? It's just gonna get all wet and ruined," Nellie warned, sitting on the bed now, cross-legged.

"That's *so* not the point," she sighed opening the door to her closet, which was crammed with clothes. She yanked out a yellow sundress and the hanger spun onto the floor on top of others. "What do you think?" She held it under her chin.

"It's nice, but what about a bathing suit?"

"Ta da!" she laughed, flashing open her robe to reveal the skimpy blue-and-white striped two-piece she was wearing. Nellie asked if it was new. Borrowed, she said. Jill had lent it to her.

"That's disgusting!" Nellie blurted, clearly, by Ruth's annoyed expression, endangering this rare sisterly moment. "I mean the bottom part, like somebody's underwear," she tried to explain as Ruth squatted down, rummaging through the closet jumble of dusty boots, slippers, shoes, sandals.

"Not if you use a panty liner," she said, which turned Nellie's stomach all queasy for a second. Ruth glanced back. "Have you even started?"

"Started what?" Nellie knew exactly what she meant. Her face burned.

"Your menarche."

Relieved, Nellie asked what that was.

"Your period. That's what the first one's called." Ruth stood up. She'd found her tan sandals.

Nellie's half nod half shrug came with a grunt.

"When?" Ruth sounded surprised. "When'd you start?"

"I don't know." Hadn't, and hoped she never would. Every storm in their lives seemed to erupt during her mother's or sister's time of the month. Especially Ruth's, with her zits, tears, and slammed doors.

"Jeez. You can tell me. I'm your sister." She sat on the milk crate, intently buckling the intricate web of skinny straps. "I mean, it's natural. And girls, they don't get, like, all weird about it. They just, well, like . . . it's just part of life." Pausing, she gave Nellie one of those squinty-eyed oh-my-God-you-poor-clueless-thing faces she and her friends always made. Nellie stared back. Ruth came over and sat on the bed. "Look at you, you're, like, all embarrassed. Why?"

Nellie shrugged. "So is Linda the one with the unibrow?" she asked, subject changing often the easiest ploy with Ruth—but not this time. Her voice had been too thin.

"Oh, Nellie!" Leaning close, Ruth put her arm around her. "I feel awful. It's like, all this stuff's going on, and all of a sudden you're, like, this whole other person, and me, I'm just, well, tryna be all, like, okay, I'm okay, nothing's wrong here, you know what I mean?"

It seemed best to shrug, nod, grunt again. Pulling her closer, Ruth smelled like the sweet, white flowers in bloom a few days every May on the tall shrub outside their kitchen window. By Memorial Day their drifting petals covered the lawn like fragrant snow.

Her voice was different, whispery. Close to Nellie's ear yet from a distance, someone Nellie used to know was saying she could always trust her. There wasn't anything she couldn't tell her. No matter what it was, she should always come to her because she was her big sister, and Nellie probably didn't know this, but when she was little all she'd ever wanted was a baby sister, so when she woke up the morning Nellie was born and found out her prayers had been answered, she promised God she'd never let anything happen to her. Ever.

Mock orange. Those were the flowers, the sweet drift from her hair, even her armpit so near Nellie's chin. It was true, Nellie realized with a surge of relief over something she didn't even know she'd lost. She did love Nellie, and Nellie loved her. Until only a year or two or three ago, she had been her beloved older sister. And now that she had the old Ruthie back, she wasn't about to lose her again. Or at least that's what she would tell herself days later, standing on the front porch, foreign-posted letter in hand, but right then, at that moment when Ruth was asking if she ever got cramps or anything, she could honestly answer, "No. Never."

"You will," Ruth declared of Nellie's bleak future. "Same as me and Mom." With every roller plucked from her head, she confided another misery of her menses. Headaches, nausea, clots and heavy flows, stained clothing, tender breasts and sore nipples, swollen feet, greasy hair, the grim list endless.

"There's this one girl, she even gets the hives with hers. And Ginny from work, she gets, like, the worst diarrhea. Usually right before, though. Which is how she knows . . ."

Knows what, that she'd never let Ginny from work scoop an ice-cream cone for her again, Nellie thought, staring straight ahead trying to look unfazed by the looming perils of womanhood. *Why did girls always have to talk like this? Boys didn't. Not that she ever heard, anyway, except for that grossest thing of all, Bucky peeing on Henry. With everything else going on she'd practically forgotten about that. Where was her* Get Tough! *manual? She hadn't seen it in a while. Too bad Dolly hadn't known some of the holds. If only she'd shown her, it could've saved her life, one of the release holds anyway, the one from a stranglehold because that's how it had happened, Des La Forges had told her mother on the phone. Dolly had been choked to death. Mr. Cooper's hands weren't very big, not like Max's.*

"And I've got all my old bras," Ruth was saying. "So when your—"

"You know when Dolly first came?" Nellie interrupted. "Remember that guy, her boyfriend, how big he was? Well, it was him! He's the one that did it. I just thought of it! They'd have these, like, wicked fights. She told him not to keep coming around anymore. He was just too immature. All he wanted was . . . one thing."

"What're you talking about?" Ruth made a face.

"Sex!"

"Not really." Ruth cringed back.

"But that's what happened. He came back and she said no, and they had another fight, they did! So then he killed her. Her old boyfriend," Nellie added seeing her consternation. "He's the one!" Of course. It made such perfect sense because Max was innocent, and that way, Nellie wouldn't have to destroy the entire Cooper family.

"But he was in Pennsylvania. He moved there. He wasn't anywhere near here," Ruth said.

"How do you know?"

She held her shrug. "Everyone knows."

Everyone but her.

LATER THAT SAME night Ruth got caught sneaking in from the pool party forty-five minutes after curfew. The voices from the downstairs hallway drifted in and out of Nellie's sleep.

"You can't keep doing this!"

"I know! I know I'm late, but the thing is I was hoping you'd be in bed because I knew if you were still up, I was afraid I might say something because it was bothering me so much, even though I promised I wouldn't."

EIGHT O'CLOCK IN the cloying stillness of the morning, Nellie became a woman—in the hearts and minds of her family, anyway. Both her windows were propped open by old store rulers stamped PECK HARDWARE, each letter marking an inch. The limp curtains barely stirred. Every now and again a bird managed a listless chirp. Nellie was in bed reading *Copperspiece Tales,* the first of the three books on her required summer reading list for school. It was about an American Indian family on a reservation in New Mexico, or Native American family, as Ruth had already corrected her. The story was all right, it was just that so far that summer real life had far outpaced anything she could possibly find in a book.

With her mother's footsteps in the hallway, she peered over the book, expecting the door to fly open as she raced in, zipping her pants or blotting her lipstick on her way to work. If Nellie wasn't downstairs before she left, she always ran up to say good-bye and remind her of the list of chores on the kitchen table, even though they were usually the same: make beds, unload dishwasher, sweep crumbs from kitchen floor, spend time with Henry, and make sure he brushes his teeth. Henry had let the family down by being the first Peck kid to have a cavity before the age of twelve—not just one but three, and with no dental insurance, it was another financial blow. But on that morning the door creaked slowly open. Her mother closed it with another slow creak, then sat on the bed, regarding her with sadness.

"Oh, Nellie!" she gasped, and Nellie knew by the pain in her voice that Charlie had died. "My little girl," she cried, pulling her into her arms. And then Nellie's next thought was poor Boone. What would become of him? They'd just have to take him, that was all. Ruth could get allergy shots and her mother and Henry would get used to him after a while. She'd walk him three times a day and train him not to bark. He could sleep up here with her. But she knew enough to wait, bide her time, let her get past the grief before she said anything. "I'm sorry. I'm so, so sorry. With everything that's happened, everything that's gone on, you couldn't tell me, could you, so you just did it all yourself, you took care of it, didn't you? Oh, my little trooper, my tough little trooper, after all you've been through . . . I just feel so awful, my baby, my little girl, that you couldn't come to me. I should've been there for you, and I wasn't," she sobbed into Nellie's hair, promising it would never happen again. Never, ever again would she be too busy or distracted, upset, or worried when Nellie needed her, which clearly was right then.

No way on earth could she admit she'd never menstruated while her mother was struggling to compose herself by inquiring after her first flow—had it been heavy or light, cramps no cramps? Did Nellie prefer pads or tampons? Pads, Nellie quickly agreed after her mother said she should probably wait to use tampons until she was a little older. Nellie didn't ask why—and, oh God, didn't want her telling her what Jessica already had, all about stretching and things slipping out later on. What things? *That* thing! To her mother's last question, her next period, when was it due, Nellie gave her usual shrug-grunt. Later that afternoon after work, her mother presented her with a belated starter kit, a package of sanitary napkins and a special calendar to mark the days.

"Some girls, their skin breaks out right before. Others can tell when they get a little sensitive here." Her mother's hand grazed her own bosom, like Ruth's, fuller than hers would ever be. "And sometimes you can get really irritable right before, like so emotional the least little thing and you can fly off the handle. But it doesn't last too long, thank goodness." Sighing, she ran her hands through Nellie's hair. "And in the end it's all worth it," she said, and Nellie knew by her troubled gaze that that wasn't true.

So from then on, in addition to a lot of other guises, she was going to have to be a pseudomenstruator, flipping out once a month like clockwork and walking around with her arm slung protectively across her tiny, tender breasts. But at least Ruth was interested in her. A few days passed without anyone wanting to discuss cycles again, but her parents were treating her differently. Her mother had grown more attentive, watchful. Nellie would say something and her mother's gaze would hold, alert to clues, signs. It was the way she often looked at Ruth. Her father seemed uncomfortable. Wary. His guarded eyes said it all: she'd changed. For all he knew, his little Nell might be wearing a sanitary napkin. Actually though, it was more than that. She just didn't know it yet.

A FEW DAYS later Mrs. Cooper called her mother and invited Nellie over. Jessica had asked Nellie three times already and each time she'd said she couldn't. She had to take care of Henry, the true and perfect excuse.

"Well, that's awfully nice of you, Claudia, but you have enough of your own. You certainly don't need two more," her mother was saying. "Are you sure?"

Nellie couldn't believe it. Jessica had gotten her mother to invite Henry, too.

It would be a miserable visit. Embittered by Henry's actual presence, Jessica was as mean to him as Nellie'd ever seen her be to anyone, and that was going some. The worst came when Nellie went into the bathroom. Jessica raced downstairs where Henry was watching television. She told him they'd had a big fight and that Nellie had stormed out. He'd better hurry if he wanted to catch up to her, Jessica said, because Nellie had taken off running. Actually, she'd been reading *People* magazine, trying to kill as much time away from her as she could. Jessica knocked on the bathroom door again. "I know what you're doing in there," she said. "Going through the medicine cabinet. You're stealing drugs, aren't you?"

"Be out in a minute!" She continued reading. The latest issue and she only had a few more pages to go.

"Just don't take the Xanax. My mother counts them."

"Go away," Nellie groaned, flushing the toilet to keep her at bay.

Finally, when Jessica began banging on the door, she came out. She wanted to show Nellie something in her brother's room. Lou was a year older than Ruth and really cute. For once, Nellie would have something to report back to Ruth. But where was Henry, she asked, following Jessica up the stairs. She wasn't sure. Nellie said she'd better go look for him. He's down in the kitchen, Jessica said quickly. Talking to her mother. Which sounded reasonable enough as they went along the long, yellow hallway, flanked by many cream-colored doors. Each of the Cooper kids had their own rooms. Lou's was like a cave, dark blue with a red plaid border on the walls. Clothes were strewn everywhere. The bed had been halfheartedly made by pulling the red corduroy comforter over the rumpled sheets. Nellie was surprised. In her house making the bed was the first thing everyone did when they got up. Apparently, in this as well, Mrs. Cooper was a lot more laid back than her mother.

Jessica opened the closet and reached over the door frame for a small key. "Wait'll you see this," she said in her low, evil voice as she dragged out a gray metal file box from under the bed, then inserted the key. The lock clicked open. Inside were clear plastic sandwich bags filled with dried, ground-up leaves. "Pot," she whispered, opening a bag and inhaling deeply. She held it out.

Backing away, Nellie told Jessica no. She was scared. Horrified. Drugs. She couldn't believe this. She was in the same room with drugs.

"Lou's a dealer. But just to his friends." Jessica licked her finger, stuck it into the bag, then slurpily sucked off the pot. "Same as smoking it," she said, trying not to make a face with her dry chewing. She kept working her tongue over her green-flecked teeth. "See! You get, like, whoo!" she said, waving her arms for balance.

"Jessica!" Mrs. Cooper called. "Jessica, where are you?"

With her mother's voice nearing, Jessica stuffed the bag back into the file box, locked it, shoved it under the bed, returned the key, and was still closing the closet when Lou's door opened.

"Jessica!" Mrs. Cooper was red faced with fury, so angry she seemed unaware of Nellie's cringing presence. "Didn't you hear me?" She grabbed Jessica's arm and yanked her into the hallway. "How many times have you been told to stay out of your brothers' and sisters' rooms? How many times? How many?" she shrieked. Jessica's indignant sputters only seemed to enrage her. Nellie had slipped out behind them and flattened herself against the wall, trying to be invisible because she couldn't get past them to the stairs. She'd seen her mother mad but never like this. Mrs. Cooper was hysterical. Forever after, when she would hear someone described as "going nuts," this is what she would remember: Mrs. Cooper shaking Jessica and screaming into her face. "You have no respect for anyone's privacy! Always sneaking in and out of all our rooms, it's creepy, Jessica! It's just . . . so creepy! Why do you have to act like this? Don't you know how creepy . . ."—Nellie cringed, dreading having to hear her say, *how creepy you are?*—". . . it is?" she said.

What was creepy was Jessica's smirk and slitted eyes, not only un-fazed by her mother's tirade, but savoring it. Looking at Nellie now, Mrs. Cooper said she was sorry that she'd been involved in this, and maybe she should go home now. *Maybe?* All she wanted was to find Henry and get out of there. Out of this crazy drug den.

That's when Jessica snapped. "No! No!" she screeched, reaching out—as if for protection from this dangerous mother.

There was a thud then as her mother pinned her against the wall. "Stop it!" Mrs. Cooper hissed. "You just stop it!" Mrs. Cooper was taller, but Jessica was heavier.

"That's not fair! Don't make her go! Nellie!" she bawled, grabbing for Nellie as she tried to edge by. "Nellie! Nellie!"

Nellie felt terrible, not only for being part of this craziness but guilty as well. Once again she hadn't been tough enough. If she'd just avoided her the way everyone else did, none of this would be happening.

"Let her stay! That's not fair!" she screamed and charged, fists fly-ing, punching her mother's chest.

Nellie froze, not knowing what to do, throw a hold on her to help Mrs. Cooper or to run.

"Stop it! You just stop it, right now!" Mrs. Cooper gasped, strug-gling to keep her at arm's length as Nellie fled down the pale carpeted stairs.

IT WAS THE most disturbing scene she'd ever witnessed in a family. Her head hurt as she raced through all the downstairs rooms, calling for her brother while overhead the frenzy raged on. Henry was nowhere to be found. Figuring the commotion had scared him, she looked outside, everywhere, front yard, backyard, pool cabana, even in the amazing three-room tree house Mr. Cooper's carpenter had built for the children. Twenty frantic minutes later, she finally arrived home. On the hot front steps sat Henry, tear- and grime-streaked face set bitterly against her. The doors were locked and she had the key.

"You're in big trouble," he warned as she ran up the walk.

"Me?" she panted, trying to catch my breath. "I've been looking for you. Everywhere! All over the place!"

"No! You and Jessica, you just wanted to get rid of me!"

"Oh, God," she sighed, flopping next to him on the dusty step. "You have no idea; you don't have a clue what just happened." She described the ugly scene she'd left behind.

"She hit her mom?" Shocked, he folded his arms for a long, quiet moment. "You think she's crazy? Like, insane?"

"I don't know." She must be, Nellie thought, pinching off the tip of a lilac stem. "But everyone's so mean to her. Maybe she just can't help it anymore."

"Yeah, cuz she's so mean to them!" Henry wasn't buying it.

"Like Mr. Cooper, he's not even nice to her, her own father." Nellie watched from the corner of her eye. She wanted to share her suspicions with him. With someone. But what if she was wrong? "He's not—"

"Remember that day at Charlie's?" Henry interrupted. "The time the dog bit me? Well, she thought it was funny. The whole time, Jessica, she was, like, smiling."

"She was just nervous. That's what she does." She was surprised to hear herself defending Jessica, but she'd known her since kindergarten, and it was true.

"Max *saved* me," Henry countered as if arguing with someone.

"Yeah, I know." Talking about Max was hard. The thought of him locked up in jail made her feel helpless. Weak for not saying anything. Cowardly. But then again, what if Mr. Cooper really had been looking for her father that day? What if he had tried the store first, but the door had been locked? Her father did that sometimes, especially when he was writing. Maybe she just liked Max better than Mr. Cooper. And when it came to the darkness in a man's heart, what more did she know of Mr. Cooper than she knew of Max Devaney? After all, she'd known Mr. Cooper practically her whole life. And Max Devaney only a few weeks. But there's knowing a person in the way they want to be known, every detail letter perfect, and then there's the kind of knowing that's all inside, like still feeling ripples in the air even when that person's gone.

"You think he did that? Killed Dolly?" Sometimes, she thought Henry could read her mind.

"I don't know. He killed that dog, don't forget. Some people, killing's not a problem for them. I mean, his own family, they blamed him for his brother dying. Maybe that's what happened." There. She'd said it. And now, on board with everyone else, maybe she'd feel better. "Probably just got easier, that's all." She even yawned.

"What? Killing people?"

"Maybe."

"Yeah, well." He seemed troubled. "He's still a hero though, right?"

"I guess."

"Can you be both?"

"What do you mean, both?"

"A hero and a killer."

No, she wanted to tell him. You couldn't be both. And Max wasn't. She just knew he wasn't.

"WE HAD THAT stuff last night!" Henry groaned as her mother uncovered the steaming blue casserole dish, almost dropping the lid.

"Stuff?" her father warned peering over his glasses.

Her mother had come home from work in a bad mood. Speaking louder than they realized, two women under the dryers had been discussing the murder in "Sandy's house and how the killer'd lived in the junkyard with her father. Charlie."

"It's called leftovers," Nellie told her brother with a long nudge of her foot.

"Shepherd's pie" her mother said, glowering at him. "And if we don't finish it tonight, then we'll have it tomorrow night, too."

A grim prospect, given the lumpy, gray mass, corn and peas being the most recognizable ingredients. It was her father's favorite meal, which he'd missed last night because he'd worked late at the store, and Ruth's, too, but tonight she was at work. Nellie usually ate it out of cowardice, loyalty, and hunger—in that order.

"I'm not hungry." Henry sulked in his chair, empowered by the day's rejection.

"Fine!" her mother said with surprising bitterness. Halfway through dinner last night she'd let him leave the table when he said his stomach felt sick. "But tonight you can just sit here and watch the rest of us eat."

He wouldn't be seeing very much, though, with the kitchen getting so dark. Outside, the twilight sky had turned almost black with a far-off rumble of thunder. Her mother reached back and switched on the light over the table. Her father started to get up to close the windows, but she said not to. It was too hot and muggy and, besides, it still hadn't rained. He didn't say anything, just looked at her. Usually, the minute there was thunder she'd run around shutting all the windows. She was terrified of lightning, though she'd always tried to hide it from her children. She didn't want them burdened by her fears.

"Can I have some cereal?" Henry asked as they began to eat.

"I thought you weren't hungry," her mother said.

"I am, but not for *that*!" Henry pretended to gag.

"No, Henry, *that* is dinner," Benjamin said with a rare scowl. "You either eat it or you don't."

"But—" Henry began.

"No! And not another word!" he barked, pointing his fork—at their table, pointing one's fork was an unforgivable gesture.

Nellie could tell by the sag of her mother's shoulders that she felt terrible. Nellie continued eating, swallowing dryly and clearing her throat. Henry sniffed, eyes quickly red with tears he was struggling to contain. Knowing what a lousy day he'd had, she felt bad for him but worse for her mother.

In the close and perfect stillness, Nellie was conscious of how fragile she looked, how her father's eyes seemed to avoid her mother's. They ate in silence, as if one wrong word might unleash the looming storm. Even the thin curtains did not stir against the sill. After a while the sky began to turn a heavy, bruised yellow from which rain seeped gently but steadily. Henry concentrated on placing his flatware at various angles.

"Thanks, Sandy, that was delicious," her father said, getting up. He had to go back to the store, where he'd been cleaning out the cellar for the last two nights. The young fellow he'd hired to help was coming back at seven. He told Nellie to clear the table and put the dishes in the dishwasher. Henry could get up, he said, after he apologized to his mother. Her father left and Nellie began rinsing the plates in the sink, while at the table the uneasy stalemate continued. A part of her was enjoying Henry's fall from his usual high perch.

"Well?" her mother finally said.

"I'm sorry," Henry said bursting into tears.

Holding out her arms, her mother pulled him close. Now she was crying, too. Lulled by the running water in the sink and their murmurous apologies, Nellie kept loading the dishwasher. Conflicts just about always involved Ruth. But in the last few days she'd been the perfect daughter and sister, which surely meant trouble ahead. But at least she wouldn't be running away. Her daily check of the mailbox had yet to turn up anything from "the land down under." She turned off the water, stunned to hear Henry describing his eviction from Jessica's house. Not only hadn't Nellie done a thing to stop it, but she'd stayed there playing with her after he was gone.

"Because I didn't even know! I thought he was downstairs," she insisted, but her mother wasn't buying it. As the older child it was her responsibility to know where her brother was at all times.

"I trusted you, Nellie. And you let me down, and you let your brother down. It's that simple," she added as she got up from the table. She filled a bowl with Cheerios and set it in front of him. Nellie leaned against the counter, glaring, while he shoveled spoonfuls of cereal into his mouth, but he never looked up. A dangerous game. He had a lot more on her than she had on him. She waited until he'd finished eating and had left the kitchen before she told her mother exactly what had happened. Everything, even about Jessica eating her brother's pot. She was never, ever going over there again, and she wanted her to call Mrs. Cooper.

"She was probably just showing off in front of you. And besides, I'll bet it wasn't even pot," her mother said.

"Then what was it?" she demanded, indignant at the double betrayal, first by Jessica and then by Henry. Triple betrayal, really, because her mother had forced her to go there in the first place.

"It could've been anything. You know Jessica." Once again, she checked her watch. A woman was coming to see the apartment tonight, Miss Schiff, their first prospective tenant, and she was twenty minutes late. The ad had run in the paper for two weeks, but as soon as people heard the name and address, they weren't interested. Lazlo had called last week about getting his old apartment back, then called the very next day to say he was looking for something a little bigger. Maybe even with a studio. And who could blame him, her mother had said. He didn't want to live in a crime scene either.

"Yeah, and because of her, Henry might've gotten lost or kidnapped." Point by point, she was brilliantly building the case both for her innocence and for never having Jessica forced on her again.

"But he didn't," her mother said.

"But he could have! And if nobody tells them, then how're they supposed to know what's going on? And what if it happens again? To some other kid? Think about it, how guilty you'd feel. I would, anyway."

"Oh, Nellie," she sighed. "They know what's going on, what they're dealing with. Believe me, they know. Especially Claudia. She's such a good mother." So here they were again, same full circle: The Coopers were wonderful and Jessica needed a friend.

"What about Mr. Cooper? You think he's a really good father?"

"Yes. Of course I do."

"Even if he had a girlfriend? If he cheated on his wife?" Nellie held her breath.

"Where did you . . . What're you . . . Nellie! That's a terrible thing to say."

"But it's true. And you wanna know how I know? Because I saw him. He used to go see Dolly. And you know the day of the murder, well, he was there then, too. He was out back by the bushes and his face was all scratched and he was really nervous, like, he couldn't believe it. Like, oh, my-god, after what'd just happened, and there *I* am, this kid he knows, talking to him."

Her mother looked puzzled, as if she'd heard every single word but in another language.

Nellie tried speaking slowly, but couldn't. "Max didn't kill Dolly. Mr. Cooper did." With the terrible weight lifting, she felt lighter inside. Free.

"Nellie!" She kept shaking her head. "I'm sure you *think* it's true. I mean, I can't imagine you'd make up something like this up just to get back at Jessica so you don't have to go over there." Her eyes widened. "You wouldn't, would you?"

"No! It's the truth. Really! I swear it is!"

The doorbell rang, and she jumped up.

"Now listen to me, Nellie." She leaned close, talking fast. "Sometimes we want things to be a certain way so we start questioning everything. Especially if we're mad or we don't like somebody." She started for the front hall. "Then that just makes it all the easier," she called back, then opened the door. "Hello!" she greeted the soaking wet woman on their doorstep.

Miss Schiff was a fashionable older woman in a belted black raincoat. She gave her umbrella a vigorous shake, followed by a sharp rap on the step before coming inside. "Yes," she said with a distracted nod when Nellie was introduced. Was this also the entrance to the apartment, she asked uneasily. No, that door was on the other side of the house, her mother said, then suggested they go down through the cellar instead of out into the rain again. Miss Schiff followed her into the kitchen. "It's just been painted," her mother said in a high, forced lilt of breaking-point nerves. "Moonbeam cream, I think it's called. Actually, it's the same as this." She pointed to her own walls. "But you could always paint it another color," she said when Miss Schiff made no comment.

"Oh, I'm not much of a painter," Miss Schiff said.

"No, not you. I didn't mean you. We would. We do all that," her mother said, turning back.

"All right, but first I . . . I mean, I should've told you on the phone; I was going to, but then I didn't think of it until afterward. The thing is, you see, I have a cat."

"A cat," her mother repeated.

"Yes, and if that's a problem, then I won't take up any more of your time. He's ten years old, an indoor cat. He's declawed," she added weakly.

"Oh," her mother said. "Well, I hadn't thought of that. Of a cat."

"The ad didn't say anything about pets." Miss Schiff sounded nervous.

"No, that's right, it didn't, did it?"

"So," Miss Schiff said, frowning, "do you not rent to pets?"

Not to pets, just to people, Nellie thought wanting to clarify what was becoming a strange conversation.

"Well, I don't know . . . I mean, I never have."

"Well, then, I'm sorry. I should've said something before. It's just that the ad didn't—"

"But that doesn't mean I wouldn't," her mother said quickly. "It just never came up, really, but I suppose if it's a nice cat, well . . . and I'm sure it is."

"So does that mean you would?" Miss Schiff gripped her umbrella close to her chest.

"Yes. A cat. That's fine."

"What's—" *the cat's name,* Nellie was about to ask before being interrupted.

"So why don't we go see it now." Her mother reached for the cellar door knob and their eyes met. *Don't say another word,* hers warned.

She could hear them perfectly through the bathroom wall. With the matter of the cat settled, Miss Schiff sounded much friendlier. She had grown up here in town, but had lived the last forty-two years in Seattle, working in a doctor's office. A dermatologist. When he retired and closed the practice, she decided to move back even though she had no family left here. They were next door for about twenty minutes. Miss Schiff wanted the apartment. She'd said it was perfect for her, her mother told her father later, when he came home from the store.

"She said she likes having a family in the same house," she said from the couch, her legs curled under her. She was in her nightgown. She'd been waiting to tell him the good news. Henry had fallen asleep earlier, and Ruth wasn't home from work yet. Ordinarily, Nellie would have been in bed, but she'd been writing a long letter to Max at the wobbly, old Hitchcock desk in the living room. It had occurred to her that he probably wasn't getting any mail. His family didn't care what happened to him, and she couldn't picture Charlie writing back. She didn't mention her suspicions about Mr. Cooper. In fact, her only reference that came close to the murder was telling him about Miss Schiff maybe moving into the apartment and how excited she was about having a cat in the house, even if she probably wouldn't get to see it much, she added, then told him she'd seen Boone quite a few times, *not true,* but she knew he'd like hearing it. She ended the letter by asking when visiting hours were. "Your good friend, Nellie," she signed it. After she'd sealed the envelope, she realized she didn't know the exact address of the jail. But tomorrow she'd go see Charlie, get it from him, and that way spend time with Boone.

Writing the letter was a relief. She couldn't prove or even be sure of Max's innocence, but at least she'd done the right thing by telling her parents about Mr. Cooper. All she could do now was wait for the wheels of justice to start turning. And turn they would. That she was sure of.

In the other room her father was asking about the cat. He didn't understand. What about Ruth's allergies? Or had the woman paid the deposit and then said she had a cat? he asked. Oh no, Miss Schiff had been very upfront about it, her mother said. But didn't the ad say no pets? he asked. The first ads had, her mother admitted. But not this time. For whatever reason. Misprint or something. No big deal.

"Besides, she's way up on the third floor now. I mean, how far can cat dander travel?" her mother said.

"Hm, good question. I'll get back to you on that," he said, and Nellie smiled.

"Plus, she's probably outgrown it all now." Her mother sounded tense.

"So'd you tell her?" he asked after a moment.

"What?"

"Sandy."

"I don't see how that's my responsibility. Besides, she probably already knows."

"You just said she doesn't know anyone in town."

"I said she had no family left here."

"What're you going to do, let her move in and then find out?"

"I don't know." Silence. "Besides, once she's settled and loves it here, then it won't seem like such a big deal."

"Sandy."

"What?"

"You've got to tell her. It's the right thing to do, that's all."

"Oh, that's all? That's all? Easy for you to say."

"And if she doesn't want the apartment, then someone else will."

"No they won't! Of course they won't! *I* wouldn't! Just going in there tonight made me sick to my stomach!"

"Then that's the way it has to be, Sandy. For now, anyway."

"*For now anyway!* Everything's always just for now, isn't it?"

"Sandy. C'mere."

"No. You don't know how hard this is for me. And it's not just the money, it's everything. It's all so horrible. And here we are, stuck in this mess."

"We're not stuck. And we're not in any mess. Bad things happen and they happen to everyone, not just us."

"All the talk, I just hate it." Her voice broke.

"You'll see, hon. In a few months, this'll all be over and forgotten. I can't tell you how many tragedies I've discovered that've happened in this town through the years. And this'll be just one more, that's all. One more historical nugget."

"Nugget! Oh, God," she gasped.

"You know what I mean. Listen, tomorrow you call Miss Schiff and you tell her the truth, and who knows, she probably won't even care."

WELL, MISS SCHIFF did care. The apartment would remain empty. Her mother stopped running the ad. Why throw thirty dollars down the drain every week? Every day after work she would ask Benjamin if he'd heard anything from Andy Cooper yet. And every day the answer was the same. He kept leaving messages, but Andy wasn't getting back to him.

———

THE LAVENDER WAS being overtaken. It was a hot Sunday afternoon and they'd been weeding the herb garden. Kneeling halfway into the bed, her mother was digging out the last of the invasive mint. Nellie stood over her, waving away the bees they'd disturbed.

"We're gonna get stung," she warned again as she gathered the straggly stems and threw them into the wheelbarrow.

"We'll be fine," her mother murmured, which Nellie heard as a cool stillness. This was her mother's happiest time, though lately she'd barely been able to keep up with all the yard work. Nellie's father had taken over the lawn mowing, but after beheading the front-yard petunias with the Weed Whacker, her mother had reclaimed the trimming.

Her mother's sweaty, red shoulders were flecked with soil from the weeds she was so furiously yanking out. Grunting, she leaned in farther to pick up the long, dusty worm she'd just displaced. She dropped it, wiggling, into a hole and smoothed soil over it. The backs of her mother's legs were getting burned. Nellie took a few steps to the side trying to shield her from the sun.

"I can't see," her mother called up from the shadow and Nellie moved.

She loved her mother, but not with the same easy pleasure that she loved her father. An ache was how she loved her mother, with a sympathy she did not understand.

A bee buzzed close by her ear. She screamed and ran toward the porch.

"Nellie!" her mother chided, rattling through the tool bucket for her trowel.

"I might be allergic, too!" she said, coming back. Like Ruth, who carried a bee-sting kit in her purse.

"Don't worry, you're not." Her mother sat back on her heels and stretched.

"But what if I am? You don't know. What if a bee stings me and my tongue swells up and I can't breathe, then what do I do?"

"Well, then I'd run inside and get Ruth's EpiPen and give you the injection." Her mother seemed amused. "You don't think I'd let anything happen to you, do you, Nell?" She got up and put her arms around Nellie. "Do you?" she asked, and Nellie shook her head. "Well, what is it, then? Come on, hon, you can tell me; you know you can."

"I'm gonna tell the police about Mr. Cooper, I have to!" she blurted and her mother stepped back.

"No, you don't *have* to. And you won't. Absolutely not. Do you hear me? Do you understand what I'm saying?"

She nodded. "But I don't think *you* understand," she said in a small voice, determined not to look away from her mother's stare. Even with the bee at her shoulder she would not flinch.

"Oh, my God, Nellie, you've really got to stop, you can't keep doing this. You're only thirteen so you think everything's so simple, but it's not."

"I don't think it's simple. I didn't say that."

"No, but you want it to be. Because you're very idealistic—you always have been and that's wonderful, but comes a time, Nellie, when you've gotta listen to us, and trust us. Your parents. You just have to."

"Even if I'm right and you're wrong?"

"Oh, for God's sake, Nellie," her mother sighed. "You know what I think? I think a lot of this is drama, okay? And I'm not trying to belittle you or make you feel bad. Because we're girls, we've all been through it. Sometimes we get these feelings, these ideas, not so much in our head but in here," she said, tapping her chest. "And they can take on a life of their own, and before we know it, it's like an obsession, we can't even think straight anymore. So not another word about this, okay, hon? Please? Things are hard enough right now, don't you think?" Her bucket rattled as she picked it up and started toward the house.

That's why loving her mother was so complicated, Nellie thought as she struggled to push the heavy wooden wheelbarrow into the barn. Because they weren't the same, they weren't at all alike, which made her feel bad for both of them.

Chapter 16

—

I T MAY HAVE BEEN THE DWINDLING DAYS OF SUMMER OR MAYBE Henry just felt safer now, but he had resumed work on the tree house with a feverish intensity. The rickety walls had been cross-braced. The roof was almost finished. While scouring the neighborhood for usable boards, he'd discovered a house on Cork Street being renovated. He had climbed into the Dumpster when a carpenter drove up and caught him trying to hoist an old window over the side.

"What the hell're ya doing in there?" the carpenter yelled, so Henry told him. His tearful honesty was rewarded when the carpenter not only put the window in his truck but dropped it off at their house on his way home from work.

Right after breakfast Henry headed out to the tree house only to be ordered back inside. He had to wait until at least ten. Last night Miss Humboldt had called to say that Tenley hadn't been feeling well lately, and the early morning hammering was disturbing his sleep. At ten sharp Henry's labor began. *Bang bang bang* rang his steady hammer strikes through the open window. It was a beautiful morning, sunny and crisp, its perfection tinged by the fading hydrangeas, a sure promise of fall, another day nearer the start of the new school year. The phone kept ringing. Every time it did, Nellie cringed, afraid it was Miss Humboldt. So far the calls had all been for Ruth from her friend Torrie. This last one had been going on for almost an hour, and Nellie had to use the phone.

"Hang up!" Ruth barked when Nellie lifted the receiver again. She told Ruth she'd been on the phone long enough and she needed to call the salon to ask if she could go to Charlie's because Ruth would be home with Henry. "Hang up! I'll be off in a minute! Just hang up!"

Ruth yelled, and Nellie realized Torrie was sobbing on the other end of the line. She hung up without another word.

Soon after, Ruth came thumping down the back stairs into the kitchen. She slumped over the table glaring while Nellie dialed the salon. Of course she could go to Charlie's, her mother said, sounding rushed. When all her chores were done, she added.

"That's really rude, you know, picking up the phone every two minutes!" Ruth said when Nellie hung up.

"It wasn't every two minutes," Nellie said, wiping off the counter-top.

"That was a really private phone call," Ruth said.

"Well, how was I s'posed to know?" She turned on the water and wrung out the sponge.

"Every time you picked up, Torrie, she was, like, a wreck."

Nellie didn't say anything.

"The thing is, she's having a really hard time," Ruth called over the running water.

"That's too bad." Feigning disinterest, she shut off the water and started to leave.

"And it's hard on me, too. Being the only one that knows, that is."

"How come? I mean, how come you're the only one?" Nellie had no clue what she was talking about, but if she asked, she'd never be told.

"The thing is, her parents think she's such a saint, and, plus, her mother's this big pro-life fanatic."

"Oh," Nellie said. Maybe Ruth thought she'd been listening on the line. Or maybe she just needed a sounding board.

"She wants me to bring her in to the clinic. On Thursday. And I said I would, but I don't want to, and I don't know how to get out of it. I mean, I feel like I'm letting her down, but then there's the other part of it. You know what I mean?"

She didn't, but she nodded.

"I just keep thinking, I mean, what if Mom had done that? I mean, I wouldn't be here right now. I never would've happened. For Torrie it's just like this awful problem she's gotta take care of, and then when she does, everything'll be the same, back to normal again. But not for me it won't. I mean, if I help her, it'll be like getting rid of myself in a way, because I know what the other part of it's like. The being unwanted part."

For a moment they just looked at each other. Her sister's eyes were red and glistening, but she wasn't crying. Nellie was.

"Mom wanted you. You know she did," Nellie said, rubbing her nose on the back of her hand.

"Yeah, but she was the only one," Ruth said, then burst into tears. "My own father, he just took off."

"But he was in high school—his family made him." Or so the story went.

"He's not in high school now."

Again, Nellie nodded. They were both sniffling.

"You know how many letters I've sent him? Four! And he hasn't written me back, not one single letter."

"Maybe he didn't get them." Her mind was racing. If she gave Ruth the letter she'd hidden, she'd be in huge trouble, and Ruth would be even more hurt by her father's brush-off.

"That's what I keep thinking," she said.

Outside, the hammering suddenly stopped. There was a car running in the driveway. Then a knock at the door. It was Detective Des La Forges, asking for their mother. He wanted to tell her something. She was at work, Ruth said, quickly adding that he shouldn't go there looking for her. It would be too upsetting. The jowly faced man said he understood. He'd call her later at home.

Nellie was leaving for Charlie's when Ruth told her to wait. She looked in the refrigerator for something to give him.

"Here," she said, wrapping the end of last night's meat loaf. "Tell him he can heat it or make sandwiches with it."

She walked to Charlie's, not quite sure what to make of it all. Maybe her father was right, and life would get back to the way it used to be, happy and simple, when everything was still possible, even Max's innocence. And her own.

She walked around the junkyard, calling for Charlie. He wasn't in the barn, and she couldn't tell whether he was in the house or not because the front door was locked. Figuring he might be in the woods, checking on Boone, she followed the narrow path past rusting bar-

rels, junked oil tanks, half-buried paint cans, and the bittersweet vine–
entangled shells of old stripped cars. She was ashamed. Charlie was
an environmental menace, but she couldn't very well report her own
grandfather, could she? And yet wasn't that what was wrong in the
world, people always looking the other way, making excuses, each lie
and omission shoring up the next. Afraid to tell the truth, afraid to
take a stand. Like her trying to rationalize the irrational sight of Mr.
Cooper huddling in bushes mere feet from the doorway to a murder.
The fallout had to be considered, her father had said. The collateral
damage. But didn't every action cause a reaction? Wasn't there always
fallout? Why was Mr. Cooper's reputation more important than Max
Devaney's? What if Charlie's hazardous waste was seeping into ground-
water that fed the very springs they'd filled their gallon jugs from? She
thought of how her father had pointed up at the brilliant night sky and
explained that some of those stars were dead, and had been for mil-
lions of years. You can't tell the difference with the naked eye. But the
light still exists. Though she couldn't have explained how, she knew it
was all connected in that unfathomable, unnamable way of things that
exist both in and outside the realm of childhood experience.

Once she was beyond sight of the house, the going got rough. In
their spindly struggle for light, trees grew closer here, some shooting
straight up from the queer hummocky ridges marking decades of bull-
dozed debris. The weedy mounds glittered with bits of broken glass.
Until the town had served him with a court order, Charlie had been
dumping trash out here for years, his own and for anyone else willing to pay. No questions asked. When she finally came to the old
truck, Boone was gone. Only the thick, frayed rope dangled from the
truck bed.

"Hey, Boone! C'mere, boy, c'mere, Boone!" she called, waving away
mosquitoes as she headed deeper into the woods. Traffic sounds in the
distance meant she was nearing the outer reaches of Charlie's property.
Thinking she'd heard voices, she stopped and called again for Boone,
but softly, almost in a whisper. It occurred to her then that she was all
alone, and if anything happened, no one would know she'd come this
far into the woods. She decided to head back but wasn't sure of the
path. No need to panic, she kept telling myself. After all, these woods

were right in the center of town. Sooner or later she'd come out onto a familiar street.

"Kun-ka-too!" came a dull shout, followed, as if in answer, by a long piercing cry, whether of pain or surprise she couldn't tell, but every hair on her frozen body stood on end. Here it was, the very moment she'd been preparing for, and not a single hold came to mind. She could barely breathe. Footsteps. Crackling twigs. The leafy rustle of parting branches, and suddenly Boone sprang at her, wiggling and whimpering happily. Someone had been running behind him and now came to a dead, panting stop. He was tall, dressed in black with red slashes crossed across both cheeks like war paint. It was one of the twins, Rodney, and on his heels, Roy, also in black. Yellow-and-bright-green circles had been painted on his cheeks. His acne-pocked nose glistened with sweat.

"Hey!" she called with a nervous laugh. She braced her feet to keep Boone from knocking her down. They both just looked at her. She couldn't tell if they were embarrassed, but she knew she was. She'd caught them at something strange and they all knew it.

"He got untied," Roy said. Even in school he was always first to speak.

"We were tryna catch him," Rodney said.

"Well, I got him now," she said, as if this were all perfectly normal.

"Okay," Roy said, and Rodney nodded.

"So you guys're what, Indians?" she asked.

"Native Americans," Roy said. "Passamaquoddy."

"Who're they?"

"They used to live around here," Roy said.

"A long time ago," Rodney said, and she asked how he knew. Because of all the artifacts they'd found, he explained as they began to walk with Boone trotting behind. She followed them over the rise, then down the densely wooded incline that ended behind their house. At least from here she'd find her way home.

"Wanna see some?" Roy asked, sliding open the black metal door of their garage. Cars hadn't been parked in here for a long time. But there were two odd-looking bikes covered with homemade gadgets and gizmos. Each bike had a small motor attached to the hub of the back wheel. The garage was filled with unrecognizable metal contraptions.

Some resembled modern art structures with gleaming pylons attached to metal discs by coiled springs. Others seemed to be wacky machines with moving parts, levers, chutes. Rodney was demonstrating one fashioned from a car battery, clock face, radio innards, and a narrow circuit board connected by thin wires to a series of spur gears that, turning, produced a deep robotic voice that droned, "Warning, warning. Security has been breached. Warning, warning. Once unleashed, the force will destroy you. Warning—"

"Cool," she said as Rodney aimed a remote that clicked it off.

"It works off of infrared beams," Roy said. "But the detection range is still too short."

"Yeah," Rodney agreed.

"Cool," she said.

Sweat beaded on their fuzzy upper lips. She tried not to look at it.

Now Roy was showing her the weather instrument he'd been working on. Not only did it measure humidity, but could detect changes in air pressure hundreds of miles away. She was pretty sure such a device had already been invented but didn't want to hurt their feelings. Elbowing each other out of the way, the twins moved excitedly from gadget to gadget, pushing buttons and turning wheels. Lights flashed, motors hummed, bells rang as their voices overlapped with eager descriptions. It was like being inside the belly of some huge mechanical beast, and she was their first guest. Boone sat by the door, clearly used to the cacophony.

What about the artifacts, she asked, and Roy slid a large flat box from under a workbench that was covered with tools and cans of spray paint. Inside were dusty arrowheads, chips of earthen pottery, and oddly shaped stones that he said were used to make digging implements as well as hunting tools. To Nellie it all looked like a bunch of rocks, but the twins treated it with great respect. Roy was talking about Chief Passaconaway and the Great Spider Mother. Rodney kept interjecting facts and elaborating on Roy's details. They'd been digging for years, they said. The artifacts were so easy to find because most of the junkyard had never been disturbed.

"In fact, we just found a whole new place," Roy said.

"Yeah, down by the willow trees," Rodney added.

"Just scoop your hand in the muck and there it is," Roy explained.

"All kindsa stuff," Rodney said.

"C'mon, we'll show you." Roy lurched for the door.

When she said she'd better bring Boone back to her grandfather's, their faces fell. They'd found the dog last week, roaming the woods, so they'd been feeding him. He'd been hanging around ever since. That was nice of them, she said, but she had to give him back. Charlie was taking care of him for someone else.

"Taking care of him!" Roy sputtered. "Poor dog, he never even had water."

"So we did, we filled his bowl," Rodney said. "Brought him treats, too."

"I know, but his owner, he wants Charlie to have him," she said. "That's what he said."

"He's the one in jail, right?" Roy asked, and she said yes.

"He killed our dog," Rodney said. "It was in the paper. My mother saw it."

"That was your dog? The white pit bull? He bit my brother. He, like, almost killed him, but Max saved his life. I was there. I saw the whole thing. Believe me, that was not a good dog."

"He broke off his chain!" Roy said.

"Max was a hero," she said.

"We used to see him. He didn't think we did, but we did. We weren't s'posed to talk to him. My mother said he was strange."

"She thinks everyone's strange," Rodney interjected, grinning every time she looked at him.

"He followed us," Roy said. "We'd look around and he wouldn't be there, but then he would. He'd be, like, hiding."

"Yeah, like, behind a tree or something."

"That's weird," she said.

"Yeah, maybe he wanted to kill us, too, that's what my mother thinks anyway," Roy said.

"And that's *really* weird," she scoffed.

"Yeah, he even talked to his dog. Sometimes we'd hear him: 'So what d'ya think, gonna rain today or what?'" Rodney said, and his almost pitch-perfect imitation of Max's deep voice gave her the creeps.

"Well, I better get going. C'mon, Boone!" she called from the doorway, holding out the packet of meat loaf, but the dog remained rooted at Roy's feet, looking at her. She called again, this time with more urgency, but he didn't move, and it made her sad. It seemed as much a rejection of Max as of her. Boone knew Max wasn't coming back, and he knew she hadn't tried to help him, and he knew Charlie didn't care, so he'd made his choice. Her face grew hot as she stood there. "Just so you'll know—Max—he never killed anybody. The only reason he was watching you is because he used to have a brother, too. He said that, how you reminded him of him and his brother. That's all he was doing." And with that she marched off, but down their road. She might be afraid of going back through the woods. But she wasn't going to be afraid of speaking her mind.

Charlie was sitting on his front steps, bare chested and reading the newspaper. She gave him the meat loaf, then sat next to him, but he raised the paper higher and kept reading to the end of the article. He said he thought he'd heard the doorbell, but he'd been napping and didn't want to come all the way downstairs. Hillman County Jail, he said when she asked for Max's address—that's all the letter would need. What about a cell number or something so he'd be sure and get it, she asked, and he chuckled. Don't worry, they'll find him; he'll get it, he said, but she'd better ask first. He didn't think the star witness should be writing to the accused, especially with the trial so near at hand. As a matter of fact, he hadn't even answered Max's last letter.

"How come?"

"I got enough problems without being some killer's pen pal," he chortled, liking the way that sounded.

"You mean you think he did it, killed her, Dolly Bedelia?" She was stunned.

"Well, lemme put it this way. I don't think he just went and, you know, *killed* her. I think it was something that happened. I mean, the man had one helluva temper." Charlie snapped his fingers. "Quick as that and he'd turn. Like that time with the dog. Made my blood run cold. Smashing that dog's head like that."

"But he was tryna save Henry. The dog was biting him, chewing his arm. It wouldn't let go." Her voice quavered, and she took a deep breath. She knew better than to say whose dog it had been.

Right then Charlie did something strange, looped his arm over her shoulder. "Hate to be the one to tell you, kid, but some people're just born bad to the bone, and that's all there is to it. Nothin' you can do."

And some're just born ignorant, she wanted to say, but didn't, couldn't; instead, she hunched over her knees with an intensity of anger and aversion until he lifted his arm.

Chapter 17

—

NELLIE SAT ON THE FOOT OF HER MOTHER'S BED, GROWING more bothered as she watched her in the mirror. What was the point of the makeup? She looked perfectly fine without it. She dipped her pinkie into a tiny glass jar, then rubbed a smear of blue onto her eyelids. Now she was putting on lipstick that was way too bright, too red for a mother to be wearing. *Why? Why is she trying to look different from who she really is?* The last time Nellie'd had these feelings was the first morning she'd gone off to work with a feathery new hairdo and a black smock over her arm. Capping the lipstick, she turned her head this way and that, smiling into the mirror. *My God, who is this person?* She pinched lipstick from the corners of her flaming mouth, and Nellie had to look away.

"When's Ruth coming home?" Nellie knew but felt the need to make some point, though wasn't sure what.

"Nine or ten, depends how long the takeout window's open." She leaned closer to the mirror and ran her tongue over her teeth.

"What if Dad's late?"

"He won't be. He knows when they're picking me up." It was the birthday of one of her girlfriends, so they were taking her out to a dinner theater in Georgetown.

"How come you have to go?"

"I don't *have* to go." She was teasing the hair at the crown of her head. Nellie'd never seen her do that before. "It's just a nice break, that's all."

"Break from what?" The way she'd said it made Nellie feel bad. Break from her family, that's what she meant. From Nellie.

"The routine. You know, work, and then coming home and doing more work." She made her life sound so miserable.

"Dad does all the dishes. And the laundry, he even does that now. And I keep things picked up, plus I have to mind Henry all the time. He's the one, he never does a thing, and Ruth, she just leaves her dirty dishes in the sink and food all over the place. And nobody ever says a word to her. The minute you leave for work she turns on her air conditioner and all she does is talk on the phone the whole time."

Her mother had turned from the mirror. "Nellie?"

"What?" she stared back.

"What's wrong?"

"Nothing." She didn't dare blink for fear she'd cry.

"Are you . . . your period, is it—"

"No!"

"Well, something's wrong. Is it because I'm going out? It is, isn't it? Oh, hon, c'mere." She held out her arms, but Nellie wouldn't budge, so she sat down next to her. "I know, I'm gone all day, so when I come home you just want your mom here, right?" She hugged Nellie. "That's okay. I understand, especially with everything that's happened." She smelled of lilies.

She laid her head against Nellie's, which made her feel worse—selfish and mean. "Torrie Blaine, she's pregnant," she sputtered, and wasn't sure why, except maybe for needing some anchor to keep her mother in place as belonging to them instead of being her girlfriends' girlfriend. "And she wants Ruth to help her get rid of it, and Ruth doesn't know what to do because it's like what happened to you. The same thing."

She sighed, and Nellie was relieved to see the light gone from her eyes under their pale blue lids. Nellie had snatched her midflight from her carefree verve. She was Nellie's again, but now she was ashamed.

"Oh God," she sighed, getting up from the bed, and Nellie felt terrible. It had nothing to do with Torrie or Ruth or even her mother's going out. It was this growing knot of dread like the twins' robotic voice in her head. *Warning, warning.* Something bad was near, darkness gathering, and nothing could stop it.

A FEW DAYS later she was loading the dishwasher after dinner when the doorbell rang. Her father was scrubbing the spaghetti sauce pan, so he told her to see who it was.

"Your mom or dad home?" Detective Des La Forges asked through the front door screen. Instead of a shirt and tie, he wore a black T-shirt and baseball cap.

"They both are," she said, reaching for the latch.

"Whoa!" he said. "You shouldn't be opening the door like that."

"Why? Don't you want to come in?"

"What if I was a stranger or something?"

"But you're not."

"Well . . . technically, no." He had that overly stern look adults get when they suspect you're on to them. "But what you should do is go tell one of your parents I'm here."

"Okay." She paused, to see if he really meant it. Or if he was kidding.

"Go ahead. I'll wait," he said through the screen, then lifted his eyes, scanning the overhead clapboards, as if for danger.

"You didn't let him in? He's still out there?" her father said, shutting off the water.

"He wanted to," she tried to explain as he hurried out of the kitchen, drying his soapy hands on a dish towel. Her mother was already in the front hall, apologizing for his wait. No problem, that was fine, he told her as Nellie watched from the alcove into the study.

The trial was scheduled for the first week in October. He'd wanted them to hear it from him first even though official notification would be coming from Finn Cowie, the assistant DA in charge of the case. Cowie would fill them in on all the details. No one spoke. It seemed that until that moment her parents had been living an existence parallel to the reality of all that lay ahead. So what did this mean? Was there something they should be doing? These were her father's nebulous questions. Her mother's were more precise. Who in the family would have to testify? Would they all have to attend every day of the trial? How much time would she have to take off from work? She'd need to know because some of her clients booked monthly. When would the jury come to look at the apartment? Their old tenant wanted to move back in and if he had to wait because of that, he might change his mind. Just last night Lazlo had called to say he wanted the apartment.

"Lazlo's easy," her father said with a dismissive wave. "Don't worry about him. We'll work it out, one way or another."

"Really? And how do we do that?" Her mother's voice bristled.

"He can . . . stay with us! Up in one of the spare rooms," her father said, adding for the detective's benefit, "we've got enough of them. In fact, maybe that's what we should do, rent them all out, Pecks' boardinghouse. Little notoriety might help." He laughed. Her mother kept looking at him. "That's what happens," he continued on his faltering course. "Like the Biladoux house? In 1897, the niece, first she poisons the two cats and the dog, then she slips the same brew into her aunt and uncle's favorite stew—"

"Ben!" her mother gasped.

"But they never did prove it," Des La Forges said. "A gas leak, that's what they think happened."

"Gas leak! There was an empty arsenic bottle under her buggy seat," her father said, persisting in his details, his thin face flushed with the pleasure of these old tales he knew so well. "Millie Boden. Yes, that was her name, the niece. Six feet tall, and strong as a man. She'd walk down to—"

"Well, anyway," her mother interrupted, putting her hand on his arm. "We've taken up enough of your time," she said to the detective, her most gracious smile frozen in place. "We'll let you get on your way."

"Good seeing you," Des La Forges said, adding that he was on his way to a softball game. He was the pitcher and they were in the finals, which reminded Nellie's father of a team the hardware store used to sponsor. Won the league championship. Must have been '68 or '69. He'd been a kid, but he remembered how delighted his father had been. There was a picture of it somewhere, his father and the team with Johnny Hale holding the trophy.

She felt sorry for her father. Couldn't he tell Des La Forges wasn't interested? That he was just trying to be polite?

"Remember Johnny?" her father persisted, grinning. "The old barber?"

"Oh yeah, sure," Des La Forges said, quickly opening the door.

"As a matter of fact," her father said, "now that I think of it, Johnny's father, old Charlie Hale—you're too young, you wouldn't know him—but he did all the Biladoux yard work, and I remember my father talking about it, too, the arsenic, and how it was—"

"Ben," her mother implored. "Bob has to go, he just told us."

"Oh sure, sorry. All this talk about trials . . ." His voice trailed off.

"Puts us a little on edge, I guess," her mother said with a nervous laugh.

"Ah, who knows," Des La Forges said through the screen. "Maybe there won't even be a trial. Last I heard there was talk of a plea bargain. Pretty tight case they got."

After he left, her mother started to go upstairs, where she'd been mending sheets on her sewing machine.

"I didn't want to say anything, but I'm afraid the detective's facts are a little, shall we say, shaky? I know for a fact it was poison," Benjamin called after her, and she turned, looking down with an iciness that sent a long shiver through Nellie. "I'll send it to him tomorrow, a copy of the article. The old *Ledger*—they followed the trial every single day." His brow furrowed over a pensive smile. "I'll track it down. I know it's in there." He meant his files, musty records of all the obscure events of which he was the most devoted chronicler. "Take me a while, but I'll find it."

"You're serious, aren't you?"

"Of course I'm serious," he said with a cocky nod.

"Tell me something," she said, chewing her lip. "With everything that's happening, how on earth could this possibly matter?"

"It's a fact, and facts matter. The truth. That's all."

Maybe he was distracted. Maybe he was mentally riffling through files, but to Nellie his voice sounded distant, unconvincing, and she felt it again, that thing, like dampness underfoot, wanting to rise.

———

LAZLO HAD PUT up with all the snide remarks about his "hokey paintings and dead-end job," but it was James's deceit, the constant lies about his whereabouts and phone calls and strange e-mails that he couldn't take anymore. If James couldn't be in a monogamous relationship, then he wanted his old life back—peace of mind and self-respect. (*Monogamous*—it was obviously about being gay, and as Nellie ran around the side of house to her mother's herb garden, she made a mental note to look it up.)

It was early Saturday afternoon and Lazlo didn't have to be at the restaurant until 3:30. He and her mother were sitting in the rickety green rockers on the front porch sipping the peach ice tea he'd brought in a cooler. Hoping she hadn't missed anything, Nellie raced back up the steps with the warm sprigs of pineapple mint she'd been sent to get. She looked on smiling as her mother pinched off the stems and dropped the crinkly green-and-white striped leaves into each goblet of the cloudy brew. There was a glow about Lazlo, a motionless blur of dazzling energy that made her feel lighter and life seem easier in this perfect moment with her mother's gleaming Waterford, the fragrance of mint in the steamy air, and Lazlo in his bright, patch-plaid Bermuda shorts and polo shirt a shade of eggplant, and his wavy hair trimmed close. Even his narrow bracelet of woven leather was exactly right. No gaudy gold or jewels. It was just like the old days, having Lazlo here.

Benjamin was still at the store, her mother was telling Lazlo. This was the second day of the Springvale Merchants' Summer's End Bazaar. She hoped sales were good because they'd been trying to reduce inventory. She leaned forward, and he did, too, in their easy way of sharing confidences. Things were looking up: someone was very interested in buying the store, but please don't say anything, she added, already regretting telling him. No, no, of course he wouldn't, he assured her, and if only he'd known it was Bazaar Days, he would've gone down and bought some things for the apartment. Nellie couldn't imagine what. The sale items displayed on folding tables in front of the hardware store had looked pretty bleak, even to her. She'd worked there yesterday and this morning, and all she'd seen sold were a gray plastic funnel, two car mats, a dusty roll of bubble wrap, and a wooden window screen.

"I know Ben's just painted everything," Lazlo was saying. "But you know me, I like color. A little more zing maybe than moonbeam cream." He drew back his head and laughed. "Oh, oh, I know that look. I know what you're thinking. Lazlo's going to go way over the top here."

"No, I wasn't thinking that," her mother said.

"Actually, I'm thinking of yellow, kind of mangoey and warm but not orangey. Like that," he said, pointing to Nellie's shirt. "Nellie, we'll go to the paint store, and you'll wear that shirt. And after, we'll go down by the depot and get a lime fizz."

"Okay!" She jumped up from the step. Lazlo always had time for the things most adults didn't. Like charades and crazy eights and bicycling through the Harness Falls woods with lunch in their backpacks.

"Next week." He checked his cell phone. "I'm off Monday."

"Okay! Great!" she said. Finally, something to look forward to.

"The thing is, Lazlo," her mother began slowly. "I can't have you changing your mind again. I mean, if you and James patch things up, then where does that leave me?"

"That's not going to happen. Believe me!" Lazlo said, but with a long sigh that even Nellie recognized as wistful.

"You left us in kind of a lurch, you know that, don't you?" she said.

Don't! Nellie wanted to shout. *Don't spoil this! Please!*

"It was impulsive. Believe me, I've learned my lesson," he said.

"I never would've rented to . . . to Dolly, you know, to someone like that, but things were getting really tight and, oh God, what a mess that's turned into."

"Sandy!" Lazlo set his glass onto the round wicker table. "You're not blaming me for that, are you? Because I moved out?" His jaw clenched.

"No! I'm just saying, it's . . . it's just been really hard, that's all." She picked up her napkin and daubed her eyes, sniffling as Lazlo took her free hand and held it in both of his.

"I know. But you've gotta turn the page, Sandy."

"I know. I know, but, you see, then I had this other tenant. I was even going to let her move in with a cat, of all things, but then you said you were going to move back, so I told her no, and then you changed your mind, and by then it was too late. She'd found another place."

Miss Schiff. Nellie couldn't believe what she was hearing. Her mother was either crazy or a liar. Or maybe a crazy liar. A desperate crazy liar, apparently a good one, because now Lazlo was trying to convince her how absolutely sincere he was in his decision. In fact, he'd even sign a lease if she wanted him to, he said, hesitantly, as if expecting her to insist that wouldn't be necessary. It never had been before.

"Well, now that you mention it, that's probably a good idea. That way you're protected, too." She took a quick sip. "This is just the best tea. Isn't it, Nellie?" She gave a little cough behind her hand, trying to hide her discomfort.

"It's good," Nellie said. A weak response, but she had ruined the moment as surely as if she'd taken a knife to their hearts. She was embarrassed. From then on, she would regard her mother with distrust. And with an uneasy respect. Part of her understood. Somebody in the family had to get tough.

Chapter 18

———

EVERY DAY SHE CHECKED THE MAILBOX FOR A LETTER FROM Max. A week had passed since she'd written. She didn't think she'd said anything to offend him, but she wrote another letter. Mostly it was about Boone and how happy he was. She wrote about things she hadn't done but wished she had, like taking him for long runs through the woods and crashing through underbrush after him, even following him along an upended swamp maple that had fallen at an angle, lodged between two pines. She wrote about how he kept making her throw back slobbery tennis balls for him to retrieve, and about his diving into the mucky brook for sticks, then emerging in a triumphant muddy mess. She didn't mention his being tied to the abandoned truck for weeks or that the twins had taken him home. Or that he wasn't the least bit interested in her because Boone had long ago learned how to get by in this hard world: the truth, but what would have been the point?

Into her thoughts came one of those conversations a kid half listens to but doesn't quite get, the tangled strands now suddenly making sense. Her father had been telling Lazlo about the historian's responsibility to recognize the difference between literal truth and ideal truth. When it came to Boone, she had chosen the latter, a story of life as it should and might still be, so that Max wouldn't give up hope.

Some things were absolutely true. Charlie was the same, she wrote, except for an outbreak of shingles that finally sent him to the doctor. Wanting it to be a long letter, one that would help pass the time in his lonely cell, she wrote about how Lazlo had moved in, and how Henry had half the roof done on the tree house, and even though Max didn't know him, how Tenley Humboldt had installed a floodlight aimed directly at the tree house. It came on with a motion detector, so they'd be illuminated if they went into the tree house after dark, which was a really strange sensation, like being in a space ship. She told him a little about Ruth and the reason she was finally acting human again, which was because Patrick Dellastrando had practically told her to get lost. She'd gone from heartbreak to grievous insult, now to a state of general dreariness. Nothing could make her too angry or too happy. She was flat-lining through the days, off to the takeout window every afternoon, then home at night no later than nine to shower off the vestiges of hot fudge and strawberry sauce before stopping in Nellie's room to philosophize about how life sucked and what a raw deal she'd gotten, having a father who didn't care if she even existed. Nellie even told Max about Danny Brigham but not that she'd intercepted his letter to Ruth.

She also wrote about how much fun it was hanging out with Krissie Potek again. Not only didn't Krissie mind Henry always tagging along, but she actually thought he was funny, a quality lost on Nellie lately. She thought Max would find it interesting that Krissie was a good fisherman ("or is it *fisherwoman?*" she wrote, she wasn't sure). Krissie had been fishing with her father and older brother ever since she could remember. She said she'd asked her father if Nellie could come next time they went, but so far it hadn't happened. Krissie had admitted that while her father liked teaching, he didn't really like kids that weren't his own too much. So what do you think that's all about? she asked Max, hoping to engage him, and, if not, at least make her letter seem more conversational. She pictured him dragging in from the hot, shadeless prison yard (doing what? she wanted to ask, but figured she'd save that for her next letter) and looking forward to stretching out on his bunk and reading her letter again, probably for the third or fourth time that day. Maybe no one else cared, but he'd know she did.

"Well, anyway," she wrote on the twelfth page, "school starts in three weeks." *And the trial, a couple weeks after,* though she hadn't written that, but probably would in her next letter. Her family might be dreading the trial, but it had occurred to her that Max might be looking forward to it. Given the chance to finally tell what had really happened that day, he'd be moving that much closer to freedom.

Jessica's calls wanting Nellie to go hang out with her or asking to "come here" had gotten so persistent that, now, everyone checked caller ID before answering the phone. The message box—squawk box, her father called it—was filled with her plaintive begging and infuriated demands that Nellie please, please call her back. "Goddamn you, Nellie!" she finally screamed in one. "I know you're standing right there listening to this, you selfish bitch. Pick up the phone! Pick up the goddamn phone!"

A brutal mistake and Jessica knew it, immediately calling back, and for the rest of the day leaving messages of apology and regret, but it was too late. The entire Peck family had played the message, even Nellie's mother, who listened in shocked silence. When Nellie played it for Krissie, she hugged her arms and said, "That's scary. That's really scary."

"She's like the last person I'd be scared of," Nellie laughed.

"She's just so mean. Her feelings, they're not, like, normal. Like when she hurts people, that funny look she gets," she said, which surprised Nellie.

Krissie was usually making excuses for Jessica. Because Mrs. Potek and Mrs. Cooper were good friends, it was a loyalty Nellie'd had to swallow. But apparently not anymore. Krissie began telling her how last May, Mrs. Cooper had complained to the high school principal when Mr. Potek refused to let Patrice Cooper take a makeup test when she got a B on her math final. Mrs. Cooper said Patrice had told Mr. Potek right before the final how sick she felt, but he had made her take it anyway. That B had kept Patrice from being class valedictorian, and the complaint had gone into Mr. Potek's record.

"You're kidding." Nellie couldn't wait to tell Ruth.

"My mother couldn't believe it. She was, like, really upset."

"I bet."

"My father said she's not the nice, sweet lady everyone thinks." Krissie grimaced. "But you can't tell anyone that," she added, wide-eyed. "He'd kill me."

"Don't worry, I won't," Nellie said, eagerly repaying the confidence with her tale of Jessica's sending Henry home so she could show her Louis's stash of pot and then how Mrs. Cooper had flipped out on her with Jessica giving it right back, and Nellie feeling trapped like she was in some kind of asylum where the guards were as crazy as the patients.

"Really?" Krissie whispered, her long black hair falling across her pale face.

"Yeah," she whispered back. With Jessica out of the picture, it would be good having Krissie to herself.

"Wow. So maybe that's what's wrong," Krissie said. "Maybe they're all screwed up and Jessica, she's the only normal one."

"I don't get your logic."

"I know," Krissie admitted. "But now I feel bad for her."

"Well, don't," she said, and would wish she hadn't.

SHE'D QUICKLY FOUND her seat in the back row. The first few minutes of class were noisy with students' looking for their seat assignments. Mrs. Duffy was their homeroom teacher. She stood by the door scanning her chart to make sure no one switched seats. Mrs. Duffy was young and pretty but really tough. And very pregnant. Nellie tried looking everywhere but at her big, round belly, which just didn't seem right somehow for a teacher. No matter how hard Nellie tried not to, she kept thinking about how she'd gotten that way. Roy and Rodney Shelby came in and sat next to her in the back row. She smiled, but they stared straight ahead. "Hey!" she said across the aisle. "How's Boone doing?" she asked Roy, who was closer. He nodded, then hunched over his notebook. Charlie had told her mother that Mrs. Shelby had asked if they could keep Boone for good. Charlie had said he didn't care. Unfortunately, Charlie hadn't been caring about much lately. It wasn't just the shingles, her mother said, but the trial and having to testify. Nellie knew how nervous she was starting to feel.

"What's that?" She leaned across the aisle to see Roy's drawing. He ripped the paper from his notebook and passed it to her. A quick sketch, but it was a perfect likeness of Boone with his head tilted to one side. She'd forgotten the twins' talent for drawing.

"Excuse me, Miss Peck. If you don't mind," Mrs. Duffy said, already halfway up the aisle, with her hand out.

"It's just a dog," she said, eyes level with her belly as she snatched the paper. "His name's Boone," she added, hoping to defuse Mrs. Duffy's anger, but she was already crumpling it up. Nellie shook her head in blurry disbelief, so angry the lenses on her glasses were fogging up.

Krissie glanced back with a sympathetic pout.

"There'll be no notes passed in this class, thank you very much!" Mrs. Duffy declared, waddling to the front of the room. She dropped the ball of paper into the wastebasket. "And from now on, save your drawings for art class, Mr. Shelby." She glanced at the little squares on her chart. "Roy, that is."

Roy squirmed, shrinking miserably into his seat. To Nellie's knowledge, and they'd been in school together since first grade, neither twin had ever been reprimanded by a teacher.

"Thanks anyway," Nellie whispered, but he stared straight ahead.

The bell rang and Mrs. Duffy checked her chart. One empty seat. The intercom sputtered on as Mr. Perkins, the new principal, began a staticky speech welcoming everyone, himself included, to Timmony Middle School, an experience he likened to an astronaut returning to Earth from the moon, and if it was a joke, he'd either forgotten the punch line or lost his train of thought. Nobody seemed to get it. Even Mrs. Duffy looked puzzled. Then, as the Pledge of Allegiance was ending, the door opened. Hand high over her belly, Mrs. Duffy looked back as her tardy student slipped behind his desk with a wink.

Not only hadn't Bucky Saltonstall gone back to wherever he'd come from (by then Nellie'd lost track of his tall tales), but he was enrolled at Timmony. In eighth grade, team B, her homeroom. After the announcements, Mrs. Duffy called Bucky up to her desk. As she spoke, she sniffed at him. He kept shrugging.

"Excuse me, class," she said, getting up. She and Bucky left the room. Twelve minutes into the very first day of school he was being escorted to the assistant principal's office, late and smelling of cigarettes. His turned-out pockets contained only a book of matches, and a fifty-dollar bill. Following school board–mandated protocol, Mr. Hadley drowned the matches in a glass of water. The money was another matter. Arriving within minutes, wearing a yellow rain poncho over her housecoat, Bucky's grandmother explained how she must have given him the fifty by mistake, as lunch money, thinking it was a five-dollar bill. Bucky said he'd walked to school behind two construction guys who'd been smoking, which is how the smell must've gotten on him. Obviously, his grandmother agreed, sniffing his head. There should be laws against smoking near children, she declared.

Bucky looked handsome in his new school clothes. His thick, sun-tipped hair had been trimmed, and in this new setting Nellie was impressed by his manners. As the day went on, even Mrs. Duffy seemed to be softening a little. Bucky was very smart and way ahead of practically everyone in math, except, of course, for Roy and Rodney, runners-up in last year's state math tournament. "Yes, sir or no, ma'am," Bucky would answer teachers, a maturity she found stirring. His voice was deeper than the other boys' and he was a head taller than most. He sat by himself at lunch and ate slowly, all the while looking around. He seemed so self-contained, at times even mildly amused, more like an observant adult than a loner. At recess he cruised the playground, hands in his pockets, moving from group to group, pausing to watch them playing basketball, soccer, Hacky Sack. Nellie was playing foursquare with Krissie, her cousin Betsy Potek, and Brianna Hall, the most beautiful girl in eighth grade. Jessica stood on the sidelines, demanding to play, even though she knew she had to wait her turn. Their ball handling was flawless. Nobody wanted to suffer Jessica's tirades once she got in, her inevitable name calling and cries of cheating.

"Come on! The bell's gonna ring!" she yelled. "You're not being fair!"

Arms crossed, Bucky had been leaning against the chain-link fence, watching. Really watching Brianna, Nellie could tell.

"Hey, look out!" he cried, jumping at Nellie, causing her to drop the ball. "Your turn," he told Jessica, who yanked at the crotch of her tight pants and ran into her square, laughing.

At the end of the day, Nellie lingered outside the classroom door. As soon as Mrs. Duffy left, she slipped back in and rummaged through the wastebasket. The crumpled drawing was at the bottom. She smoothed it out and put it in a notebook. She was going to send it to Max.

NELLIE AND KRISSIE were headed downtown. She had a dollar in her pocket and an hour left before she had to be home for Henry. "What a jerk," she said, meaning Bucky.

"He was just tryna help Jessica," Krissie said.

"Bucky Saltonstall never helps anybody but himself, believe me."

"Well, he seemed nice to me."

"Oh, God," Nellie groaned, hearing a familiar voice.

"Wait up!" Jessica called, running to catch up. "I was looking for you guys. I even went in the park." Panting, she tried to catch her breath. Her cheeks were bright red. She kept pulling at the back seam of her pants as she walked. Other than the weight she'd gained since Nellie'd last seen her, little had changed. She acted as if nothing had happened between them. She couldn't stop talking, mostly about Bucky. She'd seen him smoking in the park this morning and then again a few minutes ago, as soon as he got off school grounds, and guess where he'd hidden his cigarettes? In a French dictionary.

"He showed me." She hurried to keep up. "He, like, cut the pages in the shape of the pack."

"Ooh, that's original," Nellie said, rolling her eyes.

"He's gonna get caught. It's just a matter of time," Krissie warned in her teacher's-daughter voice.

"He drinks, too," Jessica said. "Beer. In his yard he's got this, like, underground thing. He dug it out and put a cooler in, and that's where he keeps it."

"What a loser," Nellie groaned.

"No, he's not," Jessica said with a scornful look.

"Right." Nellie quickened her pace.

"You're just jealous, that's your problem," Jessica said.

Just then a horn tooted. Mrs. Cooper's silvery blue BMW pulled up alongside. "What do you think you're doing?" Her face was gray.

"I'm going with them. Downtown," Jessica added in a weak whine.

"I have been sitting outside of that school for the last fifteen minutes waiting for you. And then I went inside looking for you. And now you're late."

Late for Jessica's therapy, Nellie knew. It had always been on Mondays, right after school.

"I forgot!"

"Get in the car!"

"Well, if I'm late, then just call—I can go another day!" Jessica said.

"Jessica." Mrs. Cooper fortified herself with a deep breath. "Get in this car and get in right now, and let's not have any problems about this. Let's just move on from here. Okay?" she said with a forced smile and warning eyes. She had yet to acknowledge the other girls.

"No, just make another appointment, that's all, and then I can—"

"Jessica—"

"—go with them. I never have a chance to be with my—"

"Stop it!"

"—friends, and now you won't let me."

"Are you going to make me get out of this car?"

Yes, Nellie thought, *please get out and wrestle her to the ground, so we can be on our way.*

"I just want to go with my friends, that's all," Jessica whined with a punch on the car door.

"Well, maybe you can all go tomorrow. How does that sound, girls?" Mrs. Cooper asked, the steel leash of her gaze locked on her daughter. "Sodas'll be on me!"

"Okay," Krissie agreed in a wan voice.

"I'll pick you all up after school. It'll be fun!" Mrs. Cooper called out as Jessica climbed, still whining, into the front seat.

"I can't!" Nellie called back the minute the door lock clicked. "I've gotta do stuff. Thanks though!" Ignoring Mrs. Cooper's glare, she waved. She had to get free of Jessica's control somehow. Jessica might not get it, but surely her mother would.

"See! I told you!" Jessica was shrieking as they drove off.

As always, the first thing Nellie did after school was bring in the mail. Still no letter from Max. But here on this warm September day right after the advertising circulars and bills was a pale green envelope postmarked Australia. The return address sticker said Blair Brigham.

She ran into the kitchen, turned on the electric kettle, and waved the envelope through the rising steam. The flap curled quickly and she peeled open the envelope. Inside was one page of the same pale green stationery.

Her hands shook as she read the grim, black-inked script.

Dear Ruth,

   I am Mrs. Daniel Brigham. The reason I'm writing is because I'm the one who opened your letter. It was the first I knew of your claim against my husband. In a way I wish I hadn't because now I'm in the uncomfortable position of having to tell you that Daniel doesn't want to hear from you again. He says he has already told you this in his letter answering yours, but you keep writing anyway. You say you have a lot of problems at home, but we are in no position to help you, financially or emotionally. And there is also the matter of not really knowing who you are or what you want. If you continue sending letters here, we will be forced to turn them over to our lawyer.

Sincerely,
Blair H. Brigham

"Ohmygod, ohmygod, ohmygod," Nellie panted, taking the stairs so fast her glasses slid down her nose and she kept tripping. Ruth would be home soon. She locked her bedroom door, dropped to her knees, and frantically clawed out dust and shoes from her closet floor. She lifted the strip of linoleum, then slid the letter under the loose board into the dark, gritty cavity that now held two. And if she didn't get Ruth to stop writing to Danny Brigham there'd be more, or worse, maybe even a lawsuit. She couldn't very well give her this letter and not the first one. Here was the rueful liar's conundrum: the entire truth or none at all. But maybe she'd think the reason she'd never gotten Daniel Brigham's letter was because it had gotten lost in the mail. Sometimes that happened. Just last week hadn't Nellie heard her father telling her mother that maybe Mr. Cooper's copy of the signed purchase and sale agreement had gotten delayed in the mail. But then again, did she want to be responsible for her sister's unhappiness? She knew how hurt *she* had felt reading Mrs. Brigham's letter. She couldn't imagine how painful it would be for Ruth to read. It might just push her over the edge, though exactly where and to what depths Nellie couldn't begin to fathom, beyond the gleaming, dagger-point, paralyzing certainty that one way or another she was going to be in more trouble than she'd ever been in her entire life.

Downstairs, the front door banged shut, then came the thump of Ruth's tossed backpack onto the floor. Nellie crawled back into the closet and pulled up the linoleum. She'd just destroy both letters and pray that'd be the end of it. But no, that was fear. This was no time for panic. She had to stay calm. She had to get tough. She needed to think. She dropped the linoleum and shoved the shoes back in. She'd learned her lesson. Never again would she interfere in someone else's life. Certain things had to follow their own course. Their own destiny.

Chapter 19

——

"IT'S JUST BEEN OUR BEST YEAR. GARDENING, I MEAN," Miss Humboldt added, filling the doorway and breathing hard. The walk over had winded her. She had to get right back, she said, when Nellie's mother invited her in. Sweat dripped down the sides of her face. She kept shaking the neck of her muumuu and puffing air into it.

Nellie's mother was admiring the two sturdy trug baskets overflowing with zucchini, summer squash, bell peppers, radishes, cucumbers, pole beans, and tomatoes so richly red they didn't look real. "Look at the size of this eggplant," she marveled, then held it to her cheek. "And still warm from the sun." She was touched and deeply grateful.

With no extra money for back-to-school expenses, Nellie's mother had done something she'd vowed would never happen in this family. She had gotten a credit card. Finally! Never had Nellie been so proud as the moment in the shoe department at JCPenney when her mother opened her thin red wallet, and from one of three slots, the other two containing paltry library card and driver's license, she removed that sleek plastic ticket to treasure. MasterCard. Its slow, reluctant passage from her mother's hand to the clerk's came with a swell of triumphant music. Or maybe it was just the soaring of Nellie's heart, because now, finally, they were like everyone else. Whatever their necessities or desires, they could now be satisfied on a whim, at the drop of a hat—just hop in the car and get it, no more living according to the stingy dictates of the checking account balance. Nellie had spent the last few days poring over catalogs, earmarking pages, circling item numbers, and roaming the aisles of Walgreens' breathless with the possibility of it all. She had new faith in her parents.

Her mother offered Miss Humboldt a cup of coffee. It was Sunday morning and she'd just made a fresh pot. But Miss Humboldt couldn't stay. She had to get right back. It was Tenley. His nerves. But at least he was back on his medication. She was hoping and praying he'd stay on it this time.

"Same as always," she said when Nellie's mother asked how she was doing. She said she was looking forward to the cooler weather. "The summers are just getting too hard what with the yard work and the gardens, and . . . all the other things . . ." Her voice trailed off.

"I know," her mother agreed. "And this year with so many hours at the salon I've barely kept up with the weeding. In fact, that's on today's list, right, Nell?"

"Right." Nellie nodded. First time she'd heard of it, but she knew that bright, burbly lilt was trying to fill dead air.

"And trimming the front shrubs," her mother went on, peering at her now as she fretted about forsythia gone wild and low-hanging tree limbs. "Everything's getting so overgrown. And all of a sudden there's all this bittersweet everywhere I look. And you know how—"

"Sandy?"

"Yes? What? What is it, Louisa?"

Miss Humboldt's face was buried in her hands. Her great shoulders trembled.

"Nellie," her mother said, "go . . . just . . . go somewhere . . . please."

So she darted around the corner.

This was just the worst thing she'd ever had to do, Miss Humboldt was saying. Even as a child Tenley had been single-minded, obsessive, paranoid—call it what you will—but she'd always known how to handle him, which usually consisted of hearing him out, letting him have his say, however unreasonable or angry it might be, and often was. And for years he'd listened and let her talk him down. But not anymore. Not since that terrible night, being attacked in his own yard, and then, to confirm his worst fears, the slaughter of that poor young woman right next door, here, in this very house.

"Slaughter?" her mother said. "You mean killed. Murdered."

Same difference, Nellie thought, "But that's how Tenley sees it. And now he thinks there's more to come. He's afraid!" Miss Humboldt cried. "He's absolutely terrified!"

"But they've got him, the man, the person that did it. He's in jail."

"I know, and I keep telling Tenley, but he won't listen. And now . . . now he's got a gun," she said with a gasp.

"Oh, my God," her mother said. "Have you called the police?"

"Well, no. I can't. It's perfectly legal. I mean, he filled out all the paperwork. He's got his permit."

"But that doesn't mean he should have a gun. Especially when he's so . . . so troubled."

"I know. I know! And I keep thinking I'll just take it, that's what I'll do, I'll hide it, but he's got this holster. He wears it. Night and day! Even when he goes to bed. But I'm working on it. I watch him. Every minute. All the time, believe me. He goes into the bathroom and I tiptoe around the corner, and I wait. I listen and I wait for him to come out. I just feel so . . . furtive."

Nellie knew the feeling well, cheekbone hard against the door frame.

"Where is he now?"

"Asleep, thank goodness. But not for long. He never is."

"Are you afraid, Louisa? Afraid he'll hurt you?"

"Me? No! Oh no! It's your family, the children. When they're in the tree house. I'm afraid one of these times Tenley's going to . . . to startle. That's why, that's why I'm here. To ask you to get rid of it. Please. Ever since it's gone up, it's just been one thing after another."

"But it's just a tree house," her mother said in a faltering voice. "The children . . . they play there . . . Henry built it . . . he's worked so hard on it . . . I can't imagine making him take it down. And I know that was a terrible thing, the night when that boy, the things he said, and then throwing all those candy bars at your brother . . . of course he was upset, but the children, Henry and Nellie, they didn't do it. They—"

"It's the tree house. The fact of it. And I don't think we should have to be subjected to it anymore." Miss Humboldt's tone grew shrill. "Especially Tenley, not right now, not when he's so fragile. And as much as I hate saying it, Sandy, it is an eyesore."

There was a moment's silence. "I don't know what to say." Her mother sounded hurt.

Say you're as nutty as your brother, and that's your problem, not ours, Nellie telepathically urged.

"He says if you don't take it down, then he's calling the building inspector."

"Louisa!"

"I'm sorry, but I have to be loyal."

"Well, here then," her mother said, handing back the produce-laden baskets. "I don't want them."

IN A WAY, Max had written back. He wasn't allowed to send her a letter, but in his to Charlie, he said how much he'd enjoyed hearing all about Nellie and her family. He told Charlie that he appreciated the time she was spending with Boone. He really missed Boone and even dreamed of him. Sometimes the dreams seemed so real he'd try not to wake up from them. It almost felt like being with him again, the two of them tramping through the woods or out in the boat, floating down the river, even watching the doodlebugs make circles on the water. He said to thank Nellie for the picture of Boone. He'd hung it up.

"Just that. The last line," Charlie said, when she asked if Max had said anything about the trial.

The last line read, "Can you please get my money in the box? I need some for a shirt and tie for court. Can you give it to my lawyer? Thanks."

"Did you? Did you give it to him?" she asked.

Charlie shrugged. "Don't know what he's talking about."

"In that trunk, the metal box, you told me there was money. You said you took it so the cops wouldn't."

Charlie grunted in his struggle to get comfortable in his recliner. His chest was bare and surprisingly bony. The mere touch of cloth against the shingles was unbearable. "I told you the cops took it, that's what they do."

"No. You said you did so they wouldn't take—"

"Go on, get outta here. I don't wanna hear anymore!"

"That's not right, and you know it's not. What's he gonna wear, his jail stuff?"

He sat up and pointed his taloned, yellow finger at her. "I don't give a—" He caught himself. "It's not my problem, okay? He did what he did and now he can damn well pay for it, goddammit, bringing all this shit down on me. I got enough problems. And tell your mother, next time, send some other kid. I've had it with you and your mouth."

"But he didn't do it. I know he didn't!"

"Oh, you do, huh?"

"Yes. I do."

"How?"

"Because. I do."

They stared at each other. A grin twitched at the damp corners of his mouth.

"I know some things." Maybe Charlie did, too, she thought. Between them maybe they could help Max. She spoke slowly. "Things nobody else does."

"Yeah? Like what?" His shrewd eyes narrowed as if to haggle over the price of some scrap metal she'd brought him.

She folded her arms. She had to be sure she could trust him. An entire family's fate was at stake. Her father's admonition had taken deep root in her conscience, its burden heavier with each new day. But what about Max? nagged the constant voice in her head. Wasn't his future just as important? Last week the district attorney's office had called her father. They wanted to talk to her. It was becoming harder and harder to pretend none of this was happening. Or that it didn't involve her.

"Like, about her," she said. "Dolly Bedelia."

"What?" He snickered. "What d'ya know, little miss smart-ass, that nobody else does?"

If he hadn't looked at her like that, leering almost, if he hadn't called her that name, she would've told him, right then and there. And it would've been over. For once and for all.

"Never mind," she said.

In order to avoid Jessica, Nellie'd been taking a completely different route home from school, even though it meant walking alone. As much as she missed Krissie, who lived near Jessica, at least she wouldn't be constantly reminded of the pain she was about to cause, not just to Jessica but her entire family. She tried to tell herself that in some ways Jessica deserved whatever the fallout would be. She'd always been mean, but usually to others, though Nellie'd long ago given up making excuses for her. She was probably the most selfish person she knew, though again, not with Nellie. And as she guiltily realized, Jessica's generosity had been their surest bond since they'd been little, sharing her toys, her television, and for a time, buying Nellie whatever she wanted—candy; magazines; water balloons; magic tricks; once, even a new backpack instead of Ruth's shabby hand-me-down—until Nellie's mother put a stop to it. As much as Nellie wanted to be strong, Jessica had always cultivated her weaknesses. And she'd resented her for it. Until the day last spring when she discovered Major Fairbairn's manual.

She'd read it so often that now whenever she summoned the major's words, the voice in her head was clipped and British:

There will be some who will be shocked by the methods advocated here. To them I say, "In war you cannot afford the luxury of squeamishness. . . . We've got to be tough to win, and we've got to be ruthless—tougher and more ruthless than our enemies."

Every civilian, man or woman, who ever walks a deserted road at midnight, or goes in fear of his life in the dark places of a city, should acquaint himself with these methods. Once mastered, they will instill the courage and self-reliance that come with the sure knowledge that you are the master of any dangerous situation with which you may have to cope . . . once closed with your enemy, give every ounce of effort you can muster, and victory will be yours.

As she marched along, she wasn't sure who her enemy was, but she couldn't let it be herself.

Bucky had just caught up. He was smoking. She walked faster.

"Hey, what's the big rush?" he said, easily keeping pace. She was weighed down by a backpack sagging with books while his hung flat and empty on his back.

"Your smoke—it's corroding my lungs."

"Jesus," he said, taking a last drag before flicking the butt into the gutter.

He was complaining about his gym teacher. Mr. Feldman had caught him sneaking out of class, so he told Bucky to run five laps around the track. Bucky had refused. He said he had a heart murmur.

"So he goes, 'Well if you do, nobody told me!' The asshole. 'Well,' I go, 'I just did, didn't I?' So he goes, 'Sorry, Bucko, that's just not good enough.' 'Jesus Christ,' I go. 'What d'ya want, a fucking X-ray?' which totally pisses him off, so he gives me a week of fucking dentention. Jesus Christ!"

"Watch your mouth, okay, Bucky?"

His hand flew to his mouth. "Are you fucking serious?" he laughed.

With that, she turned and stepped off the curb, right into the passing traffic. Horns blared and brakes screeched, but she didn't care. Courage. As long as she was the master of any dangerous situation, no harm could come to her.

"What're you tryna do?" bellowed the driver of a red plumbing van.

The right thing, she knew as she reached the other side.

Blinders, that was the trick. Ignore all threats. Forge ahead. Sweat poured down her sides and her heart was pounding, but with elation, not fear.

"That was smart." Bucky had crossed and was walking beside her.

"Shut up."

"How come you hate me so much?"

"I don't hate you. I hate the stuff you do, that's all."

"Kinda the same thing, don't you think?"

She didn't answer. Their sneakers made sticky *plat-plat* sounds over the recently hot-topped sidewalk.

"I do have a heart murmur, you know." He coughed and patted his chest.

"So does 10 percent of the population."

"Who told you that?"

"I read. You should try it sometime."

"Yeah, you don't have TV, right? That's what Jessica said. Your family, they're like—" He wiggled his fingers. "—out there."

Her first impulse was to shove him off the sidewalk.

"But that's okay. Hey! *I'm* a freak. I like freaks. Long as they don't think they're better than me."

"See ya," she said stopping in front of her father's store.

"I'll come with you. I need some nails." He held out his arms. "For the crucifixion."

"It's not open." She stood in the doorway, blocking him.

"Yeah, what's that all about? Jessica said your father's stalking them. They see his name and they won't answer the phone." His grin was like Charlie's, hungry and snide.

"Jessica ever tell you about *her* father?"

"No, what?"

"He's . . . an asshole!" she blurted, shaken by how close she'd come.

"Hey, watch your pretty mouth," Bucky whispered, holding her arm and pulling her against him. Just as his mouth touched hers, she drove her *"knee quickly upwards into* [her] *opponent's testicles."*

"Fuck!" he moaned, doubled over as she ran up the street, best she could, under her shifting burden of books, praying her father hadn't seen anything, or worse, that Bucky wasn't staggering into the store begging for help.

Chapter 20

—

NELLIE'S FATHER HAD TAKEN HENRY'S SIDE. HER MOTHER wanted the tree house torn down immediately. Calling it an eyesore had been Miss Humboldt's master stroke. It had become another reminder of Sandy Peck's connection not just to the junkyard but to all things unseemly. She now despised it as much as the Humboldts did. The tree house would stay, Benjamin declared. It in no way endangered the Humboldts or impinged on their property. Henry's hard work was not going to be in vain just because they found it aesthetically displeasing. Part of her father's stubborn stand came from his own frustration. Everything had stalled, not just selling the store but getting his life's work published. Luminosity Press had finally written back. They would publish the history, but in three volumes because of its length, at a cost to her father that was three times higher than their initial "guesstimate."

It was early evening and her father was out in the yard with Lazlo. They were sitting in the pale blue Adirondack chairs Lazlo had brought with him. He had moved in last week after painting the apartment in parrot greens and mango tones. At that point, her mother would have agreed to fuchsia, black—any color—as long as there was rent money coming in. Lazlo had refinished the hardwood floors himself. His plan had been to retile the bathroom, but two days after his move, the new manager at the restaurant fired him. Her mother was shaken, but Lazlo was philosophical, even buoyed by his misfortune. It was karma. Now he could devote himself to his art. Not to worry, he assured her mother, he could live on his savings, for a year anyway. And even better, he could help with the jewelry parties. In fact, they could be partners. She wanted a partner about as much as she wanted an unemployed tenant but couldn't tell him that, so, for now, the jewelry business would be on hold.

Both men were sipping white wine. Nellie sprawled on the back steps, eating a pear. Henry sat in his tree house for no other reason than to justify its existence. Ruth was in her room doing homework. She was starting off this school year the way she always did. Determined to be an excellent student, reading every assignment, copying over her notes. Nellie gave her until Halloween, if that, before she fell by her well-rutted wayside. Nellie was the student in the family. No one ever had to check her homework or call school asking to speak to her teachers. And, but for his daydreaming, Henry would have been right up there with her. Her mother was still at work. Frederic's was doing all the models' hair for the Springvale Hospital Ladies Auxiliary Fashion Show that night. Her mother had agreed to work, only to find out later it was for charity. She wouldn't be paid. Not one penny, she'd grumbled on her way out the door. But it's for such a good cause, Nellie's father called after her. She hadn't answered.

Lazlo's easel stood by his chair. Until the sun began to set, he'd been sketching the tree house. Now, with nightfall crouched in the cooling shadows and a few crickets chirping weakly, Nellie was remembering how serene she always found the company of these two peaceful men.

Her father had been talking about his childhood. More and more lately, her mother had little patience for these slowly spun out reminiscences. Just the other day she'd rolled her hand for him to get to the point. Nellie hadn't been sure if he even noticed, but she'd found it as alarming as her father's description of the flood years ago: water seeping in under the door.

Now he was telling Lazlo about the Humboldts' wanting the tree house torn down. Lazlo remembered running into Louisa Humboldt on the street a few times. But in his three and a half years here, he'd never met her brother. Tenley was very private, her father said. Always had been.

"Probably just kids he hates," Lazlo said. "Not the tree house."

"Maybe. He took his share of abuse as a kid, I'll tell you that."

"Yeah, well, growing up's hard enough, but try being gay. I mean, talk about a square peg in a round world."

"I know, couldn't've been easy. But I don't think that's Tenley's problem."

"Problem? Oh, that's very enlightened of you." Lazlo sounded hurt. He was convinced that's why he'd been fired.

"I'm sorry, but you know what I mean."

"I guess," Lazlo sighed. For a moment there was only the faint chirping.

"Anyway," her father continued. "Tenley was one of those kids, you know, just always out of his element. If he ran, he'd trip over his own two feet. You'd throw him the ball, and it'd hit him in the face. Seems like he was always running home, crying. Then he just stopped coming around. I don't know, I always felt bad, as if he blamed me or something."

"Probably did. Blamed you and everyone else he thought fit in better than he did. The pain you go through as a kid—half the time you don't even know why. Then, by the time you do, it's too late. Too deep," Lazlo said, tapping his chest.

Nellie sensed he meant himself as well. She watched the bats swooping close to the tree house.

"Maybe you're right," her father agreed.

"So just go talk to him," Lazlo said. He was looking up at the tree. "I would've given anything for that when I was a kid."

"Oh, well," her father said with a slap of his thigh.

"A place to feel safe in," Lazlo was saying.

You're safe here, Lazlo, she wanted her father to say. As safe as anyone would feel, living in a crime scene, though that wouldn't occur to her until days later.

Suddenly there was a loud bang, and Henry scurried down the ladder from the tree house. Her father and Lazlo jumped to their feet. It had been a car backfiring, not Tenley Humboldt "startling."

IT WOULD BE a peace mission. On Saturday morning her father announced that they were all going to walk over to the Humboldts' and discuss "the matter of the tree house." They would present their case neighbor to neighbor. Her mother lowered the newspaper.

"You mean me?" she asked.

"Yes, all of us. What I'd like," her father explained with a nod, "is for Henry to state his reasons for building the tree house and then Nellie—"

"Please, Ben, stop it. Don't we have enough to worry about?"

"That's exactly my point. Let's defuse the situation. Handle it in a civilized manner. I've known the Humboldts my entire life. There's no reason for this kind of rancor."

"Nellie." She took a deep breath. "You and Henry, go make your beds, okay?" She was struggling either not to cry or not to lose her temper. Or both.

Damn. Nellie didn't want to leave the kitchen. This promised to be a blowout, no two ways about it. But Henry wanted no part of it. He ran upstairs and closed his bedroom door. Nellie lingered on the stairway. She intercepted Ruth on her sleepy way down. She was still in her nightgown. Nellie could hear them, but not what they were saying. Ruth hunched behind her on the top step, their cheeks against the balustrade. The muffled volley suddenly stopped.

"Who are you?" her mother suddenly cried. "I don't even know who you are anymore! Do you even know what's going on? Do you care? We have no money for anything! We're involved in a murder trial, a murder trial, Ben, and all you can think about is that damn tree house out there?"

"Sandy!" her father called as a door slammed.

"Poor Mom," Ruth sighed.

"What do you mean?" Nellie asked.

"It's like she's just seeing it all for the first time."

"All what?"

"Like." She winced the wince of the obvious. "Like, Ben."

"What?"

"C'mon, Nellie, get real, will you? He's, like, from another planet. You think that's how fathers are? They just let everything go to hell like that?"

"Shut up, Ruth! Just shut up!"

"You're the one that asked me," she sniffed past her down the stairs.

"He's your father, too, you know!" Nellie spat after her. And with that, Ruth glanced back but clearly knew better than to say what she was thinking. As did Nellie.

THEY DID GO to the Humboldts'—Nellie, her father, and Henry. Miss Humboldt's chin quivered as her father asked if they might speak with her and Tenley. She left them on the porch while she checked to see if her brother was up to a visit.

"That's a golden chain tree," her father said, pointing to the pretty tree next to the steps. "Don't ever eat the seeds though. They're poisonous."

As if we would: Nellie and Henry exchanged glances. The argument with her mother had drained all fervor from her father's high-minded mission. But now it was a matter of principle. And so there could be no backing down—even if he was nervous, which Nellie was surprised to see that he was.

Returning, Miss Humboldt opened the door and led them into the blindingly beautiful living room. In the far corner Tenley sat cross-legged on an enormous white chair. His folded arms hugged a gold-tasseled pillow close to his chest. He was wearing a silky black shirt and silky black pants and on his feet what looked like ballet slippers, soft and black. His hair fell loosely to his shoulders.

The three of them sat on the long curved sofa across from him. Miss Humboldt lowered herself into the chair next to her brother. Her father began by apologizing for not having come here first and telling them that Henry wanted to build a tree house. And once Henry got started, the project had taken on a life of its own, the way such things do when you're young. Just eight years old, her father said, and Tenley's grip tightened on the pillow. In any event, her father continued, the tree house was there, and he was sure, given their long relationship through childhood till now as neighbors, as well as being the longest residents on the street, that they could come to some mutual agreement here. For instance, if privacy was the issue, the tree house window facing the Humboldt's could be boarded up. And anytime the children got too rambunctious, all Tenley or Louisa had to do was call.

"Call?" Tenley repeated. "So here it comes now, full circle." With every indignant glance at his sister, she blinked, lips moving wordlessly.

"Well, it's only fair," her father was saying. "Children can be noisy, and why should you have to put up with their commotion?"

"Hm, that's right. I still can't expect peace in my own yard, can I?" Tenley said.

"Of course you should," her father said. "That's your right. That's exactly why we're here."

"Oh, really?" Another glance at his sister. Her face reddened.

"Remember us, all our commotion?" Her father smiled with the memory. "All the children on the street? Twenty, anyway. Two or three in every house. Never a lack of playmates, that's for sure."

"Some things you don't forget. Ever. They persist and persist."

Her father's head drew back with the sibilance. "Of course. I'm sure they do."

"No, Ben, because you have no idea what I'm talking about. None. None at all."

"Well, I'm sorry for that, then. Because I want to."

If only she could have sat next to Henry instead of her father. She needed someone to jam her leg into. She couldn't take the pressure. And worst of all, her father wasn't getting it. Miss Humboldt was, though. Staring at her brother, she looked ready to burst.

"All I ever wanted was to be left alone. What was wrong with that?" Tenley asked.

"Nothing. Nothing at all," her father answered quietly.

"Then why wasn't I? The apples, those disgusting, slimy, rotten apples, it felt like hundreds of them hitting me. Like explosions, smashing into me. In my own yard. Why? What did I do wrong? Why couldn't you just all leave me alone?"

For a moment her father seemed in deep scrutiny of his clasped hands. But his eyes were closed. He finally spoke. "Because we were just children?" His ragged question hung in the silence. "I don't know. But, Tenley, I . . . I . . . I don't think I ever d . . . d . . . did any of that. I didn't. I'm pretty sure—"

"Actually, you were the worst."

He sat forward. "How? What did I do? I never—"

"Oh no, you never did anything! You just let it happen."

And with her father's sigh, she knew that it was true.

Chapter 21

———

"I'M TOLD THIS FINN COWIE'S A REAL GENTLEMAN. YOU'LL BE in good hands," her father said as he drove.

Even though it was a cool, bright September morning, the sky looked milky, probably because her glasses were so smudged. Squinting through a two-day scrim of fingerprints and water spots had soft-focused life to a dreamlike state, turning tension and agitation to this blur of passing cars and buildings as her father continued to assure her over the persistent, racing whir from the engine that there wasn't anything to be nervous about. This was way beyond nerves. She didn't want to be here, didn't want to be on their way to the district attorney's office when she should've been in class like every other normal kid in America. Her backpack was next to her on the seat. Afterward, she'd be dropped off at school.

"Don't worry, I'll be in there with you. The whole time," he called over the noise. He drove even slower. Probably nothing, he'd assured her mother as they were leaving; fan belt's a little loose, that's all. The whirring pitched higher now that they'd stopped for the red light.

"It's just to go over everything before the trial starts. Pretty routine, that's all. The law, you see, it's all about formality and procedure. Certain ways of doing things. Steps to follow. Keeps us civilized," he said with a punctuating nod. "I almost went to law school. Sometimes, I—"

Behind them, a horn blared. The light had changed to green. They turned, and there it was, almost a block long, grim, dull orangey brick with sandstone columns. The courthouse parking lot was full. She wondered how many murder trials were going on in there. They found a space farther down the street.

"Don't worry, you'll be fine," her father said, turning off the noisy engine. He patted her leg. "And you look lovely, by the way. Very pretty."

They were both dressed up. According to her father in his dark gray funeral and wedding suit, it showed respect for the law. There was no way her tacky outfit showed respect for anything other than her mother, who'd refused to let her wear pants. So here she was in her sister's hand-me-downs, a blue-and-yellow skirt that was too short and a frilly white blouse that was baggy. Her mother had insisted she carry Ruth's fringed leather pocketbook. Just in case, she'd said. In case what? In case you need it, she'd said with her warning look. *For what, a little shoplifting afterward, like Ruth?* she wondered, trying to lighten her foul mood. The navy-blue flats, also Ruth's, were rubbing her heels raw.

"You haven't had much to say," her father said. "Nerves, huh?" Ticking his fingers on the steering wheel and clearing his throat, he was the nervous one.

"Sometimes I just like to be quiet, that's all." She yawned. If she seemed calm, then maybe she'd feel it.

"Okay," he said softly. He checked his watch. "We've got a couple minutes. Unless you want to go now."

"Not yet!" she said before he could open the door. They sat, staring at traffic. She kept thinking of Mr. Cooper's tie, up and down, up and down, a pulse beat on his shirt front. She wondered if he'd been angry or scared. It couldn't be a very nice feeling, having a kid in charge of his entire future, especially a kid whose name he couldn't remember half the time. Maybe she should just confront him. Tell him time was running out and she couldn't keep his secret for much longer, not with Max's life on the line. At least if he turned himself in, then he wouldn't have to be always worrying about being caught, a dread she well knew, having lived it last summer, always afraid of Bucky implicating her and Henry in the stolen bike scheme, which could still very well happen, she realized, a cold sweat prickling her back. Just then, there came a roar. "Daddy!" she gasped as the earth rumbled and the whole car shook.

"Just a garbage truck," he said, looking in the mirror. "But he's going way too fast."

"So! How come you didn't go? To law school, I mean," she asked in a rush, needing containment, safety, even if it was only his voice.

He sighed. "Sometimes it's a matter of thinking too much. Of wanting so much to make the right decision that you end up not making any decision at all. You know what I mean?" he asked, as if still trying to make sense of it.

"Not me. I just do things," she said with a shrug. Though in a million years it wasn't true, not with the Australian letters under the floorboard and Jessica's relentless pestering and her guilt about Max. But her father needed to tell her things he couldn't share with anyone else, and she wanted to help him. It pained her to think Ruth might be right, that he was hapless and weak. "You know that book *Get Tough!*?"

"Sure. Uncle Seth's book. Now there was a man of action. Omaha Beach. Three times they shot him, and he just kept crawling and crawling."

"No, I know," she said quickly. "His book, that's what I do. I know all the holds, I study them, and it makes me feel—" She groped for the word.

"Strong?"

"More than that. Something else."

"Empowered?" he asked, smiling when she said yes, that was it, kind of. "Very good," he declared with the wag of a warning finger. "But a lot of people make that same mistake. They think it's all about physical strength. And most of the time force is the greatest weakness of all. You can't go too far wrong if you just remember this. Mark Twain said it. 'How curious that physical courage should be so common in the world, and moral courage so rare.'"

In the stray of his eyes to the traffic again and the solemn lift of his chin, she saw the virtue he felt possessing such a truth, and how apart it set him, safe from her and her petty problems. And suddenly she was stung by his smug dismissal of everything she'd discovered and needed to be true, stung by the quiet tyranny of his kindness, the serene self-absorption that never needed or asked a thing from her or from anyone. For the first time she understood her mother's frustration. He could as well live alone with his books, on an island somewhere, unreachable, and be just as content as now.

"I hate these stupid shoes!" she said, kicking them off. "They're killing my feet. I don't know why I had to wear them or these stupid clothes."

"Nellie." He took her hand in his. "I wish you didn't have to go through this. If I could, I'd go in there and do it for you. Bad enough putting any child through something like this, but when it's your own—" He shook his head. "Just doesn't seem right."

"So do you think he's innocent then?" she asked, more challenge than question.

"Oh no. That's not what I meant. It just seems they have all the evidence they need, so why drag you into it?"

"Because I was there," she said bitterly. "I'm the only one that was."

By the time she'd wedged her shoes back on and was limping up the wide granite steps, they were late. "Wait!" she said before he pushed open the glass door. "I'm going to tell them the truth, you know."

"Well, of course."

"You know what I mean." A breeze kept lifting the hem of her stupid skirt. Two women hurried toward them so they stepped aside, next to one of the massive fluted columns. With the cold stone pressing against her arm, she knew what she had to do.

"You mean Mr. Cooper?"

She nodded. It would be the hardest thing she'd ever done. But she had courage, she did, more than enough, more than he knew, physical *and* moral.

"Nellie, you know why he was there. The offer . . . I told you. He couldn't get me at the store, so he came to the house, and I wasn't there, so he called me."

"He made that up! He lied! Why don't you believe me?" she said so insistently that the young man opening the door looked back at them.

"Listen to me, Nellie," he said in a low voice. "Everything that happened that day was ugly and horrible. And you haven't been able to forget any of it, not a single moment, because you've had to go back and try to keep it all straight in your head, every detail, from the beginning of the day, to the end. And I'm sure I can't begin to understand your pain and anxiety, but just because Andy Cooper happened to come to the house that same day doesn't make him guilty of anything. Don't look away. Listen to me! What about me? I was there! That morning, I was down cellar. I even knocked on her door. I was going to remind her about the new hot-water tank. But she never answered, so I figured she was still asleep. Then I left for work. But I was there. Not even out in the yard, like Andy Cooper, but right there, on her cellar stairs, right outside her door. So I don't know, maybe that makes me a suspect. The police don't think so, but maybe you do. Well, do you?" he asked as she stared down at her big, miserably pinched feet in the stupid blue flats.

They took the elevator to the second floor. The receptionist who led them into the district attorney's office was wearing pants—so much for respect for the law. She apologized and said they'd have to wait a few minutes. District Attorney Cowie was running late. For such a large room there was little in it: the desk and leather chair, four wooden arm chairs, and a tall glass cabinet of law books. Nellie could smell dust, and something else. Pot, she realized sniffing inside Ruth's purse. She closed it quickly, wondering if the courthouse had any drug-sniffing dogs roaming the halls. She and her father sat facing the empty desk. They spoke in low voices.

"Not very fancy, she whispered, breathing on her glasses and wiping them clean on her blouse.

"Austere." Her father looked up at the high tin ceiling. "Bet that was the ice storm. Last March." He pointed to the brown-ringed yellow stain above the window. "That was something, huh? Lucky for us we had a generator. The old store came in handy then, didn't it?"

"I knew I should've worn pants." She hugged her arms, shivering.

"Want my jacket?"

She rolled her eyes in reply. "Not even any pictures," she said, looking around.

"Lots of diplomas, though. That's what counts."

The door opened, and a wide block of a man entered, carrying an armload of folders. He towered over her father, who stood up to shake his hand. He had silvery black hair, bushy black eyebrows, large eyes that stared, bright and unblinking, above an easy smile that made her want to like him.

"Finn Cowie," he said, introducing himself and repeating their names as he shook her father's hand, then hers.

"I know you probably hate missing school," he said, winking as he sat down.

"Actually, I do," she said stiffly. She hated it when adults said such lame things to her.

"Nellie's a very good student," her father said. "And very conscientious, which is why she understands the necessity of coming here today."

Equally lame, she thought, glancing at her father, then saw how nervous he was. Was he afraid of what she might say?

"Well, this won't take too long." Mr. Cowie was opening a folder. "Just a few questions," he murmured, turning pages. Which did she prefer being called, he asked, Ellen or Nellie?

"Nellie's fine, thank you," she said, braiding the fringe on the useless purse.

"Just so you'll know, Nellie, when the time comes for you to take the stand and testify, all you have to do is answer the questions as best you can. Don't be scared or nervous. You don't have to please anyone. You don't have to be afraid of saying the wrong thing, because there aren't any wrong answers. It's going to be about facts, the things you saw, the things you heard, and it's that simple. Really. Nobody's going to be shouting or yelling at you. It's not like you see on TV."

"We don't have a TV," she said, not knowing why, other than to offset a whole new fear, the thought of being yelled at in front of a courtroom filled with strangers. Or worse, people she knew.

"Really? Well, you're probably a great reader then." He seemed amused. "I'll bet you read lots of books, don't you?"

Not true, lately, but she nodded, then wondered: was she under oath and lying right now?

For the next few minutes, Mr. Finn Cowie proceeded through the same list of questions Detective Des La Forges had asked. Her answers were the same. And as the detective had, Mr. Cowie asked some again, rephrasing them, as if to be sure of every detail.

"So were you down there with Max Devaney, in the cellar, every minute, the entire time he was working on the water pipes?"

"Uh-huh."

"Nellie, in the courtroom you'll be expected to answer yes or no."

She nodded, and he repeated the question.

"Yes," she said.

"And you never left? Not even once?"

"No." She didn't like the way he was looking at her.

"You stayed right down there with him."

Uncertain if these were questions or statements, she nodded. And for good measure, added, "Uh-huh, yes."

"Doing what? Standing there? Talking? Helping?"

"Mostly watching. And talking, I guess."

"Really. Some people think Mr. Devaney's a pretty scary guy. How 'bout you? Did he make you nervous? Or afraid?"

"No! Max was always nice to me. Really nice."

"Your mother didn't like him, though, right?"

She looked at her father. "Well, just because he was in jail once, that's all."

"That's right," he said. "After we found that out, my wife was, well, uneasy having him around. But, of course, we didn't know then, all the details, that is."

"Does *she*?"

"Yes, we've talked to her."

Who, me? she wanted to ask, glancing between the men, but knew her father wouldn't like it.

"We've asked her, and we're satisfied that—" Her father cleared his throat. "That nothing of an untoward nature happened."

Nodding, Mr. Cowie considered this, as he folded a scrap of paper into smaller squares. "So, Nellie, how was Mr. Devaney nice to you? Did he give you things? Or take you places? What did he do to be so nice?"

"Nothing really, he just was . . . nice, that's all. He'd, like, talk to me, tell me things."

"What kinds of things would he tell you?"

"About when he was a kid." She shouldn't have said that. Her mind raced to stay ahead: *The way his brother had died had been in the paper. But why bring up anything negative?* All she wanted was to help. "Things he did, fishing, how to stack wood so it won't heave, stuff like that. And his dog. We talked about him a lot. Boone, that's his name. Plus, he saved my brother's life once."

"Yes, that's right. And I can tell you're a very sensitive and forthright girl, and you like Mr. Devaney, so do you think you owe him something for that? A favor or something?"

A trick question, because saving a life was the highest form of courage and selflessness, so of course Max deserved something. If not a favor or award, at least her respect and gratitude. But that wasn't what Mr. Cowie meant. "I don't know. No." Her stomach felt shaky.

"What do you mean? What kind of favor, Mr. Cowie?" her father asked. "If I don't understand you, I'm sure Nellie doesn't."

Mr. Cowie rubbed his chin on clasped hands, the pause unsettling. There was something unpleasant he didn't want to say. "It's just that there's quite a discrepancy here. Nellie says she was down in the cellar the entire time Mr. Devaney was working down there. But Mr. Devaney says she left him alone down there twice. I don't understand, that's all. On the one hand, it's not to Mr. Devaney's advantage to say he was alone down there, and on the other hand, why would Nellie say she was with him the whole time if it's not true?"

"Because it is true!" She'd spoken too quickly, too heatedly. She saw the alarm in both men's expressions.

"You're not afraid of him, are you, Nellie?" Mr. Cowie looked concerned.

"No." She had to stay calm.

"Here, let me read this from Mr. Devaney's statement," Mr. Cowie said, running his finger down a typed page. "I was alone down there two times. Both times the girl went out to check on the dog."

Her face flushed. Being called "the girl" really bothered her, but then again, he'd also said "the dog" instead of Boone. "He just must've forgot, that's all."

"Hm. He was pretty specific. He said you were worried about the dog being locked up in the hot truck."

"Well, yeah, but we just talked about it."

"He said you told him a neighbor had called to complain."

"I know. But I only said it so he'd let Boone out of the truck."

"So you made it up?"

"Yeah. To him. But for a good reason. It was hot in the truck. But he didn't care. He was mad, so I just . . . I was just there."

"He was mad? Mad at you?"

"No! At Boone. He said he had to stay in the truck."

"Why? What did Boone do?"

"I don't know. Barking, I guess." Her foot was tapping a mile a minute.

"But Max seemed mad, angry, upset. Is that what you're saying?"

"No, bothered. But just about Boone, that's all."

Her father's foot nudged hers, so she locked her ankles together.

"Nellie." Mr. Cowie sighed. "There's nothing Mr. Devaney can do to hurt you. Nothing at all. You do know that, right?"

She nodded.

"But you're afraid." He leaned closer. "Why? What're you afraid of?"

Of telling the truth, of getting up there and telling everyone exactly what I'd seen that day. Afraid where the truth might take us all.

"I'm just a little nervous. About the trial, that's all," she said in a weak enough voice that Mr. Cowie assured her, as her father had earlier, that there was nothing to be nervous about. All she'd have to do is answer his questions. They went over a few more details, which she could tell was just his way of trying to make her feel better. Before they left, he gave her his business card and said she could call him if she thought of anything else they hadn't discussed. Or if she remembered something or had any questions. Or if she just wanted to talk. She thanked him, and as she dropped the card into the purse, it amused her to picture Ruth discovering it among the illicit shreds of whatever substance she'd left in there.

Chapter 22

———

STRANGE, WHEN YOU'RE YOUNG, HOW QUICKLY PROBLEMS DISappear. If you don't have to think about them, if no one's talking about them, or better yet, if no one knows about them, then they cease to exist. And so it seemed with the Australian letters, lost in the blurred cascade of half-forgotten summer days. Surely by this time the dusty pages had been nibbled into oblivion by the autumnal influx of field mice, which were being caught in their cellar traps at the rate of one or two a day. For Nellie's mother, the removal of each small gray corpse was more sickening proof of their hastened decline. For her father it harbingered winter's premature arrival, deep snow, thick ice. He wondered aloud if he should double his shovel and salt stock at the store. Her mother didn't answer. Instead, he pounded red-and-white driveway reflectors into the ground earlier than he ever had.

The trial was starting. Jurors were being selected, a slow process, according to the district attorney's office. They'd been keeping the Pecks informed, though at home, the trial was never mentioned. Not in front of the children, anyway. Far more pressing for Nellie were the history paper she had to write and a report for English class on Steinbeck's *The Pearl,* both due in a week, and nightly worksheet pages of advanced algebra problems to solve, as well as the flattering and complicated attention of beautiful Brianna Hall to negotiate.

The newspaper's most recent account of the murder had run with a front-page picture of a younger, sweeter-looking Dolly, taken from her high school yearbook. The article mentioned "Ms. Bedelia's thirteen-year-old neighbor, who had discovered the body, along with the accused." In Brianna's eyes Nellie had become a most desirable friend, a burgeoning celebrity touched by life's darker forces. It was all she could talk about. Every day she presented a new scenario.

"You know that guy, the killer—"

"He's not a killer—"

"—yeah, well, what if you say something he doesn't like, and he knocks the defense table over and attacks you?" she mused as they trudged uphill under the ever shifting weight of their backpacks.

"He wouldn't do that. And besides, I won't be saying anything bad about him." She'd said the same thing yesterday.

"Yeah, and my father said there'll be all kinds of police there, too. I hope it's not like that show last winter. Remember? *The Prosecutor?* They're in the court and the killer, he's got this, like, knife thing he made, like, all pointy and sharp, like, from a spoon or something . . ."

Nellie enjoyed Brianna's company, in spite of her fascination with serial murderers. She said her parents had an entire bookcase filled with crime books, and they loved watching the Crime Channel, which, until then, Nellie'd never even heard of. Brianna told her all about Ted Bundy, this handsome guy who lured pretty college girls to their doom by wearing a fake cast on his arm so they'd take pity on him. She told her about this sicko who'd dress up like a clown and kill kids, then bury them under his house. And then there was the guy who killed an apartment full of nursing students. It was the first time she'd heard these stories, and they were a numbing distraction in their creepy way. Dolly's murder scene paled compared to Brianna's gory tales. Nellie could almost think about it without feeling dizzy.

"Imagine," Brianna mused while they waited for the light to turn. "Everything you say, every single word, someone'll be there, writing it all down. You'll be like, oh, my God, what if I say the wrong thing, they're all gonna be, like, flipping out all over the place," she said, tenderly adjusting the strap on Nellie's backpack. For one so conversant with violence, she was very caring.

"Not really," Nellie said. "It's not like on TV. People don't yell and scream. They just don't." More and more lately she found herself making important pronouncements. She was starting to sound like Ruth.

"Wait!" Brianna stopped, and in her admiring gaze Nellie saw her well-earned place in her pantheon of all things strange. Brianna was taking a camera from her backpack.

"Smile!" She took a picture. "Now, look upset, like, oh, my God! *What's that?* Like you just discovered the body."

With the second flash, Nellie said she'd better get home.

"Okay, and then you can show me where it happened, the murder." She said she'd call her mother from Nellie's house. Nellie told her she couldn't, that she had to work on her paper. Telling her she'd see her tomorrow, she hurried off. All Brianna's crime talk was starting to get to Nellie. In that way she was like Jessica: once latched on to a subject, she couldn't get off. Lately though, Nellie hadn't had to worry about avoiding Jessica. She was always with Bucky. They'd even been caught smoking in the Coopers' pool cabana. If Mrs. Cooper had any concerns about Bucky, she'd surely overlook them as long as Jessica finally had a friend.

At home the mailbox was stuffed with catalogs. When Nellie pulled them out, the regular mail fell onto the porch floor. On top was a long manila envelope. *Mr. Daniel Brigham,* read the return address label. She ran straight up to her room. Sealed shut, then taped, there'd be no steaming open this one. With it trembling in her hands, she sat on the edge of her bed. Why so thick? Was it some kind of warning? A threat? A lawsuit? She might have confiscated the other letters, but Ruth had kept right on writing. Nellie ripped open the envelope.

There were two handwritten sheets of lined paper. Folded inside was a newspaper clipping headlined ROBBERY FOILED BY STORE MANAGER. The grainy picture showed a paunchy, round-faced man. Balding, with wire-rimmed glasses, he stood next to a supermarket register. Instead of a wild Hawaiian shirt he wore a snug, dark jacket with a store logo on the breast pocket. Brigham had tackled an armed robber fleeing the supermarket in broad daylight, with receipts from the office.

What propelled Mr. Brigham into action was seeing the robber shove a woman carrying a small child out of his way as they were entering the store. Mr. Brigham said, "It was hard losing the day's receipts, but company policy says to do whatever the thief wants. They don't want us risking harm to customers or ourselves, and I was in full compliance. But then I saw the punk knock the mum and her baby down, and, well, that was just too much for a man to take. Pure reflex, that's all. So off I went, and took him down."

The article called him ". . . a genuine hero, bringing the thief down with an American football tackle. Brigham's actions may contradict company policy, but his employees say they're not surprised by his quick-thinking bravery. Lucille O'Day, head cashier, describes him as "a fair boss who runs a tight ship but is always kindhearted and pleasant."

"Dear Ruth," began the letter's almost illegible scrawl. Nellie had to decipher each word, reading sentences countless times to understand it.

After I received your last letter, I felt very bad. I didn't under-stand why you kept ignoring me when I asked you not to write. It was so upsetting to me that I finally told my wife and asked for her help. She said she would write and explain how I felt. But you kept writing anyway. And to tell you the truth, that only made me angrier. You see I haven't had an easy time of it lately. My wife has had many health problems and has been let go from her job. Our youngest daughter (we have three) has spina bifida and requires spe-cial care. Our middle daughter has severe learning disabilities so she has to attend a specialized school that is almost an hour's drive from home. Thankfully, our oldest girl is blessed with good health and normal intelligence. I tell you all this so you'll understand why your complaints about your lot in life fell on such deaf ears.

But then came the incident at work—you'll see what I mean in the clipping. Anyway, it was one of those breakthrough moments. It has taught me a great lesson. It's made me realize that what's most important in life is confronting difficulty straight on instead of look-ing the other way or running away. The Brigham family may not have a lot, but we have each other and that is the most important thing. I hope you will forgive me for not being more welcoming

*when you first wrote. Even though I always knew this might happen,
I guess I was still too afraid of the unknown. But now I'm not. In
fact, I would like to get to know you. I have your picture, and I plan
to show it to my daughters and tell them that they have an American
sister.*

Your father,
Daniel Brigham

With the pillow over her head, Nellie sobbed until her chest ached
with loss. Their family was coming undone. Ruth would surely leave,
her only sister, now with her pick of Aussie sisters and accents she'd be
only too eager to imitate. Of course, she would prefer her own heroic
blood father over her disappointing stepfather. And after Ruth, who
then? Her mother, who'd been so nervous lately, so beaten down, who
now, in addition to weekdays, was working Saturdays and two nights
a week.

She threw open the closet door, swept out the shoes, and laid to
perpetual rest this deadly letter with the others. A few days passed. Life
went on.

HALFWAY THROUGH DINNER there was an urgent tapping on the door
glass. Agitated, short of breath, Mr. Cooper rushed in, clutching a peat
pot of burgundy mums to his chest. With his quick desperate glance,
Nellie's legs locked around the chair rungs. At last. Tormented by guilt,
he'd surely come to confess. A devout churchgoer, he couldn't let an
innocent man be tried for his sin. She was already dredging her heart
for forgiveness. She'd known him all her life. He must have been pro-
voked, maybe even trying to protect himself. Though she didn't de-
serve to die for them, Dolly's explosive rages were no secret to Nellie.
She would tell everything she'd heard and seen, all the while respecting
Dolly's memory and the tragedy of Mr. Cooper's helpless infatuation.
Knowing he was married with a bunch of kids, she'd gone after him
anyway. She was good at getting what she wanted, flirting with Max
so he'd get her car started, flattering her landlady instead of paying her
rent on time. Promising ice cream, she'd even lured Nellie and Henry

into her ploy for meeting Mrs. Cooper. Nellie'd been her easy victim, too.

Mr. Cooper apologized for barging in, but he'd just left Ray Mikellian. After weeks of excuses and unreturned calls, he'd finally marched into the bank president's office, demanding answers. He stood by the table, peering over the mums. Her father had pulled out the extra chair, but Mr. Cooper didn't seem to notice.

"'Shouldn't be a problem, shouldn't be a problem,' that's what he kept saying, which, coming from Mikellian's good as gold, and you know that, right, Ben? There's never been a time, not one single time, in all my dealings with the man when he's gone back on his word, so I just wanted you both to know so you'd feel better about this whole thing. Especially now, and you're right, you're right to hold my feet to the fire. It's the economy. Money's tight everywhere, but I made you folks a sincere offer and I don't want you thinking for a minute I'm backing down, because I'm not. Of course I wouldn't. So just be patient a little while longer, that's—"

"But every day that goes by, Andy, it's—" her father tried to say.

"I know. Believe me, my friend, I know. The press of time, I know it well." Mr. Cooper finally slipped into the chair across from Nellie. Her mother's eyes followed the streak of dirt from the pot he was pushing to the center of the table. "But things're bad everywhere. Right now I've got three deals just barely holding together. It's not just me. Everyone's got the jitters. Everyone."

Her mother got up and carried the mums to the counter. She wet the sponge then wiped the table clean. Mr. Cooper's pale blue shirtfront was smudged with dirt. The two men were discussing the art supply shop on Main Street, which was going out of business after twenty-three years in the same location. Sign of the times, Mr. Cooper said. So much of their merchandise was easily available online.

"Or Target," Ruth interjected. "That's where we went, right, Mom?"

Her mother didn't reply. She tapped the rim of Henry's plate. He hadn't touched his peas. He hunched over, gripping his belly.

"Last year, the dance posters, remember?" Ruth persisted. "It was, like, so much cheaper." The new mature Ruth was struggling to be part of the conversation. Little did she know the strange forces driving it.

"There's no competing," Mr. Cooper agreed, as Nellie stared, boldly, accusingly. She was prepared to give him every ounce of understanding and support. But he had to confess.

"America's gone off course, that's what Mr. Barnes told us in Gov. One," Ruth continued. "We've, like, lost our way. This whole immigration thing, it's like thrown everything off-kilter. They take all the jobs and suck up all the benefits."

"That's not only an inaccurate statement, Ruth, but it ignores the fact that we're all descended from immigrants. Unless we're American Indians," her father added.

"Native Americans. Careful, Ben," Mr. Cooper warned with a sly smile.

"I was talking about illegal immigrants. That's what I meant!" Ruth was miffed.

Henry was eating his peas, gulping each one whole, no chewing. Ruth sulked through her father's often told story of his maternal great-grandmother coming alone as a sixteen-year-old from Galway to Boston. Peg O'Riordan had been hired right off the boat as a housemaid for a wealthy family. She'd only been working a few days when she was accused of breaking the hand off a prized porcelain statue. More benevolently, instead of firing her, the lady of the house withheld the pittance that would have been Peg's first month's wages. To Jesus, Joseph, and the chaste Virgin Mary, she swore her innocence, but had no defenders. The statue had actually been knocked over by the oldest son's climb through a window after a late night of drinking. Rather than betray their dissolute brother, his teenage sisters let poor Peg slave for weeks, unpaid.

"Imagine," Mr. Cooper sighed, clasping his hands while Nellie glared at the slender fingers, imagining their lethal squeeze around Dolly's thin neck. "All that our ancestors had to put up with. The indignities, the injustice. But look at this fine family," he said with a sweep of his hand. "I'd say you've done old Peg proud."

Old Peg? Nellie could see father bristling.

"Same thing in Australia," Ruth was saying. "Only most of them were criminals. Not my relatives, though. They immigrated from here."

"Emigrated," her father corrected, jaw still tight.

"My grandfather's company, he got, like, transferred," she continued.

"That's right," Mr. Cooper said. "Arnie Brigham. Salvo Systems. Actually, they moved the whole company there, didn't they?"

"Yeah, Danny, my father, he was, like, in high school and he couldn't even finish the year," Ruth said, grinning, with the joy of being able to have this conversation. Her mother was looking her way, but with a kind of desolation.

Mr. Cooper remembered Danny. "Pretty good football player. I think he made varsity his freshman year. And all-state his sophomore . . . no, maybe junior year. He looked at her mother. "Is that right?"

She nodded. "Both years. Danny was a good athlete."

"Not much of a student, though, right, Mom?" Ruth said so happily and easily that Nellie flared with jealousy. Ruth and her mother shared another existence, a connection beyond this family.

"He was very intelligent," her mother said. "Just not too interested in school, that's all."

"Tell me about it, I got a few of those at home," Mr. Cooper laughed and stood up.

Nellie's eyes smoldered. So that was it? And now he would leave? Not a remorseful bone in his body?

"Which reminds me, we never see you anymore, Nellie. How come?" he said.

"I've been busy. Getting ready for the trial. The murder trial."

"Shame you have to go through all that. You and your family," Mr. Cooper sighed, shaking his head.

"Nellie'll be fine," her father said. "She'll be okay."

"All I have to do is tell the truth," she said, her gaze hard on Mr. Cooper, but he was looking at her father not at her. "Everything that happened that day. Everything I saw."

"Andy," her mother said quickly. "We can't wait much longer. We really can't."

He held the door open. "I know that. And, believe me, I'm trying. I'm doing my best," he said, a sting in his voice.

"Maybe you should try another bank," she said, but the door had already closed.

The kitchen seemed smaller, the light bleaker. Her father began clearing the table. "At least he's trying—gotta hand him that," he called over the rinse water, but her mother had gone upstairs with Henry. Claiming "a ton" of homework, Ruth followed, leaving Nellie to load the dishwasher.

A little while later Lazlo came over. Grateful for the company, her father poured them both red wine. They sat at the table while her father did most of the talking. Lazlo kept glancing toward the hallway. Would Sandy be coming down soon, he asked. With her father's worried look Nellie knew they were fearing the same thing: Lazlo's moving out again. She might have dozed off, her father said. She did that sometimes: lie down on Henry's bed and just fall asleep. A few more minutes passed. No, he said, when her father went to pour more into his glass. He must have nodded then or made some gesture, because her father told her to go finish her homework. He'd wash the pans. Instead, he went upstairs and got her mother.

Lazlo told them that he had seen Ruth coming into the house this morning at nine. Soon after that her girlfriend had arrived. At two o'clock, he'd been in the yard working on another sketch of the tree house when they came outside. Seeing him there, Ruth was quick to say they'd had early dismissal and had just gotten home, which he knew wasn't true. Lazlo felt terrible. The last thing he wanted was to get Ruth in trouble, but he'd seen her slip into the house midmorning more than once in the last few weeks. Later, when confronted by her parents, Ruth swore that was the only day she'd skipped; Lazlo didn't know what he was talking about.

The next morning her mother canceled her first two appointments so she could meet with the principal. Since September, Ruth had missed school four times. She had signed her mother's name on every absentee note in her file. Stunned, her mother called the salon and took the rest of the day off. When Nellie and Henry came home from school they found her in the dim front parlor, staring out at the leaf-blown street.

"Did you quit?" Henry asked, delighted to find her there. No one had felt her absence more in this last year than he had.

She didn't answer.

"No." Nellie elbowed him. "Mom has to work. We need the money."

Her mother burst into tears, much of her lament lost in sobs. *Things* didn't matter, new cars, fancy clothes, new furniture. No. All she'd ever wanted was a happy family and now everything was crazy, just one big mess, and it was all her fault, every bit of it. No, it wasn't, Nellie insisted, but her mother shrank from her touch and cried even more. Now Henry was crying. Nellie called her father at the store. He hurried home, his usual abstracted air giving way to panic. There was nothing he could say or do. Every assurance made her feel worse. He sent them outside. They climbed into the leaf-filled tree house, their fragile world shakier with every gust of wind through the swaying limbs. "Like Ronnie-Don Rufus!" Nellie hollered to make her brother laugh, as the wall boards rattled and branches creaked. Henry said he was going in before the whole stupid thing came crashing down.

Ruth had come home. Up on the third floor, she sobbed in her mother's arms. She was sorry, but she hated school, and she hated her life. Dolly had been the one person she could talk to, the one person who knew what she was going through. Nobody else understood or even cared. Her friends were sick of hearing how alone she felt. They'd never been abandoned the way she had. Not once, but eight times, eight letters begging her father to please write back. And nothing, not one letter, not one single word back.

"What's wrong with me?" Ruth wept.

"There's nothing wrong with you. I couldn't ask for a better daughter," her mother cried, and something broke in Nellie's heart.

"But I'm *his* daughter, too. Doesn't he care what happens to me?"

Nellie crept into her room and closed the door. The house was still. She lifted the floorboard, scattering the shoes to the side of the closet.

SATURDAY. TODAY WAS the day. It's what she should have done in the first place. She'd barely slept last night. Her mother was down in the kitchen. She'd be going to work soon. Better to tell her right before she left. Less time for the misery Nellie knew she deserved. The smell of sizzling bacon drifted up the back stairs. She was starving. A tap came at her door.

"Breakfast," Ruth called. "Mom said to tell you." She opened the door and looked in. "Are you coming?" Her eyes were red and puffy.

"I don't feel good," Nellie said, holding her stomach.

"Nellie? What's wrong?" Ruth sat on the edge of her bed. "Poor kid, you look awful." She leaned closer. "Have you been crying? You have, haven't you." She tried lifting Nellie's chin. "What is it? Come on, you can tell me. I won't say anything. I promise."

Nothing was wrong, Nellie said, but Ruth wouldn't believe her. She said she could tell. Basking in the glow of her own redemption, Ruth knew only love and sympathy. Her little sister was hurting, and no one knew better than she did the loneliness of keeping it all pent up inside.

"I mean, you were the first person I told about writing to my father." She pressed her forehead against Nellie's.

"No, you told Brenda first."

"Well, the first person in the family, then."

"You told Dolly," Nellie said, guessing.

"That was different. Dolly was like that. You could just tell her things. And that's how it should be for *us*. You can tell me anything, Nellie. Anything at all. Whatever it is. And believe me, I won't tell anyone. Not a soul. I swear." Her clear blue eyes held Nellie's with such warmth that there was no way she could confess so callously, so easily hurting her. "So tell me. Tell me what's wrong."

Nellie couldn't even shake her head.

"Okay, how's this then—let's trade secrets." Her grin made it worse. Oh, how Nellie hated this game. Ruth was always so much better at it because she had all the secrets and Nellie had to make up hers to get any back.

"Look." She lifted her nightgown and pulled down the side of her panties. There, just above the tan line on her lower hip was a small blue star, its tails of light ending in even smaller stars. "My first tattoo. I got it last summer. I went with Patrick."

"Dellastrando?" All Nellie could utter. Her sister had done that? Lowered, maimed herself for Patrick Dellastrando, the hairy thug around the corner who wouldn't even speak to her anymore. Viewing her defiled maidenhead would not have been as shocking.

"Like Dolly's, remember? Okay, your turn," Ruth said. "Go ahead, just get it out." She squeezed Nellie's hand until it hurt.

"I don't have periods," Nellie blurted surprising herself. She'd thrown out the first box of sanitary napkins, but her mother had quietly replaced them in her closet.

"Oh, my God. What do you mean? Why not?"

"I just don't, that's all."

"You're probably just late. Irregular. That happens, especially when you're just starting."

"No, I'm not having any. I just don't, I didn't, that's what I'm talking about."

"Are you worried?" She kept taking deep breaths and looking around.

"No! I haven't started yet. But Mom thinks I did, because you told her, and it's embarrassing."

"Oh!" Ruth sighed. "But why did you say you did if you weren't? I mean, that's kinda weird, don't you think?"

So THEN IT was Sunday. Nellie'd been next door interviewing Lazlo for her history paper. She needed to talk to a veteran and he'd served in the Gulf War. He told her a lot of interesting stories, but she was very distracted. Not only was it the first time she'd been in the apartment since Dolly's murder, but she kept hearing strange thumps from next door. She left, promising Lazlo she'd show him the paper when she got it back from the teacher.

Apparently, there was more trouble in the house. Angry stomping up to the third floor. Ruth's door slamming. Her mother and father barely speaking to each other. Henry said Ruth had used the new credit card to buy designer jeans at the mall. She'd signed their mother's name. The bill had sat in the dreadfully growing pile, unopened until this morning. Her mother demanded Ruth hand over the jeans so she could return them. But they'd already been worn, Ruth said. Didn't matter, with a forged signature the sale was invalid, her mother said. When a ransacking of Ruth's room didn't turn them up, Ruth admitted she'd given them to Ashley Dellastrando. They hadn't really fit her very well and it was Ashley's birthday. Henry said her mother trembled all over, like she was trying not to throw up. Ruth was a wonderful girl, her father kept telling her. She was going through a difficult time, that was all. And some day they'd look back and laugh about it all.

"That's when she got really mad." Henry had to whisper because her father was in the next room, reading the Sunday papers. "She said, maybe he could laugh, but she was done."

In Nellie's estimation, Ruth had gone too far this time. Truancy and thievery, not to mention the secret tattoo. She'd pushed their mother over the edge.

Nellie lifted the letters from their gritty tomb. She wasn't sure whether she wanted to save Ruth or just be rid of her, but somebody had to do something. She knocked on her mother's bedroom door. She didn't answer. Calling in, Nellie said she had to show her something. It was very important. Her mother said she'd be down later.

"It's about Ruth." Silence.

"I'm through worrying about her. Your father can deal with it."

Nellie was halfway down the stairs when she stopped. She ran back to her room. All she had to do was destroy the letters, tear them into a thousand pieces, and no one would ever know. But she would.

Her father was in the kitchen. Slouched over the table, he gripped an empty coffee cup in both hands.

"Dad?" she said, and he looked up with a weary smile.

"What are these?" He meant the envelopes she was holding out.

"Letters. From Ruth's real father." He nodded as she tried explaining her sincere intentions. "And so then, the last letter was nice, but that meant she'd find out about the first two." She told him about the newspaper clipping and Brigham's heroism. "I was afraid she'd think he was this great guy and she'd just leave."

The worry in his eyes was a relief to see, and then he said, "You did a terrible thing."

"Just read them, you'll see."

"I can't, they're Ruth's."

"I was afraid she'd choose him over you." She could barely speak.

"That's your sister's decision to make, Nellie, not yours. You can't control another person's life. You had no right to do this." He held up the letters and looked at her with a disappointment she'd never seen before. And would never forget. "Imagine if someone tried to keep us apart. Think how you'd feel." He reached for her hand, and she grabbed his.

Chapter 23

———

FINALLY, IT WAS HERE, NELLIE'S DAY TO MOUNT THE WITNESS stand and save Max Devaney. She had a bad cold and her glasses were crooked on her runny nose. The little hinge pin had fallen out as they were leaving the house. Her father had stuck a strand of picture wire through the hinge, but the glasses were so wobbly she had to hold them straight. They arrived at nine, expecting to go straight into the courtroom. Instead, their witness advocate escorted them to a small, overheated conference room off the main corridor. Her mother fanned herself with a gardening magazine from the dog-eared stack on the wobbly table. A matchbook cover would do the trick, her father declared, leaning to look at the leg. But who even carries matches anymore, he said to no one in particular.

Miss Chapley, a petite woman with round, rosy cheeks, had been filing her nails. It was giving Nellie the chills. Seeing her shiver again, Miss Chapley said she shouldn't be nervous. Nellie said she wasn't. Filing faster, she said Judge Vasquez was very patient, especially with children. Nellie told her she was thirteen. She looked surprised. Her godchild was thirteen, she said, as if Nellie must be mistaken. An interesting age, her father was quick to add, *whatever that meant.* Miss Chapley said her godchild was turning into just the biggest social butterfly, eyeliner, girlfriends, parties every weekend. Silence around the table, everyone surely thinking what a loser Nellie was, squinting through her cockeyed glasses and breathing through her mouth because her nose was so stuffed up. Not just a loser but a pariah in her own family. The Australian letters had ruined her life. Selfish, Ruth had called her, a pathological liar and a sneak, and no one had said a word in her defense. Suspected of everything, trusted with nothing, she knew how Max must be feeling.

Her mother asked if she could open the door, the heat was too much. It had to stay closed, Miss Chapley said. Her father suggested opening a window. He could try, Miss Chapley allowed, but it had been painted shut. He banged on the window frame a few times with the heels of his hands then fished something from his pocket. Miss Chapley glanced up from her nails with the shiny blade's first score down the painted sash.

"Is that a knife?" she gasped.

"Swiss Army," he grunted, working to free the other sash.

"My God!" Miss Chapley sprang for the door.

"Ben! We just went through security!" her mother said. "You can't bring a knife into the courthouse."

Miss Chapley hurried back in with a court officer, who smiled seeing Nellie's sheepish father. They'd been Eagle Scouts together. The court officer's son was in Ruth's class. Apologizing, her father unhooked the tiny knife from his key chain and handed it over. Nellie imagined Ruth's laughter as she described him smuggling a concealed weapon into the murder trial, but then she remembered: not only wasn't her sister speaking to her but refused to be in the same room with her. Together, the grunting men managed to open the window a few inches. Miss Chapley resumed work on her nails. Holding her glasses straight, Nellie flipped through a boating magazine, the file's steady rasp deep in her bones. She considered asking if nail files weren't also a security breach, but she couldn't risk any more of her parents' annoyance. Especially her mother's.

Charlie's testimony on the trial's opening day had been in the paper. Recycling, he answered when asked his occupation. Someone chuckled, and he looked out into the courtroom and said, "Well, what the hell would you call it?" The judge reprimanded him. "Just wandered in one day," Charlie said of his first meeting Max Devaney. "Asked if I had any work, odd jobs, whatever needed doing. A lot needs doing, I told him, but there's nothing to pay you with. Bad enough nobody wanting old things anymore, now nobody wants old bucks like me around, either." More chuckles. Inspired by his appreciative forum,

Charlie complained about all the town's restrictions, their fees and outrageous fines just about putting him out of business, which was really their goal, his property being so valuable right in the heart of town, but the judge nudged him back on track. "Patiently," the paper said.

"So having Mr. Devaney willing to work for room and board was helpful then, wasn't it?" District Attorney Cowie continued.

"I paid him some. When I could. He was okay with it." Charlie revealed details Nellie hadn't known. Toward the end Max had been cooking for the two of them. He'd started painting the dining room, the plan being to move Charlie's bed downstairs. Some nights they even watched television together, though Charlie said Max wasn't one to sit still for long, unless it was something he liked to watch. "Crime stuff, mostly, and horror, like those Halloween movies. Myself, I couldn't watch 'em, though," Charlie added. "Way too much blood and gore."

"That's what the defendant preferred, though, right? More violent, the—" Cowie was cut off by Eggleston Jay Wright's objection. Judge Vasquez called both men to the bench. The rest of Cowie's questions concerned Dolly, whom Charlie said he'd never met or heard mentioned. And, yes, Max had gone out a few nights, and from the way he got all spiffed up, Charlie figured it had to do with a woman, but he never asked and Max never said. Closemouthed as he was.

After that, her mother hid the newspaper. If she could have, she would have removed every paper from every front step in town. Further details came from Brianna Hall. Two of Dolly's friends, both dancers, she said, had testified about seeing Max Devaney in the club. The first time he just sat watching. The next time he tried to pay Dolly to sit with him. She refused and he lost his temper. After that, she was really scared of him. She told them how he used to show up at her place all the time. He knew she couldn't do much about it because of his close ties to her landlady's family. Hearing that, Nellie felt bad for her mother, the legacy of her father's junk still darkening her days.

There was a lot Nellie would learn later. When it was too late—or didn't matter, depending on your point of view. The child he'd left behind was about her age. For the boy's sake, his wife said, common law, she admitted uneasily, a plain, thin-faced woman explaining how she'd tried to make it work, both of them having been so young, along with her guilt that he'd gone to jail for having done something only wrong in the eyes of the law and her family, as well as his, who never forgave him for the brother's death, leaving him only additionally marked, killer and deviant. Everywhere they went, scorned. So she kept taking him back after each time he just up and disappeared, until it just got too hard, the effect of such terrible rage on the boy. The night she finally said it, the night he came in bloodied from yet another fight, she told him to go, and he didn't say a word, just put his big, cut hands on her shoulders and shook her until her legs gave out, which probably saved her life, him being so dead inside, anyway.

But for Nellie, Max Devaney's history began the day he stepped from the glare into the dark heat of Charlie's barn and sniffed at the pot roast. So her facts were pure, uncluttered by memory or misunderstanding. He existed only as she knew him, in a child's view, its own complete and unassailable reality.

The stern, frizzy haired judge was leaning so close Nellie was sure she could hear her stomach growling. It had been a mortifying entrance into the oak-paneled courtroom. Not wanting to keep holding her glasses straight, she'd taken them off, so certain details were blurry. Like the steps leading up to the witness box. She'd gashed her knee in the stumble, but assured the judge she was fine. The baliff peeled open a Band-Aid and Nellie pressed it over the cut. With her glasses back on she couldn't help grinning at the first face she saw. Max stared back from the defense table, expressionless. With his bushy hair cut and the ruddiness faded from his pitted cheeks, he seemed smaller. He was wearing a dark, pin-striped jacket and faded blue pants from the Salvation Army store. With the rest of the court's fifty dollars, Eggleston Jay Wright had also bought the tan shoes there. Buttoned to the neck and tieless, the limp white shirt was Max's own. He'd keep on looking for the money, Charlie had promised Eggleston when he came for the shirt.

After she was sworn in, the judge asked a few questions. Was she comfortable? Was she nervous? Did she understand the difference between a lie and the truth? Yes, no, yes, which set her foot tapping. She *was* nervous, so with her first untruth she tried to smile as District Attorney Cowie walked toward her. From this height they were almost eye level. He seemed more threatening than in their first meeting. Of the five men and seven women in the jury, there wasn't a single smile among them. Most of the seats in the courtroom were taken. Her parents were right behind the prosecutor's table. She wondered if it was like sports where you sat on your team's side. She didn't recognize anyone on Max's side.

"Hello, Nellie," Mr. Cowie said. "Hope that knee's not hurting too much."

"It's okay. Thank you, sir."

"That's good. Well, anyway, I'm going to ask you a few questions that probably seem real obvious, but it's just to get it all in the record here."

She nodded, and he asked her full name and age, her address and who else lived there besides her .

"And Lazlo Larouche," she quickly added, after naming family members. "He's our tenant," she explained when Mr. Cowie asked what Lazlo's relation was to them.

"And where exactly does Mr. Larouche live?"

"In the apartment, in the back of our house."

"Yes, that's right, and before Mr. Larouche, who else lived in that apartment?"

"Dolly did." Her nose had started running again.

"Do you mean Dolly Bedelia?"

She nodded, and the judge reminded her to answer aloud so everyone could hear her.

"Yes. Dolly Bedelia. She lived there after Lazlo." And as soon as she said it, she knew by the buzz of confusion how every word counted. Eggleston Jay Wright might be in a daze, but neither the judge nor Mr. Cowie were taking anything for granted. With the order of tenancy clarified, Mr. Cowie's questions mostly concerned Dolly. He described her as a struggling young dancer still naively hoping for her break into show business. Most of his questions began with statements. She knew she was only supposed to answer the questions, so she wasn't sure how to handle the other parts.

Now Mr. Cowie was asking where she'd first met Max Devaney. In Charlie's junkyard, she told him, explaining, before he could ask, that

Charlie was her grandfather. Not only was she feeling more confident, but she liked being the center of attention, everyone hanging on her every word. On her mother's side, she added, smiling out at her. Her mother's smile back was uneasy, but she didn't have to worry. Nellie could tell she had a knack for this. Testifying was like hand-to-hand combat, all about instinct and reflex, and thanks to Major Fairbairn, she was well practiced. Maybe she'd be a lawyer, she thought, which would please her father. Maybe this was what the major's book had been preparing her for. Defending the weak, the unjustly accused.

"Now, the next time you were in Max Devaney's presence something quite terrifying took place, didn't it, something that—"

"You mean the dog?" she interrupted, her thoughts agile as jabs. *Heel of the hand, full force, fingers to the eyes. Strike.*

"Yes, the dog that Max Devaney killed in front of you and your little brother. Will you tell us exactly how the dog was killed?" *Killed. Killed.* Just saying it, the word, his counterthrust. "Nellie, exactly how did Max Devaney *kill* the dog?"

Attorney Wright was on his feet, objecting. "This has no relevance to the matter at hand."

Judge Vasquez called both men up to speak to her. Their conversation fizzed in whispers. "Pattern of violence . . . rage," she heard Mr. Cowie say. Returning to his seat, Attorney Wright made a big show of shaking his head. Brio. She liked that.

"Anyway," Mr. Cowie said. "I'd like you to tell us exactly how Mr. Devaney killed that dog."

"With a hammer."

"And exactly where did Mr. Devaney hit the dog with the hammer?"

"In the head."

"Ooh." He winced. "Mr. Devaney must've been awfully angry to—"

"You left out a part," she interrupted. Straightening her glasses, she looked out at Max. Still no expression. Nothing. Unafraid because he had faith in her, faith in the truth. "About the dog attacking my brother. Henry, I mean. He bit him, like, took this chunk out of his arm." She even squeezed her forearm for emphasis. "Henry was down, flat down on his back and the dog still kept tryna bite him and Henry was screaming and Max just picked him up and *threw* him against the barn! The dog I mean, but even that didn't stop him, so that's when he hit him, when he started back after Henry, he took his hammer, I'm not sure if he had it in his hand or maybe picked it up, but he hit him with it."

"So, Max Devaney *killed* the dog by *smashing* his head in with the hammer?"

"He didn't smash his head in, he just hit him. Like, boom!" she said with a sharp strike of her hand.

Mr. Cowie made a show of flinching, as if startled. "And then what happened?"

"Well, then Henry had to get stitches. Twenty-two, I think." Seeing one of the lady jurors cringe, she looked at her as she continued. "It was really deep. And now he's more scared of dogs than ever."

"And who can blame him?" Mr. Cowie said, obviously trying to score points with her, but it wasn't going to work. She was way too quick for that. He wanted to depict Max as a violent man, but she'd shown his heroism.

Had *she* ever been afraid of Max, Mr. Cowie asked. No, she said quickly. He asked if she considered him a friend. She told him she did. What kind of friend?

She thought a moment. "Well, not a friend friend. I mean, well, you know, he's a grown-up."

"Yes, a grown man. An adult. But, still, you liked him, didn't you?"

"Yes."

"And did he like you?"

"I think so." She couldn't help smiling at Max who was hunched over the table.

"Did he ever do anything?" He paused. "I mean, to show that he liked you?"

"No." The way he'd said that gave her the creeps. "He was just nice, that's all."

"Did you enjoy his company?"

She nodded. "Yes."

"Even though you weren't supposed to be alone with him. Your parents had told you that, right?" He tried to look puzzled.

She shrugged. Everyone was watching. Including her mother. Wide-eyed, she was straining to tell Nellie something. But it's not that easy, she tried to tell her mother with her return stare, not that cut-and-dried. She couldn't find her tissue. She wiped her nose on the back of her hand.

"Well, they never really said it, I mean they didn't actually tell me, but . . ." Again, she shrugged.

"But you knew. You knew there was something. You knew they didn't want you alone with him, is that right?" Cowie was trying to get Max's sex offender status into the testimony, but she wouldn't know this until later. Meanwhile, she was walking the tightrope of not putting her parents in a bad light while still helping Max.

"I don't know. I mean, well, they might want me to do things sometimes, but they don't always say why."

"But if you asked, they'd certainly tell you, right?"

"Actually, we're not supposed to ask why. We're supposed to just do what they say, that's all."

A few people chuckled, and Mr. Cowie rubbed his chin. She'd thrown him off balance. She wiped her nose again. "Here," the judge said, looking a little squeamish as she held out a tissue box. She took one and thanked her. She gestured for Nellie to take more.

"Good idea," Nellie said, trying to blow her nose, not easy to do with everyone watching. And Mr. Cowie waiting. And soiled tissues piling up in her lap.

"Well, in any event, on the day in question, Monday, August 19, the day of the murder, you and your brother Henry were home alone . . ."

Details: the hot-water tank in the truck, the two staircases at either end of the house leading into the cellar, theirs and Dolly's, the huge commercial fans and how loud they were in the cellar, the same things he'd asked weeks before in his office, only this time she was prepared. Where was she standing, what was she doing, what was Max doing? And had she heard any sounds coming from Dolly's apartment? Not then, but before, she said. Before Max came. Really? He seemed surprised. Like what?

"Like thumping, bumping kind of sounds. Then, like, kind of, maybe a voice, I don't know."

"And whose voice was it?"

Her eyes locked on Mr. Cowie's. She didn't dare look anywhere else, and it seemed by his fierce gaze back that he understood and wanted to help. This was her chance, both their chances. She needed him to peel back the layers and let the truth shine through. Her heart was pounding. "I'm not sure." Which was true. She hadn't been sure. Not then, not until she saw Mr. Cooper out by the bushes.

"Was it a woman's voice?"

"I don't know." Her eyes, magnets to his.

"So, could it have been a man's voice?"

"Maybe." *Ask me,* she silently urged. *Ask me the rest. Ask if there was anyone else there that day. Ask who was trying to disappear into the lilacs, because I can't just say it on my own.*

As if with a sudden thought, Mr. Cowie frowned and walked back to the table.

Max sat up and folded his arms. This had to be the first he knew she'd heard noises in the apartment earlier that day. She wanted him to be encouraged but couldn't tell if he was or not. He did seem more attentive, though, watching Mr. Cowie turning page after page in his note book, then watching him return with his next question.

"So, then, Nellie, after you heard those disturbing noises and what might have been a man's voice in the apartment, how much time would you say passed before you saw Max Devaney come out—"

"Objection," Attorney Wright called out. "That's not at all what—"

"Rephrase the question, please." The judge stared over her glasses at him.

"Of course," Mr. Cowie said with a respectful nod. "All right now, Nellie, when you next saw the defendant at the crime scene, what—"

"Objection!" Attorney Wright said, and the judge called both men to confer with her.

She'd been trying not to look at the jury but now was intensely aware of their scrutiny. One, an older lady with dull black hair and dangly turquoise earrings, was smiling at her. When she smiled back, the woman glanced away, and Nellie realized it was the conference at the bench everyone was so focused on. Judge Vasquez was reprimanding Mr. Cowie. Nellie could only make out snatches of the conversation, but Mr. Cowie was clearly annoying her.

Attorney Eggleston returned to his seat with a fair bit of swagger. Mr. Cowie resumed his questions. He asked Nellie if she'd noticed the cut on Max's hand when he arrived with the hot-water tank. No, she answered, explaining that there hadn't been a cut then because he got it while he was working on the pipes. She glanced at Max, but couldn't tell if he was looking at her or at the judge.

"Oh, okay," Mr. Cowie allowed. "And how do you know this? Did you actually see it happen? Did you see him cut himself?" He was standing in front of her, arms folded, a wall between her and her parents.

"I saw the cut. It was from, like, a jagged pipe or something, I think he said."

"Oh. So, he *told* you, he *explained* how he got the cut. You didn't actually see it happen, did you?"

"Well, not the actual pipe." She crossed her ankles to lock her tapping foot in place. He had her cornered. "The cellar, it was kind of dark down there," she said so weakly she hated herself.

"Were you down there the whole time with the defendant, while he was there?"

"Pretty much." She was surprised he'd ask this. He already knew what she'd say, knew it wouldn't help his case against Max.

"Pretty much? Hm, I'm not sure what you mean, Nellie. Did you leave? Were there times when Max Devaney was alone down in the cellar?"

"Sometimes I was on the stairs. Like, looking down. Watching." She hung over the railing to show what she meant.

For a moment, Mr. Cowie continued staring at her. "Now, I know you come from a fine family, Nellie. And you've been raised to tell the truth, haven't you?"

She nodded with a dry swallow. "Yes, sir."

"But there's a discrepancy here. According to Max Devaney's own statement to the police, there were times down in that cellar when he *was* alone. Once, you went outside to check on his dog, he said, and the other, he wasn't sure where you went, just that you were gone, that he was alone down there. So which is it?" he asked, his back to her, walking now to stand at the corner of the jury box. "Did you leave the cellar while he was there?"

He looked at her. Everyone did. It was them against her. Even Max. The rushing noise in her head was like wind.

"I was on the stairs." She barely heard her own words. Less than the truth, less than a lie.

"So were you in the cellar the whole time Max Devaney was there?"

"Well, I guess . . . I mean, if I was on the stairs." Shriveling inside and getting confused, but she couldn't show it.

"What is it? Why can't you answer yes or no? Maybe it's because you're so young. Maybe you don't understand the seriousness of this."

"I understand." She wished he'd come closer. His standing over by the jurors now and close to the spectators had left her feeling stranded. It was all of them, and her here, alone, the only kid.

"Are you afraid of Max Devaney?"

"No."

"Do you want to protect him?"

"No." She wished she hadn't shrugged.

"But you have feelings for him, I mean, you care what happens to him. You do, don't you?"

"I guess."

"Is that a yes or a no?"

"Yes."

Nodding, he was quiet for a moment. "Nellie, did something happen in the cellar that day? Something that Max Devaney said or did to you that you're afraid to tell us. Did it?"

"No!" she said, sickened by what he was suggesting.

Across the way Max stirred angrily. His feet shuffled under the table. Both bailiffs turned as his chair scraped back. He muttered something and Eggleston patted his arm.

"Then why did he say he was alone down there for part of the time?"

"Because . . . because . . ." She took a deep breath, and even the court stenographer looked up. "Because—"

"Just tell him the truth, girl. It's okay!" Max called out. The judge was tapping her gavel. "I can handle this."

As the judge admonished him, he held out his hands in exasperation, whether with Nellie or the judge, or both. Wilting in the chair, she closed her eyes. The judge asked if she was all right and she nodded. "Are you sure?" Not a sound in the courtroom, silence before the avalanche. Nellie covered her face, and the judge called a brief recess.

Miss Chapley escorted her into the ladies' room. She waited by the door. A woman left the stall next to Nellie's and turned on the water in the sink. The hand dryer blasted on. Nellie sat there crying as the enormity of her foolishness became clear. She kept flushing the toilet. If she could have, she would have stayed in there forever. What had she done? What had just happened? She'd never seen her mother look so distraught or her father so sad. She'd ruined everything for everyone. Miss Chapley knocked on the door and said they'd better go back in. Crying had made her even more congested and her glasses were filmy.

When she was back on the witness stand, Judge Vasquez asked if she was okay. Nellie said she was. She recognized the loyalty in her mother and father's strained smiles. Disappointment she might be, but she was theirs. Mr. Cowie's approach was as hesitant as his voice. He began by saying how difficult it must be, being so young with all this pressure on her to recall so many details. Especially under the burden of perjury. "Even adults get mixed up sometimes. It happens," he added.

"I'm not mixed up." He couldn't hear her, so she had to repeat it.

"All right then, Nellie. So, *did* you leave the defendant alone in the cellar?"

She nodded. "But not for long. Just two times." A male juror smirked so she looked right at him as she spoke. "Max didn't do anything wrong and I'm the only one that knows that. The only one that can help him." She could tell by all the lowered eyes that people felt bad. Embarrassed as they were, her parents continued to smile.

"Nellie," Judge Vasquez urged, the wide sleeve of her robe grazing her shoulder as she leaned close. "You're not here to *help* anyone. You're here to tell the truth, and that's all you have to do. Do you understand?"

"Yes." She'd really messed up. Now her every word would sound like a lie. That she'd admitted to perjury meant nothing then. She didn't even know it was a punishable offense. Later she would realize how kind everyone was trying to be. For her parents' sake.

Testimony resumed with Mr. Cowie's checking his notes, particularly when it came to the discovery of Dolly's body.

"So Max Devaney asked you to open Miss Bedelia's door, is that correct?"

"Yes."

"Why did he ask you to?"

"Because he thought it was locked. I did, too."

"And was it? Was it locked?"

"No."

"And when the door opened, what did you see?"

"Dolly." A shiver of memory tore through her. "She was on the floor, and things were all tipped over. Chairs and things."

"And did you know she was dead?"

She nodded sadly. "Yes," she whispered with a sharp metallic taste in her mouth.

"How did you know?"

"Because . . . because you could just tell."

She's dead. That's what he'd said from behind. Just like Boone, he already knew. He'd known before she even got there, waiting for her, for his witness, for *her* hand on the knob. But she couldn't tell anyone that. They wouldn't understand how things aren't always what they seem. That just like the best holds, words can be used against you, and once you're down, they can kill you.

Mr. Cowie asked a few more questions, the call to her father, the police arrival, and where was Max Devaney during that time?

"In the truck with Boone."

"His dog?"

"Yes."

"And what was he doing?"

"Nothing. Just sitting there." Waiting. Same as then, staring, looking out at nothing. Looking empty.

"That'll be all, Nellie. Thank you. I know this hasn't been easy," Mr. Cowie said quietly as if it were just the two of them in this huge court-room. He started to turn then looked back at her. He knew. There was something she wasn't telling him. *But it's not what you think!* she was silently screaming.

Attorney Eggleston Jay Wright came next. His thin, nasal voice was a relief after the pressure of Mr. Cowie's low, slogging intensity. The first few questions he asked she had already answered. Some he kept rephrasing, like a cloudy glass he was trying to get clean, rubbing, then holding it up to see, rubbing some more, checking again. He brought up the two times she'd left Max alone in the cellar. For how long? Not long, she said. A couple minutes, that was all. And what was he doing when she got back? Same thing, still working on the pipes.

"And to your knowledge, Mr. Devaney never once went into Dolly Bedelia's apartment the whole time he was there?"

She wasn't sure whether to answer yes, he never once did, or no, he didn't. "He never went into her apartment." Couldn't be clearer than that.

"Now, earlier you said you heard a commotion coming from that apartment. Was Mr. Devaney there when you heard it?"

"No."

"How do you know, how can you be certain he wasn't there?"

"Because he hadn't come yet, I mean, his truck, it wasn't there."

"Not in the driveway, you mean."

"It wasn't in the driveway, or the street either. And I know because I kept looking. Henry, my brother and me, we were supposed to go to the mall, but we couldn't leave until Max came. Which is when I was supposed to call my father. For him to come, so we could leave." There! She was getting back on track.

"So the first time you saw Mr. Devaney, the very first time you heard him or knew he was there, was when his truck pulled into the driveway. At three-fifty-five. Five of four in the afternoon, is that correct?"

"Yes."

"You're a very observant girl," he said with a cocky nod.

"Thank you." She liked Wright. She'd been wrong. He was as tough as she was. Together they'd set Max free. She frowned, anticipating the next key question, the lethal blow.

"So at five of four you actually saw the truck pull into the driveway, is that correct?"

"Yes, but first I heard it. The truck—it's loud," she said, not that she really remembered, but to make her point.

"So if the truck had come at any time before that, would you have heard it?"

"Oh yeah. It's really loud, like rattling, shaking-all-over kind of loud."

"Pretty loud then." He looked amused.

"Yeah, even with the fans so loud, I would've heard, it's so loud."

"I see." Wright gave a stiff nod.

Her mind raced, needing to make this work, to put the fans in logical context. "And then right after that Max turned the fans off so I would've heard. I mean . . ." She stared at him. "I mean when I went upstairs. Those two times. I would've heard. If anything happened, I mean."

Seeing Wright start to turn, she panicked. "Oh, and there's something else!" she called out. "I just thought of it, Max's cut, the one on his hand. When I came back down, the first time, that's when I saw it. And the reason I know he got it in the cellar's because the cloth he wrapped around, it was from the ragbag next to the dryer." Her lightning bolt, proof he hadn't cut himself in an earlier struggle with Dolly, but as he'd said, on one of the pipes. "Green-and-white striped, from my mother's old nightgown," she added and saw her mother's fingers twisting in her lap.

Wright's eyes flickered in wild assessment, struggling for some way to turn this to his client's advantage. Instead, he thanked her, then told the judge he had no further questions of the witness.

No further questions? she thought, stunned by the brevity of his effort. Was that it? His best defense of an innocent man? As she left the witness stand, she paused, looked right at Max and smiled. His hand covered his mouth, but his eyes told her he knew she'd tried.

Chapter 24

T HE CAR DOORS WEREN'T EVEN CLOSED AND SHE WAS COM-
plaining about Max's lawyer. "Why'd he quit like that?" she
sputtered from the backseat. "It's not like he ran out of time
or anything. He's just lazy, that's why." Seat belts clicked. No one answered. Her father started the car and her mother stared out the side
window. Did she want to be dropped off at the salon, he asked. No,
she was way too drained, she said. All she wanted was to climb into
bed and pull the covers over her head, she sighed, which should have
been Nellie's cue, but indignation and frustration had far surpassed
shame. "I mean, look at all the questions Mr. Cowie had," she said.
"The other guy, he just wanted to finish. Like, *that's it*! *Don't wanna
hear any more!*"

"I think we've had enough legalities for one day," her father said.
"Let's not talk about it."

"But the rag proves it," she persisted. "He—"

"That's enough!" Her mother's first words to her since they'd left.
She looked back at her.

"Sandy," her father warned.

"Well, he's not a very good lawyer," Nellie muttered, when she
turned away. "Hardly even tried."

Her mother spun around on the seat.

"But it's true!" Nellie cried.

"True?! Excuse me, young lady, *you* want to talk about what's true?
I mean, why did you do that? How could you? How could you get up
there in front of all those people and lie? With us sitting right there!
And under oath, no less. Nellie, I don't even know what to say to you.
I don't think you know the difference anymore between the truth

and a lie. That wasn't some game you were playing back there, som[e]
school play. That man's on trial for murder. Murder, Nellie! And you
look right straight out at people and tell one lie after another? Oh, my
God!" She kept shaking her head.

"One, that's all I told," she said quietly, sliding low onto the seat.
"And I'm sorry."

"One? You kept saying it!" She gripped the top of her head with
both hands. "So of course he didn't want to ask you too many questions. He was afraid!"

"Now, Sandy, that's a little too—"

"What? What, Ben? A little too honest?" she cried.

The car swerved a little as her father pulled out of traffic, and into a
parking space. With the engine running, he sat with one arm over the
back of the seat. He reached for Nellie's hand, but her arms stayed folded.
They'd been going to wait for this discussion until they got home, he
said, but some things were just too important to be put on hold.

"You see, Nell, that's the trouble with a lie," he said. "It taints everything. You should've told the truth right from the start and let the
chips fall where they may."

"I did, but you wouldn't listen!" She began to cry with the futility of it all. "You didn't believe me! I told you about Mr. Cooper! You
know I did!"

"Stop it, Nellie!" her mother demanded, and now she was crying,
too. "Stop it right now! What're you trying to do, destroy us? And besides, who on earth would believe you now? About anything?"

Nellie curled up on the seat.

Her father pulled back into traffic and delivered his weeping family
safely home.

THE TRIAL CONTINUED without her. She wasn't called back for any
more testimony so, apparently, her mother had been right. In a way
it was a relief, though at least, she could have seen Max again. She
thought of him often in the next few days, how depressed he must be,
how helpless. She'd only made things worse for him, and for that, she
hated herself, her indecision and weakness, her fear. She had to believe

he'd be found not guilty, but there was no one she could talk to, no one. Her lie under oath had not only fortified her position in the family as a habitual liar, but now there was talk of her emotional problems. She'd sneezed suddenly the other night and everyone had jumped. Even Henry was treating her differently. Her mother wanted her to see someone. Her father agreed. As long as it was the right person, he said. Of course, her mother said. A search had been launched, and Ruth was deeply involved. Or so she had Nellie believing.

They'd made an appointment with Dr. Willington, Ruth told her, but had canceled it when she reminded them that Alicia Boudreau was Dr. Willington's stepdaughter. Alicia was in Nellie's class.

"So now they're checking out shrinks from some other town," Ruth said from her desk. She was doing math homework on her calculator.

"I don't care," Nellie said, moving around her room. She'd come up looking for a clear cover for her history report. She was only allowed in here with Ruth's permission, and never alone.

"Well, you should. You should care about something, don't you think, instead of yourself all the time," she said, and Nellie rolled her eyes.

"So are you gonna go?" Nellie was reading the most recent letter from her sister's "real" father, as Ruth took great pleasure in saying. Alongside his newspaper clipping, the letter was tacked to Ruth's bulletin board. He'd invited her to come stay with him and his family for a few weeks next summer: "The girls can't wait to meet their big sister." Nellie bristled, wondering where she'd fit into this new constellation, half stepsister, step half sister?

"Well, yeah! I just need enough for the plane ticket."

"How much is that?"

"Three thousand."

Might as well try and raise enough for a ticket to the moon, she wanted to say but didn't. The dribs of Ruth's forgiveness were still being eked out. Sometimes she made it seem as if Nellie was the reason her father had ignored her existence from birth.

"What about him, your real father, can he give you any?" Nellie knew he couldn't.

"I've already got eight hundred, and Mom and Ben'll help. Soon as they sell the store. Few more weeks and we'll be rich, rich, rich." She swiveled around on her chair. "Hey, how come you're not friends with Jessica anymore?"

"I don't know." Nellie hated it when she called him Ben.

"Well, you must know. You always used to be friends."

"Well, for one thing, she's really mean. Especially to Henry. And she steals stuff. And she's always talking about how much she hates her mother. She even said she—"

"Well, guess what," Ruth interrupted, rolling closer on her chair. "Guess who Louie Cooper wants to go out with?" Grinning, she held out her arms. "Moi!"

"He's a drug dealer!"

"Oh, my God." Ruth shook her head. "You've gotta stop, you can't keep doing this, Nellie. It's—"

"But it's true! I saw it. With my own eyes. Jessica showed me. Bags of it, pot, in his room. She took the key down—she showed me."

Ruth wheeled back to her desk, opened a drawer and pulled out a clear plastic cover. "Go," she said, flipping it onto her bed. "Will you please just go?"

WHEN THEY FINALLY saw Lazlo's completed painting, she and Henry were disappointed. They stared, not knowing what to say. It looked like their tree house, but it didn't. His was a nest of boards and sticks, without nails or bolts, more image than structure. More hope than reality. An idea that with the first strong wind would come crashing down.

"What do you think?" Lazlo asked.

"Very nice," they answered in unison. "I like the colors," Nellie added.

"Our tree's bigger though," Henry said, and she pressed against him, hoping to stop him there.

"You're right," Lazlo said, taping more bubble wrap around a painting. He'd been packing them for his booth at Art in the Park. "Mine's not as substantial as yours." The wrapped paintings were stacked by the front door, waiting to be carried out to his car. It was Saturday and her father and mother were both at work. Not wanting them to stay in the house all day, they'd left a list of things to do. After helping

Lazlo, they were supposed to walk down to the store and help their father pack up all the junk in the cellar. Every day he brought some to Charlie's. Mr. Cooper had finally gotten financing. He was hoping to pass papers on the property sometime before Christmas. It was up to the lawyers now, only a matter of scheduling, he'd assured her father.

"And," Henry said, peering closer, "we don't have electricity in our tree house.

The tree house in the painting glowed against a darkening sky. "Maybe it's just a reflection," Lazlo said, lifting it off the easel to be wrapped. "Or a candle, or the Humboldt's motion detector."

"How come you don't know?" Henry asked, and Lazlo laughed.

"That's so not the point, my young philistine," he said, then waving a strip of bubble wrap toward the kitchen, asked him to get his car keys. They were hanging over the sink. Henry cringed back. Each gestured for the other to do it.

He asked you, Nellie mouthed, pointing, then seeing her brother's fear, forced herself to enter that tiny kitchen where Dolly still lay even with gleaming vinyl flooring and fresh paint, her head near the table, her soiled feet by the cupboard door. Had she run in here trying to escape to the cellar? Or was this where her killer had found her? The door had been painted, forever obscuring Max's bloody thumbprint. Had he left it on his way in or his way out? The only signs of struggle had been in here. She snatched the key from the hook and hurried back to Lazlo.

"How can you live in here?" she blurted. "Don't you get freaked out?"

"Sometimes. But don't forget this was my home a long time before that happened. Plus, I didn't know her like you guys did," Lazlo said as they carried out the larger paintings first. He arranged them in his trunk, layering blankets between the frames. "That's probably the hardest part. Right?"

"She wasn't a very nice lady," Henry declared.

"What're you talking about? You hardly even knew her," Nellie snapped, which triggered one of those volleys of bickering they'd had so many of lately.

"Like that time she was mean to Max, I heard what she said."

"So did I."

"Not all of it. You went inside, and she said if he didn't stop bothering her, she was gonna call the police and tell 'em he shouldn't be hanging around us kids all the time. He said something, so then she called him a pervert and he got in his truck real fast and peeled out."

"I knew that."

"No, you didn't!"

The tree house painting took up most of the backseat. She rode up front with her brother squeezed in back, close against the wide silver frame strapped firmly in place by a seat belt.

"If we crash, Henry," Lazlo called back, "your one mission is to save the painting. Got that?"

"Yes, sir," Henry answered. "But what if I can't? Who gets saved, me or the painting?"

"Well, thank goodness Nellie's here. She'd have to save you while I'm rescuing my painting. Unless," he laughed, looking back in the rearview mirror, "we have to sacrifice you for the sake of the art. And sometimes that happens."

She looked out the window. Sacrificed—*but for the sake of what? Convenience, comfort?*

"I'm more important than a painting!" Henry protested.

"Who says?" Lazlo laughed.

"I'm a person!" Henry called back.

"Who says?" Lazlo laughed.

Their sparring continued all the way to the park. *What was Max doing on this warm fall morning as he waited for the jury to decide what the rest of his life would be like?* The leaves on the trees were edged in reds and yellows. The park was already filling with people, anchoring their tent poles into the ground. *No matter what they decided, Max had been serving his sentence for a long time. Life couldn't be that unfair, it just couldn't.*

She and Henry helped Lazlo carry his display tent. They walked up and down the paths trying to find number fifty-six, his assigned spot. Many of the artists knew Lazlo. "That's too bad," a pretty young woman was telling him. Number fifty-six was on the far end, on the other side of the bandstand. Lazlo looked discouraged as they dragged the metal poles and rolled canvas to the last numbered placard. They were at the end of the longest path, next to a trash barrel.

"How about over there?" Nellie pointed to all the space in the middle of the park where vendors were setting up pizza, frozen slush, and popcorn stands. A balloon cart had just arrived.

"We can't. There's no numbers," Lazlo said.

"There will be now," she said, picking up the placard and heading toward the food vendors, but Lazlo raced after her and took it back. He'd stay where he'd been assigned. But that's not fair, she said, and Henry agreed. Nobody was going to come down this far. Such was life, the luck of the draw, Lazlo sighed; not everybody could get the best location.

"But you got a bad one last year, too. And you didn't sell any paintings, remember? Not one single one," she reminded him. She knew because at the end of the day they'd helped carry them all the way back through the park to his car. She felt bad. She could tell she'd embarrassed him. But what was the point of going to all this trouble when nobody would see his paintings?

"This'll be fine." He worked quickly in his remote spot, lacing the canvas to the poles. They held them straight while he pounded the stakes into ground. "Plus, I'll be in the shade here."

Deep darkness was more like it with all the trees and bushes, but she kept quiet. It took three trips for them to carry all the paintings to Lazlo. When they were finished, he tried giving them each five dollars, but they told him they'd get in trouble if they took it. He insisted, saying not to worry—he'd take the heat for them.

When they got to the store, their father was in his office, talking on the phone. He seemed very distracted, almost as if he'd forgotten they were coming. The lights were on, but the store was empty. There were still some items left on the shelves that he hoped to clear out with the week-long going-out-of-business sale he was planning in November. He told them to wait; he had to take care of the call first. Henry asked if they could go across the street and get something to eat, but her father said to wait, just wait. He had no sooner closed the door to his office when a lady came into the store, carrying two chrome towel rods. She needed four new screws for them. Nellie said she'd get her father.

"This is the second day," she overheard him say when she knocked on the door. He hurried out of his office. "Connie," he greeted the woman who gave him the towel rods. She told him what she needed.

"Shouldn't be much longer now," she said, following him to the back of the store. "Can't imagine they want to be doing this all week-end long."

"Just a quick minute," her father said, excusing himself. He opened the door to the cellar and told Nellie and Henry to go down and start filling boxes.

The harsh odor of moldy wet earth made them both sneeze. Her hands were quickly filthy. Part of the cellar had a dirt floor, which was where most of the oldest junk had been tossed. Old signs, pipes, buckets, wooden boxes of everything from rusty siphons, shelf brackets, loose nails and sheets of ceramic tiles, covered with soot and cobwebs. Henry counted sixteen water-stained bags of solidified concrete. It was pretty obvious their father hadn't been taking care of business for some time. They started dragging boxes to the bulkhead door.

After the customer left, their father came downstairs. They filled the trunk and the backseat with boxes, then drove to the junkyard. Charlie met them at the gate. "Better'n a cane," he said of the rusted grocery cart he was pushing. His hair was matted and he smelled of stale urine, but he was delighted by the arriving junk.

"Just pile it all up, and I'll go through it later," he directed, pointing to the barn. He leaned on the cart handle while they unloaded the car. When something caught his eye, he'd fish it out of the box and drop it into his cart. "Brackets'll go fast," he said. "Anything wrought iron." The front of his shirt was stained with food and his long fingernails were dirty. He started to cough, the deep rumble in his chest doubling him over the cart. He began to wheeze, unable to catch his breath.

"C'mon, Charlie, let's go in the house." Her father held his arm and guided him slowly inside.

Unloading the rest of the car went faster without Charlie picking through every single box. When they'd finished, her father still hadn't come out so they scurried up into the dark loft and stood staring at the bare cot, the sag of its body contour, deep, as if someone had only just risen from it.

"You think he'll ever come back?" Henry asked.

"Maybe," she said, and then her father was calling from the bottom of the stairs.

He drove home very fast. All he said was that Charlie wasn't doing well. Soon after they arrived, her mother and Ruth rushed out to take Charlie to the emergency room. In the time they were gone, almost two hours, Nellie's father cooked hot dogs and beans and canned brown bread for dinner. They had just started eating when Lazlo came next door.

"Sit down, I'll get a plate," her father said, already taking flatware from the drawer. Lazlo said he had to show them something. He stood over the table grinning with his hands behind his back.

"You won, didn't you?" her father said, and Lazlo held up his blue ribbon. First prize. They burst into applause, then passed it around the table.

"And!" Lazlo said, sitting down. "Some lady from New York and her husband want to buy it! A thousand dollars, can you believe it! And it's all because of you," he said to Henry.

"And Nellie," her brother said, which gave her that hollow feeling she often had lately when the happiness around her seemed more the absence of something than a presence.

The judges' unanimous choice had been the tree house painting, and tomorrow there would even be a picture of it in the paper, Lazlo told them as he spooned the dark syrupy beans onto his plate.

"It's about time," her father said. "Some good news. Finally."

IT WOULD BE another hour before her mother and Ruth came home. Hearing about Charlie made Nellie sad. He'd been admitted to the hospital. Chest X-rays showed a large mass on both lungs. For now, they were telling him it was pneumonia, which her mother said was kind of true. Tomorrow they'd know more and could better explain it to him.

"He was so strangely calm," her mother said. "As if he already knows."

"He probably does," Nellie's father said.

"Poor Charlie," Ruth said, teary-eyed again. "He just looked so small, the sheets up to his chin."

"He's never been very big, hon," her mother said, patting her hand again.

"He thinks he is, though," Nellie said, then with everyone staring at her, she tried to explain that she wasn't being disrespectful. All she meant was that he never backed down from anybody or anything no matter what they thought or said, "Kind of like in the manual, what Major Fairbairn says. How just a little exertion and you can make even the strongest, most powerful prisoner obey you. It's like this strike force—boom boom, you just . . ." Her jabbing fists dropped and her voice trailed off.

"That's random," Ruth said, shaking her head, wide-eyed.

NELLIE WAS IN bed when the phone rang downstairs. She heard her mother's and father's voices. The hospital, she assumed, then was relieved when the house fell quiet again. She'd been reading a book from the school library, *The Light in the Forest*. John Butler had been four years old when the Lenni Lenape Indians stole him from his white family, renamed him True Son, and raised him as their own. If Ruth did go to Australia, maybe her real father would give her another name, maybe one from his family, his mother's or grandmother's. Or maybe some kind of strange Australian name, she mused, staring up at the ceiling's hairline cracks, like rays in the plaster streaming out from the old brass light fixture. If she did go, Nellie knew she'd never come back, and then what would happen here, to all of them? Well, one thing, with the third floor empty, she could move up there, but she'd keep her sister's room exactly as she'd left it.

Her eyes were starting to close when there was a knock on the door. Both in their bathrobes, her mother and father came into the room. They knew it was late, they whispered, but they had to talk to her. Her whole body stiffened. Charlie—she could tell.

"Oh, Nellie, my sweet little girl," her mother said, sitting on one side of the bed. Her father sat down on the other. Her mother kept shaking her head. "I blame myself. I should've just let that apartment sit empty. That was the beginning. From that point on, everything's just been a mess. The whole summer, it's just been so crazy." She took Nellie's hands in hers. "And then the trial, we never should've let you do that."

"Well, what choice did we have, Sandy? I mean . . ." her father said softly.

"We should've had her talk to someone."

"Well, it was going to happen, regardless."

"But she's a child. Look at her, we forget she's a little girl. She shouldn't've had to have all that pressure on her. We weren't thinking. It's like we just threw her to the wolves. We did, didn't we?" she said, starting to cry. She hugged Nellie, who let herself collapse into her mother. "We didn't protect you, and now you're paying the price." Her mother kept stroking her back.

Nellie still hadn't said anything. Part of it was aching to be held and comforted and part was confusion. What was the price? Did they think something was wrong with her? That she was disturbed? Crazy?

"The verdict just came in," her father said, and she pulled free. One look, and she knew. "They found him guilty, hon," he whispered.

"That's not fair!" she cried. "It's not right, and you know it's not!"

"Shh, shh," they kept saying, though their sadness and concern were for her, for her state of mind, her already fragile moral equilibrium. They had no doubt of Max Devaney's guilt. Whether in rage or cold blood, he had murdered an innocent young woman, gone home to freshen up, then returned to install the hot-water tank and wipe down the crime scene, hoping to cover his tracks. Simple as that, their most compelling evidence his bloody fingerprint just inside her door. And just below it, where it had fallen to the floor, the bloodied strip of rag that had been on his hand. Everything else was insubstantial. Even the scrapings under Dolly's broken fake nails yielded no traceable DNA. The few fingerprints they did find were unidentifiable. In that always messy apartment the killer had taken both time and care to wipe off practically every surface. And he'd used one of the bigger pieces of that same green-and-white striped cloth from their ragbag in the cellar.

So Max would spend the rest of his life in prison for a crime he hadn't committed. For the next few days she could barely eat. Charlie had terminal cancer. Her mother begged him to at least try chemo and radiation, but he didn't see the point. He'd had a good life, he said, and wasn't about to mess it up now. His plan was to get a little stronger, then go back home and do what needed doing. Charlie was only getting sicker and no one wanted to hear about her troubles anymore. She was thirteen years old and it was time to think about her family.

"Care what happens to us for a change!" her mother had lashed out a few nights before when she pushed her plate away, saying that every time she thought of Max she felt sick to her stomach.

"Sandy," her father tried to soothe her. "Some things, Nellie just needs to say, that's all." Which only made her mother cry.

"Come here, honey." Her mother held out her arms. "I'm sorry. Daddy's right," she wept, though that didn't mean there'd be any more talk of Max Devaney, Nellie knew. As far as her mother was concerned, he'd gotten exactly what he deserved.

Do what needed doing, Charlie's words had become a calming and urgent mantra.

OVER THE NEXT few days her father tried to answer her questions. She couldn't understand why they hadn't told her many of the details before the trial. That way she would have been better prepared. He was driving her to school for the third morning in a row. He thought she'd overslept again, but the truth was she didn't want to run into anyone. He was the only person she could talk to, the only one listening, or at least with any patience. Everyone else had moved on.

"Like the rag, I wouldn't've said that," she groaned as he pulled in front of school.

"No, Nellie. Now, stop thinking like that. That was just one thing, one element among many. And besides, this was completely out of your control. It's just something you were caught up in. And what happened, happened. Both before and after, and you have to accept it."

"But it's wrong! They're wrong!" Again, the same go round and round and round. Bewildering, how the most sensitive, ethical man she'd ever known could be so shortsighted, blind even.

"Nellie, everything points to his guilt. The evidence. Even Charlie didn't know where he went that morning. He was gone for hours."

"Because he was fishing! He told me."

"But no one saw him fishing."

"That doesn't prove anything. Just because no one saw him doesn't mean it didn't happen. You said that before."

"Nellie. Come on, hon." He looked at her wearily. "You're going to be late."

"You told me. Like a star, you said. And just because we can't prove it doesn't mean it didn't happen, that it never existed. We still have the light. You told me that! You know you did!"

"All right, yes." He took a deep breath. "Yes, that's true. But you can take that same argument, Nellie, and turn it the other way. Some things just are the way they are. One person takes the facts and interprets them his way. You take the exact same facts and interpret them your way. It doesn't mean the original act didn't happen. Like where Max was all that morning. He had to be somewhere, that we know."

"Yeah, he was fishing!"

He put his hand on her shoulder and took a deep breath. "All right, think of it this way: two blind men come upon this huge animal. They both walk around, touching it. Neither one knows what it is. The first fellow says, 'Oh, okay, I get it; it's some kind of a hose.' But then the other keeps feeling and he says, 'No, it's trees, four trees.' And for them, that's their truth, their truth of the animal, their experience of it. They really believe that. But here's the thing. It's an elephant. It is what it is, the sum of all its parts. It's real, even though the two men can't actually see it. Do you know what I'm saying?"

She nodded. "Yeah. Same as me, that he's innocent."

His next words were lost in the blare of the school bell. A few stragglers ran up the steps and into the building.

"Come on, Nell, better get a move on now."

"He's innocent, Dad. He is, and I know he is."

For a long moment he studied her. "Because your experience of Max tells you he's innocent. But you've never experienced his guilt. You don't know who he really is, his true morality."

"Just like Mr. Cooper, you don't know who he is, who he *really* is."

"I've known Andy Cooper a long, long time, hon, and he may have his flaws, like any one of us, but he is *no murderer*. Believe me."

"Knowing someone a long time, that doesn't prove anything."

"Okay, Nellie girl," he sighed. "That's enough." He set her backpack on her lap. "What do I have to do, carry you in?" He was trying hard to smile.

"But, Dad, wait! Wait. You always say you'll help, all I have to do is ask, so what if Max didn't do it, and it really was Mr. Cooper, and I'm the only that knows it, what should I do?"

"You shouldn't ruin a good man's life, damn it, Nellie, that's what you shouldn't do!" he said so bitterly that she was stung, shocked into silence.

But which man did he mean?

ONCE SHE HAD made up her mind, she could almost see better, further, more clearly. "We've got to be tough to win, and we've got to be ruthless—tougher and more ruthless than our enemies," urged the major's voice, and as she walked slowly from school, resolutely, could feel herself slicing through air and time, her entire being a blade through caution and obedience. She took her time getting there. All along the way everything had changed, like her, the brightness brighter, the dark darker. Stronger, taller, older, she moved with sure and fluid grace.

"Nellie Peck," she told the secretary, a pretty, gray-haired woman who pulled her glasses low on her nose.

"Is it about the property?" She sorted through folders on her desk. "Did your father send you?"

"No. I just need to talk to Mr. Cooper, that's all," she said. "If he's not busy, that is," she added, to be polite. She didn't give a damn how busy he was. Just thinking the swear was exhilarating.

Smiling, his secretary glanced at her backpack. "Is this for school? Are you selling something?"

"No." She stared back.

The woman looked down uneasily, checked her phone. "He's on the phone right now," she said hesitantly. "It's probably going to be a pretty long call. So do you want to maybe come back in a little while, or—"

"I can't." She kept wetting her lips, her mouth was so dry. It was hard to swallow. "It's really important."

The secretary scribbled on a Post-it note, opened his door, and slipped inside.

"He said to wait," she said when she returned.

Nellie sat in one of the three suede club chairs. She didn't have to wait long. Mr. Cooper opened his door and came out, smiling.

"Well, this is my lucky day. Nellie Peck! Come on in, young lady." He held open the door to his office. "To what do I owe this pleasure?" he said, then, as if just remembering something, turned back to his secretary. "You know what, Ginny, you can go. I'll just finish up tomorrow."

Even after he closed the door and asked her to sit down, Nellie remained on her feet. She wasn't afraid of him, just afraid of losing her courage, which was the worst fear of all.

"Please," he said, gesturing to the opposite chair. "Go ahead, sit down. You're making me very uncomfortable, standing there staring at me like this." He tried to chuckle. "There, that's better," he said when she finally sat down. "So what's this all about? Something about Jessica?" He sighed and shook his head. "What's my dear daughter done now?"

"It's about Dolly's murder—"

"Dolly?" He frowned. "Oh yes. That's right. I'm so sorry, the young woman in your house. Of course. Yes. What a terrible thing. Your dad said it's just been awful, for the whole family. The trial, all that publicity and—"

"You were there that day, Mr. Cooper. I heard what happened. All the noise, and things getting knocked over, and then I saw you. You were right outside her door. You were in the bushes almost, and your face—it was scratched. And something was wrong, I knew it, I could see it, and then after you left, that's when he came, Max Devaney with the hot-water tank, but she was already dead. And you know she was, don't you?" Panting, breathless, talking so fast, hearing only her own voice, not his, though he was speaking, trying to, *because once closed with her enemy, she had no choice but give every ounce of effort she could muster, and victory would be hers. And Max's.* "And all those other times—I saw you going in there, even a couple nights before, late, really late. I saw you leaving—almost running, you were in such a hurry. And she told me about that time on the boat and looking up at all the stars. And that was when she got the sunburn, the same time. And that hat you bought her—"

"Stop it!" he'd been saying. "Will you please just stop it!" he demanded.

"And I don't know how you can let an innocent man go to jail for the rest of his life for something you did. How can you do that?"

If he thought she was crying, she wasn't, not really, not tears of weakness and fear, only relief, seeping out of her.

"I'm sorry, but I don't know what to say to you, Nellie. You've worked yourself into quite a state here." With gleaming gaze fixed, frozen like a blade midthrust, he paused as he spoke, the same staged calm as that day. "This is crazy . . . absolutely crazy. Are you listening? Do you know what I'm saying?" He reached across the desk and she jumped, which startled him. "Settle down, just settle down. All I'm gonna do is call your dad and have him come get you. But if it makes you feel any better, I'll just go call him from the other phone." He stood up slowly, as if not to alarm her, and slipped into the outer office.

She sat perfectly straight, staring over her backpack. "Ben," all she heard him say, the rest muffled.

"Your dad's on his way," he said, from the doorway. "He should be here any minute."

"You killed her, Mr. Cooper. And I know you did." Teeth chattering, bones trembling, an explosion, pieces falling, settling around her. All energy spent, she'd done what needed doing. Finally. The rest, now up to him.

"Nellie!" Her father took her backpack.

"I'm okay," she kept saying as he gripped the arm of this fragile, shaken creature he was trying to lift from the chair.

"I'll call you," he said on their way past Mr. Cooper, who looked sad, and very ashamed, she was pleased to see.

Chapter 25

——

THERE WERE TWENTY BAGS OF LEAVES IN FRONT OF THE HOUSE waiting for the town's fall pickup. Days of cold winds blowing had stripped most trees bare. November felt like midwinter. Usually youth was its own best narcotic until those awful moments when she would be seized by sudden guilt. Mostly she felt limp. Gone was the terrible urgency of needing to make every part fit sensibly together. After all, what had she been hoping for? That Mr. Cooper would suddenly confess, that science would prove the truth, that jurors would have been so impressed, so touched by her declaration of Max's innocence that they'd doubt the only evidence they'd been given and believe a girl whose own family not only didn't but thought she was way too tightly wound and going through some kind of adolescent, premenstrual breakdown. Still, though, they tried to be patient and loving. "Teenage girls, tell me about it," Mr. Cooper had said, sighing, when her father tried to apologize. Andy had seen more than his share of hysterical meltdowns Claudia Cooper had assured Sandy when they met for coffee, a humiliation her mother felt compelled to endure.

At the kitchen table her parents had been waiting for her to come downstairs. Still in their pajamas, they looked exhausted, but they wanted her to know they finally understood. Everything made sense now. It had all started last summer with the stolen bikes, hadn't it? That awful Saltonstall boy had told Jessica and she had confided in her mother, but only because they were all so concerned about Nellie, who suddenly didn't even care that they knew. How could it matter? They were talking about something that had happened a long time ago to someone else. If anything, she was amused by the facile weave, every strand tucked into place.

They'd already spoken to Henry. At first he wouldn't tell them much, her mother was saying (seeing how uneasy her grin was making her mother, Nellie forced a frown), but then he'd confessed everything and explained how easily taken in they'd both been by the more "experienced and sly Saltonstall boy," her mother's words, she knew, not Henry's. And, of course, along with that had come Nellie's fears about losing her only sister, Ruth, and then *everything with Dolly and the trial*, which was how it was referred to now. Murder with all its chilling violation had been reworded to a state of murkiness, a complication they were in the process of putting right by moving each piece, each fact into place, because that's what parents did, helped you understand what had really happened, and why. Which is why they wanted her to know that they understood how her problems with Jessica along with their own financial difficulties could become so complicated and confusing that, in her mind, Mr. Cooper was to blame for everything. They were each holding one of her hands and fighting tears, especially her father.

"So I must be really messed up, huh?" *Strange to feel this giddy.*

"Oh, honey," her mother said. "Listen, these things happen."

They do? Really? To whom? she wanted to scream.

"It can all seem so overwhelming sometimes," her father said. "Especially when you're so young. And that's why we want you to talk to someone. A therapist. Okay?"

THE FIRST APPOINTMENT had to be in the evening so that her parents could be there. Once, she would have been eager to have someone willing to hear everything she had to say about whatever was on her mind. But tonight the most she could muster was mild curiosity. Mrs. Fouquet was a tiny woman with dark, intense eyes and short brown hair fastened back by bobby pins she kept fiddling with. Under her faded denim jumper she wore a red plaid turtleneck with a pearl necklace. In Nellie's opinion, a really bad combination, but the message was clear: her mind was on more important matters than fashion coordination. Mrs. Fouquet and her parents had been talking for at least twenty minutes. Mostly about the makeup of the family. The many secrets of Nellie's furtive summer: they made it sound as if she'd been running with Hells Angels. And then, *everything about Dolly and the trial.*

"That's a great deal of pressure to put on anyone, especially a child," Mrs. Fouquet said, and Nellie saw her mother's head tense back.

Seeing her so nervous was puzzling. After all, Nellie was the one under the microscope, not them. Nobody thought *they* were disturbed.

"We wish we'd had her see someone right away," her mother said. "Right after the discovery."

The discovery—they called it that now, not her finding Dolly dead on the littered floor, murdered, strangled, the thin red trickle from her button nose and the corner of her pretty mouth.

"We thought we could handle it," her father was saying. "Nellie's always been so up front about everything. You know, whatever's on her mind she tells you, right then and there."

Nodding, Mrs. Fouquet looked from one to the other. She seemed to like Ben and Sandy. *Probably feels bad such nice people have to have such a lying, thieving, nasty-minded screwup for a daughter.*

"And she's so intelligent," her mother was saying. "Like her father, the two of them, the things they talk about. Sometimes I close my eyes and it's like two adults talking." She flashed Nellie a quick smile.

"So like everything else, I guess we just assumed Nellie was so well grounded she'd get through it okay," her father said, his wistful glance for the daughter he'd thought he had. "She's a good girl."

"Actually, most of our problems have always been with our oldest, with Ruth," her mother said. "But I guess that's what happened— all the turmoil with Ruth, meanwhile, everything with Nellie's going under the radar."

Pretty valid observation, Nellie thought, roused by the realization of how good she'd be at this, therapy, helping people cut through their own bullshit, which was probably her surest skill, and best of all, being paid to do it. Some people she'd spot the minute they came through the door. *Boom, kleptomaniac! Next. Narcissist! You! Pathological Liar!* But then they probably wouldn't want to pay for the whole hour, so she'd have to drag it out, something she'd had plenty of experience doing after all the hours of half listening to Jessica's tales of woe just long enough to get to the end of a show.

"And what about you, Nellie?" Mrs. Fouquet was asking. "What do you have to say about all of this?"

"I don't know." She shrugged, scrambling to take her proper place in this dialogue. Deciding to become a therapist had given her a surge of confidence along with a sense of clinical remove. In addition to the three adults analyzing Nellie Peck, there would be Nellie Peck herself. The problem was that the one thing that needed saying was the very reason they'd brought her here to try to talk her out of.

"You've had to go through a great deal. It couldn't have been easy," Mrs. Fouquet coaxed.

Sympathy, Nellie noted, *bullshitting the bullshitters.*

"What's been the hardest part of it all?" Mrs. Fouquet asked.

"Not being believed." She looked at each of them.

"Not being believed by who?"

Whom, she wanted to say. "Nobody believes me about anything. Except maybe my brother. I think." *And they'd probably brainwashed him, too.*

"Why do you think that is?" Obviously, going for the kill, Mrs. Fouquet repositioned her chair. "That nobody believes you about anything."

Interesting technique, Nellie thought, *the way she reframes each answer.* "Well, first of all, it's probably because I'm a kid, which I get. And maybe even because I'm a girl and I'm supposed to be all hormonal and emotional all the time, which I'm not. Hormonal, that is. But I guess the part I don't really get is how people can call me a liar just so they can keep on lying to themself. Themselves," she quickly corrected.

"No one's calling you a liar!" her mother gasped, to which her father added, "And we never would. That word is not in our lexicon," he informed Mrs. Fouquet.

"Just because you don't say the word doesn't mean you're not thinking it," Nellie said in her most precise diction.

"Nellie," her mother implored, shaking her head.

"Excuse me, Nellie, let's try something," Mrs. Fouquet said. "Put yourself in your parents' shoes, switch places, so to speak. Now, every time they tell you a story, you have a hard time believing it, and the reason you can't is because of all the things they've made up before that weren't true. So then one day there's a terrible incident and they come to you and try to explain exactly what happened. But by then, you'd have a hard time believing them, wouldn't you?" Mrs. Fouquet's face glowed with cleverness.

The little boy who cried wolf? That was weak. Better not to get tangled up in the analogy, Nellie decided, opting to sidestep that one. "But they never do, they never lie. Mostly, they just don't tell us things. They wait till we leave the room. So I usually just try and figure things out myself," she said, eliciting wan smiles from her parents.

"We don't argue in front of the children," her mother tried to explain. "We never have."

"But you must argue sometimes," Mrs. Fouquet said. "Most couples do."

"Not really," her mother said with a quizzical look at Nellie's father.

"Disagreements, the quick kerfuffle," he said. "And the occasional slammed door. Or frosty silence," he intoned in a deeper voice, so stern faced that her mother giggled. "Icicles." He shivered, and Nellie smiled, observing them across a barrier only she knew was there. She loved them, she did, which made their tenderness toward each other only the more isolating. And bewildering.

Now came Nellie's time alone with Mrs. Fouquet. Her parents left to sit in the waiting room, relieved and grateful, their burdens already lighter. Mrs. Fouquet wanted to stay on the subject of Nellie's figuring out things for herself. Nellie got right to the point. She explained what she couldn't actually say to her parents. There was only one reason they didn't believe her, and one reason only. They needed Mr. Cooper's help.

"Do you really think your parents would do that just to sell some property?" Mrs. Fouquet had gone skeptically squinty eyed on her. A bobby pin dangled over one ear.

"Maybe they don't think of it that way, but that's what they're doing."

"You sound angry. Are you? Are you mad at them?"

Nellie thought a moment. "Not really. More like disappointed, I guess."

"How so?"

She cringed with the annoying expression. It made her more determined to say exactly what she meant. "Sometimes I think it's easier for kids when their parents are all messed up. They don't know, so they have to find everything out for themselves. They're tougher then, stronger in a way. In my family there's the right way and the wrong way, so it always seemed easy. You know, just follow the rules. But it's like this muscle you never get to use. Then all of a sudden when you have to, you find out, whoa, wait a minute, there's all these other reasons, but we won't talk about those, so you just do what we tell you." She looked up, conscious of the warmth and the low light in the room, the watchful silence. "I'm sorry. I can be very loquacious sometimes. Actually, most of the time."

"Oh no, not at all. I'm impressed," Mrs. Fouquet said, repinning her hair. "You're very mature and you have a great deal of insight, which is a gift, but it can also be difficult when you're young. And confusing."

"Because people think you don't know what you're talking about, right? I mean, when you're a kid."

"Sometimes the hardest part of being a kid is accepting when something's out of our control."

"But it's not! Out of my control, I mean, because I'm the one that can make things right. The way they should be."

Air ball, not even close, Nellie realized, seeing Mrs. Fouquet glance at the glowing red numbers, the tiny digital clock on the side table, unobtrusive, but strategically placed. "In any event, Nellie, that'll take some time," she said, closing a folder. "And patience. A lot of patience, both on your part and your parents'." She reached across the desk and shook Nellie's hand, her firm grip holding a moment. "And by the way, that muscle, that's a good muscle to keep flexing," she said with a wink.

RUTH HAD GOTTEN all A's on her midterm report. Henry had a boil on his cheek that had just been lanced. His description of what came oozing out made his sisters beg him to stop. Charlie was back home, most days spent in bed. He had agreed to a visiting homemaker and nurse after her mother threatened to petition the court for legal guardianship. Benjamin's half-filled application for a job at Home Depot was still on the kitchen counter. Her mother was working on invitations for the jewelry party she was planning to have two weeks before Christmas. Might as well turn the notoriety to some commercial advantage, she'd decided. Lazlo regretted selling his prizewinning painting, he told Benjamin. It had left him with a great emptiness, which he admitted didn't make sense. Maybe it wasn't emptiness so much as the well he needed to keep filling, her father suggested, likening it to his own experience. He was still trying to find a publisher, but in the meantime he'd started the research for his next book. It would be about George C. Humboldt and his connection to the old railroad line, a subject few people knew anything about. After two very long and productive visits with the Humboldts, he'd already filled an entire notebook. Tenley had begun sorting through ancient family papers, boxes of them in their attic. Louisa said she hadn't seen her brother this engaged, this excited about anything, in years. If ever.

NELLIE HAD STARTED a letter to Max. Twelve pages long, it was mostly fiction, Charlie feeling better, her long walks with Boone, but she couldn't seem to finish it. Something needed saying, though she wasn't sure what. Or maybe there was nothing to say, no good ending. Not a satisfying one, anyway. Maybe she just needed to keep on writing. Maybe that was it, her connection.

SHE HAD BEEN sent to keep Charlie company. Mrs. Kirkley, his day nurse, had to leave a little early, and Nellie could fill the gap until the night nurse arrived. She came directly from school. She was almost at the junkyard when the Shelby twins drove by on their souped-up bicycles with Boone leashed to Rodney's handlebar. ASTRO BOWL-ERAMA, said the bold white stitching on their satiny black jackets. They stopped and rode back.

"Boone! Hey, Boone." She dropped to her knees and hugged him. "How're you doin', big fella?" The dog's tail whipped back and forth and he nuzzled his head against hers. *He knows I tried*—she could feel it, rubbing his broad chest. "His heart," she said, looking up, "it's beating so fast." The brothers were grinning at each other.

"Cuz he likes you," Rodney said.

"No, I don't! *You* do, you're the one!" Roy said.

"I meant him." Rodney pointed to Boone.

"You both do, then," Roy said, rocking back and forth, an awkward attempt to calm himself that had amused many tormentors over the years.

"Shut up!" Rodney swiped his brother's arm.

"It's true. You even told Mom," Roy said, and Rodney's face turned red.

Saying she'd better go, Nellie stood up. Her own face felt hot.

"Hey, that crazy guy, he was guilty, huh?" Rodney said quickly.

"He wasn't crazy." She started walking. Rodney rode slowly next to her, with Roy trailing.

"Well, I wouldn't exactly call him normal, okay?" Roy said then gave his snorting laugh.

"Yeah, like sneaking around, spying on us all the time," Rodney added with such grating self-importance it was all she could do not to run.

"He was a pervert, that's why. A registered sex offender. My mother said she should've called the police; if only she had, that lady'd still be alive," Roy called from behind.

"That's so weird! Why do you say such weird things all the time? No wonder people are always making fun of you!" She pulled open the creaking gate, hurried inside, then banged it shut, shaking the rickety fence on both sides.

Nellie sat across the room, with her history book open, waiting for Charlie to wake up. Still agitated by her run-in with the twins, she couldn't concentrate. She felt terrible. She shouldn't have said what she did, especially when she was the only person they ever talked to, probably in the whole town. Trusting her, they'd let their guard down and she'd turned on them. The worst of it was realizing she was just as mean as everyone else.

Charlie lay propped up against pillows. His cheeks were sunken and unshaven. His eyes were closed. Even from here she knew he wasn't asleep. She could tell by his breathing, and sleeping people didn't keep licking their lips.

"Charlie?" she whispered, getting up. She wanted to talk about Max. "Are you awake?" She asked again when he didn't answer. "Charlie?" She stood over the bed. "You still sleeping?"

"Jesus." His eyes opened wide. "Not anymore I'm not." He closed them again.

"Want some water? Your cup's here."

When he nodded, she guided the straw to his mouth. One sip and he pushed it away. She asked if he was hungry. No, he said. Could she get him anything? No. One of those hard candies on his night stand? No, nothing. How about the TV, did he want it on, she asked hopefully. He didn't. This morning's paper, she'd read it to him if he wanted.

"You know what I want?" He looked sideways with one eye open. "To get this over with, that's all the hell I want."

"Get better you mean?" She knew what he meant.

"No point dragging it out. A sick animal—you wouldn't think twice, right? Put it out of its misery, that's what you'd do. Hey! Why'nt you go get that hammer and—" He thumped the side of his head, then turned away with a sour laugh.

"You think Max'll write you again?" she asked quietly.

He snorted. "Dead men don't write letters."

"What do you mean?" Her voice was strident.

"Like he wanted for his dog." He slashed his finger across his throat. "Better'n being caged up, don't you think?"

"No. There's always hope." Even the word sounded bleak.

"Got news for you, girlie. Guys like Max, they got nothin', and they're born with less. I seen enough to know. Poor bastard, last of the losers. Last one I'll know, anyway." His mouth trickled into a wan, wet smile.

"I thought he was a very nice man." Her voice broke.

"For all the good that does. 'Specially when you're so far down from the get-go."

She got up and stood by the window, arms crossed, looking out at the sea of discarded, unwanted, useless trash Max had tried to organize. Caught in the wind, a torn cardboard box tumbled the length of the rutted driveway. She didn't want Charlie to see her crying. For a few moments the only sound was the rasp of his labored breathing.

"What're you doin' over there, crying? Jesus!"

"I just feel so bad." She covered her mouth.

"Well, don't. Guy like him's just not worth it, that's all."

"No!" she cried, spinning around. "That's not true, and you know it! He worked so hard around here, and he really liked you. And I don't know why, because you didn't even care, did you? Making him sleep up in the barn like he was some kind of bum."

"He *was* a bum! But I was damn good to him, and look how he pays me back, goddammit. Like I haven't got enough goddamn problems. And now I gotta listen to you?" Charlie gasped, straining to squeeze out the words between pants as she grabbed her jacket and backpack and headed for the door. "Yeah, go! Go on! Go! Just get the hell outta here, will ya. I don't need this shit, especially from you . . . you—" Coughing, he couldn't catch his breath. Wide-eyed, he writhed from side to side, struggling to sit up. She slung her arms around him and pulled him up, then had to hold him so he wouldn't fall back. His head hung heavily against hers as his chest rose and fell with each long, desperate wheeze for air. When he tried to speak, the words came like water sloshing in his lungs.

"Breathe, Charlie, please breathe, please," she whispered against his cold, bristly cheek. "Please!" She couldn't believe what she'd done, first to the Shelby twins, then to her poor, sick, old grandfather.

"Lemme go," he gasped, and she told him, no, because she wasn't going to let him die, she wasn't. "I gotta lay down," he pleaded, so she eased him back onto his pillows, then stood watching until the pace of his breathing slowed. His eyes finally opened. "You still here?"

She nodded.

"Max." He closed his eyes again. "He liked you."

"He did?"

"Only one he ever talked to. Besides me."

Chapter 26

————

SHE COULD FEEL THE COLD GRAY SKY PRESSING DOWN AS SHE hurried along, determined not to look back.

"Wait up! Wait up!" Brianna Hall kept calling until Nellie finally turned around. "I been running the whole way!" Brianna was out of breath.

"I didn't know it was you," Nellie lied, shifting her backpack.

"You saw me," Brianna panted. "Then all of a sudden you go the other way."

Just as Nellie'd gotten to the sidewalk, she'd seen the Shelbys' car pull up next to Rodney and Roy in their shiny black jackets. Sitting next to Mrs. Shelby was Boone, his big head high over the dashboard, the way he used to ride in the truck with Max. Attached to the car, on what looked to be a homemade rack, were the two bicycles. After the twins took them down, they opened the door, tossed their backpacks inside, then pedaled off down the hill. As Mrs. Shelby drove by, Boone stared straight ahead, not even a yip of recognition.

In the week since seeing the twins on her way to Charlie's, she'd tried to at least smile at them in class, but neither one would look her way. She'd been eliminated from their necessary field of vision as completely as everyone else who'd ever been cruel to them.

Brianna was asking Nellie again to come to her house. Her older brother had just gotten two new video games and he'd be at football practice until suppertime.

"I told you," Nellie said irritably. "I have to be home for when my brother gets there." Having lost sight of the twins, she walked slower. Probably just as well. Even if she did catch up, anything she said would only make things worse. And maybe it was best this way. Mrs. Fouquet said she shouldn't always be trying to be all things to all people, because it held her back from being her true self, a conundrum because her true self was the very person no one wanted her to be, including herself. She woke up every morning with this same emptiness inside. And the worst part was not knowing what was missing. In their last meeting, she had shown Mrs. Fouquet her *Get Tough!* manual. She told her how excited she'd been the first time she'd read it. But now when she looked through it, it seemed ridiculous. Embarrassing, even. She couldn't understand why it had once seemed so important to her. So meaningful.

"Because your world is changing. You're changing," Mrs. Fouquet told her. "It's like climbing a mountain. The higher you get, the smaller things seem back in the distance. The more insignificant."

So maybe that was it. A depressing thought. Worse, though, was the fear that perhaps nothing had ever been the way she'd always believed. Not just Max's innocence but her own for thinking all things were possible and within her grasp, her power.

"Eighteen hours in labor," Brianna was saying. "Can you imagine? By that time, I'd be screaming for them to just cut it out of me." Yesterday during last period, Mrs. Duffy's water had broken in front of everyone, dribbling down her swollen ankles, staining her tan shoes. The principal had driven her to the hospital. Julia Marie Duffy had been born at eight A.M. A great cheer had gone up in the classroom this morning when it was announced over the PA system. And for some reason, Nellie had almost cried. While nothing could make her happy, happiness left her feeling only more hollow inside.

"I'm not going to have any kids," Nellie said.

"Yeah, right. You'll probably have, like, ten or something," Brianna laughed.

As they came down the hill, Nellie noticed a crowd at the far end of the park. There were a few girls, the rest boys. Four more boys ran along one of the paths toward the swelling group. Whatever the attraction, it was taking place near the flagpole.

"Let's go see!" Brianna hurried ahead in a half trot. "C'mon, I think it's a fight!"

Like so much else lately, Brianna's excitement was only wearying to Nellie. Her feet felt like cement blocks as she dragged farther behind.

The hoots and howls filled her with dread. She'd just keep walking. All she wanted was to get home so she could be alone. A fight was the last thing on earth she wanted to see. Brianna came running back.

"It's awful!" she said, grinning. "Poor Rodney, Bucky's got his crazy bike halfway up the pole and everyone's laughing."

With Brianna in the lead, Nellie plodded on. Her feet were too heavy. It wasn't until she'd reached the edge of the giddy pack that she understood.

The bike had been hoisted almost to the top of the flagpole. Bucky stood below, holding on to the rope, which Rodney kept grabbing at without daring to get too close, the way you'd try snatching a stick from a roaring fire. Roy sat on his bike, black satin shoulders hunched, staring at the ground.

"Sorry, Freak!" Bucky howled with each of Rodney's fearful attempts. "You had your chance and you blew it!"

"Give it to me!" Rodney grunted, head down like an abused dog.

"All I wanted was a ride," Bucky said, smirking as he wound the rope around the pole cleat.

"No, you took it. You just took it, that's what you did," Rodney said, his dull voice breaking.

"Aw, c'mon, Bucky," a boy finally called.

"Okay, I'll trade you," Bucky told Rodney. "Gimme your jacket."

"No!" Rodney crossed his arms, hugging himself.

Two younger boys next to Nellie and Brianna laughed nervously.

"Jesus, you gotta give me something." Bucky's leering eyes scanned his audience, savoring their attention, their uneasiness. It wasn't the bike he wanted or even Rodney's misery, but this, control over everyone, their disapproval all the more exhilarating for him. "Fair's fair, right, Nellie?" He smiled at her.

Maybe if her glasses hadn't been so smudged she might have acted sooner. Or maybe because they were so smudged everything around her was blurred enough so that when she stepped forward, all she could see was shape, a featureless outline on brittle paper, the pages so fragile, the old, turned corners would crumble in her fingertips.

"Give him his bike."

"Oh, okay, Nellie. Sure, whatever you say."

"You feel really important, don't you?" Fear and loathing—she could smell both in his nasty breath.

"Go fuck yourself, okay?" The excitement of his breathing pounded in her own ears.

Just as she touched the rope, he unwound it from the cleat, then shoved her out of the way. The bike fell onto the concrete pad in a crash of mangled metal parts.

"What the hell'd ya do that for?" he laughed. "You wrecked it!"

"You jerk!" she yelled, storming back at him.

Reaching out, he snatched off her glasses. "You're fuckin' cross-eyed!" he howled, staggering with laughter.

She grabbed for her glasses, but he danced back, ducking and weaving, dangling them high over her head, laughing as he told her to stop, please stop, because she was just going to get hurt. And with that she lunged at him. He swung back, punching her so hard her head shook with the jolt and her arms dropped to her sides. A shrinking pinprick of light gleamed through the end of the long, narrow tunnel.

"Leave her alone!"

"Jesus," someone said.

"Oh, my God!"

"Nellie!" Brianna screamed.

Rodney Shelby was lifting her to her feet. Brianna was trying to put her glasses back on her. Bucky pushed his way through the shocked children. They'd never seen such a thing before. Roy was rocking back and forth on his bike.

SHE WAS ON the couch. Henry kept pressing a bag of frozen peas against her cheek. Her father ran into the house. Ruth had called him at the store. She was afraid Nellie had a concussion. She'd looked it up in their medical encyclopedia and Nellie had all the symptoms.

"You're falling asleep again. Don't! You can't!" Henry told her again, his bony shoulder pressed into hers. Ruth said he had to keep her awake. Every time her eyes closed, he'd nudge her and call her name as if she were in another room or outside. She'd never felt so strangely, distantly weary.

"She got in a fight," Ruth whispered. "Bucky Saltonstall."

"What do you mean, a fight?" her father asked.

"A fistfight!"

Looking stunned, her father sat on the edge of the coffee table, facing her. He removed her glasses, then with two fingers lifted the lids in each of her eyes and peered closely. She smiled with his touch.

"Nellie, what on earth is going on? You had a fight? You hit someone?"

"It wasn't her fault!" Henry said. "She was just tryna do the right thing."

"Since when is hitting someone the right thing?" her father asked, but he was looking at her.

"When someone hits you first because you're tryna help somebody?" Henry's voice quavered. "That's when!"

"But this keeps happening, doesn't it, Nellie?" her father said, shaking his head. "And every time it get worse, doesn't it? Every single time."

"Dad!" Ruth said, coming into the room. "You don't even know what happened. And besides, look at her, she's so out of it."

She was trying to stand up. Her legs were still wobbly so she had to sit down. Her head ached, but things were starting to clear. She knew what came next. Her father told Ruth to call her mother at the salon and tell her he was taking Nellie to the emergency room.

"No," Nellie said, standing up again, this time managing to stay on her feet. "That's not where I'm going."

"Come on, hon." Her father had his arm around her on their way to the door. He called back for Ruth to get her sister's jacket. A light snow had begun to fall, the first of the season. Ruth asked if she and Henry could come. He wanted to—she said he was crying. All right, her father said. Go back in and get him.

"No," Nellie said. "Nobody can come. Not now."

"All right," her father called after Ruth. "Nellie's right. We'll do this. We'll be right back. Tell Henry I'll call from the hospital and let him know what's going on."

He was looking over his shoulder and backing out of the driveway when she said she had to go see Detective Des La Forges. He thought she wanted to report her injury to the police. White flowers were falling. Lacy petals melting on the windshield. Snowflakes.

"But first let's make sure you're all right, okay?" he said as he turned on the wipers.

"Just a little dizzy, that's all."

He drove slowly down the street, trying to avoid bumps and potholes. "And then after, we'll figure out what to do. Probably the best thing—and I'm sure Mom'll say the same thing—is to call his grandparents. They should—"

"No, that's not why. I have to tell him about Mr. Cooper."

"Nellie!"

"I know, and if I'm wrong, then . . . then that's okay." Her eyes wanted to close. The swish of the wipers back and forth, back and forth was making her stomach queasy.

"Oh, Lord, Nellie, please, let's not—"

"I'm just gonna tell the truth, Dad, that's all." Her tongue felt stiff.

He kept driving, his knuckles tight on the steering wheel. They were two blocks from the station. The closer they got, the slower he seemed to drive. So far, they had stopped at every yellow light. The next one was turning yellow when he suddenly sped through it. He drove past the police station.

"You're not gonna take me?" She was stunned.

"Nellie," he pleaded. "Don't. Don't do this."

Springvale Hospital was another mile ahead. With every blue H sign they passed, her thoughts became clearer. He didn't have to come with her. No one did. She could do this by herself.

"Here we go," he said, turning into the emergency room parking lot.

He had parked and was coming around the back of the car to open her door, but she was already out and walking away from the hospital toward the street. He hurried after her, insisting she go back and see a doctor. He kept trying to reason with her. She wasn't thinking straight. The most important thing was her health, making sure she was all right, and that's all he was trying to do here, he explained, protect her, keep her safe. That's all he'd ever wanted. She did know that, right? And not just her, but all of them. "Your mother, Ruth, Henry." He was growing breathless. "This whole thing, it's all been so . . . ugly. And what's the point? Why on earth would you put everyone through all of that again? *Especially* your mother!" He took her arm and stopped her. "Why?" he demanded so desperately she didn't know what to say. "Don't you know what this will do? Don't you care?"

She didn't answer—just kept walking with a dizzying sense of elation. He kept pace, both of them silent now, the only sound from cars whizzing by on their way home from work. It was suppertime. Her stomach was growling. For the first time in weeks she was hungry, but not for food. She felt bad for her father. She had a jacket on, but he didn't. His shoulders and the top of his dark hair were skimmed with snow. *Odd,* she thought, *how it melts when it hits the ground, but doesn't on his head.* Her glasses were wet.

Gripping the railing, she walked up the front steps of the police station with him close by her side. He pulled open the door and held it for her. Instead of what she expected, policemen milling around a large room, they were met by a glass partition. Behind it a woman with spiked orangey blond hair spoke to them through a grate. She asked her father why he was here. She didn't even look at Nellie, who recognized her as the parking meter lady.

"To drop off an accident report or file a complaint?"

"Is Detective Des La Forges here?"

"Sure, but he'll wanna know why."

"We'd like to speak with him, that's all," her father said and the woman rolled her eyes.

"Name, please."

"Benjamin Peck. And this is my daughter, Nellie."

"Oh yeah, sure!" the woman said. "From the hardware store. Hey, I heard you're closing. That's too bad."

"Thank you," her father said.

"Yeah, jeez, what am I gonna do now every time I need a key made?"

"Buck Buster's, on State Street—they make keys," her father said.

"Yeah, that's where I went last time. Only cuz your machine was broke," she added, then pushed a button on her console to tell the detective he had people waiting to see him.

Detective Des La Forges looked thinner than the last time Nellie had seen him. And sure enough, he was telling her father that he'd lost twenty pounds and had never felt better. Well, he certainly looked great, her father said. Soup and salad, the detective explained, for both lunch and dinner. And three fruits for breakfast. Any three he wanted. With yogurt. Low-cal, of course.

"Sounds easy enough," her father said.

Detective Des La Forges nodded, then peered at Nellie. "Everything okay?" He pointed to her face. "Looking pretty bruised there." He looked back at her father. "That why you're here?"

"Is it? Is that why?" her father asked gently, hopefully, as if to give her one last chance, then before she could answer, he said, "No. No, it isn't. We're here b . . . b . . . because Nellie wants to . . . she wants to talk to you about something."

"Sure," the detective said, looking at her. "Anytime, I told you that. Even when it's over, people still have questions. A trial—there's just so much information, it can be confusing."

"It's not about the trial. It's something I didn't tell you. I should've, but I didn't." She took a deep breath to contain the whirling dizziness.

Des La Forges held up his hands. "Stop right there. No explanation, no apology needed. That was a heck of a lotta pressure for a kid, and you did a good job. You got a little off course there, maybe," he said, rapping his knuckles on the desk. "But then you rallied."

"Thank you," Nellie said. "But that's not what I want to talk about."

"Oh. Sure. Go right ahead then. So what's going on?" He flashed her father the quick smile of a commiserating parent.

"My father doesn't think I should tell anyone this, but the thing is, I don't think one man's life is more important than anyone else's. And I know not telling the truth is just as bad as telling a lie." She wondered if she was making sense. Afraid she was slurring, she tried to speak more slowly. "That day, when Dolly died, well, there was another person there that day, at our house. It was afternoon, about one o'clock. And he didn't want me to see him. He was, like, trying to squeeze back into the lilacs. And his face was scratched, but it couldn't've been from the bushes, I know it wasn't."

"Who? Who was it?" the detective asked.

"Mr. Cooper," she said.

"Huh?" the detective shook his head.

"Andy," her father said with halting gravity, as if he were exposing his own daughter as well. "Andy Cooper. Nellie, she came out and saw him. Looked like he was trying to hide."

"Andy Cooper! I don't get it. What's the connection?"

"Mr. Cooper was Dolly's boyfriend," she said certain now that she was going to have to go through everything all over again.

The detective looked stunned. "How do you know?"

"Because I used to see him there sometimes. And because I just know, that's why."

THE SNOW WAS falling faster as they walked back to the hospital parking lot. When she told her father she didn't need to see a doctor, all he did was nod. He was upset. The most he'd said was to warn her about the slippery sidewalk and wonder how much snow would fall tonight. There hadn't been anything on the news. When they got in the car, he turned on the heat but not the wipers, then sat looking at the windshield and its snowy stare back. He took a deep breath but instead of speaking, groaned.

"Don't be mad at me. Please, don't," she begged in a small voice but knew he wasn't angry. He was disappointed, once again, painfully disappointed in her, and couldn't begin to hide it.

"I'm not mad. Why would I be?" He tried to smile but only looked sadder. "You did what you had to do, what you thought was right."

"Maybe they'll prove it wasn't him, and then—"

"No, Nellie, that's not it." He closed his eyes a moment and then he looked at her. "You see, even when you were a baby, I knew how very special you were. And how . . . how good I'd have to be as your father. But then . . ." He kept nodding. "The time came when you needed me most, and I let you down. I failed you. And that, that's the worst thing, the worst thing of all."

"No, you didn't!" She couldn't bear seeing him so distraught. "You just didn't know, that's all. I mean, I'm just a kid and I say all these things and—"

"No, I knew. I knew something was going on. And Cooper, he

knew I knew. I'd seen him coming out of there a couple times. But neither one of us said anything."

"Why not?" She sank back against the door.

"Weakness." He shook his head in disgust. "Such an easy companion. Always tells you exactly what you need to hear. I couldn't stand the thought of letting your mother down again, the way I always have, so I just told myself, 'No, that's not what it is, it can't be. Impossible.' Even after, when you told me, I didn't want to hear it. I couldn't."

"But why?"

"I wasn't good enough, strong enough." It almost seemed like a question, the way he looked past her, tilting his head, puzzled and ashamed. "I wanted to be. But I wasn't."

Yes, you were! You were! she wanted to reassure him, instead, cried, "But why? Why weren't you?"

"Because it wasn't just you I couldn't hear it from, it was me. I stopped listening to what's in here," he said, hand pressed to his chest. "I wanted to keep believing that everything I'd always believed in still mattered, that everyone was good and decent, so I started making excuses for myself and everyone else, and then, it was just easier to look the other way and tell myself that as long as *I* did the right thing, as long as *I* led a good life, everything would be all right in the end."

"But all those things you said, Dad, all those things you told me, and the whole time . . . I mean . . . poor Max!" she sobbed.

"I know. But I kept thinking, what if it was. What if it *was* Max, how could I do that to the Coopers? What right did I have?"

"But it wasn't up to you, Dad. Was it?"

"I know, and I'm sorry," he groaned, leaning his forehead against the wheel. "I'm so, so sorry."

They both were. But what she felt most keenly in the cavelike closeness of the snow-covered car was the great expanse between them. The one fixed point in her life, and he was a blur. If she hadn't known her own father, who then could she know?

Chapter 27

———

T HE DAYS THAT FOLLOWED MOVED SLOWLY. NELLIE WANTED
to be hopeful for Max, hard though with such uneasiness,
such dread in the house. She could tell that her father was
relieved, but now whenever he tried to be upbeat, it seemed thin and
forced. Especially with her mother, whose initial shock had given way
to fear. Of everything, Charlie dying, another trial, their future.

Mr. Cooper had only been questioned. He hasn't been arrested,
Nellie's father had to keep reminding her mother. "Who knows how
this'll play out? We just have to be patient, that's all," he said.

"Oh, sure, Ben, sure. If he did do it, then he goes to jail. And if
he didn't, then he's really going to want to do business with us, right?
And if he did it, but they can't prove it, then what? We've gotta always
be worrying about this killer who hates us? Especially Nellie?" The
butcher knife chopped in double time on the cutting block.

Her mother was dicing celery for the turkey stuffing. Thanksgiving
was two days away, and she'd been really busy at the salon with all the
last-minute appointments, so she was trying to prepare as much of the
food ahead of time as she could. This year Lazlo would be bringing
his sweet potato and marshmallow casserole that they all loved. Aunt
Betsy and Uncle Phil were also coming, but because Aunt Betsy was a
terrible cook, she was only ever asked to bring canned cranberry sauce
and bakery rolls, which she inevitably had some big story about—how
the first bakery had been closed, and the only other decent one was way
up in Mountcliff, then after creeping through bumper-to-bumper traffic, the parking lot was full and the only spot she could find was two
blocks away, which meant she'd had to walk through just the worst gale
force wind, and once she got inside, she'd had to wait in line for almost

an hour, only to get them home and find one bag three rolls short, so, believe it or not, back she'd gone. Every year was a new version of the extraordinary effort it took to buy two dozen snowflake rolls, which always left Nellie conflicted, guilty if she ate one, guilty if she didn't.

"No, Sandy," her father was saying, "all we're going to worry about is having a wonderful holiday. Okay?"

In spite of Charlie having been admitted to the hospital again, though no one said it.

"Oh, Lord," her mother sighed. "Lord, Lord, Lord." Then suddenly roused by yet another fear, she called out, "Nellie! Where are you?"

"Here, Mom. In the pantry," she called back. Assigned the task of checking Grandmother Peck's sterling silver for tarnish, she'd been wiping each piece with a special cloth.

Every night her mother sat on the edge of Nellie's bed, talking, until Nellie would close her eyes, pretending to sleep. There was so much she'd never told anyone, especially not her children, all the disturbing people and incidents she'd endured in her childhood, and how confusing life had been with her mother practically an invalid and her father without a tender bone in his body, though she'd long ago accepted that that's just the way he was, so, then, when it came to being a mother herself, she was so afraid of making mistakes that she held everything in, herself included, which was probably why Ruth had so many problems. But from now on, she wanted them all to be completely open with one another and say whatever was on their minds, no matter what it was. Which, though Nellie didn't say it, was the very trait that had always gotten her in trouble. More than anything, what Nellie needed right now was for her family to stay the same as they'd always been.

"Come in here a minute," her mother called, and when Nellie did, her mother hugged her. "My little girl. My poor little girl," she sighed into Nellie's hair, then stood there patting her back.

"I'm okay, Mom," Nellie said.

"Look at you," her mother said, holding her at arm's length. "Taller than me. You're probably going to end up as tall as your father. Lucky girl."

Not what Nellie wanted to hear, but she smiled.

"You should go out for basketball—you'd probably be the center," commented Henry from the table, but she ignored him. He was peeling apples with their father, each vying to see who could do it in just one long peel.

She went back to rubbing each fork tine and knife blade and spoon hollow until they shone. Ruth had made the mistake of coming downstairs looking for a snack and now she'd been pressed into apple-slicing duty. The three pies—apple, pumpkin, and mincemeat—that were being assembled tonight wouldn't be baked until tomorrow night.

They hadn't changed, not really, but she had, Nellie realized, listening to them in the kitchen. They were the same as they'd always been. She loved her father but with a forgiveness that tinged everything he said and did, diminishing him with her pity. Ruth had been right all along. As had her mother. Now there was just Henry, only Henry left to admire him. Only Henry who didn't hear the fear in his father's voice, or see in his intensity the desperate need to keep everyone at bay, them and all their petty problems.

WEDNESDAY, THE DAY before Thanksgiving, when school ended at noon, so no danger of running into Jessica at lunchtime recess. She had been absent all week, to Nellie's great relief. She had told herself Jessica must be sick, even though she knew from Ruth that Louie hadn't been in school either.

The headline in yesterday's paper had been LOCAL BUSINESSMAN QUESTIONED IN HOMICIDE, with Mr. Cooper's picture on the front page, a smiling file photo. Most of the story was a rehash of Dolly's murder and the trial. But it did report that because new information had come to light, police were questioning Mr. Cooper about his relationship with Dolly Bedelia and his whereabouts immediately prior to the murder. After initially speaking with Mr. Cooper in his office last week, the police had contacted him again requesting DNA samples, and he'd refused. Mr. Cooper's attorney described his client as not only "incredulous" but seriously considering a defamation of character lawsuit against any number of people, Assistant District Attorney Finn Cowie, chief among them, and Eggleston Jay Wright, Max's lawyer, who was demanding the investigation be reopened.

Almost home, Nellie was stunned to see Jessica coming down Oak Street. Her first impulse was to run by her, but she kept walking. The drumbeat in her head kept time to each of Jessica's plodding footsteps. Closer, closer, now inches apart.

"Bitch," Jessica growled, hands on her hips. "You're so gonna pay for this. You have no idea what's coming, do you, bitch?"

"I'm sorry," she said, speaking as fast as she could. "It's not like I was trying to cause trouble for anyone, especially you, Jess. I mean, we've been friends ever since first grade. I just had to tell the truth, that's all. It's not like I was trying to hurt you or anything." Nellie cringed, a feeble ending.

"Oh no, not me, just my whole fucking family, that's all!" Jessica said, adding with an eerie laugh, "Everyone's, like, going nuts. Thank God Patrice is home from college. At least someone's cooking. My mother's, like, locked up in her room twenty-four/seven, and my father, all he does is drink vodka and cry. You ever hear a man cry? It's really, really weird, like this high eeee-ew! eeee-ew! Like some kind of sick animal."

They stood in Nellie's driveway as Jessica's dispassionate report continued. Things had gotten so bad with her father throwing and breaking things, even punching his fist through the study wall, that Patrice had to call a doctor, who came in the middle of the night with medicine to calm him down. He'd been sleeping all morning.

"I better go in," Nellie said, her arms prickled with goose bumps.

"Yeah, me, too," Jessica said, and Nellie told her no. Her mother was too busy cooking, which wasn't true. She was at work. "Please, please!" Jessica begged. "I just wanna be in some normal place, that's all!"

All right, but not inside, Nellie conceded, swayed by guilt and sympathy. They'd have to sit on the steps, though, because the porch furniture had already been put in the barn for the winter. Even with a jacket, Nellie was soon shivering, but not Jessica, who wore only a thin, tight sweater. She looked heavier, Nellie thought, with all the turmoil she was probably eating constantly. As if reading her mind, Jessica said she was starving. Could they just get some food and eat it out here? Nellie said they couldn't go in. But she had pretzels somewhere in here, she said, finding them in her backpack. Jessica ripped open the bag.

"Guess what happened to Bucky," Jessica said through a mouthful of pretzels.

"Like I care," Nellie said, though it was better than hearing about all the misery she'd caused the Coopers.

"His grandmother caught him stealing some money from her closet. He knew where the key was, so he'd just go take, like, ten or twenty, whenever he wanted."

"What a jerk."

"Yeah, well, but they're rich," Jessica said, devouring the last pretzel. She kept wetting her fingers and dipping them into the salt at the bottom of the bag.

"No, they're not!"

"Well, anyway," Jessica said between smacking sounds as she sucked salt from each fingertip, "they never gave him any money for anything. So, I mean, poor Buck." She shrugged. "Now he has to go live with some aunt and uncle in Albany."

"Poor aunt and uncle," Nellie said.

"Poor Albany," Jessica laughed. She folded the bag into a tiny square and stuffed it into her pocket, along with all the other empty bags and wrappers she would be sure to dispose of before she got home.

"Now, I'm like, wicked thirsty," Jessica said, biting the side of her thumbnail.

"I told you, we can't go in."

"You can, and I'll just wait."

Nellie ran inside, then hurried back out with a glass of water.

"Jesus, this the best you can do?" Jessica scoffed, then guzzled it down. "Anyway," she said with a bitter laugh. "I don't think my Mom'll be buying any more Cherry Coke for you."

Nellie could only nod.

"Guess I'll be coming over here from now on," Jessica sighed. "I mean, if we're still gonna be hanging out, that is."

With a score of horrible scenarios crashing through her thoughts, Nellie continued nodding.

"And *I'll* buy the fucking Cherry Coke!" Jessica said, then burst into heart-breaking, blubbery tears.

"Don't cry, Jess. It'll be okay. It's probably just—"

"He did that to *me!*" she sobbed. "When he gets mad . . . it's like he goes crazy. He puts his hands on your neck, and you don't dare move, and the whole time he's yelling right in your face, like, 'Yah! Yah! Yah!' spit getting all over you, and you just have to stand there, because you know if you move or say one single word back, something bad's gonna happen." Suddenly, she grabbed Nellie's wrist and squeezed hard. "But don't you tell anyone! That's a secret, Nellie. That's just between you and me, and if you do, if you tell anyone, if you tell one single person, like that bitch, Brianna Hall, I'll kill you, I swear I will!"

"Okay."

"Say it! Promise you won't."

"I won't tell anyone. I promise."

Shoulders touching, they sat staring down at the steps. Poor Jessica, she kept thinking, even in this, so disconnected, whether happy or sad, never really in quite the right place. What an awful life. No wonder she was so strange. Strange enough even to still want to be friends. Or maybe that's exactly what kept her going. Her persistence.

"Hey, Jess, I just thought. I've got this book, you want to see it? It's got all these holds and things, like ways to protect yourself in case of attack, or like, if all of a sudden someone comes up from behind and grabs you, you do this kind of spin-around thing," she said, on pivoting feet now, arms and hands flying in demonstration.

"Are you fucking serious?" Jesssica said, squinting up at her.

"Yeah. It's called *Get Tough!* It's by Major Fairbairn. He's, like, this really cool English guy."

"Yeah, well, not right now, okay?" Jessica said with a disbelieving sneer.

"Okay." Nellie knew enough to drop it, even though it was probably the very thing Jessica had needed all along. Empowerment.

NELLIE WOKE UP in the morning to the smell of turkey roasting in the oven. Her first thought was of Max waking up to the holiday in a prison cell. She wondered if he was feeling just a little bit thankful today. Attorney Wright had told her father that even if the police did reopen the case and arrest Mr. Cooper, there'd still have to be another trial. The only way Max could be released from jail before a trial would be if Mr. Cooper confessed to the murder, which probably wasn't going to happen anytime soon, so Max was just going to have to be patient. But at least now there was hope. Sitting up in bed, she put on her glasses and reached for the notepad containing her long letter to Max.

Today is Thanksgiving, she wrote, *and when my father asks us at dinner to name something we're thankful for, I'm going to say I'm thankful that I told the truth. I hope you won't be mad at me for not telling the police right away about Mr. Cooper. I wanted to, but I was afraid. It really is true what Mark Twain said—physical courage is great, but it's moral courage that really counts, but I'm sure you probably already know that.*

Anyway, I'll finish this later. My mother is calling me. We have to eat breakfast early so we can get the kitchen ready for the big feast ahead. She scratched out *big feast* and just wrote *day.* No point in making him feel worse than he already did.

Ruth had finished breakfast and was washing her dishes in the sink. She was meeting her friends in a half hour, even though the football game didn't start until eleven. Socially, it was the biggest game of the year, but a very lopsided rivalry. In the last ten years Springvale High had beaten Mountcliff Academy eight times. Ruth started for the stairs, saying she might be stopping by Quinn's house after the game. "They're having this, like, brunch. But I won't eat anything, I promise. I'll be starving for dinner."

"Who's Quinn?" her mother called after her.

Probably another phantom friend, Nellie thought.

"MacFarland," her father said, bending over the oven door as he basted the turkey. "His great-grandfather was Lucky Quinn. He was the fire chief when the station caught fire and burned to the ground. In 1928, I'm pretty sure. Never lived it down, remember?"

Her mother didn't answer, but her eyes caught Nellie's, then held for a second, a painful second, a look neither could acknowledge without undermining his dignity. Meanwhile, in his constant hunger for irony, Henry was begging for details, the whole story, which as his father told it was obviously the funniest thing Henry had ever heard. Just then the phone rang. Her mother hesitated before she answered. Charlie had called from the hospital last night, demanding to be picked up. He wanted to come home. Her mother called his doctor, who said it was out of the question. He was too weak. Even though it had been after ten, Nellie's father drove to the hospital and managed to talk Charlie into staying. At least through the weekend. Truth was, that's when he was probably going to go into hospice care, if a bed became available.

"Don't worry about it," her mother was saying. Her father shut the oven door quietly and came near, looking concerned. Her mother rolled her eyes. *Betsy,* she mouthed. *The rolls.* "I'm sure they're fine, Betts. The shape doesn't matter—they'll still taste great. No. Don't even think of it." She hung up, then had to hold onto the counter she was laughing so hard. "Phil. He sat on one of the bags of rolls!"

"No!" her father cried, laughing.

"Yes!" her mother gasped, "and she thinks they should get in the car and try and find a bakery that's open."

"Yeah, can you just see Uncle Phil yelling, 'Bakery! Bakery!' at his dashboard," Nellie said, putting her cereal bowl into the sink when the phone rang again.

Everyone froze in their giddiness as her mother answered, but it was only Lazlo needing to borrow some cinnamon. Her mother sent Henry over with it, then told Nellie to go upstairs and shower. But she'd just taken one on Saturday, Nellie protested, raising an arm and sniffing.

"Weekly's not good enough," her mother said on her tiptoes, reaching high into the cupboard for a box of cornstarch. "You should be taking one at least every two days. It's very important for girls, especially now that you're a teenager."

That word alone was enough to send Nellie heading for the bathroom before another discussion of female personal issues could take place, especially in her father's presence. She let the water run a long time before she finally stepped in. Groping through the lineup of bottles, she knocked half of them over as she tried to find the shampoo. Without glasses, she was practically blind in here, another reason to avoid showering. What if there were an emergency, a fire or something, she'd be a goner in here. Sometimes she'd just run the water in the shower stall while she washed up at the sink. But her mother was right across the hall now, making her bed, so she didn't dare.

The soap slipped from her hand onto the stall floor, white soap on the white tile, so she had to kneel down to find it. She reached out past the shower curtain and took her glasses from the vanity. They steamed up even more when she put them on, but at least she could see a little as she worked the shampoo into her hair. She couldn't have contacts until she was seventeen, another of her mother's arbitrary rules, like not getting her ears pierced until she was sixteen. Not that she even wanted to. But if she ever did, she'd only get one in each lobe, not three like Ruth had. She'd gotten in trouble for it, but like everything else with her sister, it hadn't lasted very long, and no one had ever dragged Ruth to a therapist. Apparently, having two fathers absolved her of a great many sins. She wasn't about to admit it to anyone, but she liked her sessions with Mrs. Fouquet. But now that she thought about it, maybe Jessica had liked her therapy sessions, too, in the beginning. Maybe that's how it started, getting so into yourself you didn't even notice people looking at you funny every time you said anything they didn't understand.

"Nellie?"

She peered around the curtain. The shape in the doorway seemed to be her mother, holding out her bathrobe.

"Are you almost done?" her mother said.

"I just got in here!" Nellie called back, annoyed. Her mother left the robe on the hamper, then closed the door. *Message received,* Nellie thought—the days of leaving the shower wrapped in just a towel were over. She quickly rinsed out the shampoo, then turned off the water. Her mother obviously thought she'd been in here too long, wasting hot water and holding up everyone else. She wrapped her hair in a towel and dried her glasses, then put on the robe.

"I can't see—that's the problem. That's why it takes so long," she complained, opening the door, surprised to find both parents in the hallway.

"Why don't you dry your hair, hon," her mother said into the billows of escaping steam. "And then get dressed. Dad and I are just . . ." She looked at him, blankly.

"Go ahead, hon, just get dressed. Mom and I are just getting things ready here, that's all," her father said, stricken as he looked, yet managing a weak smile. "Go ahead."

"What? What's wrong?" Nellie said. Nothing, they kept trying to tell her, but if it was nothing, why were they out here? Why was her mother's chin trembling? Why was her father raking his fingers through his hair? Why did they both look so helpless, as if they were waiting to be told what to do next? "Tell me!" she insisted. "What is it?"

"Honey, we just got a call," her mother finally said. "From Aunt Betsy. They just heard it on the car radio. It was about Mr. Cooper. He died last night."

"Oh no! What happened? How'd he die?" She was as confused and stunned as she was relieved and troubled by all the inappropriate questions racing through her brain. What about Max? What did this mean? Was it good or bad for him? At least she wouldn't have to go through another trial. Or maybe she would.

"Pills, they think. Looks like he committed suicide," her father said. His face was white and his hair hung lank over his furrowed brow.

"How could he do that? I mean, to his family?" Her mother shook her head, as if to shake off water or snap herself from a spell. "Those poor children."

"Poor Jessica," Nellie finally said because they expected her to. And because she wasn't about to betray her friend's confidence. Not now, anyway.

"I know," her father said, pulling her close and holding her tightly. "But you can't be blaming yourself for this. You just can't!"

"I won't." Acutely conscious of her nakedness beneath the robe, she hunched away from him, but if he noticed, it was only to think her overwhelmed by guilt.

"It's not your fault!" He sounded angry.

"I know, Dad."

"You did the right thing, Nellie. And don't you ever, ever for a single moment doubt that," he said through clenched teeth and breathing hard.

"I won't."

"No, I mean that." His voice broke. "Because you're the strongest, most courageous person I know."

"You are," her mother agreed with the faintest note of surprise.

"Fearless! Absolutely fearless!" her father cried, and her mother chimed in, telling her what a wonderful daughter and sister she was. Her father agreed, citing examples of her kindness and goodness, her generosity and selfless spirit, as if she were already a legend, one of his tales from the past, more than she was, more than she could ever hope to be.

Nellie listened as they comforted one another in their familiar way of smoothing down the jagged edges of memory, tucking each raw end into place, every doubt and fear about themselves, struggling to make sense of it all, needing containment, answers to their children's questions, a story, so that life would right itself, be steady again for all of them, and safe. But it was Dolly she was thinking of, and poor Max. And Jessica. She couldn't understand how life could get so messed up.

Or maybe that's just the way it is, she thought. Maybe it's the same for everyone as they get older, little by little, truth losing its energy, until, like particles in the air, it's almost invisible. Maybe that's just part of being an adult, rationalizing experience, changing it around until you forget a lot of the important things, things nobody has to tell some kids because they just know, that's all. And remember.

Chapter 28

————

SPRINGVALE IS A LITTLE BIGGER THESE DAYS. SOME BEAUTIFUL houses have been built in its once wooded purlieus, now manicured enclaves called Larchwood Estates and Montgomery Run and the tongue-tying Ridgechester Chase. The older homes in the center of town continue their paint-to-peeling cycle of beauty and blemish. A few old neighbors remain. The Humboldts are gone, moved to Naples, Florida. Two of the tree house walls blew down in the winter's first blizzard, the rest in pieces, fragments through the years, though the weathered platform remains, to this day, stubbornly wedged between the three main branches.

Charlie had to endure his cancer only a few more months, and though it took years, the junkyard has finally been cleared. Because Sandy and Benjamin couldn't afford the enormous cost of the stringent environmental cleanup, they transferred most of the land to the town. They held on to two back lots, hoping to sell them someday to a developer—their retirement, Nellie's mother says. Peck Hardware is no longer. In its place a gift shop came and went, followed by a high-end women's clothing store that closed after one year. Not much of a businessman, maybe, but Benjamin Peck's always there when you need him, a man with a big heart, everyone agrees. And in the end, what matters more? Nellie's come to that now, respecting the man her father wants to be.

He teaches history at the high school, where it is well known that Mr. Peck has never flunked anyone. His principal and fellow teachers admire his work but continue in their exasperation with lectures that run too long, overlapping their classes, and his easy penchant for veering off the subject. But there is always a waiting list for his courses and his students return every few years eager to share their successes with him. His typewritten history of the community fills four thick notebooks and is kept in the Springvale Library archives. It can't be checked out but is available for anyone interested in the long, curious life of an American town, where ordinary people do their best to overcome flaws and foibles as they struggle to do the right thing, maybe not always but most of the time.

In the end, Mr. Cooper's sad affair with Dolly was proved and widely known, as were relationships he had with other young women, many as trusting and vulnerable as she was. Even though his DNA did match evidence from the crime scene, there would always be doubt, just enough uncertainty to cloud the facts. Eventually, Max was released from prison. And yet to this very day, there are still people in town who believe he played some part in Dolly's murder.

Being the kind of man he was. Sometimes, they actually say that.

Because they don't know the man she knew, Max Devaney, however near or far away, though clearly fixed in memory, the haunted man who entered her life at that time of perfect childhood in its dazzling sphere of wildness, freedom, courage, when everything was still possible. Everything.

What do you mean?

His innocence. And her own, but she doesn't say that.

And you still think so? Even after all this time?

Absolutely.

How can you be so sure?

ABOUT THE AUTHOR

———

MARY McGARRY MORRIS was a National Book Award and PEN/Faulkner Award finalist for her first novel *Vanished,* published in 1988. *A Dangerous Woman,* published in 1991, was chosen by *Time* magazine as one of the "Five Best Novels of the Year" and was made into a major motion picture. Her next novel, *Songs in Ordinary Time,* was a CBS television movie as well as an Oprah Book Club selection in 1997, propelling it to the top of the *New York Times* bestseller list and making it an international bestseller.

Since then she has written four highly acclaimed novels, the most recent of which was *The Last Secret,* published by Crown in 2009. She lives in Massachusetts.